PRAISE FOR THE BLEED

"If you liked *Stranger Things* Season 4 and the Hellfire Club, you'll love Barry, Lich, and the gang in *The Bleed*. These metal-fueled outcasts fight back by rolling the dice against bullies, authority figures, and monsters from another dimension, proving the power of friendship is the mightiest sword. Schreffler's head-banging pulp sci-fi debut will make you cry, cheer, and scream into the mic."

—Angela Sylvaine, author of *Frost Bite* and
The Dead Spot: Stories of Lost Girls

"With *The Bleed*, Schreffler has crafted a world of real, complex characters who demand the reader's emotional investment. His style has a certain zest that channels Stephen Graham Jones, yet remains totally his own. *The Bleed* is a hell of a good time and impossible to put down. This one's binge-worthy."

—Steph Nelson, author of *The Vein* and *The Threshing Floor*

"*The Bleed* is an interdimensional tale brimming with heart, rock 'n' roll, and high school blues. Make time to read this one in a single sitting."

—Drew Huff, author of *Free Burn* and *The Divine Flesh*

"*The Bleed* is a rip-roaring mosh pit of monsters, murder, and mayhem. Barry and Lich will take you on one hell of a ride."

—R. L. Meza, author of *Our Love Will Devour Us*

THE
BLEED

CONTENT WARNING

Death, murder, violence, gore, foul language, drug use, explicit images, child neglect, torture.

This book is intended for mature audiences.

Reader discretion is advised.

Edited by Rob Carroll
Book Design and Layout by Rob Carroll
Cover Art by Butcher Billy
Cover Design by Rob Carroll

ISBN 978-1-958598-11-5 (paperback)
ISBN 978-1-958598-66-5 (eBook)

darkmatter-ink.com

THE BLEED

STEPHEN S. SCHREFFLER

For Rosalina, Delilah, and Bella. Authors of my love.

ONE HORSE, KENTUCKY

October 25, 1995

PROLOGUE

ONE HORSE, KENTUCKY, is one of those blink-and-you'll-miss-it mailbox towns. Not worth the ink required to print its name onto the *North America Road Atlas '95*—the one you must have read seriously wrong to end up there. It's home to a few fast food joints along Highway 88 from Cave City en route to Greensburg, a last-chance gas station, and an old tavern that perpetually smells like stale beer, urine cakes, and bleach applied with a dirty mop. There aren't many homes in One Horse, but the few that exist are in desperate need of repair. The trailers, too.

But One Horse, believe it or not, is also where the cosmic teeth of the universe gnash and grind as the engine of existence turns one eon at a time, because it's in podunk towns like One Horse where reality begins to tear, where the world tremors, and The Bleeding starts.

As it's doing today.

The hole opens at the epicenter of the town, small at first, just wide enough for a single ant to fall in, but it quickly grows, and soon the entire anthill pours inside. Within minutes, a pond becomes a waterfall over its edge. Minutes later, the kudzu-wrapped trees and stones behind One Horse's Chevron station bend inward and are consumed. The gas station follows, as do pumps six, five, four... A red '93 Toyota Celica is swallowed. It doesn't take long before all the houses and trailers are gone. Most are small and put up no fight. The elementary school is pulled into the pit, along with all the students inside. Moms, Dads, teachers, plumbers, fast food workers, even the one and only cop in town—all are devoured amid screams of terror and blood-curdling shouts to the heavens.

But the abyss remains hungrier than the heavens.

Once the entirety of One Horse is consumed, the hole stops growing, and all that remains is an echo from deep inside the void. It sounds like the screams of thousands, maybe millions of people—far more voices than have ever occupied One Horse. More than Kentucky, maybe. A flock of starlings dance in the twilight skies over the hole, and only The Creator knows what they see inside.

It's then that one gargantuan spider-like leg, segmented too many times and covered in hair, reaches out from inside the hole and slams down upon the edge of the crumbling pavement, attempting to find its grip amongst the rubble. Soon, another leg appears, and then another.

Two men in black suits and ties, wearing black sunglasses and black fedoras, stand there and watch the terrifying creature's emergence, unfazed, like they knew this would happen. They don't even take the slightest step back when yet another ungodly leg bursts from the hole and finds purchase upon the ground. They don't acknowledge the black helicopter thumping overhead, nor the gasp of the braking semi-truck beside them. They pay no mind to the soldiers pouring out of the semi's trailer, each one of the grunts brandishing their own assault rifle, and the two men don't watch as the men raise their weapons to the creature and start to fire. They've seen this all before.

This isn't their first Bleed, and it won't be their last.

While the soldiers battle the spider-legged creature from Hell, muzzle flashes lighting up the night like the Fourth of July, Daniel Cleeve pulls his black '86 Chevrolet Caprice Classic up to the scene and carefully selects the right shade of aviator sunglasses from the collection he keeps in a foam-padded briefcase on the passenger seat. There's maybe twelve pairs of sunglasses in total. Some have gold frames, some silver, and all have different colored lenses. This evening, Cleeve chooses a pair with a wine-red tint. He steps out of his company-issued vehicle and adjusts the collar on his blazer, then the cuffs. With a few absentminded flicks of the flint, he lights a gold Zippo and holds it to the end of a Lucky Strike cigarette that's tucked in between his lips. There's something inscribed on the casing of the Zippo, some kind of sigil he traces with his thumb. His lips move wordlessly under his handlebar mustache as he goes over the Board-approved "Next Steps After A Bleed" flowchart in his mind. A jet stream of cigarette smoke trails behind him as he walks to the edge of the pit that used to be One Horse, ready to greet whatever it is that is now butchering soldiers.

Cleeve checks the gold Casio watch on his wrist, the sanguine thrum of more company helicopters approaching from the north. Hopefully, this little meet-and-greet goes a bit more smoothly than the last one, which just so happened to be in Kentucky as well. Hopkinsville was a mess, and Cleeve doesn't have time for that right now. He has a plane to catch after this, and he'd like to be present *before* the next hole punches in from the cosmic slurry, not after. According to the techs back at the labs in Apex Door HQ, it should be happening way up north in Michigan, in a little town called Grafting. And it should be happening soon.

GRAFTING, MICHIGAN

Friday, October 27, 1995

BARRY & LICH

Roughly sixteen hours until the Grafting Quake

THE CLOUDS ABOVE Grafting are a dune-scape flipped upside down, brushed with the pale orange glow of impending daylight. They are low in the sky, and they are heavy. The people of Grafting don't know it yet, but their town is about to Bleed.

Amongst the sleepy Grafting residents is Barry, sitting with his feet hanging over the edge of his van's floorboard, door slid open to allow for some fresh air circulation this brisk, sunny morning, as he tries to smoke a Camel cigarette without hating the taste. It's not his cigarette of choice, it's just the brand he stole from the inside pocket of his mother's boyfriend's jacket. His mom Judy and her latest fling Karl are inside the trailer home next to the van. As it is, there isn't much space in there, the walls are made out of sawdust and Elmer's Glue. So, ever since Karl started showing up, Barry has been living in his long-gone dad's old van, parked in the gravel driveway underneath a trellis of dead vines.

Barry is almost eighteen, and he reckons he's got the same look his father must've had while smoking a cigarette on these very floorboards back in the old man's "lone wolf days"—that's how Senior referred to the late '70s. The van is just about all that's left of him.

Barry leans back in his cocoon of a sleeping bag and turns on the Mr. Coffee that's plugged into an adapter in the cigarette lighter next to the radio. Soon, there's a steaming mug of morning blend in his hand, and his face contorts from the first sip. Like always, he forces himself to appreciate the bitterness of the drink. He's feeling both way too old for this shit and far too young. Barry reaches for his guitar, also a relic of his father's, a vintage Gibson Explorer, all black, and he works his way through a blues bar along the twelfth fret.

Windows of the trailer are open behind him because it's that weird time of year where the afternoons are hot and the nights are cold as hell. So, you sleep with the windows open. Can always add more blankets. Barry can hear Karl's ragged snoring, but that's not the worst of what Barry has heard, sitting there since the moon was bright in the sky. He heard the other stuff, too, in the quiet between songs on his Discman.

As the dawn breaks all the way to broken, a golden beam of sunlight strikes the undeniable masterpiece of a mural painted on the van's exterior. I mean, just look at it! This is a 1980 Dodge Street Van, the round bubble-window on its side like something from Nemo's Nautilus, only it's been painted over to resemble a full moon, and three wolves, airbrushed with photographic detail, are howling at it. The van is otherwise brown…*ish*, but that graphic, man. That moon. It looks just like the real one Barry had been staring at all night. Those wolves, the way they howl, Barry gets it. He sometimes thinks maybe one of them is Senior. Middle one, probably.

Barry sets his guitar on the rumpled sleeping bag behind him and hops out of the van. He tosses the empty coffee mug into the weeds as he steps inside the trailer.

It's the kind of quiet that's unsettling, keeps you on your toes, like when you enter a sleeping dragon's chamber and you're low on hit points, which is fine with Barry. He knows all about that shit. Just the other night during a Dungeons & Dragons session, he and his party took it to a dragon, no problem. So, this is nothing. Barry knows just how to sneak through his own home.

Of course, Karl had come over last night in a pair of white-washed Lee's, and of course, those jeans are on the floor next to Judy's bed. They're like the denim version of a can crushed on a forehead, compressed from the top down, hastily unzipped and stamped out of with the urgency of middle-aged horniness. And of course, the worn wallet in the back pocket is thick as a goddamn brick.

In his Dungeons & Dragons group, Barry isn't a rogue or a thief or a weak-ass halfling. He's a motherfucking highland warrior. When they meet every other week at Sammy's house, Barry brings his sword Bludzorg, and with it, he fucks shit up. There's catharsis in being loud and obnoxious like that, like all the men his mom has brought home since Senior departed the land of the living. With Bludzorg in hand, decibels belong to Barry. Not to Karl or the others before him. Barry's the one who gets to be loud and violent. He's no slouch either. His highland warrior is unmatched in battle, but he also knows how to sneak and how to steal shit from orcs and stuff.

So, it's with ease that Barry plucks that brick of a wallet from Karl's jeans and pulls all the cash from the billfold without either snoring adult waking in the slightest. He scores eleven one-dollar bills from the theft. *Nice.*

On his way out, he thinks: *Yeah, Bludzorg can come, too.* The sword hangs in a room he hasn't slept in since who knows when. He snatches the sword, kisses the blade, and then leaves without a sound.

ABOUT BLUDZORG:

The county fair is held not far out of town, on the way to Makade City, and the county fair is like Grafting's Woodstock. This is northern Michigan, after all. I know the county fair might not mean much to you, but it does to these folks. Grafting is small, but you should see the towns around it. By comparison, Grafting might as well be Detroit. So, when the county fair is on, it's more like the "upper state fair" in this part of Michigan, with dozens of tiny towns all showing up. Barry and his friends always throw a tent out there on that weekend. The shit they get into, man.

Every year, a blacksmith pitches a yurt on the same spot along the main strip of the fair, and for years, Barry beelined to that yurt, found himself there every day, looking at the medieval-style weapons that hung from the canvas walls. Eventually, the urge to act became too great, so he stole money from the jar of cash beside Judy's bed and from the wallet of her one-night-stand at the time, then walked into that yurt, grabbed the sword—that glorious work of art—and said aloud, "This is mine!" Whispered to the sword, "You are Bludzorg."

SO, YEAH, BLUDZORG now rests against the back of Barry's sleeveless black denim jacket, frayed at the shoulders, as he raises a middle finger to the trailer door closing behind him.

"Fuck yourself," Barry says to everything still inside. Especially Karl. Fuck Karl.

Barry hops in the driver's seat of his van and sinks into the faux-sheepskin seat cover. He tries the engine, but even in mid-October, it's still cold enough to need convincing. After a few attempts, it finally turns over and the whole unit rumbles. Barry's got the defroster on blast. He presses a tape adapter into the deck, the other end plugged into his Discman, and pulls a binder full of burned CDs. He leafs through the wilting plastic pages for…something. It's early, man, so nothing heavy, not yet. Nine times out of ten, it's Misfits, The Cramps, Scorpions, Metallica, or Dio. But this morning? It's Simon & Garfunkel. He skips to "America."

Once there's a baseball-sized patch of defrosted windshield, Barry feels that's good enough to navigate the streets of Pistol River Sunrise, the trailer park he was born and raised in. Soon, he's pulling out onto Plainview Road, headed east toward town. Pistol River Sunrise is soon behind him, and the Zimmer farmlands and then Pistol River Golf Course race by on his way to the intersection of Plainview and Higgins. Higgins is the main artery running through Grafting, and at that intersection is Rotten Roscoe's, a gas station that serves as a last bastion, a sentry tower, a cairn at the edge of civility and lawless lands. The lawless lands in this scenario are from whence Barry came, and the civility is Grafting-proper, which is a right on Higgins and down the avenue some. He pulls into the station's gravel lot and rolls the van up to the brick building. He knows Roscoe and his better half Suzanna have opened the joint by now. Their house is right behind the station, and Barry saw their Rottweiler, Brick, lying in the yard as he pulled in.

Barry steps out of the van, eleven one-dollar bills burning a hole in his pocket. But what's this now, plastered on the white-painted cinder block of Roscoe's?

"Ah, there you are," he says aloud.

It's a show poster, and lettered inside a banner dripping with blood is the announcement: THE MOW IS BACK. Below the announcement are the names of five bands: Wolf Harp, Alien Organ Donor, Motel Bloody Hell, Friday the 666th, and Broodthirsty. A flying saucer hovers above the band names, and caught in its tractor beam is a cow with a joint in its mouth.

"The MOW is fuckin' back." Barry can feel the anticipation strike a match in his gut. "And I'm playing opening night. And opening night is tonight." *Hell-to-the-fuckin'-yeah.*

He pushes his way into Roscoe's.

"Hey kid, we don't want any trouble," says Roscoe. His voice is a slab of concrete, his words dredged from the other side of decades of smoking a pack of Pall Malls a day.

"Well, trouble is here, man," says Barry.

Roscoe wears a red polo, upon the chest of which his name is stitched in cursive. Wispy gray hair hangs to his shoulders.

"Yeah, I can tell. How you doin', son? Judy okay?"

Barry shrugs, makes his way to the snack aisle. "I'm fine, man. Judy's whatever. How's it hangin'?"

"Low and to the left."

Barry laughs, scans the shelves, looks past the Halloween candy for a very specific snack. "Gross, man."

"Extra brown spots this morning, too."

Barry shakes his head, "You need mental help." Then he sees it, the reason he stole whatever cash was in Karl's wallet, the reason he stopped at Rotten Roscoe's in the first place. Freshly stocked on the third row from the bottom, the waxy packaging of Donner's Cherry Pies. Man, those pies. Chunky sugar crystals over a flaky crust, sour cherries inside. Barry snatches three. Two are for him, because he's a growing boy, and one is for Lich. To complete this breakfast of champions, Barry snatches a jug of Sunny Delight from the refrigerated section, then plops his bounty on the counter in front of Roscoe.

Roscoe raises a wiry gray eyebrow at Barry. "Donner pies again, huh? You know I only stock those things 'cause of your ass?"

"Thanks, Ross." Barry smiles.

"I hear the cherry filling is really a mix of cow testicles and mouse eyeballs," Roscoe says as he scans the three Donner Cherry Pies and the Sunny Delight.

"Don't knock it till you've tried it."

"Yeah, I was young once, too."

"Oh, and a pack of Camel Reds for my dear old mom, please."

Roscoe stops, locks eyes with Barry from beneath a Neanderthal brow. "You seriously pulling this shit again, Barry?"

Barry smiles. "You never know."

"I do know, actually," says Roscoe. "That ain't even Judy's cigarette. Tell me you're not smoking Camel Reds."

"'Kay, I won't."

"Barry, seriously kid. You're not even old enough to buy cigarettes, for one."

"Eh, I'm eighteen in two months."

"Secondly," Roscoe continues, "you should keep in mind that the best time to quite smoking is before you start."

Barry rolls his eyes. "Jesus, you sound like Principal Comely."

"Just think about it, kid. You'll end up like me if you're not careful."

"A successful business owner with a peach of a wife and a badass dog? Sign me up."

Roscoe shakes his head. "It wasn't easy." He hands Barry's breakfast to him.

"Thanks, man. I'll catch ya later."

"Seriously, Barry, I think—"

Suddenly, the whole station shudders. It's as if the floor is a vinyl record that skips on the turntable. Everything shifts just slightly to the left, then locks back in. It's subtle, only violent enough to knock some snack-sized chip bags onto the checkered tile linoleum and cause the beef jerky display next to the cash register to topple on its side, but still…

Barry steadies himself with one hand on the counter, nearly drops his bag of Donner Cherry Pies and Sunny Delight. He and Roscoe blink at one another.

From the back office, Suzanna shouts Roscoe's name.

"Uh, yeah?"

Suzanna emerges. "What the fuck was that? Oh, hi, Barry. You feel that?"

"Honey—" starts Roscoe.

"Don't 'honey' me. I'm in no mood to be patronized. Didn't you see the news about the giant sinkhole down in Kentucky? Swallowed an entire town whole! Town the size of Grafting, no less. You know these things happen in threes, don't you?"

The pair descend into a whole back and forth about what just happened in their little gas station, the severity of it, what needs to be done about it, what in the store now needs cleaning, what needs to be checked on, and why Roscoe never listens to Suzanna and how that's always ended poorly for him, so Barry leaves without saying goodbye.

On his way out, he glances at the show poster for opening night at the MOW, and whatever just happened in Roscoe's is already ancient history. He climbs into the van, fires it up, and makes his way down Higgins towards the courthouse.

Higgins is still fairly empty of traffic this early. There's a couple of cars parked along the street downtown, most likely belonging to last night's most loyal patrons of Lumberjack's Tavern. So, Barry makes good time. He glances at the old abandoned factory as he passes by. It's tucked away on an overgrown private drive just down the street from the court-house. He refers to it as the Door Factory, named after all the molded doors he found piled inside, back when he broke into the place in search of copper wire to scrap—and maybe just to spook himself on the creepy vibes. Not just a few doors, either. Dozens of industrial-sized shelves loaded top to bottom with all kinds of doors in various states of manufacture and disrepair. They were covered in dust and claimed by spiders and termites and who knows what the fuck else.

That seemed like a lifetime ago, back when Barry's dad was still around and Barry would ride shotgun in the pickup. He'd spend most of the day in the front seat of Senior's Chevy, while the old man would sit on the hood, waiting. That was in the parking lot of Scott's Hardware, and Senior was offering two strong hands and capable woodworking skills to the patrons on their way out. When he was on this side of town, Barry couldn't help but reminisce about these local haunts. It was like dipping his toes into the cold springs of nostalgia.

He pulls the van to a stop in the courthouse parking lot, gathers his Donner Cherry Pie bounty, and follows the sound of a weed trimmer coming from the other side of the building. A bright orange extension cable snakes from the brick building's corner, and Barry grins as an idea forms. He shifts his payload into the crook of one arm, bends down, and unplugs the cable. The sound of the weed trimmer dies, and in that silence, he hears Lich.

"What the hell?"

Barry can hear the sound of his poor friend smacking at the weed trimmer. Then, he plugs the orange cable back in.

The weed trimmer whirs back to life, and just when Barry feels like Lich is comfortable enough whacking those weeds, he unplugs it again.

"Fuck."

Barry hears the clank of the weed trimmer being dropped into dewy grass, and finally, what he had been counting on all along: Lich's approaching footsteps. Just as Lich turns the corner, Barry leaps out at him, the unplugged extension cable in one hand and a Donner Cherry Pie in the other. "Special delivery!"

Lich leaps back with a yelp. Then the horror washes away as he sees Barry, who is on his knees, smacking the wet grass histrionically, back hitching with laughter.

And then Lich—

BUT WAIT. WHAT the hell kind of name is Lich, anyway?

Lich and Barry play Dungeons & Dragons together every week. Years ago, Lich's character died early in the campaign, and his soul was transferred into the undead lich the party had been fighting at the time. I know, maybe that doesn't explain things, but for the group, it was everything, so now he's just Lich. Barry joined the D&D group after Lich earned his moniker, so Barry doesn't even know Lich's real name. He just knows that Lich is his best friend.

"YOU DONE, MAN?" Lich asks Barry, who's rolled onto his back, catching his breath, pies, Sunny Delight, and extension cable spilled all around him.

Lying there, Barry inhales deeply, wipes at his eyes, and nods. He holds up the extension cable. "Need this? Come on, dude. You got a job to do. Weeds ain't gonna whack themselves."

Lich shakes his head, snatching the cable. He plugs it into the outlet.

"It's dangerous to go alone," Barry says in a terrible, low-register English accent, handing Lich one of the Donner Cherry Pies. "Take this."

"Oh, hell yes." Lich snatches it and tears through the packaging.

The two boys lean back against the pale brick of the court-house and eat in silence as the sun burns from blue to orange in the waning dawn hours. Barry takes a pull from the Sunny Delight, then hands it over to Lich, who does the same.

"You know," says Lich, "hedge trimmers are in the shed back there if you want to make yourself useful."

"Eh, I wouldn't know how to get into the shed."

"It's unlocked, man."

"I don't know, Lich. Sounds like it could be a liability issue. What if I lose my head in a tragic hedge-trimming accident? The City of Grafting would have no choice but to sue you, and your mom would lose everything she has—which isn't much, but still." Barry pats Lich's shoulder. "I wouldn't want to do that to you."

"What if I let you use the chainsaw?"

Barry perks up, drops the act. He's always begging Lich to let him rev that gas-powered monstrosity, wield it around like a Michigan-born Leatherface, but Lich always says no. "Wait, really?" Barry can't believe his ears.

"No," Lich says flatly. It's a satisfying bit of revenge for the power cord prank.

Barry's brow falls flat. He's been had. "You scoundrel. Hey, did you feel that weird quake or whatever it was earlier?"

"Dude, yeah. You felt it, too? I didn't think we got quakes in Michigan."

"Maybe it was the start of a sinkhole. Roscoe's old lady was talkin' about one that just happened in Kentucky. Swallowed a whole fucking town."

Lich stops chewing his pie, a look of fear now on his face. "No way."

"Yes way. But I wouldn't worry too much, bud. Nothing so cool would ever happen to Grafting."

"True," Lich agrees. He goes back to enjoying his pie.

"So, guess what else," Barry says.

"Huh?"

"Show at the MOW tonight. Want to go?"

Lich smiles. "Oh yeah? Is Wolf Harp playing?"

Barry hocks a loogie that's neon red from the Donner Cherry Pie filling. "You ready to play?"

Lich nods. "Can't wait."

"Been a while since we dusted off our old Wolf Harp tunes."

"Yeah. How do you feel about it?"

"Can't wait either."

For a moment, they just lean there against the courthouse brick, mouths full of pie.

"How'd they sneak that one past Sheriff Keller? His life's mission is shutting the MOW down."

Barry shrugs. "Our job is not to ask, dear buddy."

"Is there a cover?"

"Bet there is. Old Man Rudy may be a punk rocker, but he's cheap as hell."

"Yeah, that's true," Lich says. "We still the opener? I can't stay late."

"Dude, what? You don't want to sneak beers with me after the gig?" Barry waves dramatically. "Those are victory beers, dude. We need those."

"Yeah, I get it." Lich shakes his head. "It's not like I don't want to… Just, I don't know. It depends."

And then Barry gets it. "Oh. Your mom is pulling another Houdini?"

Lich nods.

"Fuckin' bitch, dude."

"Come on, man," Lich says quietly.

Barry sighs. "Sorry. It just seems like she's leaving you alone with the twins more and more lately. Those benders she goes on… It just pisses me off."

"Yeah. Anyway, I can't leave the twins alone too late if she's still gone after school. And even if she's back, well, probably still can't leave them, ya know?"

Barry shakes his head, takes a deep breath, and claps Lich heavily on the back. "Fuck it. We can just no-show if it comes down to it." He smiles. "That'd be pretty metal, actually. We can stay at your place and crush some *Golden Eye* instead. Besides, Sheriff Killer's probably sniffed the show out already and has big plans to shut it down. Probably best not to be there when he's hungry for blood."

Lich smiles. "You're not tired of getting your ass kicked in *Golden Eye*?"

"Look at the balls on this kid. Just keep picking Jaws, and I'll keep whooping your ass."

"Whatever, man. Real original playing as Bond."

Barry holds up his index finger like his hand is a Luger, hums the James Bond theme, then pretends to blast Lich in the face with the finger gun. "All right. We got school in like an hour. Where's those damn hedge trimmers?"

APEX DOOR

Roughly fifteen hours until the Grafting Quake

EVERY TOWN HAS an Apex Door, including yours. Most likely, you know the building. You just don't *know* it. It's that one old building off that nondescript drive, looks as if it's been derelict since before you were born. Everyone in town knows the place, but no one knows for sure what purpose it ever served. It was a grocery store once, according to a neighbor; a factory, according to a friend. Hell, your town's Apex Door might've been a dentist's office at one point. Maybe it's just a house, or an old mill missing half its lumber. But why is the building's lawn always mowed? Who hung up those NO TRESPASSING signs? Sometimes there's a car parked out front, or a truck, or several, but you've never seen anyone coming or going. Or maybe you have? Maybe they saw you, too. And maybe they recognized you? Maybe it's a building on a busy city block, or one catching seagull shit along the industrial side of the bay, or one that's rotting on some abandoned farmland. But regardless of what it looks like on the outside, inside that building is an Apex Door field lab.

The one in Grafting, Michigan, is right down the street from the courthouse where Barry and Lich are currently scarfing a few Donner cherry pies and washing them down with Sunny Delight. Barry takes a good hard look at what he coincidentally calls the Door Factory, but he doesn't see the fleet of white vans coming from south on Higgins, doesn't see them pull into that neglected asphalt drive out front. Gun Club is playing on the tape deck, so he doesn't hear the semi-truck that follows those white vans. Doesn't have a chance to catch the Apex Door logo.

The first of the fleet—a brand-new Sprinter van—pulls to a stop along the cracked drive. A short man hops out, black silver-streaked curls bouncing. He removes his horn-rimmed glasses, wipes away a fog from the lenses with a small cloth, and squints up at the building. He tucks the cloth into the pocket of his pressed white shirt, then turns awkwardly to watch the rest of the vans park. He curses under his breath as the semi-truck pulls in behind the caravan.

"Oh goodness…" he says. He's not known to curse.

He reaches into the van and retrieves a clipboard from the passenger seat that has an inventory checklist, as well as some notes on timing that he'd scribbled in blue ink around the margins. As the other vans pull in, he directs them with waving hands toward the east side of the old factory. Their drivers know to back up to the roller doors—all this was covered during the briefing back in Tennessee—and so that's what they do. He then regards the parked semi-truck, which idles loudly. The truck's driver, a hulking man with dark skin, is now leaning against the grill, smoking a cigarette.

"Dale," the driver says to his clipboard wielding counterpart.

"Please, Logan, call me Dr. Foster. I believe I've earned as much."

"Okay, Dr. Foster, I'll bet you my salary against yours that this hick-ass town has never seen a Black man within its city limits until now. I'm a goddamn trailblazer." He hocks a loogie that steams on the truck's grill.

"Decorum, please," Dr. Foster chides. "A Regional Director is on his way."

Logan's shoulders drop. "Ah, shit. Seriously?"

"Daniel Cleeve, himself."

Logan whistles. "Better get to it then. Where do you want the payload? I doubt the tranquilizer is gonna last much longer, and no one wants that thing to wake early. Trust me. Big as a fuckin' T-Rex. You seen *Jurassic Park?*"

"I have not. And yes, I know all about Baby's strength."

"Baby?"

"*Babylon,* actually. Baby, for short."

"How adorable," Logan mocks.

Two forklifts approach from the loading bays. "Those forklifts will take it to the lab," Dr. Foster says. "Make sure they handle the cargo with care."

Logan squints at the abandoned factory from where the forklifts came. "Building's a bit small for an Apex lab, don't you think?"

"Oh, goodness." Dr. Foster wheezes an awkward laugh. "The lab is underground, and it's at least five times the size of what you see here." He laughs some more. "Goodness."

Embarrassed, Logan looks to the road, but the feeling fades when he sees what approaches. "Speak of the devil," he says. He squares his shoulders and folds his hands behind his back so as to stand at attention.

A black '86 Chevy Caprice rolls up the gravel drive and stops behind the semi-truck. Daniel Cleeve steps out. He's wearing a tweed blazer over a pearl-snap shirt, a gold cattle-skull bolo tie, a worn stetson, and a pair of aviator sunglasses, the lenses wine-red. He reaches into the breast pocket of his jacket and retrieves a pack of Lucky Strikes, then knocks an unfiltered cigarette into the corner of his mouth. He lights the cigarette with a gold Zippo. He places a pale hand against the semi-truck trailer and says with a cloud of smoke, "Leviathan slumbers."

Dr. Foster scurries over to him. "Mr. Cleeve, we weren't expecting you so early. What a pleasant surprise."

"You're behind schedule."

Dr. Foster checks his wristwatch and swallows.

Cleeve turns at the hip, twists to regard the fabled Head of Security and Field Extraction. A man so tough, he's legend. "Logan. I've heard good things. It's a pleasure to finally meet. Where are your men?"

Logan points toward the approaching forklifts, which have noticeably slowed upon the arrival of Cleeve. "En route, sir."

Cleeve turns to Dr. Foster. "Have you approximated the location of the next Bleed?"

Dr. Foster clears his throat, stumbles over his words. "I… uh… Once Baby is secure in the lab, I will work on the calculations."

Logan signals to one of his men, then breaks from the trio to join his team and help them move Baby to its containment chamber inside. Cleeve, meanwhile, begins a slow walk toward the factory, and Dr. Foster follows. Cleeve continues the conversation as they walk. "How is your *other* pet project going, doctor? Acclimating to the new environment?"

"Oh, yes. Doing fine, thank you. No genetic anomalies, no side effects. The opposite of Baby, really. It feels odd to say, but he's more or less a typical boy."

"What does he think of his new school?"

"I'll know today, I suppose. Assuming, of course, we're caught up, and I'm able to speak with him over dinner. He wasn't fond of moving here, resisted a bit. I think he's just tired of the constant starting-over. I know I would be at his age. Once we're done with this next Bleed, I'm hoping to stay here in Grafting through the end of the school year. The boy needs friends."

"How's his personality developing?"

Dr. Foster shrugs. "Slowly. But I'm reminded at times of my own youth. The boy has…*eclectic* tastes."

"Hmm," says Cleeve as they step through the double doors into the derelict factory.

They walk past an abandoned administrative desk stacked with dusty papers and step over a tipped-over desk chair. Rusting machinery and rotting doors clutter the place, the wood now home to all kinds of bugs and vermin. A spiral staircase leads to a small loft office in the back, but they intend to head down. They find the hidden door beneath a collapsing staircase—it's there only if you know where to look—and Cleeve pulls back an ancient light switch to reveal a keypad. He summons the elevator with a thirteen-digit alphanumeric code and a retinal scan, and down they go. Destination: Sub-Basement 10.

"You're not growing attached to the subject, are you?" Cleeve asks as the elevator begins its descent.

"Oh, goodness," says Dr. Foster. "How do you mean? I suppose that in some way I'm attached to all my projects."

"You've been entrusted with a study subject, doctor, not a son. When I deem the work done, I will end it, no questions asked. Do yourself a favor and do not become attached."

Dr. Foster swallows hard as the elevator dings and the doors open to the lab.

Inside the Apex Door underground base of operations for the northernmost region of Michigan, several key members of Dr. Foster's team scurry about like mice, carrying a binder or clipboard, or leaning over desks and consoles. Three of them are calibrating Baby's holding tank, while a viscous fluid slowly fills the large cylindrical container at the center of the lab. Several members of Apex Door's IT department are wiring the main console that controls the tank.

Cleeve presses a hand to the cylindrical glass. "One day, your subject might replace Babylon," he says. "And assuming it continues to develop as a normal human, it will be much easier to control."

Dr. Foster wipes a bead of sweat from his brow.

"When will I have your approximation, doctor?"

"I'll have them for you before sundown. The first approximation we calculated was just…different. I want to run the numbers again before I log my official report."

"Different how?"

"The data suggested two spikes, not just one."

"Two Bleeds? Simultaneously? Has this happened before?"

"No, and that's why I want to calculate again. I want to be sure it's not an error. We know such a phenomenon is theoretically possible, but practically speaking, it's too improbable to be of any statistical consequence. This new finding, if true, would change much of what we know about the Bleeds. Jill's team is working on a statistical model now, but it requires a lot of scratch code and they want to ensure that nothing fails."

"This sounds time-consuming, doctor, and time is not something we have a lot of."

"Yes, but we'll be significantly more equipped to deal with future Bleed events if we have a working model that—"

Cleeve puts a hand on Dr. Foster's shoulder and squeezes hard enough to make the man sweat. "I need your approximation, Dr. Foster, and I need it yesterday." He smiles a lizard smile. "Pretend your life depends on it."

Dr. Foster remains frozen in that icy grip, unable to speak until Cleeve removes his hand. "There is only one topographical anomaly anywhere near Grafting that is significant enough for entanglement," he explains. "The data is still too raw to pinpoint the exact location, but I can speculate. *Off* the record, of course."

Cleeve authorizes the off-record report with a nod.

"It's all empty land out there," Foster continues. "Dry and populated with scrub brush and sage. There is only one structure for miles—an abandoned maintenance-of-way building next to a decommissioned stretch of train tracks. I can give you the coordinates if you like, but I make no guarantees."

"Do that," says Cleeve.

At the far end of the lab, a massive freight elevator made specifically to move heavy machinery lurches to a halt with enough force to send a small tremor across the floor. It's large scissor-lift support compresses, and everyone turns to watch. Inside the elevator is Logan's idling semi-truck, which Logan puts into gear and lets roll into the lab without pressing the gas pedal. His men surround the vehicle, weapons drawn and at the ready.

One of the IT guys working on the holding tank climbs out from his tangle of wires and leans against the tank, arms crossed casually over his chest. This is the moment he's been waiting for. "Here comes Babylon," he says with a shit-eating grin.

THE SHOW WILL GO ON

Roughly eleven hours until the Grafting Quake

WHAT PERIOD IS this? Second? And what subject is it? Math? Science? Well, whatever it is, don't ask Barry. He has no fucking clue either. He's been on auto-pilot since the first bell. Currently, he's scribbling in the margins of a college-ruled notebook he stole from the school lost-and-found last month, and so far, he's sketched some pretty killer stuff: a capital "S" with a pyramid for a hat and an upside-down pyramid for a bottom; his best-ever freehand rendition of the Metallica logo; and a pretty decent xenomorph chasing after R2-D2. Various iterations of the Wolf Harp logo fills the rest of the page. He's working on one that has a Judas Priest vibe to it when Mrs. Camden pulls a fast one and calls on him.

Barry snaps to. Or so he thinks. The haze of stupor clears to sort of let him know that this might actually be the third or fourth time Mrs. Camden has called on him. Barry's good at improvising, but he missed the initial question, so all he's got to work with is...

"Well?"

Barry looks around the class like, *Can you believe what's happening here?* But they all just look back at him like yeah, they can.

"Barry?"

Barry finds Lich at the back of the classroom. Lich is smart and always ready to help out, and he's mouthing what is probably the correct answer, but goddamn it, Barry can't make out what he's trying to say. Barry squints, answers back with a wordless *huh?* It should be easy enough for his friend to understand, and Lich does, but all Lich can do in response is…*mouth harder?* What the hell, Lich?

Mrs. Camden spots the wordless exchange and interrupts with, "Barry, can you repeat the question to me?"

Shit. How will Barry get a whole Camden-question from his pal's terrible lip-syncing? Lich, bless him, starts to try, but no. Time for a new tactic. Time to go Wolf Harp on the situation. Do what he does when he has his Gibson Explorer—just shred in the key of Doom.

"I'd love to. But first I'd like to ask a question of my own?"

She looks befuddled. Caught completely off guard. *Perfect.* "I'm sorry, what…?"

Wait. What subject is this again? Barry's mind races. *It's, uh, well…* It can only be one of a handful of things, so he decides to roll the dice. Second period—if this *is* second period—is now American History.

"Isn't what you're asking simply a matter of interpretation?" *Because what about history isn't? Nailed it!*

Mrs. Camden frowns, and some in the class chuckle. "No," she says flatly. "Solving for x is most certainly *not* a matter of interpretation."

Barry snaps his fingers. "Oh, right. My mistake."

Second period is not American History, by the way.

Barry continues, "In that case, you just gotta figure out what y is."

Mrs. Camden nods. "And what is y?"

At this point, Barry knows he's in Algebra I, which is actually third period, not second, so at least now he can fail in key. "Uh… thirty?"

And that's when the bell rings. *Phew. Close one.*

Under the watchful eye of Mrs. Camden, Barry packs up his scribbles like they're as important as the real notes the other students took. Maybe she'll believe the answer to *What is y?* really is in his notebook if he packs it right.

He and Lich walk out of the classroom together, and there is
no confusion about what period comes next. If that was third
period, then next comes fourth, and fourth period is Barry's
favorite: lunch.

"You hungry?" Barry asks.

"Starving," Lich confirms.

LUNCH AT OTTAWA HEIGHTS:

Imagine an episode of *Nature*—David Attenborough's golden
voice strangely audible in your ear—as you survey the landscape
of foldout lunch tables and the herds of awkward teens that
gather about them. You see the lions first, because they're hard
to miss. They're most likely feasting on food paid for with stolen
lunch money, and they're totally laughing about it. Chet Springs
is the head lion and also the starting quarterback for the varsity
football team. With him are Patrick Smith, the team's middle
linebacker, George Jankowski, the school's all-conference tight
end, and State Champion wrestler, Corbin Reese. The four are
also Owls, because that's the school's mascot, but forget about
that for now.

You see the gazelle table next, because like the lions, they're
also hard to miss. They eat timidly from a cluster of sandwich
baggies they've packed for themselves even though their parents
give them lunch money every day. The gazelles know where they
stand, and they know their lunch money will be stolen, so they
plan ahead. The gazelles are weak, not stupid.

You see other types of animals, too. Chattering hyenas,
sloths baked out of their gourds, peacocks, chameleons, even
those weird little beetles that roll big balls of dung.

And finally, there's Barry and Lich.

Lich's family doesn't have much, so like all the great bottom
feeders of the world, he learned at a young age to value the
scraps. Every day after fourth period ends, he gathers up all the
empty soda cans left out on the lunch tables, and at the end of
the week, takes them to the bottle drop at the IGA, which pays

him enough money to buy another week of hot lunch. Today, he's used that money to snatch two trays of cheese pizza, sliced into squares, both of which go straight into his backpack in exchange for a butter sandwich wrapped in newspaper, which is Lich's actual lunch this afternoon. If you're not familiar, a butter sandwich is two slices of slightly stale Wonder bread separated by a thin spread of salted IGA-Select butter that's only a few days beyond it's expiration date. *Yum.*

But hey, at least the twins will have pizza for dinner tonight.

Barry, meanwhile, just chills, guzzling those half-pint chocolate milks that come in the tiny cartons, not a care in the frickin' world. Every day he slugs that shit like he's just been diagnosed with a terminal illness but is cool with it as long as this is how he gets to go out. In Barry's humble opinion, whatever the hell is in those carton-chocolate-milks is worth more than all the hot lunches in the world.

Approaching them now is Sammy. She has stringy brown hair and wears a rumpled green military jacket that's several sizes too big for her. She plops down next to Barry, who glances across the table at Lich like, *Ready?*

"Have you leveled up?" she asks, pushing her square glasses up the bridge of her nose and dropping a stack of binders and notebooks onto the table. Sammy is rare among the bottom feeders. She's got a tray with a steaming square of cheese pizza just sitting there, right out in the open.

Barry laughs. "Have I leveled up?" he asks sarcastically. He swivels his head to lock eyes with Lich across the table. "Have *I* leveled up?" The rhetorical question is even more exaggerated this time, since Barry loves to make Lich laugh.

Lich giggles, then takes a bite of his butter sandwich.

Barry levels his gaze on Sammy. "Are you seriously asking if I, Bludzorg the Dismemberer, leveled up after our last session?"

Sammy rolls her eyes, already flipping to the checklist in her dungeon master journal. "Fine. Can I assume then that you're prepared to use your new abilities?"

Barry's cocky grin droops. Quietly, he asks, "Which abilities did I unlock?"

"You gotta be kidding me," says Sammy, and she hands him the player's handbook. "Just make sure you're ready for next Wednesday, okay?"

Lich pauses his chewing.

Barry glances at his frowning friend, then back to their noble dungeon master. "Why?"

"Because," Sammy says, "next session will be a total party kill if you're not utilizing your next-level abilities."

"Fair enough," says Barry. No one wants a TPK. Still, he shrugs at Lich, and Lich shrugs back in agreement, takes another bite of his butter-wich.

Sammy folds her D&D journal shut and moves on to her movie journal. She opens it up and freehands a series of squares across a blank page, then starts sketching different camera shots within each one.

"What are you working on?" Lich asks.

Sammy turns the notebook so that the pages face Barry and Lich. She places her finger on the first storyboard panel. "Fade in," she says. "A young college girl named Mandy—brunette, cute, wears a green military jacket, totally misunderstood—watches from the backseat of a VW bus as her friends pick up one last passenger before heading to the canyon for their weekend camping trip."

She points to the next square.

"The passenger who just hopped in is their friend Billy, and he pulls out a bong and they all start smoking it. After a couple of rips, Mandy gets squirrelly and starts asking if anyone else is nervous about spending the night in the canyon. Wasn't it just one year ago that all those Boy Scouts disappeared without a trace?"

Sammy points to the third square.

"Mandy leans forward to ask her boyfriend Bradly if he's sure this is a good idea." Sammy deepens her voice, pretends to be Bradley, "Yeah, babe. All the bad things you hear about the canyon, they're just stories. Truth is a lot more boring than fiction."

Fourth square.

"Title screen." But before Sammy reveals the name of her movie, she grins. "What do you get when you cross *Night of the Living Dead* with *Friday the 13th* and *The Hills Have Eyes*?"

Barry and Lich look to each other for the answer but neither says a word.

"*The CREEPS…*" Sammy shouts, "*…of Casper's Canyon!*" A few nearby students look up from their lunches, seemingly baffled by the outburst, and Sammy settles back into her regular speaking volume without paying them any mind. "Its my new film. Just getting started." She thumbs through the rest of the storyboard. "Anyway, Barry, you're the stoner they pick up in the beginning. And Lich, well, you're one of the creeps, no offense."

Lich takes a pretend bow.

"Problem is, I'm sorta stuck."

"Why?" asks Barry. He aggressively slurps the final drops from his chocolate milk carton.

"Because," Sammy explains, "my characters have to be really dumb to investigate Casper's Canyon further. But they also have to keep investigating Casper's Canyon further."

"Oh," says Lich. He doesn't really get it. He's thinking about the square pizzas in his backpack and how he'd love to take just one little bite.

"So, whats the big deal?" Barry asks. "Just make the characters dumb."

Sammy glares at him. "*The Creeps of Casper's Canyon* is set to be my big statement to the world of cinema, my shot across the bow of all the other indie filmmakers out there. And in that spirit, I refuse to sacrifice my characters to the plot. My characters are complex. They have real motivation. They—"

"Why do they have to investigate?" Lich asks.

Sammy blinks. "Because they hear screaming," she says.

"Who's doing the screaming?" asks Barry.

"Their friend," says Sammy. "Patty. She was just stabbed to death by one of the creeps."

"Why shouldn't they investigate that?" Barry asks. "Their friend is in trouble."

"Yeah," says Sammy, "but they're not going to put themselves in danger. They don't even know if they can help."

"But Patty is their friend," Barry says. He looks at Lich like, *Why is this so hard for her to get?*

Sammy rolls her eyes. "Okay. Maybe I'll just have them call the cops."

"Patty's their friend, Sammy."

"Forget it," Sammy says, folding the notebook closed. "Hey, I saw your guys' band on a show poster out front. Are you really playing tonight at the MOW?"

Barry glances at Lich. "Maybe," he says.

"Maybe?"

"I just need to make sure the twins are okay first," says Lich.

Sammy pushes her glasses up her nose. "Your mom gone again?"

Lich nods.

Sammy sighs. "Jesus, man. First off, fuck her."

"Come on, Sammy," Lich says. "That's my mom."

"Yeah, sometimes," Sammy says. "Whatever. What if I watch the twins tonight? Would you guys be able to play?"

"Oh, shit," Barry says. He looks expectantly at Lich.

Lich mulls it over. Sammy can't be any worse than he is at watching the twins, and she'd definitely be much better than his mom. "Yeah, okay," he says.

"Eyyy," Barry exclaims in his best Fonz impression. "Hell yeah, Lich!" He climbs on top of the lunch table and starts air-guitaring right there in front of everyone. "Wolf Harp rides tonight!"

Lich can't help himself. He pulls his drumsticks from his back pocket and assaults the laminate tabletop with a God-forsaken paradiddle.

The lions don't like this. Chet looks at Patrick, who looks at George, who looks at Corbin. They should be the ones at the center of everyone's attention. Not Barry and fucking Lich. Chet is thinking about all the ways to put them in their place.

With his pinky and forefinger, Barry thrusts a pair of horns to the ceiling. With his other hand, he points at Lich. "You ready, buddy?" He shouts with fried vocals.

Lich just nods, then rips a mock drum fill across the table-top—imaginary snare, across several toms, down to the floor tom. But instead of finishing with a ghost crash, he points his right-hand drumstick at Barry.

Barry grins, then plops back down on his seat. "God," he says, shaking his head. "I can't fucking wait."

GIG NIGHT

Twenty minutes before the quake

THE EAST SIDE of Grafting, Michigan, lives off a five-day work week just like everywhere else in the country, but outside those five days, there's these two days—Saturday and Sunday—that are kind of like a pocket dimension for the town's east-side residents. To them, these days are more than just the weekend; they exist entirely outside of normal space-time. The east side landmark, Lumberjack's Tavern, for example, is packed full of familiar faces every Saturday night, and to every patron there, drink in hand, Friday afternoon is a distant memory and Monday is merely an abstraction, a thought experiment, a vague promise of something that might one day come to be. But not now. Now is Friday night. There's dancing, there's fighting, and there's drinks—cloudy drinks, warm drinks, and cheap drinks that should be even cheaper. Joe's Pub on the other end of the east-downtown sprawl has the spillover. The East Grafting residents that aren't at Lumberjack's are there. Time is meaningless in both places, because both places exist on the wrong side of the tracks.

The good side of the tracks is on the west side of downtown, with it's old brick buildings, cobblestone streets, and fairy lights strung from the manicured trees along quiet Higgins Avenue. But honestly, they can have their Copper Mill Park, with its pristine beaches along the Pistol River. East Grafting is where real Michiganders live, and where they've lived for generations. I mean, hell, someone's gotta grow all the veggies for those west-side seasonal salads, and slaughter the cattle for all their double-bacon pub cheeseburgers on toasted pretzel buns, right? The harvest and the red meat comes from east of the tracks. You're welcome.

Anyway, let's look at the MOW.

Those tracks cut a line straight through Grafting, wrapping around the downtown and eventually running parallel to Higgins Avenue, where Higgins becomes Highway 99. If you fired up an old Ford and went south along 99 on your way out of Grafting and came to where you saw the tracks running alongside the road, you might just miss a place like the MOW. Six days a week, it's an empty building full of nothing but ghosts and settled dust. Looks exactly like what it is: an abandoned Maintenance-of-Way structure beside the railroad's ballast, a building not utilized since the logging days. Well, not utilized as a lineside structure, anyway.

See, five days a week it's a tomb, but on Friday and Saturday, it's a port-of-call for all the punks, grunge monkeys, metalheads, and social pariahs in Grafting and the surrounding towns. On Saturdays, it's a venue for whatever music must only be played outside of town, in an otherwise empty building astride the railroad. Tonight's show is a lineup of stoner rock bands from south Michigan, and one local that basically no one's ever heard of but they should. Inside the MOW, it's all denim jackets with cutoff sleeves, Megadeth T-shirts, shoulder-length hair, and the musky scent of teenage body odor mixed with the tang of an older brother's ditch weed. The concrete floor is slick with sweat, spit, and spilled gas-station beer. There's a mosh pit near the stage, but if you don't want to get cracked in the skull by a flailing elbow, give that section a wide berth.

The local band tonight is Wolf Harp, a two-piece stoner metal outfit working the moshers into a frenzy with their syncopated double-kick, drop-C riffage. Screeching solos split the thunderous halftime feel. Barry and Lich, they are melting this crowd.

Playing guitar is one thing. But playing on stage? In front of what feels like a million raised hands, in the humidity of a thousand lungfuls of breath, lost in that singular haze of body heat? It's just different, man. It's just different. Your best friend is behind you, pounding the drum kit with all of the conviction of a thunderstorm. A whirling crowd amalgamates before you. Some of them are your age. Others are older than your dad would be if he were still alive. That crowd, it's an organism writhing as one unit, an ocean tide dredging up entire human bodies to float and kick and punch the air, screaming and sweating as they drift across a sea of reaching hands. Barry, smashing a vintage Elektro-Harmonix Big Muff Pi fuzz pedal, is the moon right now, and he's pulling this crowd towards him like the moon pulls the tide.

Barry drags a note along the high E string, all the way from the first fret to the thirteenth. His black Gibson Explorer shrieks in saturated fuzz like it never did when it was his dad's guitar way back when. Certainly not anytime he saw his dad wield the thing, which was only ever unplugged. Back then, the quarter-inch cable just spooled away from the jack beneath the bridge pickup and snaked its way toward the ghost of a Marshall stack that Barry Sr. had pawned at some point, for some unknown reason like always. Sometimes, dear old Dad would look back at that rectangle of permanently compressed carpeting where the Marshall stack used to be and just grieve. He was in the denial stage for a long time, until one day he looked back and faced the truth: yeah, he really had gone out and pawned it. To this day, the carpet is still stamped down in that spot. Cat lays there now.

Following the acceptance stage, Senior bragged about how much the Marshall stack was worth and even considered out loud the possibility of pawning the Gibson Explorer, too. But Barry wanted that guitar for himself. Coveted it. That's why when Senior went to pawn everything he owned, he couldn't find the black Gibson Explorer anywhere. Tore the trailer apart looking for it. Never looked *under* the trailer, though. Behind the lattice skirt, with all its purple Morning Glories.

Barry didn't go back beneath the trailer for it until a few years later, the day Senior croaked. Dug it out from a few generations of growth that had been trying to break the thing down in its hardshell case, as if it was biodegradable or some shit. He extracted it from the broken lattice, snapping away roots and shaking away topsoil. He opened the case one latch at a time and held that guitar up to the Michigan sun like King Arthur must've wielded Excalibur.

Barry screams into the mic with a deep-fried vocal. He's Merlin, not Arthur. A wizard. And he has everyone under his spell. He and Lich are playing their version of "Sad But True" by Metallica. And what Barry screams into the mic is a beckoning for nothing less than *more*. More violence, more emotion, more *fuck you*. And the crowd is responding. Devil horns and middle fingers pierce the air above the roiling crowd below.

It's Barry and Lich up there on a makeshift stage, hastily constructed in slapdash planks pulled from the piles behind this old Maintenance-of-Way structure alongside the railroad tracks. Barry screams, his face painted red beneath the stage lights, and Lich is a blur behind the drums, shirtless and wearing only basketball shorts.

This is Wolf Harp. The way Barry wields his guitar like a true axe, the way Lich pounds at those drums with his stainless steel drumsticks. Let's put it this way: Alien Organ Donor is up next, and the guys from Alien Organ Donor are considering leaving.

What could top this? I mean, look at those guys. Barry has his foot on the stage monitor, guitar propped on his knee. He's gritting his teeth all the way through a tap solo north of the twelfth fret (that's danger zone), ripping back to a chord progression in drop C, three keys below standard tuning. Closer to Hell. Always closer to Hell. And loving it.

Only the rage of Mother Earth herself can match this show. Earth head-banging on its axis—that would be the only worthy follow-up to Wolf Harp on this night.

And somehow, that's exactly what happens.

At first, it's hard to tell, because the whole building is rattling. Isn't it? Been doing that since Barry introduced a half step riff, C to C# in a specific interval with Lich's double-kick. The old planks that compose the floor began their ripple then, and the crowd worked that shit up to a tempus.

But then the stage lights fall into the crowd, and at first, its like, *hell yeah.* They fall in a shower of sparks, and the crowd absorbs that violence back into their mosh pit. But then the floor drops out and half the crowd is swallowed into a dark abyss. As the stage begins to cave in, a warm molten glow emanates from a cloud of steam and some noxious gas is expelled from the bowls of the planet's core.

But Barry, he's there to play a gig. He's a professional. Lich holds down the beat, looking a little worried, but he won't stop either as long as Barry keeps shredding the neck of his Gibson Explorer.

The ceiling is now collapsing all around them. Beams fall on the stage around Barry and Lich. Only then, and only because he has no other choice, Barry stops playing, and Lich stops too. They flee from the stage as the only sounds now are the terrified screams of more and more souls being lost to the yawning pit, and the splintering chaos of an old wooden building crumbling into the Earth's superheated crust.

Exit stage right, boys.

But before he can get off stage, some important-looking beam collapses onto Lich. Barry can hear his friend crying out amidst the madness, like it's the only sound for miles, and he goes back for him without hesitation. He flips his guitar around and props the headstock under the beam, then hoists the fallen support with his makeshift lever. He only needs to provide enough clearance for Lich to belly-crawl to freedom.

For a split second, it works. Not what Barry expected. The guitar, endowed with the power of metal, holds. Lich crawls forth from the wreckage, and he reaches a lanky arm to Barry.

Barry grips his best friend's hand tight. "Come on, buddy!" he shouts.

Lich urges forth a groan to help power his extraction, but just when he's almost free, another beam falls.

Falls right onto Barry.

In those final moments before unconsciousness, Barry can hear Lich shouting his name. He can hear the screaming, the crumbling, the disaster.

And then he's gone.

INCIDENT REPORT

Apex Door Field Assessment Unit 3

Incident/Assessment Report

Today's Date: Friday, September 8, 1995

Time: 9:03 AM

Assessor Number: 7

Assessor's Handler: Orson Caster

Location of incident: Grafting, Michigan

Person(s) affected: Calvin Purdy

Reason(s) for field assessment dispatch:

The home of Mr. Purdy was initially identified following an intercepted emergency call made to local police. Mr. Purdy described poltergeist activity that included Board-approved KIs, necessitating dispatch.

Key Indicators mentioned (please refer to the latest edition of the APEX DOOR FIELD ASSESSMENT MANUAL for updated glossary of Key Indicators to choose from):

- Levitation——furniture

- Loss of sleep

- Heightened emotional states of experiencers

- Increased tendency towards violent behavior

- Shadow figures

- Doppelgangers

- Adverse response to religious ritual (Christian)

- Leyline crux

Please describe the incident(s), including any anomalous phenomena:

We visited the home of Mr. Calvin Purdy on the morning of Friday, September 8. Mr. Purdy was initially reluctant to allow us conversation. Upon pulling up in the driveway of the residence, we were met with Mr. Purdy bursting from his home with a pump action shotgun. He greeted us with verbal warnings, indicating violent action was imminent were we to refuse his demand to leave his property. Assessor Seven was able to de-escalate the behavior before exiting the vehicle.

We met in his living room, and Mr. Purdy served me coffee.

I interviewed the experiencer and discovered he was the head of a household that included three daughters and two sons, as well as a wife. These individuals were no longer present. According to Mr. Purdy, these individuals had left him, and it was not his fault. It was my impression that

Mr. Purdy intended to "shoot" the entities responsible for summoning the poltergeist that now afflicted his home.

I was able to expand upon several of the KI material, and I deemed Grafting as meeting the criteria for further assessment, following a specific detail. Mr. Purdy had described one particular visitation from an entity not matching a shadow figure.

He described how recently following the departure of his spouse and offspring, he had been caught off guard to see his wife cross the space in the living room behind the back of his sofa. He witnessed Mrs. Purdy enter the kitchen and turn on the light. According to Mr. Purdy, she had been unresponsive to his attempts at verbal exchange. She turned a corner in the kitchen without a word uttered in response to his pleas and questioning, which included:

"Jen, is that you?"

"Jen, where are you going?"

"Why aren't you talking to me?"

Mr. Purdy pursued Mrs. Purdy into the kitchen and found no individual other than himself occupying the space. Having recalled her location (her sister's residence in Grand Rapids), he called the number, and a brief conversation made clear that Mrs. Purdy was still in Grand Rapids, a three hour drive from Grafting. The conversation over telephone was apparently brief.

Mr. Purdy was reduced to tears while describing the incident. He attempted to get information from myself and Seven. When we left, he asked how he could get in touch for a follow-up. He appeared emotionally compromised to the point of self-harm.

Assessor response:

Seven required a glass of water after its body temperature had clearly increased to detectable levels. Skin yellowed throughout conversation, sweat beaded, and cranial wire was losing security from right ear. He swallowed a stabilizer with the water and was able to continue assessment.

Seven informed me that our unit must remain in Grafting, Michigan, to explore future incidents.

Conclusion & Recommended Next Steps:

The town of Grafting, Michigan, requires further information-gathering. Seven was able to provide me with three locations within Grafting that must be visited next for further assessment.

Increased stipend to include hotel stay. Increased stipend to account for Seven's insistence that the tap water is contaminated and therefore requires Apex-issued bottled water only. Increased stipend to account for local cafe visits, as they are said to have the best milkshakes north of Detroit.

GRAFTING,
MICHIGAN

Friday, October 27, 1995

REWIND TO THE AFTERNOON
BEFORE THE QUAKE

SMALL TOWN SHERIFF

Roughly thirteen hours until the Grafting Quake

IT'S EARLIER IN the day, and we all know that an earthquake is nigh, due sometime after dark, but we're taking a look back at late afternoon when Sheriff John-David Keller is pulling his cruiser up to Rotten Roscoe's gas station on the corner of Higgins Avenue and Ninth Street. Fridays are when he tops off the gas tank. He checks his reflection in the rearview, using both hands to tuck the wavy bangs of his dark hair behind his ears. His cheeks dimple as he reaches a finger up to his teeth to pick out the remains of this morning's eggs-on-toast. Exiting the cruiser comes with a fanfare of clanging: keys, cuffs, coiled cable running up the receiver on his shoulder, snagged already on the five-point star pinned to his chest. Keller gets the gas pump going, flicks the little metal tab into place, and let's the gambit run itself while he goes inside for his favorite on-duty snack. And no, it isn't donuts, but nice try. Keller would laugh at that.

A bell jingles above his head as he steps inside the little mart, and Roscoe looks up from his book of crossword puzzles.

"Hey, Sheriff Johnny Boy. Come for the unleaded, stay for the pepperoni sticks, right?"

"That sounds about right. How are you, Roscoe? Staying out of trouble?"

Roscoe, he's one of those older guys who are as soft and kind-hearted on the inside as they are disheveled and unkempt on the outside. He smiles a broad smile that it is scarce as far as teeth go. His eyes smile, too. A haggard beard piles up on the crossword puzzle he's leaning over. He's got his red Rotten Roscoe's work polo on, looks like it's seen better days. Roscoe stands with a back bent by a life of bad decisions, something he's doing his damnedest to make up for now in his twilight years. Or as Roscoe would tell you, in his "old youth."

"Straight as an arrow, as always," Roscoe says as he snatches Keller's favorite brand of pepperoni sticks off the carousel display next to the cash register. "You feel that tremor this morning? Suzanna thinks it's a sinkhole. Like the thing that happened in Kentucky."

"Don't be mocking me now, Roscoe!" Suzanna calls from her office.

"I wouldn't dream of it," Roscoe calls back. He winks at the sheriff.

"Well, tell Suzanna that if it were something that serious, I would know about it already. Probably just some gas buildup at the landfill." Keller has no idea if gas buildups at landfills can cause small quakes, but he runs with it.

"I'll be sure to let her know. Hey, how's the old man doing these days?"

"He's alright, all things considered. Still has moments of clarity and no incidents since the last one."

The old man is Keller's dad, Bill. Truth is, those moments of clarity were getting further and further apart. And that incident? Well, back in mid-spring, when the snow was just beginning to melt during the day and would freeze into a crusty slush at night, Bill Keller had found himself lost in some memory of the second World War, dredged up by his Alzheimer's. Bill had stumbled through the streets in boxer shorts and a bathrobe, taking cover behind snow banks, shouting the names of men long since turned to ghosts. And at some point, one of those moments of clarity rushed in long enough for Bill Keller to realize that no, he wasn't in Okinawa. In fact, that whole mess had wrapped up a lifetime ago, and he was actually somewhere in Northern Michigan. Bill found himself shivering terribly in the middle of a street he didn't recognize. His eyes were the eyes of a frightened child's. He hugged himself there, teeth clattering, and all he could think to do was shout the only name he knew didn't belong to a ghost: the name of his son. Eventually, porch lights flicked on along the street, and the kinder folk of Grafting helped him inside one of their homes. They all knew Bill Keller, former sheriff for many years. A good man. A man who'd been gracious and selfless for so long that finding him in such a state was almost the same kind of tragedy as finding him dead. Maybe it was worse than that. Unlike his fellow soldiers, Bill may not have given up the ghost yet, but it was certainly haunting him from the inside out. And on nights like that one, the ghost was so close that you saw it there, swirling milky white in his terribly sad eyes. Keller had been on duty when the call came, and when it did, he felt an overwhelming sense of shame and inadequacy. The kind of anger that brings a man to tears. The church stepped in for a while to help Keller take care of Bill until the sheriff was able to arrange for a private nurse who now helps the Kellers out part-time. God bless that woman.

"You good, sheriff?"

Keller blinks and finds Roscoe looking at him, holding out the sealed pack of pepperoni sticks. "I'm not just good, Roscoe, I'm great." He winks as he takes the pepperoni sticks. The bell jingles above him again as he says, "Be good, Roscoe. I'll tell Pops you asked about him. He'll appreciate that."

Roscoe waves goodbye as the door closes between them.

Outside, Keller glances over to see a poster he missed on his way in. It's a flyer for a concert tonight at the MOW. The flyer promises to "ear-fuck you into another dimension," which, *cute,* Keller thinks. Shows at the MOW usually mean a busier-than-normal night for him and his deputies.

He walks to his car, places the nozzle back in its pump, and fires up the cruiser. Keller tears the seal to his pepperoni sticks, wishing it was the pack of cigarettes they are meant to replace, rolls down the window to let the tang of cured meats the fuck out, and heads to the Grafting sheriff's station.

LET'S HONE IN on the sheriff's station for a second. And I do mean a second (well, a handful of them, anyway), because what really is there to say about this place? It's a single-story cinder block building painted tan, as if an architect with an odd love for Brutalism built the place and then picked the most soul-less paint color imaginable just to give a second middle finger to all his haters, and it sits atop a little knot of a hill at the far end of a cracked parking lot that is in such a state of ruin, it looks like nature is winning the war to reclaim that land for itself. The lot is shared with City Hall, the tallest building in all of Grafting, with not two, not three, but four entire floors of bureaucrats busying themselves with boring shit. There's some patrol cars parked out front of the sheriff's station, and there's also a defunct school bus and some junker Grumman Long Life mail trucks amidst a couple rows of vehicles unclaimed from impound. Looks like Sheriff Keller may be running a scrapyard on the side. Inside the station, its the same linoleum tiling you probably remember from elementary school, white and speckled black to hide the dirt and grime. A painted blue line on the wall is the only color in the lifeless hallway.

The place is as quiet as a morgue.

When Keller arrives, a rail-thin woman named Danni is already seated in the waiting room. She may as well get paid by the hour, considering how often she's in there to collect her baby daddy, a dude with a bleach blond buzz cut, septum piercing, and neck tattoos.

Keller nods to her on the way in. "Morning, Danni. What's Jacob gotten himself into now?"

The young woman, and I do mean young—Danni would be a college freshman in another life—holds a newborn under a nursing cover. She shakes her head. "I swear to God, I am done with his horseshit, Sheriff."

Young Danni is always done with Jacob's horseshit.

Keller nods back without breaking stride toward his office. He tries to remember if it had been last week when Danni had said those exact same words put together in that exact same order, or if it'd been the week before.

He can't go too far, however, without Debs interrupting his step, and this time, he *does* break stride, because, well, you'll see.

"Excuse me, Sheriff. Couple calls came in you oughta know about." Debs sits in her chair at the reception desk as if she was grown there from a Petri dish, her sour tone soaked with enough brine to have fermented her personality entirely—which is probably a good thing, actually. Her beehive hairstyle would probably attract a whole colony of honeybees if she were even the slightest bit sweet. Today, she wears a gaudy Halloween sweater, black and patterned with little orange jack-o-lanterns.

Keller turns back, leans over the desk, and props himself on his elbows. "Is today the day, Debs?"

"Oh, God." She rolls her eyes.

"I think it might be. I think today just might very well be the day you and I have long been waiting for."

"Sheriff..."

"I'm gonna do it."

"Johnny," Debs says, a slow smile creeping.

"Debs?" Keller says.

"Oh, Lord, here we go."

"Will you make me the happiest man on Earth and—"

"Goodness, you're too much."

"—And marry me?" Keller takes her hand.

With a heavy sigh and a gentle smile, Debs says, "You were still in diapers when I filed for my first divorce, and you'll probably be in them again before I finalize my last."

Keller loops his thumbs in his belt straps. "Oh, you didn't know? I came out of the womb housebroken. No diapers."

"Ain't that something. Don't you have some police work you can do?"

"Nope." Keller taps the badge on his chest. "The day they pinned this on me was the same day all the bad guys packed up and headed for greener pastures."

Debs shakes her head, laughs like a snorting horse. "If only." She lifts a highlighter-pink Post-it note with her chicken scratch scribbled ineloquently in red ink. "I've highlighted a few calls for you on this Post-it. Take it, please."

He does.

"Fine, but I'm coming for you, Debs." He blows a kiss as he heads back to his office, catches her smiling more honestly than she probably had meant to, but not without rolling her eyes one last time.

The Post-it note contains three action items:

1. *The Ottawa Herald* called for a statement on the tremor this morning.

2. Doug Comely, principal of Ottawa Heights, wants a call-back.

Yeah, naw, Keller thinks. High school boys shitting in the urinal is not a county issue. *Sorry, Doug, but we've been over this.*

3. The third item is a complaint about kids skateboarding in Copper's Park, and Keller knows that this complaint didn't come from any phone call. This is Debs's personal grievance…again.

A *knock, knock* at the doorframe announces Deputy Michael Pipes, who steps into the office carrying two Dixie Cups of steaming coffee. "Hey, sheriff."

"Morning, Mikey. How's life treatin' you?"

"Oh, just another day in paradise." He takes a seat in the chair opposite Keller's desk.

"If this is paradise…" Keller shakes his head to finish off the thought. "Thanks for the cup of joe."

"Don't mention it. How's your dad?"

"Better," Keller lies.

"Good."

"How about the missus?" Keller asks.

"Eh, you know," says Mikey. "Up my ass."

"Funny. Usually you're the only one up there."

"It's more spacious than you think," Mikey says. The two men share a laugh. "Hey, speaking of my wife, I was hoping to punch out early today. If you think we've got the coverage, that is."

"Early? You getting slack on me, Pipes?"

"Nah, but it just so happens to be me and Marie's anniversary. Want to get home before she's counting sheep."

"No shit? Congrats, man. Did you get her something nice?"

A lopsided smile dimples one side of Mikey's face. "I think so."

"Well?"

Mikey sighs. "Got a minute?"

"Got two if the story's a good one."

"So, you know how we honeymooned in Key West? And how Marie just couldn't get enough of the beaches there? Well, during one of our last days on the island, I went out to grab a bottle of wine from the local grocer, and while I was there, grabbed a little Tupperware container. Then, I took a quick detour to the beach she loved so much and scooped a bunch of sand and some sea-shells into the Tupperware and kept it hidden in my suitcase for the trip home. Marie was none the wiser. Last week, I had Cam over at Woody Works make a little sign that says, *Mikey and Marie's Private Key West Beach.*" He smiles, proud of himself. "I'm gonna give her the Tupperware and the sign tonight. But that's not all." He reaches into his trouser pocket and pulls out a red velvet ring box. He pulls back the lid to reveal a shining gold band with a modest diamond nestled inside the bevel.

"Well, would you look at that."

"I proposed to Marie with an onion ring, sheriff."

"A what now?"

"Back then, I couldn't afford much of anything. Marie was still in school, and I was barely out of the academy. But some-how she still said yes, man. Said yes to an onion ring, with a giant smile on her face. Before the ceremony, I ponied up for something cheap from the K-Mart, but she deserves better. Took me a few years of saving, but I finally got it. So, now what

I'm gonna do is put this here ring in the mini beach I made and re-propose as part of the gift."

A smile spreads over Keller's face, the kind that includes the eyes, the ears, the hairline, everything. "Damn, Pipes. You're a modern day Casanova."

Pipes folds the velvet box shut and puts it back in his trouser pocket. "And that's not even the really big news."

"Whadda ya mean?"

"Well, sheriff, I think Marie's pregnant."

Keller falls back in his chair, which leans and then accepts his weight with a shrill squeak. Eyes alight with a mix of shock and enjoyment, he weighs the news with his hands, each one held out like opposite sides of a scale. "What? How? I mean, how do you know?"

Pipes shrugs. "I don't know for sure, but there've been signs. Hasn't been drinking, asked about whether I'd be able to support us if she ever had to take some time away from the hospital. And just this morning, I saw a little gift-wrapped box sitting out on the dining table, and the note on it said 'I have something to tell you,' and she drew a little smiley face with heart eyes."

Keller grasps for the right words. "Well…uh…that settles it then. Who else is on tonight? Art?"

"Tammy."

"Oh, well shit," says Keller. "Tam is better than two Mikey Pipes put together. Yeah, no problem, man. Take the night off. Celebrate. Just make sure you're back at the station bright and early tomorrow."

Pipes pauses, then fumbles through a response. "Oh, yeah, of course. I'll make sure to set an alarm—"

"Mikey, I'm just fucking with you. Hell, take tomorrow off, too, if you need it. I highly doubt anything earth-shattering is gonna happen while you're gone. This is Grafting we're talkin' about."

"Thank you, sheriff. I won't forget this." Pipes sucks in a nice long breathe, then slaps his knees as he exhales. "Well, I better get back to it then." He gets up and heads to the door.

"Hey, Mikey," Keller says.

Pipes stops at the doorframe and turns back. "Yeah, sheriff?"

"Should I start calling you Deputy *Pops*?"

Mikey grins. "I'll let you know tomorrow."

Keller should have ended it there, *knows* he should have, *feels* it in his core, but for a reason he will never be able to explain and never fully understand, he says something he will always and forever regret. "By the way, if you're looking for something easy to do before clocking out tonight, you can post up out by the MOW for a few hours before it gets late. Apparently there's some rock show there tonight, so it would probably be good for someone to keep an eye on things before I swing over there myself some time closer to curfew. And, hell, if things are looking tame when you get there, feel free to cut out even earlier than planned."

"Sure thing, boss."

"Oh, and Mikey, don't sweat the small stuff, okay? We're not here to bust teenagers for smoking Marlboros. I just don't want a bunch of drunk kids operating motor vehicles all over my town. Cool?"

"Cool." And with that, Pipes is *hasta luego*.

Alone once more, Keller looks to the bright pink Post-it again. No, he won't be providing a statement to *The Ottawa Herald,* and no he won't listen to more of Doug Comely's complaints, but he needs something to do, so he heads to Copper's Park to shoo the skaters away from the tennis courts. *You're welcome, Debs.* Then it's an unexpected call from dispatch about a fender bender at the IGA, so he deals with that next. After sorting that mess out, he passes a vehicle that is driving just *way* too fast, too far above the speed limit to ignore, so he pulls the car over. It's almost dark by the time that ticket's written and torn from the book. He intends now to swing by where Tam has posted up on the north side of town, just to check in, but first he grabs the two-way radio receiver clipped to his shoulder and aims it at his mouth.

"Hey, Pipes. How are things at the MOW?"

A crackle of static, then: "Looks like a real gas. Judging by the kinds of folks going in and out, I think it'll be busy."

"All right. I'm on my way to Tam now. I'll have her come relieve you so that you can clock out, get home to the missus. Doubt the west side needs her presence beyond happy hour."

"Thanks, sheriff. Keep me posted."

Downtown Grafting barely spans the length of three city blocks, so the drive is quick, but to the locals, it's more than enough. In any case, here's some of the sights you spy on that twenty-mile-per-hour cruise headed in from the north:

First, it's a Chevron station that sort of marks the spot where signs of civilization start to appear. The post office comes next, three flags whipping atop the poles out front. Then, there's a slight downward grade to the narrow bridge that crosses Pistol River, and on the other side of the Pistol, there's a few businesses that look like they used to be houses—so not your typical business-y type of structures. A hair salon occupies one, and Wendy, the owner, takes residence on the top floor. A real estate office occupies another, but its always darkened and locked up since Grafting isn't exactly a hot destination for prospective home buyers—you live here because you were born here, not because it called to you from across state lines. Another business is a hobby shop called Ant's Good Stuffs. He's got rare baseball cards in there, hard-to-find coins, and collectible stamps—that kind of thing.

After the row of house-offices, you come upon a two-story, brick building painted the color of ocean blue—that's Pistol River Pizza, and it's the only pie joint in town. Pistol River Pizza sort of establishes what can truly be considered "Downtown," or "Old Grafting," as it's also called. This is the stretch of three blocks mentioned prior, and it's nothing but old brick buildings still standing from back in the logging days, all of 'em two stories high. Next to Pistol River Pizza is the Grafting Cinema 2, and the old couple who've been running the place for what feels like five thousand years still refuse to play movies that are rated R and will only play certain movies that are rated PG-13, like *Heavyweights* and

Kevin Costner's *Waterworld*, which are both currently advertised on the marquee.

Beside the Grafting Cinema 2 is Buck's Five & Dime, where the kids all load up on snacks before heading to the movies. They scoop a mean Superman ice cream cone in the summer. There goes Lumberjack's Tavern, sort of out-of-place here, one of those watering holes that keeps Keller and his deputies busy. And rounding off the strip is Rob's Hardware, which is actually just the old First Bank of Grafting building that Rob remodeled after the lender grew too big for the office and moved out in the '70s, back when Keller was still just a kid. Rob hangs all the landscaping tools in the building's old bank vault. Says if he ever has to barricade against the commies or something, he'd like to do it in a safe-room full of chainsaws. Also, if the wrong kinda fellow went in and maybe got a bit too precious about the wares, well, that's a big-ass prison door if it needs to be.

On the other side of the street, there's a fabric shop, a pub, and the Copper's Cafe, which is open 24-hours—so, that's pretty cool. There's also Movie Knight, the video rental store, which has the most metal sign in Grafting. It hangs by two rusty rings from beneath the leveled lance of a medieval knight on horseback, the furious steed galloping toward an invisible enemy mid-joust. Keller is a big fan. He was actually disappointed to see a Blockbuster open up in Pinewood Plaza, next to the IGA up the street. So was Cal, the owner of Movie Knight, who hung a banner in his storefront window soon after. It shows the Blockbuster logo in a red circle with a line going through it, like from the movie *Ghostbusters*. These days, if you chat with him for more than thirty seconds, you'll hear him complain humorlessly about "Ballbuster" and all the ways it sucks.

On a Friday night like tonight, plenty of folks are walking up and down the downtown avenue, going from Buck's Five & Dime straight into *Waterworld*, or crossing the street with a stack of Pistol River Pizza pies in hand to rent a movie from Movie Knight—or if you're from the west side, Blockbuster.

Keller pulls up alongside Tam's cruiser, which is parked in the Pinewood Plaza. He retrieves a pepperoni stick from the bag that's been resting on the passenger seat since he'd left Rotten Roscoe's that morning, tucks one spicy end behind his molars, and steps out of the cruiser like a slick-as-hell hombre. Tam is already rolling down the driver's-side window of her own cruiser when he approaches.

"Hey, Tam." Keller flicks a wave, one hand wrapped around his belt.

Tam nods. "Sheriff." One thing about Tam is she's not exactly a socialite. She's no Zelda Fitzgerald, if you catch my drift. Woman of few words, and honestly, the sheriff could never venture a guess as to why. Either she was incredibly pissed, deeply depressed, or profoundly apathetic. Maybe all three. But he caught on pretty early that her shitty attitude—whatever the cause—was unintentional. She tried her best to seem pleasant, which Keller believed should count for something.

"How's business?"

Tam shrugs. "Couple citations."

"Hey, listen, Pipes is clocking out early tonight. It's his wedding anniversary. But right now, I have him scoping out some rock concert at the MOW. You mind heading over there to relieve him?"

"Friday night. Who's posting up downtown?"

"I know, I know. I'll hang around here in case dispatch hits us with anything. Keep a special eye on Lumberjack's." He winks, which he immediately regrets.

"Why me?" Tam says flatly.

This kind of catches Keller off guard. "Come again?"

"I'm already here. Why don't you go relieve Mike?"

If this retort came from any other deputy, Keller would tell them that he's the sheriff of this town, and he can do whatever he wants, and what he wants right now is to watch downtown while they cover for Mikey at the MOW. But when something like this comes from Tam, something just urges Keller not to get into it with her. So, he nods and says, "Good point. You got this side of town on lock-down, so why mess up a good thing? I'll cover for Mikey." He smiles.

Tam's mouth remains a flat line. She nods.

"Alrighty then," says Keller. He pats the hood of Tam's cruiser. "Just, uh, keep up the good work then. *Tally ho*, or whatever."

Tam grimaces, then rolls up the window while Keller thinks to himself *tally ho? Tally fuckin' ho?* He has no idea where that came from, feels weird about it, but more than that, he feels weird how quickly and easily he caved. Tam openly refused a direct order, and Keller just…allowed it. But she's right, though. There's no reason to get his jockstrap in a wad. *Tally ho* was a lot worse than anything else that just happened. Maybe there's a lesson to be learned here: be more like Tam and keep your words to a minimum. That might just be the cure for *tally ho*.

AS KELLER NAVIGATES the back roads to the MOW, he wonders if Mikey Pipes is feeling betrayed. Poor guy should be home already. He turns the volume up on the car's radio to better hear the current song being blasted from the towers of Z93.3 as part of the station's weekend edition of *Classic Rock Hits*. The tune is called "Pictures of Matchstick Men." It's not often that the group called *Status Quo* hits the airwaves around these parts, but when it does, it's always this song. Makes sense, though, as it was the band's only hit. A lot of folks in Grafting would use this opportunity to change the station, but not Keller, not tonight. Tonight, this song hits. There's just something about the right song in the right situation, ya know? And I truly mean the *right* song. Not just a good one, or something you heard before and liked, but the *right song, man.* Keller can't really put his finger on why, but tonight, the right song for him is "Pictures of Matchstick Men."

Outside the cruiser's window, tall pines and elms give way to juniper and sage brush. The sky is big out here, especially with no trees or buildings in the way. Keller gets why kids and rock 'n' roll old-timers chose the boonies for their shows. He's jealous, actually, now that he thinks about it. Must be nice, stepping outside after a great gig in the repurposed maintenance-of-way structure, smoking a joint beneath the stars. Nothing but good vibes and a sky full of bedazzled infinity.

Keller is smiling already when he pulls up alongside Deputy Michael Pipes's cruiser. He gets out, walks to his deputy's vehicle, and leans on the hood like he did Tam's, waits for the deputy to roll down his window.

"Look at you, Pipes, just sitting out here on your ass, catching a contact high from some ditch weed while your poor wife waits at home. And on your one-year wedding anniversary, no less. You a bad husband, Pipes?"

Pipes smiles. "The absolute worst, sheriff."

"Not on my watch. Get the hell out of here, man. You have a date to catch."

"Roger that, sheriff. And thank you. Again"

Keller swats away the gratitude like it's a house fly, and before he knows it, Pipes is gone.

Keller falls back into the driver's seat of his own cruiser and watches the MOW for activity. The muffled sound of the bands playing inside creates a sort of resonance that feels just fine over the gravel parking lot. That's when the radio crackles to life with Tam's voice.

"Altercation outside Lumberjack's. Stand by."

Keller tilts the radio on his chest, "Roger that, Tam. Let us know if you need backup."

Crackle. "It's the Zimmer boys again. Pretty sure I got this."

Ah, the Zimmer boys, trading blows outside Lumberjack's. That how you know it's Friday night in Grafting. Comforting, in a way, like low tide at sunset.

Another crackle. This one from Sandra back at dispatch. "Got a 12-29 up Pine Mountain."

Keller answers, "Copy that, Sandy. Any more details?"

"Call's from Brock Corning. Says his house is about to collapse."

A knot forms above Keller's brow. "12-5. Come again, dispatch."

"I'm confused, too, sheriff. According to Brock, his house is shaking, and the windows are starting to shatter."

"Jesus. Okay, I'm on my way."

But before Keller can restart the cruiser's engine, Pipes's voice crackles in the radio. "No need, sheriff. I'm already en route."

"No, Mikey. You're off-duty for the night. I've got this."

Nothing but the muffled sounds of the MOW. Keller can almost see Pipes waffling on how to respond.

Finally, Pipes chimes in again: "I'm almost there already, sheriff. No reason to go out of your way. Probably just a small rock slide. I'll be in and out in five."

A tremor ratchets through the parking lot, shifting Keller's cruiser. It's a sensation Keller has never felt before. It's so alien, he wonders if it really even happened. *Just a small rock slide, huh?*

Keller clutches his radio. "Careful, Mikey," he says.

Another tremor rattles everything. Keller steps out of the vehicle, fresh pepperoni stick in hand. Goddamn, he wishes it's a cigarette. He eyeballs his cruiser. Maybe it was just the old Chevy that was shaking. Probably not, though. Keller wipes two sweaty palms on his pleated pants because something just feels off. The moon has retreated behind a wisp of cloud, the stars are hazy, and the muffled rock music inside the MOW has shifted to a dissonant key. Keller is breathing sharply through his nose. He's got a look on his face that says he doesn't trust his senses anymore.

Then the radio crackles with Pipe's voice. It's frantic. Terrified. Keller has never heard a man sound so scared in his life.

"Send all units to my location now! I've got multiple homicides! I repeat, multiple— Oh my God, Keller, it's… I know these kids."

Keller nearly tears the receiver from his chest. "Mikey! What's goin' on?"

Nothing.

"Tam, did you hear that? Over."

Still nothing.

Pipes's voice comes back. "…Fuck! Is that…Chet Springs?"

Springs? The Ottawa Heights quarterback? What the fuck?

Keller tries Pipes again with no luck, so he radios dispatch. "Sandra, did you get Mikey's transmission just now? Over."

"Deputy Pipes? No, sheriff. I got nothing."

"He's reporting multiple homicides, and he needs backup. Do you have his location for me? Over."

"Are you serious? *Multiple* homicides?"

"Location, Sandra!"

"I…uh…don't have it, sheriff. I mean, last I heard, he was heading up to the Corning place. God, sheriff, who's been killed?"

The Corning place doesn't make sense, though. Brock would never let a bunch of teens hang out at his cabin, not even the star quarterback for the Owls. It's possible his daughter Amber is back in town—she and Chet used to be a thing before her parents' divorce—but last Keller heard, Corning's wife Allison took the kids to southern California after she was granted full custody by the courts. He doubts she'd allow her eldest to return alone.

"Sandra, listen to me. I need you to get that location for me, okay? I'm heading to the Corning place now, but if you hear that Mikey is somewhere else—even if he's just a few hundred yards from that house—you need to let me know asap. You copy?"

"Copy, sheriff."

Keller looks to the MOW. Whatever small infractions might happen here tonight means nothing now. He jumps back into his cruiser and cranks the engine, but he doesn't make it out of the parking lot before the earthquake hits.

The ground ahead of Keller caves, and the Chevy skids, goes airborne for a brief second, then crashes hard and tumbles. The first thing Keller's head does is smack the driver's-side window, hits with enough force to spiderweb the glass. The cruiser continues to roll and Keller's head smacks that same spot again and again. On the final smack, the window shatters completely. All of them do.

Silence, then sound.

The soft ticking of an engine, the idle spinning of tires.

Keller opens his eyes to see that he's now upside-down in his cruiser, the vehicle's roof caved in and beneath him. But before he can make out heads for tails, he blacks out.

DEATH OF A DEPUTY, PART ONE

Roughly Five Minutes Before The Quake

THIS ISN'T THE first time Pipes has turned onto the private gravel drive that winds its way slowly up the lee side of Pine Mountain and ends at Brock Corning's little getaway cabin, sequestered among the trees. He's been called to this house before. In the past, though, it's always been for low priority complaints better suited for Animal Control—a black bear in the cans, raccoons scritch-scratching on the roof, a pissed-off owl hooting its head off at three a.m. But the sheriff's department can never treat the complaints as such, because, according to Corning, every new disturbance is different—*real*—not a false alarm like last time. Tonight, he's convinced it's the apocalypse.

Pipes grumbles to himself, now regretting his urge to help the sheriff out. He should be home right now with Marie, not out here battling wildlife. But maybe this is why she loves him. He's loyal. Dependable. Always willing to help out.

But why did it have to be Brock Corning? He's the richest man in Grafting, and he doesn't give a shit about anyone but himself. While most people in Grafting are living paycheck to paycheck, he's flying on his private jet to Chicago because the other day he had a taste for deep dish. To guys like Corning, "public service" is just another way of saying "servitude." What does it matter if he treats the grocery clerk like shit? Who cares if it's just some raccoons in the garbage cans and not an armed robber? Someone has to look into it, and that someone is Pipes. It's the man's job. He should be grateful for the work.

"He's right," Pipes says to himself, now almost to the house. "It's your job, so cut the complaining."

That's when the earthquake hits.

Pipes has never experienced an earthquake before, never even been to a state where they commonly occur, so he doesn't have any frame of reference for what should or should not be considered "normal" during such an event. All he knows is this: whatever's ahead of him, it's not normal.

What he sees but doesn't know it is the rapid approach of the earthquake. It's coming from the Corning cabin, looking less like geological phenomena and more like the shock wave from an atomic bomb. The ground ripples in a wave of exploding asphalt and dirt, boulders flying. Eighty-foot pine trees buckle in their roots.

Pipes's first instinct is to hit the brakes and swerve, but by doing so, he mistakenly positions the cruiser the wrong way relative to the incoming calamity—perpendicular, like if a surfer took a wave broadside—and his vehicle is flung toward the heavens just like the rest of the forest floor.

The cruiser whirlybirds through the air, and Pipes goes rag doll. His body smashes against the window, the center console, the steering wheel. The radio in the dash unhooks and whips about like a snake. Pens fly through the air around him, and his hours-old coffee upends itself from the cup holder and splatters inky liquid everywhere. Then the car slams back to the ground and tumbles, tumbles, tumbles, until, finally, it rolls onto its side and pauses. Momentum not yet spent, however, it wavers there for a moment, then with a long, whining *creeeaaak*, falls like a felled tree and firmly re-plants itself back on all four busted-up tires.

Pipes sits there for a moment, still buckled into the driver's seat. He takes stock of the mess around him. Tries to blink himself out of a stupor. The security lights from Corning's cabin—the ones that were shining through the pine trees just a minute ago—are now gone. *Okay...* Quake probably knocked out the power, jostled some battery wires loose. But that still doesn't explain the sound he hears crackling over the radio. It's the voice of someone familiar. Someone young. Says he's on his way right now to the scene. *Is that...? No. It can't be.*

That stupor, blink it away, Pipes. Shake that nonsense from your head. You didn't just hear what you think you did.

Pipes opens the driver's-side door, and it groans against the dents and scratches recently acquired. He's surprised he can stand up straight, though he does need to steady himself with one hand on the hood. He's got a Maglite in his other hand, feels the first hint of pain there as he tries to grip it. The way the cone of light wavers in the still settling dust from the quake alludes to some kind of injury to his wrist or hand. That, or he's just terrified. He's careful as he makes his way down the ruined driveway because this isn't just another case of raccoons. Corning is in real need of help. Pipes is certain of that.

The driveway, it's not in good shape. The manicured gravel is now a treacherous terrain of deadly hazards and pitfalls. It would be tough to navigate *without* a concussion, so the fact that Pipes is almost certainly concussed makes things more difficult. He trips a few times, adds new wounds to the ones already there. When he gets to the section of driveway where the forest opens to a clearing upon which the cabin should stand, Pipes freezes. He can't believe what he's seeing—or rather, *not seeing.* He figures it's gotta be a trick of the light, so he smacks his Maglite a couple times and tries again.

Same vision as last time.

The cabin is gone, no trace of it remains. Gone, too, is the clearing. All that remains in their absence is a smoking black crater and a dimming violet glow that emanates from somewhere inside the core. Corning's Chevy Corvette must have made it just far enough outside the event's epicenter before collapse, because there it is, still teetering on the crater's edge and slipping. The headlights are on and the engine is running, but Pipes doesn't see anyone inside.

Pipes unholsters his 9mm pistol, aims it alongside the Maglite. What are you planning to do, Pipes? Shoot the crater? Order its hands behind its back? Better safe than sorry, maybe, but really, it's just training. Instinct. He calls out, "Brock?"

Even Pipes knows how useless this is. There's no Brock. There's nothing but a Corvette rolling backwards, headlights now aimed at the sky like two Bat Signals calling for help. The Corvette loses its edge and slides slowly backwards into the pit. But it doesn't crash at the bottom, just disappears into the foggy core. The violet glow flares bright, then dims again until the light is extinguished entirely.

Pipes ain't no superhero, but he's a darn good cop, and he's ready to save the day. So even though his training says to grab his radio and call for help, he doesn't. He needs to clear the area first. He walks to the edge of the smoldering crater, watches the clatter of scree tumble in beneath his boot toward the purple center. He shines a light down on the core, and the beam animates a haze of quickly dissipating fog and smoke that smells like a combination of sulfur, copper, and gasoline.

With the smoke and fog now clear, Pipes can see all the way to the bottom of the crater. But when he moves the Maglite's beam to the center, where the violet glow used to be, the cone of light from his torch up and vanishes. He aims the Maglite away from the spot, and the circle of light reappears. *Huh.* He trains the torch on the crater's center again, but once more, the light is completely consumed. The beam remains—he can even put his hand through it— but it doesn't terminate as a circle of illuminated rock like it should, like it does everywhere else inside the crater. It just ends in total darkness.

"Son of a bitch."

Just then, a guttural sound, all wet and ragged, echoes from somewhere deep inside that black center. It sounds like someone might be hurt.

Pipes calls out again. "Brock? You down there?"

Silence.

"Mr. Corning…?"

A noise rips through the night air, almost as if in reply, but Pipes knows for sure that it's something else entirely. In fact, he knows exactly what the noise is, he just can't believe his ears. It's a rusty, mechanical growl, the last thing he expects to hear in this moment. After a brief silence, it comes again: the roar of a revving chainsaw.

Pipes jumps, aims his Maglite all over the crater's interior. "This is the Ottawa County Sheriff's Department!" he shouts. "Put down the chainsaw and come out with your hands up!"

The noise stops.

"Now come out with your hands up!" Pipes says. His voice is shaking.

A longer stretch of silence is followed by another rev of the power tool. This time, though, Pipes is ready for it, and he's able to pinpoint the sound's source. It's coming from somewhere inside those woods now, on the opposite side of the crater.

Pipes slowly backs away from the crater, light trained on the direction he knows the sound is coming from, then turns and jogs down the beaten path to his cruiser. The door is still open when he returns, and he drops like a heap into the driver's seat, shuts the door behind him. The door feels heavy on its hinges, squeals from the effort. The windshield is shattered, and the interior is a coffee-stained mess, but it could be worse. Pipes grabs the keys that still hang from the ignition and turns. The cruiser, which many would have left for dead, idles for a moment and then rumbles loudly to life. The headlights flicker; the taillights, too.

"Fuck yeah."

Pipes grabs the gear shift and presses down on the brake, but before he can put the car in Drive, he hears laughter. A male adolescent by the sounds of it. And it's coming from somewhere nearby. He swings his flashlight through a gap in the fragmented remains of the rear passenger-side window, shouts at the trees caught in its beam, "I'm armed! And I'm not afraid to use it!"

All he hears in response is the crunch of forest detritus.

Pipes grabs his weapon from the center console, steps out of the car, and takes cover behind the open door. He aims his pistol at the inky gaps between birch and pine, painted red by the cruiser's glowing taillights. He blinks the sweat from his eyes and wets his chapped lips. *Think, Mikey. Think.*

And this is when it occurs to him. He spent so much time obsessing about what tonight was *supposed* to be—the perfect dinner, the perfect gift, the perfect words to say—that he never entertained what the night *could* be. He just assumed that with enough planning it would go great. He never thought for a second about it going oh so terribly wrong.

The radio at his shoulder crackles to life. The voice on the other end sounds frantic. Terrified. "Send all units to my location, now! I've got multiple homicides! I repeat: multiple—"

That fucking voice! It's the same one from before. Mikey, man, you're losin' it.

Keeping his gun trained on the nearest tree line, Pipes removes one hand from the grip and uses it to depress the Call button on the radio. "This is Deputy Pipes of the Grafting County Sheriff's Department. Who am I speaking to? Over."

"Oh my God, Keller, it's… I know these kids."

Pipes yanks his head away from the radio, as if the thing has turned into a giant snapping cobra or something.

"…Fuck! Is that…Chet Springs?"

Mikey just listens to that voice, dumbfounded—stares absently into the middle distance. He's either hallucinating or someone in town really wants to go to jail for impersonating a police officer.

The voice on the other end is crying now. Pipes can hear it in the way it hitches. He looks around the woods. Every pitch-black gap between trunks feels like the wrong side of a one-way mirror. Feels like someone is watching him while he listens to this shitty Pipes impersonator cry into his ear. The sound makes Mikey's throat tighten. He can't remember the last time he actually cried.

"They've been decapitated," the voice continues. "And their heads… Jesus… Their heads are burning in the fire pit."

A shadow flashes in the corner of Pipes's vision, and he wheels around to point his pistol at the pool of light created by his cruiser's headlights. What he sees there nearly takes his breath away. It's the approaching silhouette of a tall, lanky individual, who is lazily dragging the black shadow of a chainsaw along the gravel road beside it. A shock of wispy hair drifts, oddly static in the breeze, as does the wisp of black smoke that wafts from the chainsaw's idling engine.

Pipes aims his pistol at the shadow and puts a finger on the trigger. "Drop the fucking weapon!" he shouts. "Do it now or I'll shoot!"

The silhouette rips the starter rope on the chainsaw.

"I won't tell you—"

Suddenly, Pipes is staring down at his gut, watching where the razor-sharp tip of a blade has just exploded from his belly in a gruesome spray of blood and viscera. He drops his pistol to the ground and grabs the whetted iron just to make sure it's real. The blade makes ribbons of both palms.

Is this...? Is this a fucking sword?

"I think I'm gonna be sick..." says the voice inside the radio.

Pipes wants to turn and face the man who just ran him through with a weapon from the Germanic low countries, circa 1200–1250 A.D., but it hurts to even think about. Hurts his organs, hurts his bones. Hurts from the inside out like nothing ever has. But he tries anyway, makes it a quarter of the way before the torque needed becomes too much and the blade is ripped violently from whence it came. Pipes feels the air rush from his lungs as the weapon exits his midsection, and he drops heavy to his knees. A quart of blood soon fills his mouth and leaks from the corners of his lips. He uses what little strength he has left to roll onto his butt and lean his back against the open cruiser door, where he can rest. He spits the blood into the gravel. "So, that's what you look like," he says to his attacker.

The swordsman is short and stout, with that same oddly static hair as the perp who wields the chainsaw. Pipes can't make out the face—too dark for that—but he does see two trails of purple smoke rising from where the eyes should be. Whatever it is laughs. It's the same adolescent laugh from before.

Pipes squeezes his eyes shut and hopes for all of this to be over soon, but in the black behind his eyelids, he only sees the gift-wrapped box and the heart-eyes note from Marie. The vision is a good one, but it's quickly sliced in half by another rev from the chainsaw. Pipes opens his eyes to see both shadows in front of him now, the two maniacs looking eager to engage in more violence. What looks like a giant mutated spider skitters across the stout one's chest and disappears over his shoulder. Pipes can't tell if he's seeing things or not. He's lost a lot of blood already. Could be delusional.

A tear falls from his eye. "Please, don't," he says.

But neither maniac listens. The short one simply lays the flat of his sword on Pipes's left shoulder, while the tall one lays the flat of the chainsaw across the sword and onto Pipe's right shoulder. Together, the two weapons make the most horrific pair of scissors imaginable, with poor Mikey's head caught in the middle.

"I'm gonna be a dad," he says. He knows this fact won't change anything, won't appeal to the pair's better angels— killers like them don't have better angels—Pipes just wants to say the words out loud one time before he dies.

The chainsaw revs, and both blades inch closer.

Pipes shudders with anticipation as tears pour down his cheeks. He shuts his eyes tight again and thinks about his unborn baby. He imagines holding that swaddled miracle for the first time in the hospital and smiling a year later at their first words. He imagines helping them take their first steps, maybe riding their first bike, and pictures himself laughing at their first bite of something sour. But the most vivid picture of all, the one that feels the most real, is the thought of his child standing on the street corner outside their house, nervously waiting for the school bus on their first day of school. Mikey stares at the back of that head with so much love that he knows he could stare at if forever if he had to. But he doesn't have to, because in that moment, the child turns back to him and smiles. The image takes Mikey's breath away, and he nearly chokes on the overwhelming surge of happiness inside him. The child waves to him, and Mikey smiles and waves back.

Meanwhile, back in the coldness of a fallen world, the chainsaw and sword lurch and sever the deputy's head clean from his neck above the shirt collar. But Pipes doesn't notice, doesn't feel any pain. He's not there. He's somewhere else. And he's experiencing something beautiful.

Your daddy loves you, baby. Always will.
Black.

INCIDENT REPORT

Apex Door Field Assessment Unit 3

Incident/Assessment Report

Today's Date: Friday, September 22, 1995

Time: 4:38 PM

Assessor Number: 7

Assessor's Handler: Orson Caster

Location of incident: Grafting, Michigan

Person(s) affected: Wendy Callahan

Reason(s) for field assessment dispatch:

Wendy Callahan was identified by scout working as a barista at a local cafe. He overheard her conversation with her friend. Witnessed distressed emotional behavior. He believed the validity of her account given the intensity of her behavior. The scout sent the audio recording pulled from interior cameras to dispatch, who agreed and assigned us to the case.

Key Indicators mentioned (please refer to the latest edition of the APEX DOOR FIELD ASSESSMENT MANUAL for updated glossary of Key Indicators to choose from):

- Loss of sleep

- Heightened emotional states of experiencers

- Doppelgangers

- Leyline crux

Please describe the incident(s), including any anomalous phenomena:

In the audio recording, Mrs. Callahan can be heard describing an experience that matches dop phenomena, which includes increased auditory activity that later manifests as corporeal encounters. She describes waking up late at night, hearing her baby's cries coming from outside the bedroom window. Upon looking through the window and opening it, the auditory manifestation continues. She wakes her husband, who corroborates the auditory manifestation. He is urged to investigate, and he does. According to Mrs. Callahan, the farther Mr. Callahan got from the home, the farther away the crying sounded.

Mrs. Callahan checked on their baby's room and found their baby was asleep in the crib where they had left her. She called to her husband from the front door, and he returned. Standard fear response to the situation. They decided it was a combination of lack of sleep, stress, and the windy night that had caused the confusion.

Mrs. Callahan described another incident that took place when she arrived home one night after a late shift at the hospital, where she is employed as a nurse. Mr. Callahan appeared shocked to see her. Mr. Callahan explained that he had just seen her walk into the kitchen approximately ten minutes prior and was unresponsive to verbal communication. Mr. Callahan assumed Mrs. Callahan was not in the mood to communicate. They explored the kitchen together and found it empty.

Mrs. Callahan also described an incident involving her mother-in-law. Mr. Callahan's mother lives in their home and watches the baby while Mr. and Mrs. Callahan are at work. The unnamed mother-in-law had recounted to Mrs. Callahan that for multiple nights in a row, she had been awakened by the sound of her bedroom door opening. The mother-in-law will see what appears to be Mrs. Callahan, quote, "peeking in" at her. Upon asking Mrs. Callahan why she was coming to her room at night, Mrs. Callahan explained that she had not been.

In the most recent event, which was the night prior to Mrs. Callahan's meeting with her friend at the cafe, the mother-in-law recounted that she had turned on the light when she saw who she assumed was Mrs. Callahan "peeking in" at her. In the light, she saw that the entity peering through the door had no face. When the light flashed, the entity ran away. This explains why the front door of the Callahan residence was open when they woke up in the morning.

Assessor response:

Seven held the physical tape of the recording. After several minutes, he began to sweat. The tape was crushed in his hand. This is especially unusual given 7's extreme care with objects and artifacts attached to areas under assessment

Conclusion and Recommended Next Steps:

Grafting, Michigan, must be categorized as a high-risk zone. It places highest among locations currently under assessment. Currently recommending SOP to place assignments on standby.

GRAFTING, MICHIGAN

Friday, October 27, 1995

BACK IN THE PRESENT

AFTERSHOCK

WHEN SHERIFF KELLER comes to, it's not all the way. Awareness arrives one wave at a time, like the tide washing in. It goes something like this:

Wave One: He blinks, understands that he is a living thing.

Wave Two: He's aware that he is inside his police cruiser, but it's not right.

Wave Three: He understands he's laying on the roof. Seat belts, wires, the cable of his dash-mounted radio receiver all dangle from above because…

Wave Four: The cruiser has been flipped over entirely. Keller wasn't wearing a seatbelt, so that's great. But why is he even here?

Wave Five: Keller relieved a deputy. Who was it? Mikey Pipes. He relived Deputy Mikey Pipes so the guy could celebrate his wedding anniversary.

Wave Six: Keller is at the MOW. It's Friday night and there was a rock show here tonight. There was also an earthquake.

On the seventh wave, Keller rests.

Then he crawls out from his overturned cruiser, elbow over elbow along the gravel lot, and looks up at where the MOW and everyone inside should be. But instead of the old Maintenance-of-Way structure, he sees a smoking pile of debris.

Adrenaline kicks him like a mule.

Keller stands, tries to run, stumbles, gets up, stumbles again, gets up, moves at whatever pace his racing brain can stomach.

A white-haired man in a black T-shirt, covered head-to-toe in Sheetrock dust, is standing at the edge of the debris and flinging aside broken rebar when Keller arrives at the wreck. Keller recognizes him immediately: Rudy Gartner, mechanic at X-Factor Auto, an expert at restoring classic cars, repaired Art's '68 Chevy Nova awhile back.

"Rudy?" The sheriff coughs from all the dust. "You okay?"

Rudy turns. He's pale, trembling, mouth slack. He blinks a few times before a light comes on behind his eyes. "Sheriff… What are you doin' here?"

Keller lays a hand on Rudy's shoulder. "There was an earthquake, Rudy. But it's safe now, I think. But listen, I need you to help me out for a second, okay? Rudy, how many people do you think were inside the MOW tonight? Do you have a guess?"

Rudy looks at the pile that was once a music hall. "Damn, sheriff, I don't know. Never been good with numbers. A hundred, maybe."

Keller reaches for the radio at his shoulder but learns it's not there. Looks like it's been torn from his uniform. Probably happened during the crash. *Fuck.* "Listen Rudy, I hate to do this to you, but I gotta head back to my cruiser so I can call this in. But I'll be right back, okay?"

"Do what you gotta," Rudy says, and he goes right back to sifting through the rubble for survivors.

The sheriff hobbles as fast as he can back to his overturned cruiser, lays down flat on the gravel, and crawls in through the shattered driver's-side window. He doesn't see the radio he lost, so he uses the one on the cruiser's dash. That's when he remembers Mikey's radio call for help. He needed back-up. Keller had been on his way to help. He reaches out and snatches the upside-down receiver. "Mikey, 9-5-2, over."

No sound.

Keller twists the knobs on the radio, realizes there's no power, smacks it. Obviously that does nothing, so he fumbles for the keys still in the ignition and turns.

The cruiser coughs, but that's about it.

Keller tries again.

The cough sustains a low growl, but dies.

He reaches up to press the brake pedal with one hand while he turns the key with his other.

The cruiser roars to life. Doesn't sound pretty, though, idling upside down. The radio lights ignite, and Keller collapses on his back, snagging the receiver again.

"Mikey, 9-5-2, over."

Nothing.

"Tam, 9-5-2, over. You copy?"

Only static at first, but then, "Copy that, sheriff. All's good here. Zimmer boys needed to be pushed apart, but then they hugged it out. Even cried about how much they love each other. Been pretty slow otherwise. Over."

"And Mikey?"

"What about him?"

"He reported multiple homicides. Is everything okay?"

"Oh, yeah. Sandra radioed me and Art about that, but sheriff, no one else heard that call besides you. Probably just interference or something. Maybe them punk boys you're spying on like to play radio pranks on police officers, you know, to scare them off."

That's when Keller realizes: Tam is way too calm right now. There's not an ounce of urgency in her voice. "How are things lookin' over there after the quake?"

A moment of static. "Quake? You mean like an *earth*quake?"

"Fuck, Tam, yes. The earthquake that just happened."

Static. "Sheriff, are you feelin' okay? You didn't smoke something out there at the MOW, did you?"

Keller huffs. "Listen, Tam, my cruiser is about to die, so I need to make this quick. I need ambulances, I need the fire department, I need every goddamn officer we have to get their ass to the MOW as fast as fucking possible. We have a mass casualty event on our hands here. Oh, and will someone please check on Mikey fucking Pipes? Fuck! Over and out."

Keller wriggles backward out of the driver's-side window and watches from his knees as a black Chevy Caprice Classic with yellow government plates pulls into the gravel lot alongside him. A man steps out. He wears black pleated pants, a gray snakeskin blazer, and gold-rimmed aviators with wine-red lenses. A cattle-skull bolo tie hangs over the topmost snap buttons of his white western shirt. He shuts the heavy car door behind him and casually puts a cigarette between his lips. He looks down at Keller as he lights the smoke with a gold Zippo, careful not to singe his handlebar mustache on the flame.

Then comes the thrum of two helicopters approaching from the east. Keller looks up at the sky to see one black helicopter shine a spotlight down on the MOW's wreckage and the other twist north towards Pine Mountain. *Mikey. Shit.*

The strange urban cowboy in the tweed blazer extends a helping hand down to Keller, gaudy, decorative rings on every finger. He's got that crook in his lip like Elvis Presley, and he plucks his cigarette from that crook to speak a warm greeting amid a swirl of exhaled smoke. "Evenin', sheriff. Quite a mess you got here."

Keller accepts the hand and allows himself to be helped up. "You FBI or somethin'? What's with the suit and sunglasses?"

"*FBI?*" Cleeve laughs. "Far from it. I'm just an ambitious young seismologist with a degenerative eye disease. Will be blind before I turn fifty." He taps the frame of the aviators. "They help with the sensitivity."

"Seismologist?"

"Yes, sir. Do you know what a—"

"I know what a seismologist is. Question is, what are you doing here?"

The cowboy points to the massive pile of rubble where the MOW once stood. "I just follow the quakes."

"Oh, yeah? And I suppose that's just some random chopper up there? And those plates, they just *look* like government issue." He points to the yellow license plates on the Chevy Caprice.

The man in the aviators ignores him, starts walking toward the MOW. "Don't worry, sheriff. I'll only be a few minutes. No one will even notice I'm here."

Keller does a sort of half-jog after him. Hobbles, really, a sharp pain rippling through his leg with each step. "Hey! Don't make me arrest you!"

The pair soon approach Rudy, who is hunched over in pain, one hand on his hip. He sees Keller and points down at the rubble beside him. Keller looks down to where Rudy points, then immediately looks away, having felt the urge to vomit. "Fuck."

It's just one arm poking out, dusted with Sheetrock powder and highlighted by streaks of gnarly crimson, but when you follow it into the pile, you see a large chunk of concrete that's wet with ragged flesh, hair, and bone. The skull beneath has been decimated.

"Sorry, sheriff, but I ain't prepared to help with a thing like that," Rudy says to the ground. He refuses to look Keller in the eyes.

"That's all right, Rudy. You've done more than enough already. Hey, why don't you go take a breather? Fire and rescue should be here soon, and they'll be able to handle this better than we can." Keller puts his arm around Rudy's shoulders and points him to a nice grassy spot a safe distance from the destruction. "Why don't you go take a seat over there. Rest some."

Rudy nods and does what Keller says.

Once Rudy's gone, the cowboy kneels down and shoves the heavy piece of concrete from the crushed skull. Keller immediately recognizes the face despite its crushed state. *Rudy Gartner?* The same Rudy Gartner who just walked that way and now sits by himself on the grass, no more than fifty yards away. Purple tendrils crawl out of the cadaver that's still half-buried in the rubble and seep with a molasses-like viscosity into the soil, where they disappear in a hiss of purple vapor.

"What the fuck…?" is all Keller can muster.

The cowboy takes another drag from his cigarette and smiles a lopsided grin. He likes knowing things others don't.

The other Rudy—the one sitting in the field—screams. "My eyes!" he shrieks. He's pressing his dusty palms hard against his eye sockets and writhing around the ground in pain. Keller jumps to his feet and rushes over to help. The cowboy follows at a leisurely pace.

Keller squats down beside the old-timer, speaks softly. "Rudy, hey, it's me again, Sheriff Keller. What seems to be the trouble with you? What hurts?"

Rudy Gartner screams again. "My eyes, goddammit!" He removes his right hand from his right eye socket to touch a spot at the base of his neck, but he keeps the eye squeezed shut. "There's something in there!" Rudy shouts. "I can feel it moving around!" He arches his back and presses so hard against his left eyeball now that he might just make it pop.

"In where, Rudy? Your neck? Here, move your hand so I can see."

"I wouldn't do that if I were you," the cowboy says, now standing right behind Keller. He presses a finger to his ear and whispers just barely loud enough for Keller to make out the words: "Target acquired."

The helicopter above them rotates slightly to better position its spotlight on Keller, Rudy, and the man who is most certainly not a seismologist. Their hair and clothing ripple beneath the downwash.

"I'll take it from here," the man tells Keller. He kneels down next to Rudy and grabs the old-timer by the chin, forces the head to turn left. With his other hand, he removes the aviators from his eyes. "There you are," the cowboy says.

And that's when Keller sees it. A large purplish tumor has appeared at the base of Rudy's skull, where the brain stem connects to the spinal cord. The skin on the tumor is stretched thin enough to appear translucent and it looks as though there is something foreign moving around inside—something alive.

Keller's head starts to pound. Is this even the real Rudy, he wonders, or is the real Rudy the dead guy buried in the rubble? The one with his skull crushed in.

The cowboy reaches into his blazer and retrieves a bone-grip hunting knife out, points the tip of the blade at the tumor on Rudy's neck.

"Now hold on a second!" Keller says above the sound of the thumping helicopter above. But when the cowboy fails to listen, instead moving the blade closer until the tip is nearly piercing Rudy's skin, Keller draws his .44 Magnum and clicks back the hammer, trains the gun on the man.

The cowboy keeps his eyes on the tumor. "No need for violence, sheriff."

"Put down the weapon!" Keller orders. He's surprised by the shakiness in his voice. *That's a first.* "Now! Or I'll be forced to shoot!"

The cowboy ignores him and plunges the knife deep into the tumor. Rudy screams, and Keller jumps back, nearly falls flat on his ass. "These things," the cowboy explains, "They're not from this world. Can't survive in our dimensional place for long without the proper nutrient bath. You know where they find that bath? They create it. Inside *us*. They're parasites, sheriff." The sounds inside the skewered tumor are sickening—slurpy and wet—but the cowboy just roots the knife deeper until there's a snap and something shrieks from inside the bloody mess. Spidery legs with too many joints shoot out from the punctured flesh and angrily clutch the blade. The cowboy adjusts the angle of the blade slightly until he has the proper leverage and, with one swift motion, digs out the little demon inside.

Rudy Gartner drops his hands from his eyes—bloodshot, Keller can now see—and his two dilated pupils roll back into his head. His body pauses, then collapses to the ground, where it lays silent and still.

The cowboy, meanwhile, raises up to his full height, victorious. With one hand on his hip, he turns the blade in his other hand to better examine his boon. At the end of the hunting knife, a creature, black and blood-slicked, glistens, its skin like shining pleather. Its hairs are stiff, and its body is thick and round like a hockey puck. Ten segmented legs clasp the blade like a fist. The cowboy turns the blade over to reveal two lamprey mouths, one on each side of the creature's body. Black liquid trickles from the lips as needle teeth bite at the weapon that's been stabbed clean through it. Eventually, the brainless movement ceases.

"Hell of a thing, ain't it, sheriff? I've seen hundreds of these little bastards, but they never cease to amaze me."

Emergency sirens sound in the distance.

Upon hearing the noise, the cowboy flings the spider from his knife and quickly stomps it into a disgusting pulp beneath his snakeskin boot. The alien mess emits a purple vapor, both on the ground and from the bottom of his shoe. He presses a finger to his ear. "Retrieve the corpse," he says. "Our time here is up."

Keller stands and turns to see an unmarked van burst from the tree line and skid to a stop next to the crushed-skull version of Rudy, corpse still trapped beneath the rubble. The alien-tumor version of Rudy is wheezing on the ground at Keller's feet.

Two giant goons in black suits and ties, wearing black sunglasses and black fedoras, exit the rear of the van and start removing heavy chunks of debris from the deceased Rudy. One tosses away a load-bearing steel beam that must weigh more than both men combined. Once enough debris has been cleared, the two goons haul the dead body free and throw it into the back of their van.

Keller watches, frozen, unable to react. He's a small town sheriff, not Agent Mulder from *The X-Files*.

"Sheriff?" The voice belongs to alien-tumor Rudy. He's awake.

Keller kneels back down beside the man. "Hey, Rudy. Just relax, okay. Medics are on the way." He looks up at the cowboy. "Who are you really?"

The cowboy smiles that lopsided smile. "That, Sheriff Keller, is no longer any of your concern." And before Keller can react, the man flips the knife around so that the hilt is pointing at Keller and stabs it into Keller's neck.

Before blacking out again, Keller sees the cowboy pull the knife hilt away from his neck to reveal a needle dripping with a glowing green liquid mixed with the sheriff's blood.

NO MAN LEFT BEHIND

THE MOON IS high when a firefighter by the last name of Nelson pushes aside the splintered wood and shingles that are piled atop Barry and pulls the boy from the wreckage. To him, it sounds like Barry comes out speaking in tongues.

"Lich? Lich? Is Lich okay?"

Nelson tries to calm the kid, "Relax, son—" But it does no good.

"Lich!" Barry calls out. Against Nelson's wishes, he climbs to his feet and starts stumbling about a sea of survivors and first responders in search of his best friend and band mate. Emergency vehicles and news vans are everywhere, parked haphazardly amid the chaos. "Lich! It's Barry! You hear me, pal?"

And that's when he sees him: the tall, lanky drummer that he couldn't navigate high school without. Lich is seated in the back of an ambulance, eyes fixated on the female paramedic wrapping his arm, blushing like she must be the most beautiful woman he's ever seen.

"Lich!"

Lich beams at the sight of Barry, and Barry rushes over to meet him. The medic finishes the wrap on Lich's arm and turns to reach for something on the ambulance shelves.

"Are you okay, buddy?" Barry asks, eyeing the bandaged arm.

Lich holds up his injury. "Oh, you mean this? This is nothin'. Just a little burn."

The medic turns back to Lich and hands him a couple of aspirin for the pain and a few pages of paperwork for the liability, the top page of which he needs to sign. Barry gets why his injured pal is blushing like a school girl. The medic is even more beautiful up close. "It *is* serious, actually," she says. "It's a second-degree burn. And it needs time to heal, so stop touching it."

Barry's heart sinks. "Will he ever be able to drum again?" He's asking honestly.

"As long as he stops touching it," the medic says. She swats Lich's hand from the bandages a second time, and Barry catches the slightest hint of a bashful smile on Lich's face.

Jeez, dude. Don't fall in love.

"I need to get home to the twins," Lich says to Barry.

"There's a satellite phone in the first aid tent if you need to call your parents," the medic says.

Barry jumps in to save Lich from the humiliation of having to explain to this beautiful maiden that his mom is probably too drunk right now to drive—probably too drunk to care. Likely not even home. "It's okay. I'm his ride."

The medic turns a suspicious eye to Barry, and Barry finds himself suddenly in danger of falling under whatever spell the beautiful gaze has cast on Lich. "Have you been checked out yet?" she says. "You've got a few nasty bruises there"—she points to his arm—"and one on your forehead. I don't want you driving if you're concussed, or if something is broken."

"That guy over there said I'm fine." Barry points back at Nelson, who has gone back to moving debris by hand. "Is Lich okay to go?" He gestures to his friend.

"Oh really? The firefighter medically cleared you to drive?" She shakes her head. Not buying it. But people with more serious injuries are in need of help. "Whatever." She takes the signed document, files it with the others. "Yeah, he's cleared."

"M'lady, it's been an honor and a privilege," Lich says, and hops down onto the grass alongside Barry. The two fist bump and then walk back to the Wolfmobile in silence, which, lucky for them, is parked a quarter mile away. Barry always parks far away for Wolf Harp shows, wants to leave the parking lot open for all their adoring fans. He's is relieved to discover that the van is still in one piece. Not a single scratch. Well, not a single *new* scratch anyway. The engine starts right up.

"Good girl," Barry whispers, stroking the dashboard gently. He turns to Lich. "Dude, we almost got sinkholed."

"Dude..." Lich bursts into laughter.

Barry is about to put the van in drive, but freezes. "Wait," he says.

"What?" says Lich.

Barry hands him a well-worn CD binder that's stained and fraying at the corners. "Pick something. I'll be right back."

Before Lich can say more, Barry leaps from the car and dashes the quarter mile back to the MOW. He zigzags back through the dense crowd of people and vehicles until he finds the spot where Nelson extracted him from the rubble. The firefighter is still there, and he's now holding the exact thing Barry is looking for.

"Oh, thank fucking God," Barry says. He carefully removes the black Gibson Explorer from Nelson's filthy gloved hands, then blows the dust off the body and inspects the neck for warping. It looks fresh off the factory floor, and Barry can't help but hug it. He wraps the instrument around his shoulders, then pulls the strap around his chest so the guitar clings to his back like a battle axe. "My deepest gratitudes," he says to Nelson, and bows. Then without another word, he just turns and heads back in the direction of his van.

Nelson, meanwhile, removes his helmet and runs a gloved hand over his sweaty brow. When not volunteering at the county fire station, Nelson fights forest fires, is a certified smokejumper with the U.S. Forest Service, so he's seen things you wouldn't believe. But watching Barry swagger off with his guitar like some rock-and-roll Conan the Barbarian, unperturbed by the chaos all around him? It's gotta be the single oddest thing Nelson has ever seen in his life.

BLUE MOON

A BRILLIANT LIGHT, incalculably distant and impossibly close—that's the first thing Keller sees when consciousness finds him. He feels his arm lifted in the careful grip of a feminine hand, the light depression of fingers against his skin. As he blinks away the retinal burn, he takes in his surroundings. *The back of an ambulance,* he concludes. That's where he is now. Whatever questions he intends to ask the paramedics examining him come out only as emphatic grunts, light on words.

"It's okay, sheriff. We're just checking you for any serious injuries," the paramedic explains.

"How long—" *Fuck,* his head hurts right now. He tries the question again, "How long is this going to take?"

"In and out in two shakes, sheriff."

Turns out that two shakes is somewhere between an hour and a thousand years. Maybe longer, had he not applied an unfair amount of pressure on the rookie paramedic, some kid named Peters. Poor gal insisted that Keller go to the hospital for a more thorough examination, but the concussed sheriff not-so-politely declined. He may also have threatened Peters with arrest at one point—should the medic refuse to comply— but the memory of that is foggy.

In fact, his memory of the entire night is foggy. He remembers the quake and blacking out in the cruiser after he crashed, but nothing else. Nothing before and nothing after. There's this hazy vision where he talks to the animated corpse of Rudy Gartner under the observation of some oil-man type, but that doesn't make enough sense for Keller to linger on it. Concussion dreams, he decides.

The field of devastation that was once the MOW is now awash in blue and red emergency lights. Powerful floodlights, too. Police cars, ambulances, and fire trucks crowd the gravel lot— they've even brought in heavy machinery to aid with excavation. Backhoes, dump trucks, excavators. Judging by the insignia on the emergency vehicles, the first responders come from a dozen different towns and counties. More than a hundred men and women are now on scene.

Keller walks aimlessly for awhile until he sees Tam amid the crowd. She's doing triple-duty: aiding survivors, directing EMTs, and keeping the nosiest of reporters at bay. Keller taps her on the shoulder with his good hand. His other arm is wrapped in a sling—nothing broken, just a sprain. When she turns, he points to his busted cruiser, laying in the gravel like a dead fish. "Mind giving me a ride back home? My old man is probably waiting for me."

Tam glances around at all the work still to be done. "Can't someone else do it?"

"You giving me a ride? Or am I taking the keys?"

"The hell you are," Tam says. "Come on."

KELLER'S FATHER IS already in bed when the sheriff gets home, so Keller grabs a bottle of Maker's Mark from the liquor cabinet and starts imbibing until he's had enough to pass out, to bring the kind of sleep he wouldn't otherwise be able to find.

It's three a.m. when his father wakes in a chorus of hoarse shouting, and although that sleep from the Maker's continues to evade Keller, it's enough to dampen the old man's outburst, so he tries to ignore him. Keller just wants to keep laying in his bed with the lights off, head swirling from the liter of bourbon whiskey in his gut, staring up at the ceiling, watching the dark shit his mind conjures in that inky blackness above him. But dear old Dad continues to shout, so Keller grunts and hauls his ass out of bed.

On his way down the hall to help his dad, Keller stops in the bathroom just to flush the toilet—things tend to get neglected after half a bottle of Maker's—and shuts off the light on his way out (God knows how long that's been left on). He makes his way to the old record player that sits atop a table outside his father's bedroom, turns it on, and drops the needle on the right groove. Pat Boone croons, *"I'll be home, my darling..."*

When he enters his father's bedroom, the old man is on the floor. His colonoscopy bag appears to have cushioned a fall that would otherwise broken a hip, but it also spilled open in the process. The stench is sobering.

It takes a while, calming down his old man. By the time Pat Boone gets to the second verse—*"I'd walk you home in the moonlight..."*—Keller's father has reverted back to a docile husk of a man. Keller cradles his father like a child in his arms and carries him to the bathroom. The busted colostomy bag spills its contents all the way down the hall, but Keller is too drunk to care. He cleans his father off in the tub, gently affixes a new colostomy bag, and carries the man back to his bed. Tucks him in.

In the hall, the *Hits of '56* vinyl album spins Elvis Presley's "Blue Moon." He glances at the darkened room at the end of the hall—a dusty nursery thats been empty since the late '80s—and hums along with the tune. The nursery is a glorified storage closet now, home to all the boxes of records that don't fit in the cramped crawl space in the basement. No baby ever lived in that room. Died in the womb with his mother.

Keller heads downstairs, away from the stench in the hallway, away from the bad memories. Maybe the sunken couch down in the living room holds the sleep Keller struggles nightly to find. It's not peace he hopes for, wrapping himself in a stained afghan. Just rest. Just sleep.

GRAFTING, MICHIGAN

Monday, October 30, 1995

WHERE SMOKE,
THERE'S FIRE

"SUPERMAN RUINS EVERYTHING," Barry insists. He slides his cafeteria tray to the left, moves with the lunch line. "He's an invincible super-dork with no friends and a pathological need to be liked by everyone. Batman, on the other hand, is just a regular dude with anger issues and a devoted man-servant. And he doesn't give a fuck what anyone thinks. That's badass."

Lich shrugs. "But that's what I like about Superman. Nothing hurts him." He holds up his bandaged forearm as evidence to why the contrary sucks.

Barry holds out his tray, and the lunch lady plops down a sloppy Joe and a handful of crinkle fries. "Yeah, but Batman's got the money and the tech and the babes," he continues. "He's a guy's guy. And he's tough as nails. Can get the shit kicked out of him all day long and never break. He *does* get hurt. *Bad.* But he still gets up and finishes the job. That's what *I* like."

Lich accepts his serving of sloppy Joe and fries and follows Barry to a table near the windows, saying, "Yeah, well I bet he would be a superman if he could be."

The Halloween decorations in the cafeteria are still up, but they've taken a backseat to student-made posters that urge financial support for all the victims of the Grafting quake and request prayers for the dead. One in particular, a sign adorned with myriad hearts and glitter, memorializes Brock Corning but refers to him as Amber Corning's dad. Flyers printed by the principal's office inform students and faculty that their will be a memorial assembly in the gym on Friday, and Barry has already thought about skipping it.

Barry plops down on his seat and stabs a paper ramekin of ketchup with a particularly long fry, then flings the ketchup from his fry at Lich, who laughs and wipes the condiment from his face. Barry starts scarfing his sloppy Joe, then stops, eyes wide, mouth full of sauced ground beef.

"Ew, dude," says Lich. He winces at the carnage in Barry's mouth. Lich's plate remains untouched.

Barry swallows hard, which somehow spews sloppy Joe juice out both corners of his mouth. "I spy with my little eye…a Lords of Cydonia T-shirt."

"Where?!" Lich looks franticly around the cafeteria.

Barry points. "My twelve."

Lich turns and immediately spots the shirt. He looks at the kid wearing it. "Who's that?"

"Dunno. Looks like a poser, though."

The stranger has flowing red hair, freckled skin, and a wad of toilet paper shoved up one nostril. His face is bruised.

"He looks hurt."

"Huh?" Barry squints. "Oh, yeah. Shit, man. He's asking for it though, isn't he?"

Lich turns back to Barry, brow furrowed. "What? Why?"

Barry begins counting on his fingers, talking through the final third of his sloppy Joe. "One: new kid."

"Oh, come on. Like he can help that."

"Two: metal band shirt. Three: ginger."

"Fuck off, Barry. You love that band."

Barry shrugs. "I don't make the rules, man."

"Maybe he's cool."

"Yeah, I doubt it."

"Why?"

Barry leans forward, smiling. "I know cool. I'm cool. You're cool. That kid is *not* cool."

"Because he's new, has red hair, and likes metal?"

"That shirt is probably why he got iced, man. Chet and his trogs love to beat up dudes in metal shirts. You know that."

"Maybe he just doesn't give a shit. Maybe he's like Batman? Ever think of that?"

Barry pauses mid-handful of fries. "Interesting."

Lich eyes his tray of untouched food, clutches at his grumbling stomach beneath the table.

"Maybe," Barry points at Lich with a crinkle fry, "that shirt is more than just a shirt." He narrows his eyes and takes an aggressive bite from the fry. "Maybe it's a smoke signal."

"A what?"

"He's throwing up the signal, man. That shirt, it's meant to signal guys like you and me. It's him saying, 'Hey, I'm new here, and I'm one of you. Please don't beat the hell out of me like Chet does.'"

"He *does* have a D&D patch on his backpack."

"Oh shit, he does." Barry turns back to face Lich, raises a single impressed eyebrow, and says in a terrible Sherlock Holmes impression, "Very astute observation, my dear fellow. *Very* astute." He then switches back to his natural Midwestern accent and says, "I think we should talk to Sammy about this."

Lich rolls his eyes. "*Any* excuse to talk to Sammy."

Barry punches his shoulder. "Shut up, dude. Seriously, she always knows what's up. Besides, if he wants to smoke signal one of us, then he's smoke signaling Sammy, too."

"Fine, dude, jeez." Lich rubs his sore shoulder. "Where is she anyway?"

Barry gathers his tray and stands. "I'm gonna toss this shit and do a quick scout. Hang tight." He heads to the pile of discarded trays atop the trashcans, sets his tray with the rest, and does a weird little spin so as to quickly scope out the entire cafeteria in one fell swoop. He must think he spots Sammy, the way his head starts to bob and weave for the angle that'll verify it's her.

Lich uses the time during Barry's absence to wrap his sloppy Joe and fries in a pair of napkins and place them safely in his backpack before anyone notices. The twins love sloppy Joes.

A moment later, Barry catches eyes with Lich and waves him over. The two reunite and begin walking toward a table near the doors. Sammy is wearing a flimsy pair of headphones that are connected to a beat-up Sony Discman, and she's furiously sketching in her college-ruled notebook, scrunched-up face hovering an inch above the paper. Her stringy brown hair hangs down to the table and blocks her vision of anything beyond her work. Barry takes a seat directly across from her, and Lich takes the seat next to Barry. Barry grins, snatches a cold crinkle fry from an abandoned tray a few seats down, and flicks it right at Sammy. It hits her square on the top of the head, and her neck snaps up in response.

When she sees it's Barry and Lich, she pauses her Discman and pulls back the headphones. "What do you two losers want?" She glances to Lich's bandaged arm, winces. "How's the arm doing, by the way?"

Lich shrugs. He's busy studying Sammy's notebook. The storyboard for her film is now a scribbled mess, a latticework of cross-outs, floating question marks, and all-caps notations shouting from the margins. "Have you figured out the plot hole yet?" he asks, nodding at the notebook. He already knows the answer, but he figures he's being polite.

Sammy just glares up at him from beneath a furrowed brow. "I don't want to talk about it," she says flatly.

"I'm sure you'll figure it out soon," Barry says dismissively. He points to the new kid, who's just now leaving the lunch line. "See him?"

Sammy turns her head to look. "Hmm. Lords of Cydonia shirt, redhead, D&D patch, looks like he got his ass kicked… Think he's smoke signaling?"

Barry slaps the table triumphantly and turns to Lich. "See? I told you!"

Lich just blinks.

"But he could also just be a poser," Sammy adds. She watches the kid take a seat at one of the far tables, then mumbles, "Hell of a time to move to Grafting."

"We need to approach him together as a unit," Barry says. "If he wants in our tribe, he's gonna need unanimous approval."

"Roll for initiative," says Sammy.

The three of them each fetch a single D20 dice from their pockets and cast them onto the table.

Sammy studies the dice like a shaman reading oracle bones. "Barry, you flank left. Lich, you go right. Take seats on either side of him. Yours truly will approach from the front and take her seat across from him."

"What are you going to say?" asks Lich.

"I've got some ideas. Now let's go. Lunch is over in five."

While sneaking their way to the new kid's table, Barry and Lich aren't really seen by anyone else. Not because they're ninja masters—far from it. Kids like them just aren't seen by kids *unlike* them. The new kid, though, he spots them immediately. He looks up from the bits of sloppy Joe he's been pushing around his plate and watches as the Beavis and Butthead wannabes take seats to the left and right of him. He brushes a long strand of hair from his face.

This is when Sammy makes her grand entrance. She takes the seat directly across from him and slaps her sketchbook and pencil bag down upon the table like a judge slamming their gavel. "I'll be the one asking the questions from now on," she says.

The kid's face bunches up into a question mark. "But I didn't ask—"

"What's your name, new kid?" Sammy asks.

The new kid's head drops a little, shoulders press in. Lich knows that look. It's that submissive posture some kids resign themselves to.

"Randall," the new kid says.

"I have three more questions for you Randall, and how well you answer them will decide if you can be one of us."

"Who says I—"

Sammy holds up a finger. "One: Where did you get that Lords of Cydonia T-shirt?"

Randall looks down at his shirt. "At a show."

Barry's mouth falls open. "You've seen Lords of Cydonia *live*?"

"Yeah, so what?"

"Whadda ya mean, 'so what'? How fucking awesome was it?"

Sammy holds up a finger to silence Barry. Her wide eyes are telling him to shut it. "What if I told you I don't believe you, Randall."

"Why?" Randall and Barry blurt in unison. Barry looks more hurt by the accusation than the accused. He wants to believe.

"The Lords of Cydonia have never played live in Michigan."

"Ah, shit," says Barry. "I knew it."

"I didn't see them in Michigan. I saw them in West Virginia."

"Name three songs," says Sammy.

"Is that the second question?" Randall asks.

Sammy suddenly looks flustered. "What? No! Its a follow-up of the first. Question 1-B. Three songs, let's hear it."

"In fairness, it's not technically a question at all," Lich interjects.

Barry quickly catches Lich's eye and gently shakes his head in a way that says, *not the time, dude.*

Randall shakes his head. "Fuck this." He pushes away the tray of sloppy Joe, gets ready to storm off, but Sammy grabs hold of his wrist and holds up a second finger, which just so happens to also make the peace sign.

"Two: What's your favorite movie?"

"I don't know. *Alien?*"

"Not bad," Barry mumbles beneath his breath. He's starting to believe again.

Sammy holds up her third finger. "Three: Why in the hell would you wear a shirt like that, with hair like that, to a school like this, and think it was a good idea? Don't you know you're playing with fire?"

Randall touches his injured nose and winces from the pain. He shrugs. "But I like this shirt."

"Good answer," says Lich.

Sammy's eyes narrow. "Yeah," she agrees. "It is."

Barry throws his big arm around Randall's shoulders and squeezes him tight—squeezes like they're the oldest of pals. "I told you guys it was a smoke signal," he says with a smile.

"Wait…" Randall says. "Because I answered your questions correctly, that makes us *friends* now?" He says "friends" like it's the first time he's ever used the word.

Barry pulls his arm from Randall's shoulder. "Let's not rush to any conclusions," he says. "You've only made it past the first interview."

"Forget it then," Randall says.

Barry thinks for a moment. And that's when he sees them: Chet and his goons passing out flyers for the annual Halloween party at the Sandpit. It's not a formal invitation. It's the Sandpit, after all. It's not like Chet owns the place. Every teen in grafting shows up at the Sandpit for Halloween, with or without a flyer. The only thing truly required for entry is a cheap six-pack of beer.

"Wanna chug some brewskis with us tomorrow night at the Sandpit? Big Halloween party. Everyone will be there." Barry and Lich will use any excuse to chug said brewskis, even if it means being around people they hate.

"What's the Sandpit?" Randall asks.

"I thought it was canceled," Sammy says. "You know, because of the quake."

Lich nods his agreement.

"Nah," says Barry. "Look." He gestures to Chet flirting with a group of cheerleaders as the star quarterback hands them each a flyer. "Chet and his merry band of morons got the bright idea to re-brand the event. Now it's a bonfire vigil for the quake victims. Halloween costume optional. Randall, you bring the beers, okay?"

"How am I supposed to get beer?" Randall says.

"You'll figure something out," says Barry. Then to the group: "So, are we in agreement? Sandpit tomorrow?"

Lich smiles, spins a stainless steel drumstick in one hand while he throws up the devil horns with his other, his own special way of saying, *Hell yeah, we're in agreement!*

"Really?" Sammy says to Lich. "Last Friday night wasn't enough for you?" She sighs and rolls her eyes. "Fine. What time are you picking me up?"

GRAFTING, MICHIGAN

Tuesday, October 31, 1995

HALLOWEEN NIGHT

THE SANDPIT

GRAFTING DOESN'T OFFER much in the way of teen entertainment. There's the Grafting Cinema 2, but as you might remember, the owner refuses to screen anything over PG-13, so no thanks. Then there's the roller rink, which is great if your idea of fun is a body-odor saturated building full of hyperactive children and their nosy mothers bopping on skates to the latest edition of *Now That's What I Call Music*. You can grab a slice of pizza at Pistol River Pies, then rent a VHS from Movie Knight, even play some pinball while you're there, but that's really more of a Barry and Lich kind of evening, and no one wants to be like Barry and Lich. So that just leaves bonfires at the Sandpit.

During the day, the Sandpit is just another community garbage dump (not like the county landfill, there are fees for your old mattress at the county landfill). It's a heap of rusted vehicles and old appliances with trees now growing out of them, and enough bicycle tires for a Tour de France. Plastic bags, broken bottles, cigarette butts, expended shotgun shells. But on Friday night, the Sandpit comes alive. Sometimes, it's just a pickup truck with a few kids swinging their legs off the tailgate, crushing cheap beer next to a small, dwindling fire. Other times, though, its an event; *the* event. On these nights, all the bored youth of Grafting show up because in the afternoon word got around Ottawa Heights High that its gonna get primal tonight at the pit. Most often, it's the farm boys who show up to the party first. Mennonites and 4-H kids arrive in their pickups or John Deeres just before sundown and start piling scrap wood until their arms give out, until the pile is taller than the tractors they rode in on. When night finally falls, they drench the wood in lighter fluid and toss a match. Then *woosh!* It's on, baby. Tonight's not Friday, it's Tuesday, but the farm boys and all the rest of the teens are already on their way because it's not just any ordinary Tuesday, it's Hallo-fucking-ween. I's also a vigil or something for the victims of the Grafting quake, but that part is still super vague, so you'll have to ask Chet for more details.

Either way, you know just the van that's about to show up. You see it turn down Grey Road off Higgins, high-beams tearing a path ahead through the darkness of enclosing conifers that look older than time. Barry's taking the twists and the turns like a champ, and Lich, who is in the passenger seat, is dropping a burned CD into the Discman that's plugged via adapter into the Wolfmobile's tape deck. Sammy's in the back. She's hunched over her Panasonic Palmcorder, display flipped open, watching back whatever footage of *The Creeps of Casper's Canyon* she filmed most recently. She's shaking her head in disappointment. And Randall is there, too. He's dressed like a greaser from *The Outsiders,* leather jacket, collar popped, head moving awkwardly to the beat of the Lich's music selection, holding the cigarette Barry gave him like it's an alien artifact. He somehow scored a six-pack of Coors Light, though, so Barry gives him a break.

"Think a lot of people are gonna be here?" Lich asks.

Sammy doesn't look away from her camcorder. "Who cares?"

"Well, I know someone who's for sure gonna be there," says Barry, "and she's been asking about *you,* Lich."

"Me?"

Barry nods.

"Girl?"

"This is a *woman,* Lich."

"Who? Do I know her?"

Barry maneuvers the van down a discreet two-track off the endless Grey Road. "Oh, you know her, all right."

Lich looks back at Sammy, who's rewinding through the tape in her camcorder. Randall shrugs when they lock eyes. Lich tries to lean into Barry's periphery. "Who is it, dude?"

"Oh, you know…" Barry reaches into the interior pocket in his black denim vest. "Little someone who goes by," he plucks a joint and offers it to Lich, "Mary Jane."

Lich smiles, punches Barry, "You dick, dude."

Barry's laughing.

Randall's laughing.

Sammy is shaking her head at what she sees in the Panasonic Palmcorder.

Barry navigates one last bend in the two-track until the road before them opens up to a grassy field and the heaping mass of garbage that is the Sandpit, a raging bonfire at the center. The fire dwarfs Barry's van, licks the sky some thirty feet above. The light of the blaze illuminates in detail the van's interior and the four wide-eyed faces inside.

"Wow," Randall mumbles.

Barry grins as he pulls up next to a line of parked second-hand vehicles on the grass.

Randall leans forward into the van's cab, his head now between Barry and Lich. "I've been to bonfires before, but nothing like this. Is it safe?"

Barry throws the van in park. "Nope."

The four of them make their way to the fire. Barry lights the joint, takes a quick drag to make sure its working right, then passes it to Lich, who confirms that, yeah, it sure is. Lich then hands it to Sammy, but she just rolls her eyes and passes it to Randall without taking a hit. Randall eyes Barry and Lich and then hits the joint hard. The kid immediately hacks a lung, offering it back to someone, anyone, while he buries his coughing in the crook of his arm. Lich claps Randall on the back, and Randall smiles through watering eyes.

Just like the wildest of Friday nights, all the bored youth of Grafting are gathered around the bonfire, drinking, smoking, laughing, dancing to the music that blasts from a boxy 1989 sedan parked near the fire, every door open to the elements. "Rocket" by The Smashing Pumpkins is playing. A number of kids are wearing Halloween masks in celebration.

Barry, Lich, Sammy, and Randall stand before the flames. Barry spreads his arms like he's the one holding this fire together. He howls like a werewolf. They laugh.

Sammy pulls out her Panasonic Palmcorder, starts filming. "I think this will be a great scene for *Creeps*," she declares.

Barry eyes her. He's drawn to the way the camcorder hides almost all of her face except for her smile. Barry beats his chest like an ape, ooh-oohing into the lens because he doesn't know what else to do about that smile. When she laughs, he feels good. He laughs, too. He doesn't mind that she pans away to the bonfire. He made the most of his moment, stoked the personal bonfire burning in his chest.

More cars continue to arrive, as do more partygoers. There must be three or four songs playing from different car stereos now. The amount of alcohol available is impressive. Everyone's doing their part to pitch in, make sure the booze continues to flow. The skunky odor of some dank schwag fills the air, rises in chiefing plumes.

Barry hops into his van and fires it up. The shitty speakers start blasting Stone Temple Pilots. He throws open the rear doors, and he, Lich, and Randall sit their asses down on the frayed shag carpeting and relax to the soothing melody of "Interstate Love Song." Sammy has gone full Spielberg, is just lost in her *Creeps of Casper's Canyon* project, ducking and weaving through different groups of partygoers, getting the perfect shots, pausing here and there to sketch in her storyboard journal by firelight.

"I don't know, man," Randall is saying. "Rush was never my thing."

Lich goes rigid. "What are you talking about, dude?"

"Oh, boy…" says Barry.

Randall shrugs. "I don't know. It's like, why am I going to sit here and listen to an hour-long song?"

"Ohhhhh boyyyy…" Barry scoots away from the other two.

"Oh, come on. What songs have you heard?"

"I don't know, man. I just know it was long. Felt like I was at the London Philharmonic or something."

Lich shakes his head, a manic grin on his face like he just can't believe this. "I get it. You don't appreciate sophisticated art."

"Yeah, I do. It's called Nirvana."

Lich's mouth falls wide open. "But they're not… Their songs aren't… You can't be… *Dude.*"

"You don't like Nirvana?"

Lich slumps into himself, looking like the world just isn't worth fighting for anymore. "No, Randall, I don't."

Barry's been shaking his head at this entire conversation. He doesn't really have a dog in the fight—no one has slandered Dio or Sabbath or Danzig—but he knows what Rush means to Lich, knows the way Lich gets bummed out when someone doesn't like his favorite band of all time. Randall basically insulted Lich's god, his prog-rock lord and savior.

Barry fights with a lighter that's either too cold or too dry to function, and his thumb is starting to develop a blister from the chainwheel. He pauses his attempts with the lighter to stare cross-eyed at the end of the unlit joint in his mouth.

Lich raises a bewildered eyebrow. "What are you doing, dude?" he asks Barry.

"Checking to see if maybe I have laser vision and don't know it," Barry replies flatly.

Randall looks ready to say something but is stopped when a high-pitched scream pierces the night, causing him and his two stoned compatriots to jump. The voice belongs to Sammy, and she sounds like she's in trouble.

Barry scans the crowd until he sees her. She's being shoved back by the glowing silhouette of Mr. Quarterback himself, Chet Springs. Barry chucks the lighter away, tucks the joint in his breast pocket, and hops off the van's bumper. His periphery is going red.

"Barry?" Lich says, running to join his friend. Randall is close behind.

As Barry approaches the commotion, he can hear Sammy pleading, "It was a mistake! I'll erase it!"

"Are you fucking stupid?" Chet says.

Chet's goons are standing beside him. Patrick's thick arms are crossed over his chest. Corbin is laughing. George is just shaking his head, hands stuffed into his letterman jacket pockets.

"Hey!" Barry shouts.

Chet turns. "If it isn't the captain of the retards."

"Leave her alone."

Chet smirks. "Oh yeah? That an order, captain?"

Lich and Randall stand behind Barry.

"I didn't mean to, okay?" says Sammy. "I can tape over it, Chet. Come on."

Chet turns back to Sammy and snarls. He grabs her arm and squeezes tight. "Don't lie to me."

"What did she even do?" Lich blurts, his voice a bit shaky. He takes a timid step forward and then a resolute step back.

"I know what you're up to, you little bitch, taping us drinking like that," says Chet. "Principal Comely has a zero tolerance policy. If he finds out, I can get suspended. I can lose my spot on the team!"

"It was an accident!"

Chet shakes Sammy by the arm, and Barry's vision goes crimson. He sees nothing but red. He charges.

Patrick, however, is adept at chasing down runners, and he reacts to Barry like he's the rival team's running back on a draw play. He hits the gap between Chet and Barry at top speed and tackles Barry to the ground with such tremendous force, it elicits a chorus of stunned noises from the crowd. Barry has the wind knocked out him on impact. He struggles to escape, but he can't get the football player off him.

"Damn, Blueberry!" Chet exclaims, genuinely surprised by what just took place. "I didn't know you had it in you."

Patrick raises a calcified fist and brings it down hard on Barry's face.

"Stop it!" Sammy shouts. "I said I can erase it! Please!"

"Too late for that," Chet says. He tears the Panasonic Palmcorder from Sammy's grip. "Say goodbye to your narc box." He rears back, ready to throw it into the bonfire like only a star high school quarterback can, but he stops when Sammy's body goes limp in his grip. Chet doesn't bother to break her fall, just lets go of her arm like she's dead weight, watches her crumple to the ground in a heap. "What the fuck is that?" he asks. He's looking down at Sammy's storyboard journal that she'd kept tucked in the armpit of her free arm. It's now splayed out on the ground beside her. Chet snatches the journal before Sammy can notice it's free and starts leafing through its pages. An evil smile stretches over his face, and he decides to show George and Corbin the hilariously strange shit he's found.

"What a freak," Corbin laughs.

"Come on, man," George says, forcing a smile. "Just give the dork her book back."

Barry fills his hands with the fabric of Patrick's jacket, tries to throw him off. Tries with all his might. Can't though. Just fucking can't. No matter how hard he curses, spits. Patrick returns the gesture with another blow to the face, this one right in the eye. A star goes supernova in Barry's vision. When his eyesight finally returns, he sees two Lichs holding back two Randalls in front of a blazing inferno that refuses to stay level with the horizon.

"Please, Chet," Sammy says quietly. She's on her knees, not in supplication, but defeat. She's begging. Sammy never begs. "Don't."

Chet sighs. "Okay, fine. But only because you asked so nicely." He holds the journal out to Sammy.

With the fire shining in her wet eyes, Sammy reaches for the sketchbook, relieved. But before she can grab it, Chet tosses it like a frisbee into the flames. "Oops," he mocks.

Randall sheds himself of Lich's embrace, leaving Lich with his leather jacket, and Corbin is too slow to stop him. Randall barrels through the wrestler's outstretched arms and crashes into Chet, tearing the strap of the Palmcorder in the process. The camera falls to the dirt beside Sammy while

Randall and Chet tumble through the edge of the raging bonfire in a shower of sparks and slag. The two boys roll free of the flames, but Randall isn't finished. He jumps on top of Chet and starts beating him with both fists like an enraged chimpanzee.

Corbin and George share a curse, then rush over to save their friend. Corbin puts Randall in some championship-caliber pin in no time, while George pats out the little tongues of fire still licking at Chet's hair and clothing.

Chet spits an incoherent stream of swears as his eyes go from startled to raging. He stands and pulls at Corbin's shoulder. "Let me at 'em!" Corbin steps dutifully aside, leaving Randall on his belly, the boy scrambling to crawl away. Chet pounces, straddles Randall. He wraps a bicep around Randall's neck and pulls it back into a violent headlock. "You think you're tough, new kid?" he says through gritted teeth. He flexes to increase the pressure of the headlock, and Randall, now struggling to breathe, slaps at Chet's arm, desperate for the much bigger youth to let go.

Lich is helping Sammy to her feet, but he's wishing he had the strength of ten more of him, had the power of flight, heat vision, and superhuman speed. That he couldn't feel pain.

And that's when Barry shows up, throws all of himself at Chet, takes the bully straight into the bonfire. What's left of the stacked pallets tumbles behind them as they burst through the other side in a shower of sparks and slag. They land hard on the other side and roll across the ground, snuffing out in the dirt whatever little flames had time enough to catch.

The star quarterback is stunned, the wind knocked completely from his chest, just like Patrick did to Barry. It's, like, the transitive property of beat downs or something.

Barry stands. Pain courses through his ribs, and the foul stench of singed arm hair stings his nostrils. His knuckles are white, clenched into the tightest fists he's ever made, and his upper lip is curled into a lupine snarl, his teeth wet with his own blood. He can end Chet right here, right now, and both boys know it. With one solid punch, he can erase every offensive play call from the quarterback's tiny brain. Can make the bully speak with an impediment for the rest of his life. But the blow never comes, because for some reason, Barry can't bring himself to release all the anger burning inside him. Not even a little bit. *Doesn't he want this?*

Before he can find the answer, someone grabs him from behind and flings him aside with ease. Barry stumbles away without falling and looks ready to rush back into the scrum but stops himself when he sees that it's a sheriff's deputy who has broken up the fight. The deputy stands between Barry and Chet, both arms extended, signaling for the boys to stay apart or else.

Then comes the whoop of a police siren and a flood of red and blue lights. A spotlight is trained on the party, and from the light, the silhouettes of two more police officers storm the Sandpit.

The students of Ottawa Heights scatter like roaches, and within minutes, a dozen vehicles or more are roaring to life and peeling out of the grassy parking lot in a cloud of swirling exhaust.

George is slapping at Chet's shoulder. "Come on, man!" he's saying. "Let's fucking go!"

Patrick shoves Barry aside as he runs past. "I'm not done with you," he warns. But Barry hardly registers the words. He's too busy observing the chaos that has broken out all around him. It reminds him of that night at the MOW, of the quake, of all the dead and dying. His adrenaline vaporizes, and the world begins to spin. Suddenly, he feels every second of the beating he's just taken, and he thinks he might need to vomit. He stumbles once to his left and collapses to the ground.

Lich rushes in to help. "C'mon, dude! We need to split!"

Barry is trying, he really is, but he just can't stand up. His legs refuse to work.

Randall stumbles over and loops one of Barry's arms over his neck and shoulders. Lich does the same with Barry's other arm. Together, they're able to lift Barry to his feet and help him hobble to the van. Sammy is walking with them, crying gently as she wipes the dirt from her camcorder.

The still-open rear doors accept the human offering that Lich and Randall bring. They set Barry in a seated position on the shag carpet and allow him to scoot back gingerly until he's fully inside. The three others climb in through the rear and shut the doors behind them.

"Fuck," is all Barry can say, breathing like a beached whale.

Lich reaches between the front seats and turns off the car. He gives the keys to Barry and takes a seat beside him.

Randall watches out the bubble-window in the back. "Shit," he whispers. "They're full-on arresting kids. Another cop car just pulled up."

"What do we do now?" Lich whispers.

Sammy tucks the camcorder in its canvas case, zips it safely inside. "We wait here," she says. "Until its over. They won't bother us if the van looks empty. Plenty of assholes out there to keep them busy."

But then the van doors open and an officer shines a Maglite on the teens hiding inside. The nameplate beneath his badge reads "Arthur Novak." He studies the wounded boys, then looks to Sammy, her eyes still red from crying. "The fuck happened to you?" he asks.

"Please," Sammy says, "Don't arrest us. My friends got beat up. We didn't do anything."

Art returns his light to Barry, and his eyes widen with recognition. "Hey! You're the kid I pulled off Chet."

"Yeah," says Barry. "So?"

Art adjusts his glasses like he's seeing the kid for the first time. "That was a heck of a tackle. Better pray you didn't injure his throwing arm." He inspects the many patches sewn into the teen's black denim vest. One in particular catches his eye. It's shaped like a frosted doughnut, with the silhouette of a punching fist at its center. Two words are stitched in a cartoon font around the outside edge: *Hurtz Donut?!* Art notes the irony, then points to a bruise forming beneath Barry's left eye. "You're gonna have one hell of a shiner tomorrow."

Confused, Barry touches the spot beneath his left eye and jumps at the sharp, stabbing pain he finds there.

"We can help him ice it when we get home," Sammy says.

Art shakes his head, then reaches for the radio on his chest. "I'm calling an EMT."

"No!" shouts Lich.

Art shines the Maglite at Lich's face.

"We can't afford it."

Art hesitates.

"Please," Sammy says. "This isn't anything new. We'll be fine. We always are."

Art squints through his horn-rimmed glasses. When the radio on his chest crackles to life and the voice asks him to check in, asks if he needs any assistance, Art pauses.

"I've been there, I get it," Art says to the Sammy, then Barry. "I got my ass kicked when I was your age, too." He snatches the radio from his chest. "All clear. No assistance needed." He waves a stern finger at Barry and friends. "Go home," he tells them, then quietly shuts the van doors and leaves.

Randall peers out the bubble-window again. "He's really letting us go," he says.

Sammy lets out a sigh of relief. "Thank God. Now let's get the fuck out of here before something else crazy happens."

Frowning, Lich points at Barry's swollen eye. "Damn, dude. Patrick got you good."

"Fuck Patrick," Barry says. "Just fuck him."

The gang nods in agreement. But what they don't know is just how well and truly fucked Patrick actually is.

DEATH OF A HIGH SCHOOL LINEBACKER

"I'M NOT DONE with you," says Patrick. And with that, he makes a break for his car. Panicked students running around in every direction are no issue for him. He's bigger than every single one and can barrel straight through them, knock them to the ground without stopping. The only people he can't simply knock over are the two county sheriff deputies parked beside his car up ahead.

"Fuck!" Patrick shouts. Usually, he'd consult Chet at this point—maybe George—get his marching orders. But when he turns to find comfort in the company of his friends, he sees that, no, they are not right behind him, had not followed him like he thought. Of course they hadn't. Chet is Chet. Chet doesn't follow. Guys like Patrick and Corbin and George do the following. So once again Patrick says, "Fuck!"

Another cruiser pulls up to the party, and for a sickening moment, the headlights expose Patrick just standing there like a cat burglar caught in the spotlight. Without thinking, he takes off for the surrounding woods.

Early winter's chill touches the air, and it's enough to shred Patrick's throat the harder he runs, the harder he breathes. He sees he's not the only rat swimming downstream. Other students are running this direction, too, like shadows in the night. He looks for something, anything he can hide behind—a fallen tree, a large boulder, an ancient car frame, *anything.*

Thanks to the light of the massive bonfire still flickering between the gaps in the trees, his eyes are unable to fully adjust to the darkness. His foot catches on some unseen deadfall, and he trips, stumbles forward, and smashes with all of his weight into the sturdy trunk of a tree. The old hemlock is unmoved. Patrick's right shoulder, however, is not.

This isn't the first time Patrick has sustained this kind of injury. He knows the feeling of a dislocated shoulder, having suffered it two other times under the Friday night lights, and he remembers how much worse it hurt the second time. This time—number three—is enough to bring tears to his eyes.

He sits with his back to the hemlock's trunk, facing away from the bonfire's light. He clutches his injured shoulder, tries not to shout from the pain. He risks a peek around the tree, sees that at least one deputy has entered the forest in pursuit. "Ah, man, I'm so screwed," he whimpers. He gathers his strength and uses the hemlock's ragged trunk to help him climb back to his feet. A searing pain in his ankle alerts him that the dislocated shoulder is not the only injury he's sustained. He can't run anymore, not on a sprained ankle, so he hobbles to a spruce just ahead, the young tree barely as tall as he is. He rests there for a brief moment, then moves to the next feature in the woods: a fallen cedar, roots ripped from the ground.

"Enough!" shouts the deputy. "I see you guys running around back there! Come back before you freeze to death!"

Yeah, fuck that. Patrick continues on. The snow is deep enough now to crunch beneath his Nikes, and the ground has started to decline sharply toward a shallow ravine below.

Another proud hemlock stands at the base of the ravine, and Patrick leans against it for support. His shoulder burns. The pain radiates through his chest and back. Busted or not, he won't be the Owls' starting middle linebacker next week. That, he knows for sure.

God, it's cold. Now that he's standing still, just listening to the sounds of the other kids running and the shouts from the pursuing deputy, he can feel the cold though his jacket. A light snow has started to fall. He wasn't dressed for this shit. He wasn't supposed to be clutching a dislocated shoulder in the dark woods of Northern Michigan. He was supposed to be chugging beers next to a giant bonfire, hitting on some cheerleaders.

Patrick reaches down to touch his ankle, but even a light amount of pressure reignites the pain. "Fuck!" he shouts, then cuts himself off, pushes the rest of the cry out through his nose. His mind is racing. Can he follow this ravine home? Should he try and get back to his car? *Think, Patrick! What would Chet do?*

A twig snaps, and something touches his shoulder.

It's the tap of a finger.

Patrick whirls around. He expects to see another terrified student waiting there, desperate to share his cover behind the hemlock. He expects that he will tell the student to fuck off, tell him or her that this place isn't big enough for the both of them. But what he sees instead, he cannot fully comprehend. It looks like someone he knows, but something is very wrong with their face. It also appears to be taller than usual. Or maybe that's just the uneven ground.

"What the fuck?" Patrick manages. "Where the hell did you come from?" He expects a timid reply, but it doesn't come.

Patrick hears the deputy calling down from the top of the ravine behind them. "I know you're down there!" He can see the chopped-up beam of light from a flashlight glassing the area around him.

"Are you crazy?" Patrick whispers to his present company. "Fucking hide, you idiot!"

The figure doesn't move.

"Are you…?" Patrick squints into the darkness.

The figure tilts its head to the side. A single yellow eye stares out from a dirty rubber eyelet. The other eyelet is black.

"…Wearing some kind of Halloween mask?"

The deputy begins his decent into the ravine. "I'm coming down! If you don't want any trouble, I suggest you show yourselves before I get there! Make it easy on me, and I'll make it easy on you! Let's be smart about this!"

Angry now, Patrick shoves the figure out to the ground. "Get lost, creep!" But he doesn't get far before an iron grip clutches his sprained ankle tight. Tears quickly well in his eyes as he bites back the cry that would betray his hiding spot to the deputy. He crumples to the snow-dusted earth.

The tall, lanky figure that Patrick pushed to the ground stands, the linebacker's ankle still in its grip. It gives the ankle a good squeeze, then stuns Patrick with a heel kick between the eyes, rendering the teen too dazed to struggle. The figure then begins dragging the hulking linebacker deeper into the woods.

The world goes by in distorted shapes and sounds, and all Patrick wants to do is sleep. He knows a concussion when he feels one. *When did the twerp get so strong?* Soon, the only sounds are the crunch of snow and his own aching groans. At one point, he swears he sees in the moonlight a pulsing purple tumor on the back of his kidnapper's neck. And another behind his ear. But all that's lost in the concussed blur.

The tall, lanky figure eventually stops in a clearing and releases Patrick at the feet of another figure, whose stature Patrick also recognizes in the dim moonlight. This one is short and squat, and his face is fucked-up, too. Patrick hobbles to his feet, where he towers over both of his freakish captors. Looking down on them gives him renewed energy. It's good to be back in control.

"You want round two or something?" he says to the shorter one. "Because I'm ready to go if you—"

But before he can finish his sentence, the short one pulls a sword and, in one fell swoop, lops off both of Patrick's legs at the knees. The linebacker's legless body drops to the ground in a terrible heap and starts rapidly bleeding out at the amputation sites. Patrick doesn't cry, doesn't call out for help, just looks over at one of his severed limbs in total disbelief. It lays there like a dismembered leg, like someone else's leg still clothed in jeans, a tube sock, and a Nike sneaker. He wants to touch it, wants to make sure that it really is *his* leg and not some gruesome practical effect, so he reaches for it and grabs it by the ankle. It feels warm, heavy...*real.* Patrick feels sick.

He inhales enough air to scream, but it's the roar of a chainsaw that fills the night with sound. Above him, the tall, lanky figure raises the gas-powered machine of mayhem and brings it down on Patrick's chest without hesitation, drives the quaking blade deeper into the linebacker's ribs. The chainsaw crunches through flesh and bone, digs its way into Patrick's right lung, shreds the organ like it's nothing. The scream that never came evacuates the wound in a wash of viscera.

If you could discern Patrick's final words from the gurgle of blood pooling in his choking throat and spilling out the corners of his mouth in shades of crimson and black, you might hear him asking one final question before he goes.

"How?"

Never gets an answer, though, poor kid.

INCIDENT REPORT

Apex Door Field Assessment Unit 3

Incident/Assessment Report

Today's Date: Friday, October 13, 1995

Time: 6:22 PM

Assessor Number: 7

Assessor's Handler: Orson Caster

Location of incident: Grafting, Michigan

Person(s) affected: The Whitfield Family

Reason(s) for field assessment dispatch:

We intercepted a call from Donald Whitfield as he dialed local authorities about an earthquake shaking his home. 7 indicated to me that this was activity directly related to the escalating phenomena taking place around Grafting and throughout the surrounding Ottawa County.

Key Indicators mentioned (please refer to the latest edition of the APEX DOOR FIELD ASSESSMENT MANUAL for updated glossary of Key Indicators to choose from):

- Seismic activity

- Poltergeist activity

- Apparition(s)
- Leyline crux

Please describe the incident(s), including any anomalous phenomena:

The call was intercepted in real-time, and it required an immediate response. We would have little time to interview Mr. Whitfield before the arrival of local authorities. Once at the Whitfield house, I identified myself and 7 as the authorities requested, and entry into the home was granted. Additionally, 7 was allowed access to the rest of the home while Mr. Whitfield and myself spoke in the living room.

Apparently, this was not the first seismic event that the Whitfields had experienced, though according to Mr. Whitfield, it was the most violent. The experiencer described it as "the straw that broke the camel's back," detailing how prior tremors affecting their property had resulted in clear paranormal phenomena (reference key indicators as selected above). Within twenty-four hours of the first tremor, the family experienced mild poltergeist activity, manifesting in the form of missing items, furniture moving, chair-stacking, etc.

Following the next tremor, Mr. Whitfield recounted how the family home had been invaded by shadow apparitions. These entities could be seen throughout the home, favoring the corners of several rooms. The youngest Whitfield child claimed to hear at least one shadow apparition communicate verbally in clear English. Mr. Whitfield, fearing a recurrence of paranormal activity, phoned local authorities immediately following this most recent tremor.

When the authorities arrived, myself and 7 were able to leave the scene without interposition.

Assessor response:

7's demeanor upon entering the home had darkened noticeably, and he appeared on guard. He only wanted to stay for as long as was necessary. He showed signs of agitation and discomfort.

Conclusion & Recommended Next Steps:

Requesting dispatch of Intercept & Recovery teams, as well as activation of the local field HQ for R&D. Grafting, Michigan, has demonstrated clear signs of Bleed. It is 7's belief that the coming event will result in rifts larger than anything on record. Full support from HQ and The Board is required. Move with haste, please.

GRAFTING, MICHIGAN

Wednesday, November 1, 1995

TESTING THE LIMIT

DANIEL CLEEVE SITS on the edge of his desk and lights a Lucky Strike that hangs from the corner of his mouth. He takes a drag from the cigarette, crosses a leg at the knee, and hunches forward like Auguste Rodin's *The Thinker* on a smoke break. "I'm disappointed in you, Logan."

Logan chews the inside of his cheek, biting back an insubordinate retort. For a moment, the only response is a loud gulp coming from Dr. Foster, louder than the bustle of technicians working in the lab outside Cleeve's office window.

Logan wipes his forehead, pretends he doesn't notice his legs going weak. He bends at the knees a bit to stretch, prevent himself from becoming too stiff and passing out. "Sir?"

Cleeve points the cherry of his cigarette at Logan, "Apex Door recently sent an extraction team to a location off of Grey Road, outside of Grafting city limits. You led this team, correct?"

"Correct."

Cleeve hops down from his perch on the desk and approaches Logan. "And did your extraction team successfully *extract* the subjects of the Bleed event off of Grey Road?"

Logan is a head taller than Daniel Cleeve, forty pounds heavier, and built like a fire hydrant. He reminds Cleeve of this fact by straightening his back and shoulders, and puffing out his chest. "No, sir. We were unable to locate the subject. This was all in my report."

Cleeve draws a hard cherry on his Lucky Strike. "You're not here to fill out reports, Logan. You're here to get results. On the night of October 27th, Apex Door sent an extraction team to a Bleed event on Pine Mountain Road. You led that team, as well, correct?"

"I did."

"And did you extract the subjects then?"

"No, sir."

"You know what this means, don't you? We have multiple Bleed subjects still out there, just roaming our reality like they own the place. *We* own this place, Logan. Not them. We do."

"Yeah, but—"

"No buts! You weren't hired to say 'but.' If you want to say that word, you can tell it to whatever mercenary outfit hires you next after we ship you out the door. Might I remind you that I extracted a Bleed target at the concert venue on the 27th without any trouble at all, and I was flying solo."

Logan sets his jaw. There's nothing the itinerant mercenary hates more than to be outclassed on the battlefield. If Cleeve weren't an Apex Door director, he'd be snoring on the concrete already. "The subjects I've been chasing are different. More advanced."

Cleeve takes a drag of his cigarette, turns to Foster. "What's he talking about?"

Foster wants to melt away into a puddle, but his solid state prevents him from doing so. "What Logan means to say is we have good reason to believe that the Bleed subjects on Pine Mountain Road and the Bleed subjects off Grey Road were— *are*—anomalies. Like nothing we've seen before."

"How so?"

"Uh, well, for one, we don't think they require extraction in order to leave our reality."

"Both times, we were on those subjects like flies on shit," Logan says. "And both times, just as we closed in, they vanished. Tracks just stopped. Bleed readings stopped, too. At some point, there was just no more evidence that the subjects were still on our plane."

Cleeve stubs his cigarette out on his desk. "So, you're telling me that a pair of Bleed subjects pulled a Houdini in the North Michigan woods last night? And prior to that, on the night of the 27th? Just like *poof*, and they're gone?" Cleeve splays his fingers wide as if he's just released two exploding puffs of smoke.

"Yeah," says Logan. "*Poof.* If that's how you want to put it."

Cleeve glares at Logan. "Trust me, that's *not* how I want to put it."

"Um…and that's only the first thing, Mr. Cleeve," Foster says. "The second point of significance—why I consider these subjects anomalies—is because I think they're the same subjects coming back."

Cleeve's eyes narrow. "Impossible."

"I have evidence. Come. I'll show you."

Foster leads Cleeve and Logan out of the office and through the subterranean lab, which is still in various states of assembly and looking nothing like the Apex Door HQ in Norfolk. Hardware hums on rack mounts or in heavy-duty travel cases, casters all locked, and wires are strewn about, ready to trip any preoccupied staffer not watching their feet. As they walk, Dr. Foster starts to explain: "A few days ago, we had a strange readout on the primary feed." He leads his colleagues around the crescent-shaped console station nearest Babylon's tank and points up to a bank of CRT monitors bigger and more advanced than anything you can find in Circuit City, maybe even The Pentagon. He points to one of the monitors. The display on the monitor looks like an electrocardiogram readout, same acid-green line rising and falling in variable peaks and valleys against a darker forest-green backdrop. A grid blankets the entire screen from edge to edge, with one of the lines on the Y-axis brighter than the rest and labeled as THRESHOLD. A young female lab tech in a white coat and sneakers sits at the crescent-shaped console beneath the monitors and clacks away at a keyboard.

"Quick refresher for—" Foster was going to say *"for everyone,"* but he changes course when he sees the threatening look on Cleeve's face. "…For Logan. This is the subfield monitoring system. It's this marvel of modern technology that will one day replace Apex Door assessors and move us into the digital age. Just like the work of assessors, this system enables us to predict high-probability Bleed events, but now with stunning accuracy—no offense to our hard-working colleagues in the field." He points to the acid-green line zig-zagging below the threshold line. "As long as that read-out remains below the X-axis, which is calibrated to zero, the membrane between realities is stable. The membrane, we think of it as a gelatinous layer of goop that separates our reality from the next closest one, to put it simply. Except it behaves more like a fluid than say…Jell-O. This line, though, the one that looks like a heart monitor, is a visual aggregate of local geothermal reads, seismographic activity, magnetic field detectors…anything, really, that can help us detect a Bleed."

Foster holds out a hand, fingers splayed. "On this hand, we have the typical ambient readout of our reality." He holds out his other hand the same way as the first. "And on this hand, we have the typical readouts of another reality. Sometimes, they go like this…" He touches his fingertips together. "When it gets bad, it goes like this…" He laces the touching fingers. "And when it's *real* bad…" He locks his fingers together to form a two-handed fist. "Bleed." He taps the lab tech on the shoulder. "Meghan, please pull up the snapshot of the Grafting Bleed event from October 27th—the one on Pine Mountain Road."

Meghan clacks some more on her keyboard until a screen recording of the readout from that night appears on one of the monitors above. The readout shows a series of blips that increase in frequency and amplitude until a much larger one suddenly spikes above the threshold line and plateaus for awhile before dropping back into the normal range, where it stays.

"Here's the Bleed from Friday night," Foster explains. "As you can see, it was quite large. That extended plateau there is what allowed for such a massive crater. Same thing happened at the concert venue. See, the duration of a Bleed event can be measured by the wave's frequency, while the magnitude of the event can be measured by the wave's amplitude." He taps Meghan's shoulder again. "Pull up the Bleed from last night."

Meghan does as instructed.

"This was the Bleed from last night. Spot the difference? No plateau. The spike is acute, nothing like a typical Bleed event, and it was quick. It tripped every alarm we have, near simultaneously. It reads like a bug, some kind of glitch, but given the evidence retrieved from the site, we can conclude that these readings are accurate. A Bleed *did* occur."

Meghan dutifully clicks through to a new data set.

Foster continues: "This is where things get *really* interesting. An hour after the initial Bleed event, another acute spike occurs, except this time, the spike is inverted. This wave starts *above* the threshold line and spikes *below* it for a brief second before normalizing. Honestly, I thought it would be months before we had any answers, but then Logan's story about the disappearing tracks got me thinking. It might not be a glitch after all. This inverted spike might be illustrating the exact moment that the anomalies quite literally disappeared."

"*Poof*," Logan says with a smile.

Cleeve steeples his fingers in front of his lips. "You understand the implications of what you're saying, right."

"Yes, sir. According to this data, the recent Bleeds in and out of our reality were intentional. The anomalies created these Bleeds on purpose, then created subsequent Bleeds here, in our reality, to go back home, wherever that may be. That's how they're evading capture."

Cleeve adjusts his aviators, a gesture seldom seen. "I want these anomalies to be Apex Door's top priority. If what you posit is accurate, and we're dealing with subjects who are entering and leaving our reality at will, we need to take them into Apex Door custody immediately. Alive, if possible."

Logan interjects. "What does it matter if they're alive? They'll just be heading for extraction anyway."

"I wouldn't be so certain of that," Cleeve says. "These subjects are— How did you put it? *Different. More advanced.*"

Just then, a familiar klaxon sounds throughout the underground lab. "EXTRACTION IMMINENT," a prerecorded voice says in the loudspeakers above.

All heads look up to watch a corrugated rubber tube, large enough to fit a human being inside, descend from the ceiling and attach itself to the top of Babylon's tank via a titanium coupling mechanism. Once coupled, a mechanical sphincter is created that, when opened, will allow whatever is in the tube to pass quickly into the tank.

Inside the tank, the shape of Babylon is obscured by its abnormal positioning and the blue fluid suspending it, but when the tube starts to descend, the many bent appendages that have been resting against the glass suddenly twitch to life. Twitch with what appears to be anticipation. It knows what's about to come down that tube, and it's excited for it.

"EXTRACTION IN 3... 2... 1..."

The mechanical sphincter opens and a days-old cadaver drops from the tube into the tank amid a flood of aquamarine bubbles. It's the corpse of Rudy Gartner—the one who had his skull crushed during the MOW's collapse. Looks like the body's been dissected a bit, too. It floats there for a sickly moment, the cadaver's long, stringy hair just waving above his head like the tentacles of a jellyfish, before Babylon lurches into action and strikes—starts thrashing about with all its massive limbs to pull the feed into its gaping maw. Within seconds, the corpse of Rudy Gartner is gone, devoured by Baby in an explosion of purple ink.

"EXTRACTION COMPLETE."

SORRY...

IT'S LATE AT night, and Sheriff Keller is standing alone in his kitchen in nothing but his whitey tighties, the stove clock swiftly approaching the witching hour. He's staring at his nighttime reflection in the sliding glass door, sizing up the ghostly manifestation that holds a glass of Scotch atop a hairy belly bloated from alcohol, bad diet, and age. He's wishing he could sleep, and he's hoping the double-pour of McClellan 12 will help. A Kool & The Gang record spins on the turntable in the living room. The current song is "Summer of Madness."

As has become common for Keller, sleep evades him. So, too, does self-forgiveness. He's been on administrative leave from the sheriff's department ever since that night at the MOW; the same night, he later learned, that Deputy Pipes was murdered up at Pine Mountain. Keller is convinced that Mikey Pipes would still be alive if it weren't for Keller's terrible decision-making that night, and he won't let himself forget it. Why did he have to station Pipes at the MOW? Why didn't he relieve him before shit hit the fan at Brock Corning's place? Why didn't he send Pipes home right after the deputy told Keller about Marie, the baby, and the little Tupperware beach?

That's when a knock comes at the front door.

At this hour? Why in the hell would someone be knocking on his door at three in the morning? Nah. He's just hearing things. He eyes his magnum on the kitchen counter but reaches for the bottle of scotch instead, adds another splash to his glass.

Silence.

See? Nothing. Just him. Always just him. The man who has to hold this town together when he can barely keep himself in one piece. He looks again to his reflection. That's years of police work right there. He's the overworked liver of Grafting, the thing that eliminates the poisons from society then dies, unheralded, of cirrhosis.

Another knock comes at the front door, louder this time, more assertive.

Keller shoots back the last of his Scotch and swaps the empty glass for his gun. On the way to the front door, he grabs his uniform shirt from a hook on the entryway wall and shoulders into the garment, affixes the bottom two buttons over the bulge in his whitey tighties. When he gets to the door, he flicks on the porch light and opens the door just a crack, gun held hidden behind his back.

A woman stands on Keller's front porch in her bathrobe. "Sheriff Keller?"

Keller blinks. *Neighbor, blue house, overly apologetic.* He can recall that much as he searches through his mental Rolodex for her name. "Yeah?"

"I'm sorry, I know it's late."

"Yeah." *The fuck is her name again? Starts with an A.*

"It's just—" She stops. Keller's puzzled look must be what compels her to explain, "Sorry, it's Anna. Few houses down?"

Anna! That's it. He was just about to flip to that name in his mental Rolodex. "Uh-huh."

Anna blushes. "Sorry. It's just… I mean… I'm pretty sure I saw your father in our yard, and—"

Keller shakes his head. "Wait. What?" He pinches the bridge of his greasy nose, sighs a plume of Scotch. "Like now? You saw him outside right now?"

Anna nods. "I heard some commotion outside, and that's when I saw someone in our front yard, hiding behind the hedges along the sidewalk. I came outside to help, but he ran off down the street. *Sorry.*"

"Okay, thanks for letting me know." Keller closes the door before the woman can say more, and he heads upstairs to check his dad's room. Bed is empty. Keller crosses the hall to his bedroom and snatches a pair of pants from the floor. He pulls them on and sucks in his gut to button them. He then shoves his feet into a pair of dirty sneakers and stumbles back downstairs.

Anna is still waiting on Keller's front porch when he opens the door. "I was going to call the police," she explains, "but, I mean, you *are* the police. I hope I'm not being a bother. It's just really cold out here, and I don't want him to freeze. *Sorry...*"

A frigid wind stings Keller's cheeks. Damn, it *is* cold. "Just go home, okay? Quick, please. This isn't bathrobe weather."

She looks down at her thin slippers and the bare ankles peeking out the tops. She nods and heads back home.

Keller hops in his cruiser and drives slowly down the street, spotlight trained on the sidewalks. The heater is taking forever to blow hot air into the cabin, and he can see his own breath. It smells hotter than it looks, coming out in frosty plumes to fog the windshield. "Goddammit, Dad," he mutters to the night. "Where are you?"

When Keller finds his father, the old man is hobbling down the center of the street, clutching himself in his arms.

Keller stops the cruiser, gets out. "Dad?"

The old man freezes.

"It's me, John-David," Keller says as he approaches him.

His father makes no movement besides the relentless shivering.

"It's me, Dad, your son. Let's get you home."

Suddenly, the old man bolts. He runs harder than he should be able to, his feeble body powered by a brain stuck decades in the past, back when it could still handle such maneuvers. He then ducks right and dives over a low row of hedges, disappears with a yowl behind them.

Keller knows this likely means a few broken bones.

The sheriff makes his way around the hedges to where his father had hurled himself so recklessly, finds the old man now frantically searching for cover. He kneels down next to him. "Dad, it's me."

"Get the fuck away from me!" his dad shouts.

Keller wraps a loving arm around his father and gently hoists him to his feet.

"Ow! You're hurting me!"

"What I'm doing is taking you back to your bed."

"No! Fuck you!" He begins to scream: "Help! HELP!"

Keller pulls a pair of handcuffs from his pants pocket and snaps them onto the frail wrists of his dad. He hates that he has to do this, especially in front of what's-her-name—*Anna*—now watching from behind the drapes in her front window. "It's not like you'll remember this anyway," he says to his dad, says to himself as he seats him in the back of the cruiser.

By the time they get back home, just a few houses down, his dad has gone from shouting to crying to sleeping. Keller parks the cruiser and opens the back door, uncuffs his father, then picks him up. Fuck, he's light. *All skin and bones*—something his dad used to say about Keller when he was a boy.

Front door is still open. That's convenient. Cold as hell inside, but Keller's already sweaty from carrying his father around. Doesn't mind. He carries him upstairs and lays him in bed. Tomorrow, he'll have to tell Martha about the old man's failed leap over the hedges. The in-home nurse will know better than Keller how to check for injuries. Maybe she'll increase the dosage on his medication so something like this is less likely to happen again.

But for now, it's back downstairs to the kitchen. He's already shed his pants again, but his shirt remains on his frame, just with most of the buttons now undone. Sheriff's badge somehow catches what little light shines from beneath the microwave. Shines that badge bright. He's about to pour himself another glass of Scotch when the phone rings. He picks it up. It's Deputy Arthur Novak.

"Sheriff, sorry to wake you."

"No problem, Art. What's up?" He pours another glass of Scotch.

"I don't know how to explain this exactly, but it's bad."

"Great." Keller shoots back the glass of brown liquor.

"There's been another homicide, sheriff. A young male this time. Student at Ottawa Heights. It's messy. I know you're still on leave, but…I really think you should come down to the medical examiner's office and see this. The wounds, they match those recorded on Pipes. Some other similarities, as well."

Keller's blood runs cold at the mention of the dead deputy's name. He looks at his reflection again, at the man who's supposed to hold Grafting together, keep its residents—his deputies—safe, just like his dad did when the old man was sheriff of this town. "I'm sure it'll be just as messy tomorrow," he says.

"Sheriff?"

"Go home, Art," says Keller. "Get some rest. Sounds like there's gonna be a lot to do, and we'll both need fresh minds to do it."

A moment of white noise through ten miles of telephone wire. Then Art says, "Yes, sir. See you tomorrow."

"Yup," Keller says and slams the phone on its cradle. He then lifts the phone back up and slams it down on the cradle again.

GRAFTING, MICHIGAN

Thursday, November 2, 1995

POSTMORTEM

WHEN KELLER SEES Patrick Smith's corpse for the first time, he says the only prayer he knows: "Jesus."

"Yeah," says Art. "Not too nice to look at, is it?"

The county medical examiner is a man in his early seventies, always one more year away from retiring. "Do you need me to stick around, answer any questions?" he says

"No, Ernie, we got it," Keller says.

"All right, then. Just let me know when you're done. I'll be in my office." Ernie hands Keller the autopsy report and takes his leave.

Keller and Art stand alone in the morgue's chilly examination room and circle the body on the stainless steel slab like vultures circling a carcass. Keller leafs through the ten-page autopsy report, but only skims the information. He's more of a hands-on investigator, so he covers his mouth with the surgeon's mask he's been holding and moves in close to the body to better inspect the wounds. "We got a positive ID yet?"

"Parents came in this morning to confirm."

"Linebacker for the Owls, right? Kid with all the tackles."

"Yeah."

"So much for a repeat championship," Keller says. He surveys the broad shoulders of the deceased. "A boy like this can't be easy to take down. Any signs of struggle?"

"None. There's evidence that he was dragged to the site of the murder, but no signs that he tried to escape."

"Could have been unconscious already, or drunk," Keller says. "They run a toxicology report yet?"

"Results are still pending."

"Ernie said he was most likely standing when his legs were lopped off." Keller looks to the sutured stumps that were once Patrick's legs. "So, this was after he had been dragged, after he saw he was in trouble. Why didn't he run?"

"Maybe he knew the attackers. Wasn't expecting them to hurt him."

"Or maybe he had met his match. You have to be a strong son-of-a-bitch to chop a man's legs clean off like this."

"Gotta say, I would never have thought it possible," Art agrees.

Keller examines the ragged chainsaw wound to the chest, now closed up by medical staples. "You said he was part of the fight you broke up, right? The one with Chet Springs and the boys. Did you get the names of the other kids involved?"

"Shit, sheriff. Probably, but I don't remember. A lot happened that night."

"I want those names. Make sure you find out when Patrick's friends are brought in for questioning."

"On it, sheriff."

"Only thing I can't figure out is how this connects to Mikey Pipes. The sword, the chainsaw—this has to be the same guys that killed Mikey. But why? What's the connection between Pipes and a high school kid?"

"They were both murdered in the woods. Maybe that's where our killers like to hunt."

"Not a bad theory. We have a patrol watching the area?"

"Tam and I have been taking turns."

"Good man."

"That reminds me. You know how I said there are other similarities between the two cases?"

Keller shrugs. "Sure. Like what?"

"Would be easier if I showed you. Field trip to the crime scene?"

"Lead the way," Keller says.

KELLER FOLLOWS ART down the steep ravine near the Sandpit and into the clearing where Patrick Smith was found dead. The killing field is overgrown with little yellow evidence markers that have been plunged into the cold earth all around them. Many have been placed to mark tracks.

"Too many footprints for two killers and one victim," Keller says. "Anyone else been taking an interest here?"

Art rubs his hands together and blows his warm breath into them to fight back the tingling in his fingers. Should have worn gloves. "Some of the evidence points to tampering. For example, varied trajectories not belonging the perps or victim indicate that at least four other individuals spent quite a bit of time on scene, most likely postmortem. All wearing the same military-issue boots, all different shoe sizes."

"Military issue? National Guard?"

"They say no."

Keller shakes his head. "Well, fuck. This just got complicated."

"Tell me about it. But that's not why I wanted to bring you here. Look." Art points to a yellow evidence flag plunged into a spot where the ground seems to…glow.

"Is that grass glowing purple?" Keller remarks.

"It is."

"Why?"

"Don't know. Some kind of chemical compound. Smells like sulfur. Samples have been sent to Ann Arbor for testing, but it will take a week or more to hear back."

Keller walks over to the glowing spot to see that it's in the shape of a footprint. There's a number of them, actually— glowing purple footprints. The sight and smell of the foreign substance sends him spiraling into a state of the most unexplainable déjà vu. His mind flashes back to the night at the MOW and to his dream about Rudy Gartner's talking corpse. "This purple substance, it's from someone's shoe?"

"Two someones. Our killers."

"So, what? We're dealing with the paranormal now?"

"Appears that way, doesn't it? Some real Ghostbusters shit, if you ask me."

Keller puts his hands on his hips to think. "Relax, Art. I'm sure there's a perfectly logical explanation for this."

"Oh, yeah? Like what?"

Keller shrugs. "Hell if I know. I went to cop school, not college."

"Anyway… Here's the really crazy thing: these same glowing footprints were also found at the scene of Pipes's murder. And that purple goo, the stuff that makes the footprints glow? Traces of it were collected by a number of first responders at the MOW, on the night of the quake."

Keller's head starts to spin. "At the MOW? What do you mean? Was there a murder at the MOW I'm not aware of?" His mind flashes to the corpse of Rudy Gartner again.

"No. Just that purple shit."

"So, our killers were there… At the MOW the night it collapsed."

Art shrugs. "It's possible." The two men stand in contemplative silence until Art decides to change the subject. "Did they tell you that Mikey's funeral is this Sunday?"

"Who do you think is giving the eulogy?" Keller says.

"Don't you hate public speaking?"

"I hate doing a lot of things, Art. Still gotta do 'em."

Art stares at the glowing purple footprint in the ground. "Ain't that the truth."

GRAFTING, MICHIGAN

Friday, November 3, 1995

IN MEMORIAM

"THIS IS BULLSHIT," says Barry.

Mrs. Bellamy is at the front of the class, instructing her students on how to exit the room one row at a time. The students seated in the front row go first, then the second row follows, then the third row... You get the picture.

"Uh-huh," Lich agrees, but he's not really paying attention. He's got one eye in his latest book of conspiracies.

Barry squints at the cover to read title, "*The Philadelphia* what?"

Lich closes the book and proudly reads the title aloud: "*The Philadelphia Experiment: Project Invisibility.* Had to request a copy at the Grafting Library. Can't believe they actually ordered one for me."

Barry rolls his eyes. "You really eat that government conspiracy shit up, don't you?"

Lich shrugs happily. "Yup."

Finally, the last row is called to exit the classroom. Last row is Barry and Lich's domain.

Randall yawns. "Anyone have any food?" he asks as he trails behind the friends.

Barry rolls his eyes. "Totally. Let me just reach into my Bag of Holding here and pull out that rotisserie chicken I was saving for later."

Lich snickers.

"What, dude? I didn't eat breakfast," Randall says.

"Join the club."

"Your eye is looking better," Randall says.

Barry touches the tender spot on his left orbital bone and shrugs. It's still pretty swollen and purple, probably needs a few more days to heal completely, but Barry doesn't mind. In fact, he kind of wants the bruising to stick around longer, thinks it looks badass. Senior probably had a few shiners in his day, too. Like father, like son.

"Still hurt?" Lich asks.

"Nah," Barry lies.

The three make their way out of first period American History, followed by Mrs. Bellamy. "Try to stay single-file, please!" she says.

Lich digs in the pocket of his basketball shorts and discreetly removes some contraband. He elbows Randall in the ribs. "Here," he whispers to him. "Take it." Keeping the item hidden from Mrs. Bellamy, he hands it over.

"Excuse me!" shouts Mrs. Bellamy from behind them. The sound is enough to make all three boys' spines go rigid. "Mr. Potts! No holding hands in school!"

Oh, good. She's just shouting at Jeremy. And yeah, enough with the PDA, Jeremy. Everyone is sick of you and Kelly always sucking faces.

"Excuse me, Mr. Potts!" Mrs. Bellamy shouts again as she abandons her post at the rear of the line to chase down Jeremy at the front. "Helloooo!"

With Mrs. Bellamy gone, Randall accepts the item from Lich and takes a good long look at the gift he's just received. He gasps at the sight. "Holy cow, dude. Thanks!"

Lich nods. "Those are the best, man."

Randall reads the label: "Donner Cherry Pie..." He runs his fingers across the logo, feels the waxy wrapping it's printed on.

"Fresh from the shelves of Rotten Roscoe's," Barry adds from over his shoulder. "Picked 'em up this morning. I was, uh, gonna tell you about them later."

"I'm eating the ever-loving shit out of this."

More lines of students appear, snaking their way from other classrooms in other parts of the building. All lines will ultimately merge at the gym.

"Oh, shit." Lich taps Barry's shoulder. "Look."

Barry turns and sees Sammy in one of the other lines of students. "Dungeon Master Spielberg!" he shouts, waving like an idiot.

Sammy rolls her eyes, then steps ahead of a few kids in her line until she's walking alongside Barry, Lich, and Randall. "This is bullshit."

"That's what I said," Barry says.

"Yup." Lich nods. "Total bullshit."

Sammy makes a face at Randall. "Really?"

Randall is devouring his Donner Cherry Pie like a starving rat. He lifts a toothy smile at Sammy, making sure she can see the sugary mess in his teeth and the goopy red filling dripping from both corners of his mouth.

"That's so gross."

The many lines of students make their way through the double doors of the gymnasium to join the rest of the student body on the bleachers.

Sammy uses the bottleneck happening at the double doors as an opportunity to sneak into Barry and Lich's line. They're all sitting together on the bleachers when Mrs. Bellamy walks by during headcount. She stops at Sammy.

"Ms. Walters?" she asks, confused.

Now, if it was Barry or Lich caught disobeying orders like this, there would be no confusion about it. Pick any teacher; they'd all agree that Barry and Lich were up to no good and that their insubordination would not be tolerated.

"Oh, sorry, Mrs. Bellamy," Sammy says in her sweetest *whoopsie* voice. "I got all mixed up, and this was the first empty seat I could find. I hope it's okay."

Mrs. Bellamy smiles like a mother might smile at her newborn baby. "Oh, sweetie, of course it is." She then makes her way to her own seat, which she has decided will be between Jeremy Potts and Kelly, much to the couple's dismay.

Barry looks to the gym's scoreboard to see a banner-sized picture of Patrick Smith in his football jersey draped over the scoreboard's display. The linebacker's birth and death dates are printed below his picture, as is his jersey number and the number of tackles and turnovers he had recorded in his career.

"What the fuck is that?" Barry says. "I thought this was a memorial for the quake victims?"

"It is," says Sammy. "But after Patrick's death, they decided to make it a memorial for him, as well."

"Okay," says Barry, "but where are the banners for the kids that died at the MOW? I don't see any of those."

Before Sammy can reply, the lights go down, and the Ottawa Owls cheerleading squad dances their way out onto the gymnasium floor to a muted round of applause. The girls are trying to smile, but it all just feels weird. They take their seats on the floor in front of the bleachers and turn their attention to the row of empty folding chairs waiting at center court. Everyone scheduled to speak at the memorial then enters one by one and takes their assigned seat on one of those chairs, just like they had practiced: Coach Simmons, Principal Comely, Mrs. Martha, some female grief counselor from Lansing, and Chet. *Fucking Chet.* And, of course, he's the first one to speak.

Chet walks up to a microphone stand and takes the mic so that he can pace back and forth with it. "Patrick Smith was more than just a linebacker for the Owls," he declares, his voice booming from the gymnasium speakers.

"Yeah, he was a dipshit too," Barry whispers.

"Not the time," Sammy scolds, elbowing him in the ribs.

Barry shrugs. She's right, and he knows it. Felt bad when he said it. But still, Patrick got what was coming, didn't he?

"He was also my friend." Chet continues.

"Oh, give me break," Barry mumbles, rolling his eyes. Sammy elbows him again. *Fine.* He won't say anything more, but he's not gonna play along, either. When the student body claps politely, Barry doesn't. It's only when he sees Lich clapping despite the pain on his best bud's face that Barry offers a few light claps of his own—you know, so Lich doesn't feel alone.

After Chet, the rest of the speakers take their place at the mic, where they dab away tears and speak about all the lost potential this past week. But mostly, the lost potential they're referring to is Patrick Smith's—how he was a model student, and how he would have grown up to become a model citizen. How he volunteered with the rest of the Owls varsity football team at town events. How he wanted to make a difference. Did things to make Grafting a better place. Perhaps he could have played for the Detroit Lions.

Barry folds his arms across his chest and shakes his head. A better place? For whom? Grafting is definitely not a better place now than it was in 1975, back when Senior was rollin' around town in the Wolfmobile. And Patrick Smith certainly didn't make Grafting better for Barry. Or for Lich. Would've been nice, though. Would be nice if someone really put themselves on the line and did something for this town, did something for kids like Barry and Lich. Patrick was just a bully.

Strikingly absent from the bloated speeches were all the times Patrick beat the shit out of Barry: the night of the bonfire; downtown next to Pistol River Pizza Pies; in the Ottawa Heights parking lot. No one talks about the time Patrick held Lich down on the shower floor in the boy's locker room while Chet and his friends hurled insults."

If Barry or Lich were to go missing or die, no one would give a shit. There'd be no memorial during first period, where Mr. Comely waxes poetic about the tragic loss of life. There'd be no cheerleading squad giving a pom-pom send-off. Local papers wouldn't care, wouldn't give them the front page of the *Ottawa Herald* like they did for Patrick. Barry and Lich would get nothing. Just look how little they've spoken about the kids who died at the MOW.

At first, Barry is angry about it, the injustice of it all, but then he starts to ponder. *How DOES he go about getting a memorial like this?* Sure, he likes laying low, prefers to be invisible, but he wouldn't mind some recognition for a change, at least in death. His memorial would be pretty cool, too, if the school allowed it. Lich would talk about

Barry's sick guitar skills and genius songwriting, and Sammy would speak lovingly about Bludzorg and all the battles Barry won. They could even park the Wolfmobile at center court, you know, to create more atmosphere during the presentations.

Patrick was a dick—to Barry, to Lich, to all the ones "asking for it"—but he also did a lot of stuff Barry didn't know about until hearing it now. Last season, he recorded the most tackles for a loss in the history of Michigan high school football. Barry doesn't know what that means, but he can tell it's impressive. Patrick also volunteered at the local homeless shelter on weekends and holidays, and coached a youth football team in his spare time. Even Lich had to nod along in respect to that little factoid.

So, what am I doing? Barry asks himself. He has his band and his buds, but no one cares about that. To everyone else, he's never been the center of anything but trouble. He gently touches the shiner beneath his eye and thinks.

After the memorial concludes, Sammy leans over and whispers, "Tonight, Lich's place. Time to conquer the next leg of the Underdark." And then she's gone, back in line with her class.

Lich looks to Barry, wide-eyed. "The Underdark? For real?"

Barry puts on a half-hearted grin. "Guess so. Hope you're hungry for Drow meat."

"Hungry?" Randall pipes in.

Barry shakes his head. He can probably show a little more mercy, too, he supposes. To Randall, at least. The kid did throw up a smoke signal, after all. "All right, buddy. I think it's time you bear witness to the best game ever invented."

"Oh." Randall blinks. "Yeah, for sure. What's it called?"

"My house," Lich says. "Six o'clock. You'll find out then."

Randall nods. "Okay, sure, I'll be there." Then after a short pause, he adds, "Will there be snacks?"

BARRY SLIDES THE miniature of his highland warrior forward three grid spaces to face one of the Drow guardians. "Eat shit," he declares at the plastic green army man representing the dark elf.

"The second Drow uses Attack of Opportunity on you!" shouts Sammy.

"Wait! I have second attack!" Barry pleads.

"Doesn't matter, dude," says Lich. "You moved across a threatened square."

"Fuck!" says Barry. "Can I use a Potion of Healing?"

Sammy gives a look like Barry knows better than to even ask. She rolls some dice behind her Dungeon Master's screen. "Seventeen damage," is her reply.

"Oh, what the fuck?" says Barry.

Sammy shrugs. "You gonna follow through with your first attack?" She leans back in her chair, bumping her knees against the foldout table in Lich's basement.

Hell yeah, Barry will. He raises his county-fair sword high. "Bludzorg gleams in the glow of the Underdark's quartz cavern," he monologues, "and I crash it down on the Drow scum!"

Sammy narrows her gaze. "What did you roll?"

"Eighteen," Barry says with a smile. He's been paying attention. He knows the Drow's armor class. Barry is good at math when he wants to be.

Sammy sighs. "It hits."

"And I cleave the foul being in twain!" Barry cuts through the air next to the table with Bludzorg.

"The dark elf cries out in pain, and her two halves fall to the wet cave floor," says Sammy.

"Yes!" shouts Lich.

Randall stands up. "Oh, damn! You killed it?"

"Bet your ass, I killed it."

"How?"

Sammy puts a hand on Randall's shoulder. "Don't worry. I'll break everything down for you tomorrow at lunch. Just keep in mind what you saw."

Across the room, Lich's siblings, twin brother and sister, work their way through world 3-3 of *Super Mario Brothers* on the NES. Their open-mouthed faces are bathed in the cool blue light of the television.

"Lich's turn," Sammy says.

"Okay," says Lich. "I cast Finger of Death on the remaining Drow."

Sammy purses her lips. "Okay. Fine. Good." She rolls a fortitude-saving throw behind her Dungeon Master screen. "That's... 3d6." Her shoulders slump.

"Plus one," Randall says, holding up a finger. The player's handbook is splayed out before him. "Oh, wait—"

"Plus one *per level*," Lich says with a grin.

Sammy bites her tongue. "Whatever. Describe the death."

Lich rubs his hands together. "The Drow freezes. A white foam bubbles from his mouth and...he starts hacking and coughing and stuff. And then he falls over."

"And then he blows up!" Randall shouts, standing from his chair.

The twins turn in unison to cast disapproving stares at Randall, then return their attention to *Super Mario Bros.*

Lich laughs. "And then the Drow explodes."

"Yeah," Sammy agrees, a mischievous grin forming on her lips. "It sure does." She's starting to look an awful lot like the Grinch who stole Christmas.

"Uh-oh," Barry says.

Lich also knows something is coming. He pulls out his stainless steel drumsticks and runs a paradiddle against his thigh in anticipation.

"What?" Randall asks.

"When Sammy gets that look..." Barry starts.

Sammy adopts an ominous tone. "The dark blood of the slain Drow seeps into the carving on the floor—"

"What carving?!" Barry demands, incredulous.

"I said there was a carving!"

"She did," says Randall. "I remember, because I was like, 'What's that carving?' But you guys didn't seem interested in it, so I thought it wasn't important."

Sammy regards the table again. "The dark blood of the slain Drow seeps into the carving on the floor. Their blood rises in a mist to form none other than…" Sammy hesitates.

"Than what?" Lich pleads.

"To be continued," Sammy replies.

"Oh my God!" Barry shouts.

Sammy giggles. "What? You in a hurry to get your butt kicked?"

"Yes, actually, I am."

Lich looks to the twins, who are still hypnotized by the TV. "Eh, I need to get the twins to bed, so we should probably call it."

"Where's your mom?" Randall asks.

Sammy and Barry exchange uneasy glances, and Barry smacks a hand down on Randall's shoulder. "Not here, Randall."

Randall takes another look at the others and gets it. He nods. He knows that families can be complicated.

DEATH OF A HIGH SCHOOL WRESTLING CHAMPION

"YES, I KNOW. I'm looking forward to it, too," Laura Reese says into the phone that's pinned between her shoulder and her chin. "Um, yeah, make that two Bloody Mary's." She laughs. "See you then." She dries her hands over the running sink, clacks the phone back into it's wall-mounted cradle, and nearly trips on the cord that has wrapped around her ankle during her kitchen-cleaning routine.

It's late, and the autumn precipitation is somewhere between snow and fat raindrops, and it sounds like their dream home is being pelted by a million tiny pebbles.

Laura washes the cookware from dinner. It's well-cleaned, but she doesn't notice. She's staring at the reflection of her own face in the window above the sink, framed in the creeping obscurity from the steam. All the light is behind Laura, only darkness exists beyond, which makes it easy to see in her reflection just how *over this shit* she is. She squeezes the plastic container of Dawn dish soap without looking, then uses an S.O.S. pad to scrub away at a dirty blender.

Upon finishing, she sets the last of the cleaned dishes on the drying rack beside the sink and looks across the kitchen to Theo, the man she married—the go-getter, the sweet talker— passed out on the family room couch like any other weeknight, arm hanging off one side, a glowing cigarette limp between two fingers. For a moment, Laura debates whether or not she should put the cigarette out.

Sure, Theo works hard—*thank you for all you do, sweetie*—but Laura's the one keeping the family together. The *only* one. Who's getting their kids ready for school while he's taking his first shit of the day? Who's driving Corbin to school at six fucking a.m. for wrestling? Who's dressing Kelly for kindergarten? Who makes Theo his favorite breakfast sandwich from scratch just so he can gobble it down without tasting it on his hurried way out the door? *Who keeps the house clean, Theo?!* You think it's magic that your first shit of the day leaves no trace on the porcelain? That your work clothes are always cleaned and pressed? That your life is just the absolute fucking best? How nice it must be to be so damn oblivious.

Dammit, Theo.

He had been in her ear every day for the past eighteen months, telling her how wise it would be to invest in this new housing development in the foothills of Pine Mountain, just outside Grafting, Michigan. "Grafting is America's best-kept secret, but it won't be for long," he had said. "It'll be a premium vacation destination in just a few years. But if we get in now while it's still early, we'll double our investment, easy." At least that's what Kale, their portfolio manager, had told him.

Kale was bullshitting, of course, but Theo still holds onto the dream. His ego depends on it. But Laura is a realist, and she can give two shits about Theo's pride and Kale's horseshit. She sees it this way: only three houses in the development have been completed so far, and of those three, only the Reese home is occupied. Construction has shut down for the winter, probably longer now because of the quake, and the other two completed homes have received zero offers since being finished nearly six months ago. *Double the investment?* They'll be lucky just to break even.

She looks to the window again, but that's when her reflection vanishes. The floodlights on their fancy new motion detector have triggered and now light up their backyard like a football field. Out across the rolled-turf lawn that has been standing in for real grass—much to Laura's dismay—the branches of a lone maple tree whip about in the wind. Theo had promised Kelly he'd hang a tire swing from those branches, but he never did and most likely never will. But wait, where the tire swing might otherwise be dangling, Laura sees something else. She cocks her head to the side. Is that…?

That's when Laura gasps.

Propped against the trunk of the maple tree is a chainsaw and what looks to be some kind of…sword? *That can't be right.* She leans in closer to the window to get a better look, but then it's too late. The floodlights shut off, and she's staring into her dark reflection once more.

She turns to call out to her sleeping husband, but before she can say a word, all her breath leaves her and she stumbles backward, her knees having gone to pudding. With unbridled force, her back slams into the drying rack that now overflows with dripping-wet dishes, and the collision sends pricey dinner plates and crystal glassware crashing to the spotless laminate floor. She tries to hold herself upright, unable to fully comprehend what she sees in the living room.

Standing above the still-sleeping Theo—who, even amid the noisy clatter, remains lost in his drunken slumber—is a tall, lanky figure, its back turned to Laura. A cluster of purple tumors pulse on the back of its neck. Purple sludge drips from its hands and feet.

All the lights in the house go off at once. Laura can't see a thing, so she drops immediately to her hands and knees and speed-crawls to the kitchen island, where she can hide. With her back against the island cabinetry, her hand brushes against something familiar. She gropes at it until she feels a handle, realizes that it's the blender that had fallen from the drying rack. Given the circumstances, Laura reasons that she may need this.

In the darkness, she can hear her husband wake from his stupor with a simple "huh" and then immediately start thrashing around. There's a muffled yelp, and then he's gagging. It's a wet, gurgling sound, as if he's drowning on something—like his own spit or blood. After a few terrible moments, the room falls silent.

Laura stifles a tearful gasp. She knows her husband is dead.

The kids!

In the quiet, she can now hear the muffled sound of Corbin's television upstairs, probably stuck on a late-night rerun of *M.A.S.H.* The TV has been like a lullaby to him ever since he was a child, mostly because his parents never did anything to discourage it. In fact, Laura's nightly "shutting down the house" routine has always included turning off Corbin's TV after she knows he's fallen asleep.

The kitchen lights suddenly go back on.

Laura freezes like a deer in headlights, her wide eyes fixed on where the demonic figure last stood. But there's no longer anyone there. Slowly, she climbs to her feet, blender still in hand, and creeps over to the couch to check on her husband.

"Theo?" she whispers.

What she sees on the couch should make her scream, but it doesn't. It doesn't make her leap back in fright like she did moments ago in the kitchen. It doesn't make her steel herself against the closest piece of sturdy furniture. It just…confuses her. She tilts her head sideways to study it at a different angle.

Who is that on the couch? That's not Theo. Not *her* Theo. That's a caricature of Theo. An obscene, yawning, ghoulish effigy of her husband, its wide, wet eyes staring up at nothing, its square jaw distended so violently that the lips have been split into a bleeding grin. That can't be Theo's mouth she can see all the way into. Those aren't Theo's cavities she can count. That's not her husband's fat, fleshy tongue, all bumpy and white, flopping flaccid out one side of the mouth. His neck doesn't bulge like that, sickening, barely supporting a head twisted so far that a single vertebrae of his spine breaks the skin from the inside.

Laura looks down to see the dim glow of purple shoe prints embedded in the carpet. They're steaming. *What the fuck?* She traces the path those shoe prints walk, her eyes like the spark trailing the wick on a stick of dynamite. They follow those prints, tracking not just goo but gore as well, stepping away from the couch and toward the stairs at the back of the house. When the spark of her gaze has consumed the wick of those shoe prints entirely, Laura panics. She associates those stairs with the most important two things in her entire existence. *Boom!* The dynamite explodes. Now she's running up those stairs two and three steps at a time.

When she gets to the top, the lanky figure steps out from the shadows of the nearest bathroom and stands menacingly between Laura and the bedrooms of her two sleeping children. Its shoulders rise and fall in controlled rhythm, and plumes of steaming breath rise hot from a disfigured face.

She wants to scream at the top of her lungs, but the words come out in a panicked whisper, "Who are you?"

The figure breathes slowly, almost sleepily, a high-pitched wheeze riding every exhale.

"What do you want with us?"

The figure ignores her questions and steps toward her.

"Stop!" Laura holds up a finger as she takes a step back. She tightens her hold on the handle of the blender. It trembles violently in her white-knuckled grip, the crossblade twisting almost imperceptibly at the base of the glass container.

Another step.

"If you leave now, I promise I won't call the police."

"*Corbiiiiin…*" the figure hisses.

Upon hearing the intruder speak her son's name, Laura turns to ice. "Get the fuck out of my house…" she growls.

The figure just tilts its disfigured head. "*Can Corbin…come out to play?*"

Laura grits her teeth and then shouts, "Play with this!" She slams the blender against the wall with enough force to shatter the thick glass, flips it in her hand, and raises it overhead so the teeth of the shattered edge are ready to bite. With one last primal scream, she slams the jagged glass and exposed blades directly into the intruder's chest, sinks it deep into the bony flesh with the nastiest and most satisfying *squelch!*

Laura is panting wildly, sweat drenches her shirt. But the figure remains unfazed. With a jerky, deformed movement, it looks down at the high-end appliance lodged into its chest in quiet observation. Laura thinks she hears it…*laugh?*

A voice comes from down the hall.

"Mom?"

"Corbin!" Laura shouts. "Get back in your room and lock the door! Do not open it, even—" Laura's vision erupts with winking stars and she falls hard to the floor. She brings trembling fingers to a stinging pain in her cheek and they come away with warm blood. With blinking motes still in her eyes, she gazes up at the lanky figure standing over her, the broken blender gripped tight in its hand. With a ragged breath, it lifts the appliance over its head, where it drips the intruder's blood in dark, viscous ropes. Laura closes her eyes and waits for the finishing blow, but it never comes. Before the intruder can bring the bludgeon down on her skull, it's shoved violently into the wall by Corbin, who tackles it down the stairs. The two bodies thunder down the steps behind her.

Laura stands and rushes down the staircase after her son. When she reenters the kitchen, she's relieved to see that Corbin has maneuvered his arms around the much taller figure and is now leveraging his small, stout stature to his advantage, like a boulder against a splitting tree. And just when the tree is about to crack in two, Corbin gets even lower, taking his opponent to the ground with a resounding thud. Upon striking the floor, the intruder loses its grip on the blender.

A new voice comes from the family room. It's not a hiss—not so ghost-like—but it's cold enough to freeze Laura. Deep and grainy, like amplified distortion, but somehow still human. "Oh, I've seen this one before," it speaks. "Corbin Reese, captain of the Ottawa Heights wrestling team, pinning my friend to the floor. Real original." This intruder is shorter and rounder than its lanky partner, face caught in the light enough for Laura to see something animal-like, a horrid amalgamation of wolf and swine.

A strange thought enters Laura's mind: *Corbin isn't captain of the wrestling team. He'd tried out for the spot, wanted it real bad, but he lost out to the Blakely boy.*

"Wait!" Laura shouts. "You have the wrong boy! Corbin isn't the wrestling team captain! The Blakely boy is! Do you hear me? He's not the captain!" In this moment, Laura feels a weird sense of hope, like this is all just a big misunderstanding that will soon be sorted out. The Blakely boy is the one who should be going through this nightmare right now, not her son. Maybe once the killers realize their mistake, they'll call the whole thing off. She looks to the telephone on the wall.

The wolf-pig approaches the wrestling match with a swagger straight out of *Monday Night Raw,* but instead of tagging his partner out, he stops, turns his head slowly, follows Laura's gaze to the wall-mounted telephone. The wolf-pig walks slowly to the phone, lifts it from the cradle, and presses the receiver against his snout.

"Hello, 9-1-1? I'd like to report a murder."

Corbin growls as he locks his foe's neck in the crook of his elbow. The lanky one's disfigured face warps.

The wolf-pig continues: "One stuck-up asshole so far. Uh-huh. No, he's definitely dead. Reese place. The new housing development up at Pine Mountain. Yes, I can hold." The wolf-pig looks up from the receiver to address Laura. "Are you just gonna stand there? Your boy needs help." It nods toward Corbin, who is now struggling to maintain his pin. "Yes, I'm still here," it says into the phone. "Okay, let me ask the victim's son." The wolf-pig kneels down next to Corbin and taps him on the shoulder. "It's for you." The monster then rapidly loops the phone chord several times around and around Corbin's neck and pulls tight.

Laura screams and rushes the wolf-pig, leaping with hands splayed wide. She claws at its face and chest, digging her nails behind one of the many patches sewn onto the wolf-pig's black denim vest. The animal kicks her hard in the gut, which sends her reeling back toward the staircase, injured and without breath, a torn patch clutched in her hand.

Corbin claws at his neck, drawing tracks of blood where he tries to wriggle his fingers inside the phone chord.

"Momma?! Are you okay?" a frightened voice asks from atop the stairs. It's Kelly. She's wearing one of her brother's old wrestling shirts, which hangs all the way to her ankles, and she's clutching her favorite stuffed animal, Honeybear, to her chest.

"Kelly, baby, run!" Laura shouts. "Run and hide and don't come out!" Laura then turns to the tall, lanky motherfucker, who's just now trying to regain its balance after suffering through one of her son's championship headlocks, and she leaps at it, knocks it back to the ground, claws viciously at its face until crimson strands of flesh are embedded deep beneath her fingernails. Only red fills her vision until from the corner of her eye she glimpses the wolf-pig release her son, and sees Corbin make no movement. She immediately stops clawing the lanky one and crawls desperately over to her eldest child. "Corbin? Corbin, answer me!"

The wolf-pig laughs as it drops the phone beside Corbin's neck and heads over to the kitchen counter to retrieve the sharpest knife from the knife block.

Corbin's lack of movement slows Laura's crawl, accelerates her wails, and she collapses in heaving sobs atop his mangled corpse. While clutching the cooling cadaver, she doesn't notice when the lanky one takes a fistful of her hair in its grip, doesn't notice how exposed the front of her neck now is.

The wolf-pig approaches Laura and presses the tip of the knife to her bloody, blubbering lips, then with a mocking sob, presses it against her throat. A spider climbs out of the creature's mocking mouth and skitters down into its black denim vest.

The last thing Laura hears is the lanky one snirking as the wolf-pig slowly drags the knife across her neck.

REESES IN PIECES

FROM A BIRD'S-EYE view, Sheriff Keller's patrol vehicle is just a small spec of flashing red and blue moving fast across an isolated stretch of densely forested road that has fully succumbed to autumn. The pines are forever green, but the deciduous trees—like the countless birch, maple, and oak—have adopted the bronze and gold colors of the season and will soon be bare.

Keller looks out the passenger-side window to where the trees part to reveal a wide-open vista. Beyond the beaten guardrail, Lake Ottawa is a sea of ichor, reflecting a warped imitation of the heavy gray clouds overhead. Frost glistens along the muddy shoreline. Keller has lived here his entire life, knows that an early frost is the sign of an early winter, which means it's going to be a harsh one—bitter cold, lots of snow.

The car radio is struggling out here, reception not so good this far from town, but Keller doesn't shut it off. Even after the hiss of distance creeps into Black Sabbath's "Planet Caravan" on Z93.3 FM, and the threat of white noise is all that remains, Keller stubbornly turns the volume up.

Up ahead is the new Pine Mountain residential development. Someday, the area will be a sought-after subdivision, filled with high-priced luxury homes, but for now, it's a landscape of rocks and dirt, crisscrossed by the tread marks of bobcats, backhoes, and bulldozers, all of which are parked, driver-less, along the unpaved road that Keller is turning down now. Three homes have been completed so far, but the remainder of the planned residences are empty plots and concrete foundations left to freeze over. Only the Reese place is occupied.

Keller sees a fire truck and an ambulance parked along the curb at the only house with a paved driveway, and he knows this must be it. The Grafting PD are missing in action—must still be on their way. He pulls to a stop behind another car marked with the gold and brown of the Ottawa County Sheriff's Department. Art is leaning against the rear fender of the cruiser, face caught in blue and red light, cigarette burning weakly between chapped lips.

Keller throws his cruiser in park and flings the door open.

"No smoking on the job," he says with a smirk.

Art plays along, shrugs. "You're gonna have to write me up then, because I'm not putting this one out."

Keller closes the car door behind him. "That bad, huh?"

Art takes a long and pensive drag, exhales. "Worse."

"You the first cop on scene?"

Art nods. "Scared the shit out of me, to be honest, being alone inside that house. Paramedics are in there now."

Keller pats Art on the shoulder. "Good man. Casualties?"

"Multiple."

"Forensics?"

"They don't have much, but yeah. State troopers are gonna set up a perimeter and help out with any possible manhunt. Hopefully Feds don't get involved."

Keller watches a firefighter emerge from the house and pause for a moment on the front porch. The fireman takes a deep breath of cold autumn air, then looks to the heavens— to God, maybe—and lets out that breath in a cloud of steam, regains his composure, buries his emotions before anyone can see. Keller gets it, knows the feeling. The firefighter is a changed man now. He will never unsee what he just saw inside that house. It will haunt him long into retirement, even after he's moved someplace far away and warm. Florida, probably.

The fireman continues across the front lawn to the fire truck, nods a silent but somber greeting to Art and Keller as he goes.

Keller exhales deeply, then nods up at the house. "Shall we?"

Art throws his cigarette to the ground and stamps it out. "After you."

When they reach the porch, Keller stops. He points at a trail of glowing purple shoe prints heading up the steps and into the house. They're…steaming. *Maybe they do that when they're fresh*, Keller thinks. "Bingo."

"Yep. I already told the medics to be mindful of the evidence. Do not disturb. You know how they are. Tend to wreak havoc on active crime scenes."

It's the smell inside the house that hits Keller first, tightens his stomach and makes him nauseous. This is not the smell of decomposition. Far too soon for that. It's the metallic smell of freshly spilled blood—*lots* of it.

Inside the kitchen, two more firefighters and two paramedics mingle. They look to Art and Keller with darkness in their eyes, nod their acknowledgment and carry on. The victims have already been pronounced dead, but the bodies can't be moved until forensics and the medical examiner shows up, so three mangled corpses are splayed out on gruesome display— two in the kitchen and one on the couch in the adjoining living room. Adult male on the couch, adult female on the kitchen floor, and one male adolescent on the floor beside her. Laura is the female on the kitchen floor. Her neck has been sliced open, a stream of hardened blood now scabbing on the defaced tile. Seventeen-year-old Corbin is the adolescent beside her, facedown in a pool of congealed blood, a phone cord wrapped around his neck. Keller assumes it's Theo on the couch, but he can't be sure from here, so he heads to the living room to inspect.

The corpse on the couch is horrific. It's certainly Theo Reese, but it doesn't look like him anymore. The jaw is distended and the arms are dislocated. *What kind of person could have done something like this? Someone huge. Really, really strong. Maybe on something, like meth.* Keller kneels down to gently touch a set of glowing purple footprints left in the carpeting next to the deceased. A rope of dark slime pulls away with his fingers. He wipes the gunk off on his pleated pants and stands back up. He'll let the boys in Ann Arbor deal with whatever the hell that is. "What's upstairs?" he asks.

"Nothing," Art says. "All the victims are down here."

Keller shakes his head. "Reeses have a little girl. She's around six years old, I think. I can't imagine she wouldn't be here."

"Well, fuck. I haven't see any sign of her."

Keller turns toward the other first responders. "Anyone find a little girl in the home, approximately five or six years old?"

Every first responder shakes their head no, but one of them speaks up, "There's a room upstairs that looks like it belongs to a little girl, but I haven't seen her. Bed looks recently slept in, so I checked the closets, but nothing."

Art turns to Keller. "Possible kidnapping?"

Without responding, Keller heads up the stairs and down the second-floor hall until he finds a bedroom that looks like it belongs to a little girl. He stoically checks the closet and beneath the bed, but there is no one there and no other spots to hide. A TV still plays in the other room. *Think, Keller. Where else would a little kid hide?*

Back out in the hallway, Art appears atop the stairs, but Keller angrily waves him away until the deputy heads back down to the kitchen. The sheriff enters the master bedroom, and once inside, he hears a soft bump and the sound of rustling clothes coming from inside the master closet. Keller quietly unclips the holster on his magnum and carefully draws his weapon, aims it at the closet's accordion doors.

"This is the Ottawa County Sheriff's Department!" he shouts. "Come out with your hands up!"

From inside the closet comes the sound of a little girl crying.

Keller's shoulders drop, but his training makes sure the magnum is kept raised. He slowly closes in on the closet doors, weapon trained, and carefully pushes one side of the accordion open.

A little girl screams. "No! Please!"

Kelly Reese sits on the floor of the closet, knees to her chest, head and torso hid behind her parents' hanging clothes. Keller re-holsters his weapon before sliding the clothes away.

"Please don't hurt me," Kelly says. She's hiding behind outstretched hands and sobbing, her face wet with tears.

Keller kneels down in front of her and speaks as gently as he knows how. "I'm not gonna hurt you. I'm one of the good guys. See?" He points to the sheriff's badge fastened to his coat.

At the sight of the badge, Kelly seems to calm down a bit. "I think my family is dead," she says.

Keller doesn't know how to respond to this, so he just holds his hand out to her and forces a small smile. "Can I help you up?" The girl is shivering.

"Is it safe?" she asks.

From outside in the distance comes the sound of police sirens. It sounds like a half-dozen patrol cars, if not more.

Took 'em long enough.

"Do you hear that?" Keller asks. "The police sirens? That means it's safe. I promise."

Kelly breaks down into sobs again. "But I'm scared."

"I know, sweetie. I know."

Kelly takes a deep breath to help quiet her sobbing, remains rigid until she can ask, "Is it gone?"

"Is what gone?" Keller asks.

"The monster," Kelly says. "The wolf-pig."

INCIDENT REPORT

Apex Door Field Assessment Unit 3

Incident/Assessment Report

Today's Date: Friday, October 31, 1995

Time: 11:58 PM

Assessor Number: 7

Assessor's Handler: Orson Caster

Location of incident: Grafting, Michigan

Person(s) affected: Brock Corning

Reason(s) for field assessment dispatch:

The local field labs identified this location and another location outside of Grafting as having been subject to potential Bleed events. The director was dispatched to one of the locations, a Maintenance-of-Way structure outside the city limits. Myself and 7 investigated the secondary location, which was a private residence on Pine Mountain belonging to a Mr. Brock Corning.

Key Indicators mentioned (please refer to the latest edition of the APEX DOOR FIELD ASSESSMENT MANUAL for updated glossary of Key Indicators to choose from):

- Seismic activity

- Leyline crux

- Vanishing of buildings

- Unexplained death

Please describe the incident(s), including any anomalous phenomena:

We arrived on the scene to find clear signs of extreme seismic activity. We had to navigate around a distressed patrol vehicle belonging to the local sheriff's station. The residence itself was nowhere to be seen. Though we had been expecting a log cabin, instead we found a crater which matches the description of Bleed residue. A crater instead of a domicile.

We found a beheaded corpse lying at the lip of the crater. Blood was still pumping from the opened arteries when we found it. The corpse was wearing an Ottawa County Sheriff's Department uniform.

The crater was hot, with a dimming glow at the center, and vapor rising from its epicenter.

Both 7 and myself heard the audible laughter of two individuals, which seemed to be coming from the nearest tree line. We can also confirm having heard what sounded to be the revving a chainsaw.

Upon further investigation, we were unable to identify the source of these sounds.

Assessor response:

7 recognized immediately that a Bleed event
had taken place. It was my observation
that 7 appeared to be highly agitated. He
indicated that the Bleed originated from
one of the worst possible origin points,
an origin point that Apex Door research-
ers have insisted is only hypothetical.

Conclusion & Recommended Next Steps:

The director must utilize every available
resource for containment. This Bleed has
the potential to become extremely pub-
licized. The director must be given full
discretion.

GRAFTING, MICHIGAN

Sunday, November 5, 1995

HURTS, DON'T IT?

DEBS HAS BEEN to Keller's office once already this morning, so when she returns for a second time, the imitation sugar in her voice loses some of its sweetness. She reminds the sheriff again that they will be leaving for Pipes's funeral soon and that Keller still doesn't have his uniform shirt on.

Keller tells her through a mouthful of pepperoni stick to "Please shut the door, Debs."

Splayed out on his desk are a number of forensic photographs from the Reese family crime scene, many of which are extreme close-ups of the wounds sustained by the victims. No sword or chainsaw were used this time, but the purple footprints were enough to tie these murders to the previous ones.

Atop the photos is a clear plastic evidence bag that contains hair samples that don't belong to the victims—wiry, black fibers that don't curl or wave, but bend and fold under stress. In a second clear plastic evidence bag is a novelty fabric patch still sewn to the black denim from whatever clothing it'd been torn from. It had been recovered near the body of Laura Reese. Forensics had been all over the house, glassed its entirety, but found no black denim that matched. The patch is of a cartoon frosted doughnut, with the shape of a punching fist at its center. Two words are stitched in a comic font around the outside of the aggressive confection: *Hurtz Donut?!*

Debs checks in again, but this time she retrieves Keller's uniform shirt from the floor for him. "It's time to go, sheriff." She shakes the shirt loose, wincing at the smell.

Keller looks up. "Yeah, it is, isn't it?"

"Mm-hm." She holds the shirt open for him.

Keller stands, turns, and runs his arms through the sleeves. Debs smooths out the wrinkles on his shoulders. As Keller works to button up the shirt, Debs says, "Art and Tam already left, so you're my ride." She pats Keller on the back as he buttons the last button. "I'll be in the cruiser. Don't make me wait forever, okay?"

Keller says, "Wouldn't dare."

Once Debs is gone, Keller angrily shoves the tails of his shirt into his trousers and buckles his belt too tight around the mess. He's about to grab his jacket and exit when he stops and turns to look at the *Hurtz Donut?!* patch once more. Something about it won't allow him to let go. Gravity. "Ah, fuck it." He grabs the evidence bag and stuffs it into his pants pocket.

No one is in the lobby awaiting booking, so Keller locks the station door on his way out. Even the petty criminals of Grafting, it seems, have gone into hiding recently. Makes sense, though. Coyotes tuck tail and run whenever a wolf shows up.

Keller heads to the parking lot. When he plops into his cruiser, he finds Debs leaning over from the passenger seat so that she can apply her makeup in the rearview mirror. "Hell of a thing we're going to," she says.

Keller isn't exactly sure what Debs means by that, but at the same time, her words make total sense. "Uh-huh." It's the best he can do right now.

A COLD DRIZZLE weighs heavy on the crowd of mourners, all huddled beneath raised umbrellas, some choosing to stand while others sit in cheap plastic folding chairs that have been arranged to face the closed casket of Deputy Pipes suspended on straps above a waiting grave. Behind the casket is a lectern, and standing behind the lectern is the sheriff. Keller looks out at the sea of sullen faces—family, friends, the entire Ottawa County Sheriff's Department, a ladder team from the county fire station, a few old hats from the local VFW, Grafting's geriatric mayor, a Michigan state congressman unpopular in these parts, and a smattering of news reporters and television cameramen, representing both local and national media outlets. But the most important person in attendance is the young woman sobbing in the front row, held on both sides by Mikey's despondent mother and father. She is Mikey's grieving widow, Marie, and she's cradling her pregnant belly like its all she has left in this world.

Keller has spent the previous week agonizing over the eulogy he's now about to give. What he's written isn't poetry, but it's honest, and he hopes it will memorialize the deputy fondly, maybe even provide some closure. He pulls the scribbled speech from his breast pocket and mentally runs through it once more. He's almost to the midpoint when a gentle hand on his shoulder pulls him from his thoughts.

"Sheriff." It's the voice of Father Muller. "Debs asked that I give you this for the ceremony." The priest hands Keller a small wooden mallet.

Keller grips the mallet's handle, feels the literal weight of the moment ahead. "Thank you, Father," he says.

Before heading back to his seat, the priest gestures to the speech in Keller's other hand. "Don't fret over being perfect, John-David. No one ever is."

Keller clears his throat into the mic, and a shriek of feedback prickles the hairs on his neck. Suddenly more anxious than before, he shoves his free hand into his trousers pocket—a nervous habit he just can't break—where sweaty fingers touch the evidence bag still stashed inside.

Hurtz Donut?!

"Pipes was…" he starts. "I mean, *Deputy* Pipes." He swallows hard. "Deputy *Michael* Pipes was…"

What the fuck did he even write last night? It was just a bunch of cop stories you tell over a laugh at the bar, during a time when everyone is alive and celebrating. Stories of Mikey one-punching the abusive husband who attacked him with a broken beer bottle during a domestic violence call. Or of Mikey arresting the naked junkie who had wandered downtown one Sunday morning and was scaring all the old ladies leaving church. Or how Mikey would show up to local Little League games on Wednesdays with sheriff-badge stickers for all the kids. Or that one time during a game when he'd forgotten his keys in the cruiser and had to call for backup so that someone would come pick the lock. The little leaguers thought it was hilarious.

The stories aren't bad, but they suddenly feel trite. Keller looks down at Marie, can only see her pregnant belly and fatherless child inside. Mikey would've been a great father. The kind of father Keller had wanted to be for his child. But unfortunately for both men, the opportunity was brutally taken from them. Keller sighs, decides to scrap the speech. He improvises two short lines instead, "I'm sorry, Marie. I wish it had been me." Before anyone can awkwardly clap, he raises the wooden mallet in his hand and initiates the 21-bell ceremony with a solid first strike. *Ding!*

Memories echo in Keller's mind with each strike. First, he sees Mikey Pipes holding the ring box.

Ding!

Sees his dad on the ground behind the neighbor's hedges.

Ding!

Sees the dead Ottawa Heights linebacker and the purplish steps fleeing from the crime scene.

Ding!

Sees the Reese home and the three dead bodies inside.

Ding!

Sees the little girl, Kelly, looking up at him from her hiding place inside the closet.

Ding!

The mess of evidence on his desk.

Ding!

The crime-scene photographs.

Ding.
The crumpled wires of hair.
Ding.
The patch.
Ding.
Hurtz Donut?!
Father Muller's hand is on Keller's shoulder again, and it's enough for Keller to realize he doesn't know how many times he's struck the bell. It must have been *at least* twenty-one times, because the priest uses his other hand to lower the mallet in Keller's grip. Then with both hands, he gently ushers Keller away from the lectern and back to his seat.

After the closing prayer, Keller watches Marie stand, approach the casket, lay a hand on it, then crumple. He has to look away before he does the same.

Art pats Keller's back. "How you feeling, sheriff?"

Keller wipes his eye. "Peachy." The memory of what he'd said at the lectern hits him. He shakes his head. "Fuck."

"What?"

"I had a big speech prepared, but…I just couldn't do it."

"Don't sweat it, sheriff. No one was listening anyway." He smiles.

"This thing threw me off." Keller pulls the evidence bag from his pocket and hands it over to Art. "I was going through the evidence from the Reese case this morning and spotted this. That thing's driving me nuts. It's not familiar to me in the slightest, but for the life of me, I can't get it out of my head. Know anyone that wears black denim and likes to sew?"

Art takes the evidence bag from Keller and inspects it. "Don't know if he likes to sew, sheriff," says Art, "But I know the kid this belongs to. He's the one that fought Patrick Smith and Chet Springs on Halloween."

"How certain are you?"

"Ninety-nine percent."

"Not one hundred?"

"No such thing."

"Okay, then what makes you so sure?"

"He was wearing a black denim vest with a bunch of patches sewn onto it, and one of those patches was this one. I remember because he had the start of a decent shiner below one eye, and in my mind, I was like, 'Hurts, don't it?' You know, because it's a play on—"

"Did you get the kid's name?"

"Yeah. Smith's buddies gave us the names of every kid there. This one's name is Bernie or Barry or something. Started with a 'B.' It's in the case file."

"Has this Bernie or Barry been questioned yet?"

"Don't think so. Wasn't much else pointing to him. Kinda became low priority."

"Well, he's high priority now. Is he a student at Ottawa Heights?"

Art nods. "Who isn't?"

Keller takes the evidence back from Art and returns it to his pocket. "Listen, I want you to get on the phone with Ottawa Heights and tell them we need to set up a meeting with one of their students. No need to go into too many details. Just have them call me about the specifics, and I'll handle the rest."

"Got it. What day for the meeting?"

"Tomorrow. First period."

"On it, sheriff."

Keller looks to the coffin as the audience disperses. "Let's nail this fucker," he says.

GRAFTING, MICHIGAN

Monday, November 6, 1995

EASY MONDAY

BARRY PULLS HIS van into the Ottawa Heights parking lot and grabs a spot. He looks back at his guitar laying in the back of the van and sighs. Slinging his backpack over his shoulder as he steps out of the vehicle, he takes one last look at the Gibson Explorer. "I'll be back," he assures. Lying next to the guitar is his black denim vest, but for some reason, he decides not to wear it. First time in forever he's gone without it.

Barry can't help but notice how easily he's able to walk up the concrete steps and into Ottawa Heights High. Usually, this is a gauntlet for him. The kind that requires Barry to pretend like he doesn't hear what his bullies are shouting at him, or that he doesn't care. They say things about his weight, about his clothes, about his mom, about his dad. They say that Senior is dead because he was a no-good crook with a slutty wife and a shithead for a son.

But today? This Monday morning? Someone didn't get the memo, because Barry is walking up those steps unscathed. In fact, it's only Randall up top in his leather jacket, offering him a high five as they walk through the double doors together. "Hey, Barry, when Sammy said you couldn't take a Potion of Healing after the Attack of Opportunity, why couldn't you?"

Barry shrugs as they stop at his locker. "Eh, Sammy explains it better. You should ask her." Barry's locker is plastered with band stickers and dick drawings and filled with morsels of rotting lunches. He hangs his backpack among the chaos and pulls his textbook for first period.

Randall continues, "But see, I was looking at the players handbook, and it says you *can* take an extra action for a Potion of Healing."

"Attack of Opportunity is, like, more important or something," says Barry.

"More important?"

"Yeah. Because it's an opportunity, and when opportunity knocks, you have to answer the door, or whatever."

"That makes literally no sense, dude."

Barry shuts the locker. "Just ask Sammy, man." He looks over his shoulder for an overdue razzing, but Chet, Corbin, and George are nowhere to be seen. Barry shrugs because, sure, he'll take an easy Monday if it's being offered. Why not? Might be the last easy Monday of his life.

"By the way," Randall says as they make their way through the loud throng and chatter of adolescence, "you ever hear Nirvana *Unplugged*? Might change your mind about them."

"No thanks."

"Oh. *Nevermind* then." The pun makes sense in Randall's head, but Barry doesn't react. Instead, they walk silently into first period and find a pair of desks next to Lich. And boy, does Lich look exhausted. With his triple-XL Misfits T-shirt and the way he folds his arms under his head on the desk, he looks like a pile of laundry.

Barry drops into his desk. "You okay, man?"

"No," says Lich from somewhere inside his folded arms. "Twins just wouldn't sleep. Wouldn't listen to me, either. Said I'm not Mom." Lich shows his face only to yawn, then digs his head back into the crook of his arm.

Barry notices something else odd. The class is still just chatting and hanging out as if the period hasn't started yet, and Mrs. Bellamy is absent. But that doesn't make sense, because that would mean Barry is early, and Barry is never early. He glances up at the analog clock over the chalkboard to confirm the miracle, but comes away more confused. He's late, like always. "Hey, where's Mrs. Bellamy?" he asks.

"Out sick?" Randall suggests.

A realization hits Lich, and he looks up from his arms. "If we have a substitute teacher, we'll probably just watch a VHS today."

Barry's eye go wide. He socks Lich in the shoulder with a smile. "Lights off. Rent-a-teacher that doesn't care. You'll be able to sleep all period, dude!"

Randall smiles and slugs Lich on the other shoulder. "Sweet dreams, man!"

But the good vibes end when Mrs. Bellamy enters the classroom, accompanied by Principal Comely. Neither of them look happy.

"Barry," Principal Comely says. His arms are folded across his chest, and he's sweating through his button-up more than usual. "I need you to come with me to my office." He points at Lich and Randall. "You two, as well."

The rest of the class exchanges amused looks—wide eyes, open mouths, big smiles. A few whisper and giggle. "Busted," Jeremy Potts jokes, and Kelly laughs, but Mrs. Bellamy silences them both with a sharp snap of the fingers and an ice-cold stare.

Barry and Lich know the long walk to Comely's office well. They refer to it as the Green Mile, partly because of the mint-green tile floors, but mostly because they feel falsely imprisoned here at Ottawa Heights High. As they approach the office, they see Sammy already sitting on the bench inside the waiting room. When they enter, she looks up at them with a mix of relief and concern—relief that she's no longer alone, but concerned about the trouble they must be in. She knows—they all know—that a meeting with Principal Comely is a harbinger of bad things to come.

Principal Comely instructs the boys to wait with Sammy on the bench until he's ready for them, then disappears into his office. The receptionist pauses her typing to look up at the three new detainees. Her eyes narrow.

"This is bad," Sammy whispers to the other three. "There's police here. I saw them talking to Mr. Comely."

"Shit," whispers Barry. "Is this about the bonfire? The fight?"

Randall points to the glass partition that allows Comely to look out of his office into the reception area. The blinds are almost always closed, but not this morning. "Look," Randall says.

Inside the office with Principal Comely is Sheriff Keller and a thin deputy who looks vaguely familiar. The deputy had opened the blinds to get a preliminary look at the kids waiting outside, and when he sees them point and look back at him, he pushes his horn-rimmed glasses up his nose and turns away.

"Isn't that the cop from the bonfire who let us go?" says Barry.

"It is," says Lich.

"It gets worse," says Sammy. "I heard him and the sheriff talking while Comely was out. There's been another murder. Corbin Reese is dead."

"Goon-squad Corbin?" Barry blurts.

"This is *so* not good," Lich laments.

The door to Mr. Comely's office opens and Sheriff Keller steps out. Principal Comely and the deputy stand behind him in the office doorway. Keller introduces himself and his deputy to the four students and then explains the situation. "So, here's what's gonna happen. We're gonna ask each of you some questions, one at a time. If you cooperate, this shouldn't take long at all."

"Are we in trouble?" Sammy asks.

Keller looks back at Principal Comely with a cocked brow.

"The sheriff just wants to ask you a few questions," Comely says.

This response does not make Sammy feel better.

Keller points to Barry. "Let's start with you."

THIS IS NOT A DRILL

BARRY IS SITTING in the chair opposite Mr. Comely's desk, his arms crossed in defiance, but the way his knee bounces at a million beats per minute suggests more than a bit of anxiety—so does the trickle of sweat running down the side of his face. Unfortunately for Keller, he's not wearing a black denim vest. No black denim anywhere. No missing patches either, as far as the sheriff can see. He really hopes Art didn't fuck this up. Keller watches Barry for a moment, allows the stress to build in the silence between them.

Principal Comely silently observes from the corner of the room while Art stands behind Barry. The deputy's arms are crossed at his chest, but his posture is relaxed. Keller catches Art's eye and nods a silent command. In response, the deputy fetches a notepad and pen from his breast pocket. He flips the notepad to a blank page and clicks the pen open, ready to write.

"You comfortable, Barry?" Keller asks. "Need anything? Drink of water, soda, snack?"

Barry's mind darts to the thought of those little chocolate milk cartons from the lunchroom, but he fights back the urge to ask and just shakes his head no.

"You sure?"

"I'm fine."

Keller smiles. "Probably not how you expected to start off your Monday, huh?"

"Not really."

"Yeah, me neither. What's your first period?"

Barry shrugs. "I don't know. American History."

Keller looks to the principal, who nods in silent confirmation.

Keller smiles. "I remember those days. American History was always my least favorite subject. I preferred World History. American History was just always kind of boring to me. What about you?"

"I don't really care," says Barry. Keller is about to move on, but to his surprise, Barry adds, "But I probably like World History more, too."

"Great minds…" Keller says, leaving the aphorism unfinished. There's something going on behind Barry's eyes that he can't quite pinpoint. A hint of familiar resentment, maybe? As if Barry knows who Keller is, like *personally* knows him and doesn't like him one bit. But Keller doesn't know this kid from Adam. *Does he?* He decides it's time for the abrupt shift. See how Barry reacts to his first curve ball. "You look uncomfortable, Barry." Keller unclips the radio from his chest, sets it on Comely's desk. Then he reaches for his gun, unsnaps the holster, and lays the firearm alongside the radio. "There. Now it's just two men talking—you and me. Forget the rest."

"Okay…"

"Want to tell me about Halloween night?"

Barry's jaw tightens. "What about it?"

"The Sandpit, Barry. There was a party that night. I'm told you were there."

Barry thinks about the deputy behind him, wonders if the man remembers him. It would be risky for Barry to lie. "Yeah, I was there."

Art scribbles a few notes in his notepad.

"With your friends?"

Barry thinks about Lich and Sammy and Randall waiting on the other side of the office window, probably scared out of their minds all thanks to him. What would they think of him if they saw him now, refusing to fight for them? Refusing to roll for initiative? What would Bludzorg think? A newfound courage darkens Barry's face to a scowl. "I don't really remember. I just remember the bonfire was crazy and there was a lot of shitty music playing. Then you guys showed up and shut it down. Everyone knows how much you pigs love busting teens."

Keller is taken aback by this reply. *Didn't expect that one.* He looks to Art for answers, but the wide-eyed deputy just shrugs, equally blind-sided and confused.

"Do you know who Patrick Smith is?" Keller continues.

The scowl on Barry's face softens. "I know who Patrick Smith is. Everyone in school knows who he is. And yeah, I ran into him that night, so you can spare me the question."

Art scribbles more notes.

"I heard you guys exchanged some strong words that night. Even scrapped a bit. Is that how you got the black eye?" This question appears to irritate Barry. *Good.*

"I got the black eye while defending my friends. Patrick and Chet and George and Corbin—they attacked us first, for no good reason. But that's what they always do to people like me."

"What do you mean, 'people like you?'"

Barry snorts. "C'mon, Sheriff *Killer*. You know. Nerds, weirdos, outcasts. Kids that listen to heavy metal and play Dungeons & Dragons. Kids who like math. Kids who watch *Star Trek* instead of football."

It takes a moment for Keller to respond. Did Barry intentionally say his name wrong? Is he trying to get under Keller's skin? Distract him? "Okay. I gotcha," says Keller. He then raises a finger as if to press pause on the investigation. "But before we continue, I should clarify that my last name is Keller, with an 'E.'" He taps the name tag fastened to his chest above his badge. "Rhymes with 'cellar.' I think you might have heard wrong when I first introduced myself."

Barry feigns bewilderment. "Okay…"

"Well," Keller continues, "it sounded like you had said 'killer' just now. I get it was probably a mistake, but it's important to address for the record." He looks Barry dead in the eye and forces a smile onto his lips. He uses the moment to search the boy's face for clues.

"I think you need to get your hearing checked," Barry says.

Principal Comely jumps out from his spot in the corner. "Mr. Aguilar!" he scolds.

"Its okay," Keller tells Comely. He turns his attention back to Barry. "Maybe you're right. Maybe I do need to get my ears checked. Not getting any younger, after all. You mentioned Corbin Reese. What was he doing during all this?"

"Laughing. Chet and his goons were trying to burn Sammy's journal in the bonfire, and they all thought it was fucking hilarious. Sammy, of all people! She's like the nicest person in school."

"Who is Sammy?" Keller asks. "Your friend?"

"Hell yeah, she's my friend," Barry says.

Art jumps in. "Samantha Walters. The young woman waiting outside with the other two boys."

Keller makes the *ah-ha* expression. "So, those boys—Chet, Patrick, Corbin, George—they all pick on you and your friends. That must make you angry sometimes."

Barry crosses his arms over his chest again. "Hell yeah, it does. One time after gym class, we were all in the showers, and Lich *accidentally* got hard. But instead of just ignoring it, Chet and his friends kept calling him gay, over and over again, like for a really long time. Lich couldn't sleep for a week after that. I don't remember hearing that little precious moment at his memorial." He side-eyes Principal Comely.

"Enough, young man." Comely is looking pale as he turns to the sheriff. "I assure you, this is not the kind of thing that happens in my school. A lie, to be sure."

Keller's stony expression almost turns sympathetic."

Keller's stony expression almost turns sympathetic. "I'm sorry to hear that, Barry."

Art flips to a clean page in his notepad and scribbles a single word in big, bold letters. He turns the notepad to show the word to Keller:

MOTIVE!!!

Keller looks past Barry to Art and nods his agreement. Keller's questions to Barry continue: "You ever think about fighting back? Ever think about getting revenge?"

Later, after Barry has put some distance between himself and this moment—when it's cold and snowing around a campfire, and his friends are all fast asleep in the van behind him—he'll think hard about his answer to this question, about what he says next, about the ensuing consequences, about everything. But even then, even when reflecting on this moment with more wisdom and clarity than Barry thought possible, he still won't regret a single word. "Want me to be brutally honest with you, Sheriff Keller with an 'E'?"

"Of course."

"I'm glad Patrick and Corbin are dead, and I hope Chet and George are next."

A dreadful sense of unease descends upon the room. Art stops writing, and Principal Comely shifts nervously from one foot to the other. Even Barry falls strangely silent.

"Barry," Keller says softly, "who said Corbin Reese is dead?"

That's when the fire alarm goes off.

"What the fuck is that?" Keller says, startled out of his shock and shouting over the obnoxious noise.

"Fire alarm, sheriff," Art says.

"I know it's a goddamn fire alarm, Art! But why is it going off?" Keller looks to Principal Comely for answers, but Comely offers only more confusion.

Thats when a frantic knock comes at the door. But before anyone can answer, the door swings wildly open to reveal Principal Comely's exasperated secretary holding on to the door frame and handle for dear life. "They're gone!" she shouts.

The three men and Barry exchange bewildered looks.

"Who's gone?" Keller asks.

"Th-the students," the woman stammers. "The suspects!" She points to the empty bench in the waiting room, where Lich, Sammy, and Randall had been sitting while Barry was being questioned. Barry resents the woman's use of the word 'suspects' in reference to his friends.

"Ah, shit," Keller groans. He points at his deputy. "Art, you stay with Barry. I'll see if I can't track down our wannabe fugitives before they get too far. Don't want them causing more trouble for themselves than it's worth." He then points to Barry, who is still seated in his chair. "Do you hear me? It's not worth it to run. So stay put." He stares down the barrel of his index finger for another beat, making sure those words hit their target.

With an impatient grumble, Principal Comely pushes past the two officers and heads out into the hallway to assess the commotion. The hallway is already overrun with swarms of giddy high schoolers all making their way to the designated exits without urgency—laughing, joking, socking each other in the arms, flirting with the nearest girls. Either they know there's no fire or they don't care if there is one. They're just happy to get out of class.

Keller joins Comely in the hallway and surveys the throng of teenagers parading by. No sign of the fugitives. He makes for the radio that's usually clipped to his chest, ready to put out an APB, but when he reaches for it, he comes up empty. He pats the empty spot where it should be until he remembers that he left the radio in Comely's office. *Dammit,* he curses to himself. Keller heads back to Comely's office while Comely pushes past him in the other direction and gets taken away by the constant stream of students.

On his way back to the office, Keller sees Art consoling Principal Comely's sobbing secretary out in the waiting room. She's seated in her chair, and Art is standing beside her, gently rubbing her back. "This is Grafting!" she's sputtering. "Things like this don't happen here. I mean, what is the world coming to?"

"Art!" Sheriff Keller blurts. "What the fuck? Where's Barry?"

"Don't worry, sheriff." Art explains. "He's still in the office. I've been watching the door." He points with his eyes to the office and the door that is still closed.

"He better fucking be," Keller warns. He marches to the office and opens the door, hoping to see Barry still seated inside, a scared baby deer without his mama. But no. The room is empty. He flings the empty chair Barry was sitting in across the room, searches frantically around the desk, topples over a coat rack dressed with jackets for every season. No sign of him. "Shit!" he shouts.

Just then, a cold gust of air brushes past his neck and that's when he notices the window. It's open. *Wide* open. Wide enough for a slightly overweight teenager to fit through. Keller rushes to the window and leans out over the dirty sill. Comely's office is on the second floor, but it's a pretty easy drop to a dense overgrowth of bushes some fifteen feet below, especially if the jumper has the right dose of adrenaline coursing through their veins. Barry is nowhere to be seen. All that remains of him are some damaged boxwood bushes below the window and a dwindling trail of broken foliage leading away from the bushes and toward the student parking lot.

Art enters the office with Comely's assistant under his arm. "Where'd he go?" he asks.

Keller slaps a cup of ballpoint pens off the desk. "Good fucking question, Art. I was about to ask you the same damn thing."

Comely returns to see the mess that Keller has made, spies the ballpoints scattered across the floor. "My pens," he whimpers.

Keller grabs his radio from Comely's desk, blurts out a county-wide APB. Four suspects: three male, one female. Approach with caution.

THE WOLFMOBILE PEELS out of the Ottawa Heights student parking lot and careens into oncoming traffic before swerving into the proper lane. Honks and angry shouts greet the new commuters.

Inside the van, Lich is slumped in the passenger seat, hyperventilating. His right hand covers his eyes. "Shit, shit, shit, shit, shit, SHIT!" Randall, meanwhile, is bouncing around the back like a rag doll, but he's not scared. He's just laughing hysterically at the chaos while leafing through one of Barry's CD binders. "Dude, that was insane!" Laying on its side next to him is his silver Magna mountain bike, which he loves too much to leave behind since it was a birthday present from his dad, his real dad that he doesn't see anymore, will never see again. His little detour to retrieve the bike from the school's bike rack almost cost Barry and crew their one chance to escape. This pissed Barry off to no end—he almost bailed without him—but when he saw Randall hustling up to the Wolfmobile, face red and cheeks puffing, pushing that stupid silver contraption by the handlebars, Barry fell victim to what a sappier person might call "a sudden change of heart."

Sammy is seated across from Randall, her back against the wall of the van, knees held close to her chest. She does not look amused. "Yeah, Randall. *Totally* insane. That's the problem." She looks to Barry in the driver's seat. He's amped up and flying high. "So, what's the plan now, oh mighty highland warrior?" She doesn't expect a reasonable answer, but he's the one behind the wheel.

Barry slaps the ceiling of the van and howls to the moon like wrestling superstar Ric Flair. "So, who was it? Which one of you badasses pulled the fire alarm? Huh?" He takes his eyes off the road to beam at Lich like a proud dad. "Was it you, buddy? Tell me it was you."

Lich is still slumped in the seat and hiding his face from pedestrian onlookers. "Not me," he says.

"Here we go!" Randall blurts from the back. He retrieves a Judas Priest CD from the binder and feeds the album into Barry's Discman.

"Sammy, was it you?" Barry asks, still searching for the hero of the day.

"Like I would be so stupid," she replies. "It was Randall. The whole plan was his idea, actually. That's why it was so stupid."

Barry almost can't believe it. "Randall? Really? No way." He takes his eyes off the road again to look back at Randall. "Good job, buddy," he says, and gives the boy a thumbs up. "You just passed the second interview."

"Breaking the Law" by Judas Priest blares to life in the van's speakers, which causes Sammy to jump. She holds her face in her hands and sighs. "We're gonna be on *America's Most Wanted*, but for idiots."

Randall closes his eyes, leans against the van's wall, and smiles. Headbangs to the beat of the song.

"We need a plan," Sammy says.

"Sammy's right," Lich agrees. "We can't just drive forever."

"And we can't go home, either," Sammy adds. "That's the first place the cops will check."

"So," Barry says, failing to see the point. "Let 'em come. I got nothing to hide."

"Hey, genius," Sammy says flatly, "I know it must be hard to think about things when ninety percent of your brain is drowning in Donner Cherry Pie filling, but in case you don't realize, I'll fill you in: as of right now, we are fugitives from the law. Any clue what that means? It means that in the eyes of law enforcement, you have a LOT to hide, and then some."

"First of all, I *do* know what a fugitive is. I've seen the movie, the one with the guy who plays Han Solo. And second, it still doesn't matter, because none of us did anything wrong. Remember?"

"Well, that's not *totally* true," Lich interjects. "Technically speaking, Randall did commit a federal offense by pulling the fire alarm."

"Well, *technically speaking*, that sucks for Randall," Barry replies.

Sammy sounds more enraged now then frustrated. "I bet it's also illegal to flee police questioning, which we all just did, but yeah, let's just act like we did nothing wrong. I bet it's a rock-solid defense."

Barry hears what Sammy's saying, remembers the incriminating shit he said during questioning. Remembers the word "suspects." He reaches for the volume knob on the van's stereo and turns the music down to a whisper. "Okay," he says, suddenly sounding serious. "So, where do we go then?"

"The Sandpit," says Randall.

"Isn't that an active crime scene?" Sammy asks.

"Yeah," says Randall. "It's the last place the cops will look."

Sammy holds up a finger in rebuttal, then lowers it. "That… actually makes some sense."

Barry looks at the van's gas gauge and the needle that is already on "E." He makes the call. "The Sandpit it is," he says.

"God, I hope you're right," Sammy says to Randall.

WOLVES

THE SANDPIT IS empty save for Barry, Lich, Sammy, and Randall. No kids partying. No cops searching the place with flashlights. No cars blasting music. Tonight it's just gonna be four friends sitting around a small fire, watching the flames dance, wondering how long they have until they're tracked down by the police and arrested on suspicion of first-degree murder.

Randall is in the back of the Wolfmobile, rear doors open, wiping down his silver Magna mountain bike with a rag he found beneath the van's passenger seat, while Barry, Lich, and Sammy gather detritus to use as makeshift seats. Barry stacks a mess of cinder blocks, Lich drags a pair of rubber truck tires, and Sammy hauls the remains of an uprooted tree stump. They gather their seats around a small campfire that snaps in a haphazard pile of kindling, and they take a load off.

Satisfied with the bike's polish, Randall rolls the silver Magna out the back of the van and shuts the rear doors behind him. He rolls the bike alongside where Lich is perched on his stack of tires, playfully kicking his heels against the rubber. Randall slings a leg over the bike's frame, and sits his butt down on the saddle. Folding his arms across the handlebars, he stares into the licking flames. "My dad is probably flipping out right now," he says.

Sammy throws a small twig into the fire. "Not mine," she says. "Doubt he knows I'm gone."

Silence.

"Anyone else's dad gonna be pissed?" Randall asks.

Lich stops kicking his heels against the tires. "I never knew my dad," he says.

"You know," says Barry, "sometimes a dad not sticking around is a good thing." He looks to the van parked close behind, its broadside being used to block the wind. He studies the three wolves howling at the bubble-window moon and frowns.

"Did your dad ditch out, too?" Randall asks.

Sammy and Lich stiffen, but Barry just turns back toward the fire, calm and collected, and states plainly, "Nah. My dad's dead."

"Oh…" says Randall. "Sorry."

Barry sighs. "My dad was a legend in these parts. He used to tell me all about his 'howling days'—that's what he called his better times—back when he was robbing Rotten Roscoe's for smokes and gambling money, and playing lead guitar for a couple different metal bands. One of his bands even opened for Motörhead."

Randall's mouth drops open. "No way."

"Yes way," Barry replies. "At a little dive bar down in Ohio, back in like '78 or something. Before *Ace of Spades*." He's almost smiling now. It's been awhile since he's been able to tell this story to someone who hasn't heard it a dozen times or more.

Next to Barry, Sammy looks Randall in the eyes and, with great sadness, mouths the words, *not true*. Randall looks to Lich in hopes he will dispute Sammy's blasphemous claim, but Lich just closes his eyes, pained, and shakes his head in agreement—*Sammy's right*.

Oblivious to this silent exchange, Barry continues: "Senior kicked so much ass that night that Lemmy Kilmister asked him to come on tour with him, but after the gig, my dad embarrassed Lemmy by drinking him under the table, so the next day, the offer was revoked."

With their eyes, Sammy and Lich urge Randall to respond. *Say something!*

"Oh!" Randall says, after catching his friends' drift. "Um… That sucks."

"Indeed," says Barry, the grief of what *could have been* written all over his face. "What about your pops, Randall? What's his story?"

"Nothing cool. He can't even play guitar."

"Spill it," says Sammy.

Randall shifts uneasily in his seat. He wants to make his dad sound badass like Senior, but he's no good at embellishing, so he gives up. "He works for Walmart, scouts locations for new stores. That's why we move all the time. Once the location has been scouted, it's on to the next. See, I told you: not cool."

Barry looks up from the fire. "A Walmart is coming to Grafting?"

"Don't know for sure, but I think so."

"You hear that Lich" Barry says. "A Walmart here in Grafting. I heard they sell CDs for cheap."

Lich raises an intrigued eyebrow. "The new Tool album comes out next year," he says.

"Rock-fucking-on," says Barry, almost sounding awestruck.

A smile creeps onto Randall's face. He can't believe his ears. "Wait, so my dad *is* cool?"

Sammy and Lich clam up, but Barry has no problem just telling it like it is. "Nah, dude," he says. "No offense."

Silence.

Randall plucks a blade of grass thawed from the fire and tosses it to the wind. "Hey, Barry?"

"Yeah, dude?"

"How'd your dad die?"

Lich and Sammy freeze. Barry has never told anyone the full story of how his dad died, not even them, but they've seen how he reacts to people who ask about it, and it's not pretty. Sammy jumps in to defuse the situation: "Barry, he doesn't know any better—" But before she can finish, Barry raises a hand to silence her. He continues to stare at Randall with quiet intensity.

Randall shivers beneath the stare, tries his best to apologize: "I—I didn't mean—"

But Barry surprises them all with what he says next. "He was murdered," he says flatly. "By Sheriff Killer's dad."

"Keller's *dad*?" Randall blurts. "Holy shit."

Lich and Sammy are equally stunned. Everyone in Grafting knows that Senior was killed in a botched robbery, but they never knew this part of the story. Lich had always assumed that Barry hated Keller for constantly closing down the MOW and for busting kids with weed. And Sammy figured that Barry just hated authority, didn't matter who. They never would have guessed...

"Shot him in the back while he was fleeing a robbery. The shittiest thing, though: Senior only had twenty-six dollars in his pocket when he died. That's all he scored from the stick-up. Barely enough scratch for a bottle of cheap bourbon. And that bastard killed him for it." He takes a moment to wipe some "dust" from his eye. "But it's okay. Senior is watching over all of us now." He turns around and points to the biggest of the three wolves painted on the side of his van. "That's him, right there in the middle. Still howlin'."

Sammy's eyes are watering. "Barry..." But that's all she manages to say.

It's quiet for a bit, but then for the second time this night, something happens that no one sees coming, not even Randall, when he thinks back on it. Randall stands, points to the moon painted on the van, and howls. Howls at the top of his fucking lungs.

Sammy looks startled. She watches with dinner-plate eyes, glances at Barry to make sure he's okay, but he's stone-faced, impossible to read. *Eh...fuck it.* Sammy stands, points to the painted moon, and howls.

Lich stands atop the pile of tires and aims his drumsticks at the painted moon, adds his voice to the chorus.

Barry's reaction starts with a twitch at the corner of his mouth, turns slowly into a grin, then a genuine smile. By the time he feels a hot tear rolling down his cheek, he jumps to his feet and howls. Howls with all his might. Howls like the universe depends on it. Like his friends depend on it. Like he depends on it.

And it feels awesome.

Awoo!

Awoo!

Awoo!

Awoo!

DEATH OF GRAFTING'S SAVIOR

ON THE NIGHT of the Grafting quake, a gnarly knocking on Chet's bedroom window had woken him from his sleep at precisely 3:00 a.m. The noise was a bit unsettling, but benign enough to ignore. *Maybe it was a small aftershock rattling things about.* But when the same exact knock occurred the following night, again at precisely 3:00 a.m., Chet couldn't ignore it anymore. He rolled over and stared at the drawn blinds from beneath the safety of his covers for what felt like an eternity, but after fifteen minutes without another sound, he closed his eyes and fell back asleep. *Maybe it was just a dream.* But then that same knocking came on nights three and four, also at 3:00 a.m., and Chet decided that enough was enough. He would catch the culprit on night five.

Chet isn't sure what he expects to see tonight on night five, sitting on the edge of his bed, window-blind pullcord in his hand, nor does he know what he'll do after the knocking comes, after he rips the blinds open to confront whatever waits on the other side, but he's ready…he thinks. He isn't used to handling a challenge alone. Usually, he has Patrick or Corbin or George around, guys who will do Chet's dirty work for him, but not now. Not ever again in Patrick's case. With the digital alarm clock on Chet's bedside table glowing 2:59 a.m., he wonders if he has what it takes to confront this thing without them.

Chet's thoughts are broken when the clock spits a fresh triplet of angry red digits onto its face—3:00 a.m.—and the horrible sound comes again, right on cue.

Knock. Knock. Knock.

But Chet never moves, just sits stone-still upon his bed, pull-cord in hand, bloodshot eyes watching the drawn blinds until morning. It's not until 7:00 a.m., when his alarm clock screeches its wakeup call, that he jumps and gets ready for school.

CHET IS USED to being revered when walking the halls of Ottawa Heights, used to being called the "The Savior of Grafting" after he became the only quarterback in Owls history to take the team all the way to the state champion-ship and win—and he did it as a Junior. But all that feels so far away now, from some other lifetime before the Grafting quake, back when all of Chet's friends were still alive, and there was no one knocking on his window at 3:00 a.m., and he could get a decent night's sleep, and the entire town wasn't in mourning and depressed.

Foot traffic in the school hallways is a blur, the students and teachers barely discernible from one another as they bob and swerve around Chet like detritus in a rushing stream. He's used to feeling like the only person that matters, but today, he feels like the only person that doesn't.

He's seated in first period, mindlessly staring ahead at the chalkboard and pondering the frailty of life, when the sound of his bedroom alarm clock screeches in his ears once more, causing him to startle in a way he didn't think possible—in the way one does when hearing a ghost. *How?!*

"You all right, man?" asks a distant voice, but Chet ignores it. Probably some nerd he doesn't like, anyway.

After coming to his senses, Chet realizes the sound isn't his alarm clock, but rather the school's fire alarm, and he sees that his classmates have already stood from their seats and started to file out the room's only door.

In the hallway now, sees Principal Comely struggling to wade through a torrent of students. Up ahead, the town's sheriff is surveying the crowd. It's like he's looking for somebody, but he gives up and darts back into Comely's office after it appears he's lost something.

Once outside, Chet's first-period teacher herds the class out onto the campus lawn, where they are to wait until given the "all clear," and it's here that the sound of tires peeling out of the school's parking lot attracts the attention of Chet. He knows Barry's van well. And he watches it hook a left out of the parking lot, listens to the engine throttle as the van disappears behind the copse of manicured Douglas firs pruned to frame the Ottawa Heights marquee.

It's not too long after that when the rumors reach Chet's ears. *"Did you hear? Corbin's dead."*

"Cops were here for Barry and Lich."

Fire engines arrive, the school is declared safe, and the students make their way back inside, but Chet heads the other direction. He crosses the yard, ignoring the halfhearted calls of a fellow student, and then makes his way across the parking lot. He never planned to disappear beyond the Douglas firs and walk down Higgins Avenue in the same direction as Barry's van, he just does. And it isn't until a quarter mile down the road that he realizes what he has done and that the school is now far behind him. But he doesn't go back.

A sickening thought enters his mind. *What if it's Barry and Lich who are responsible for the night knocks on his window?* Maybe they're also the ones responsible for the death of Patrick, and now, if the rumors are true, the death of Corbin as well.

Chet thinks back to all his interactions with Barry and Lich, none of them pleasant. He recalls all the times he picked on and ridiculed the pair, all the times he made their lives a living hell. He thinks back to the classrooms, the cafeteria, the showers. *The showers.* That prank was particularly harsh.

Then *boom!* A world-upending realization hits him. What if he, too, has played a role in Patrick and Corbin's deaths? What if he helped create the monsters that killed them?

Chet stops alongside the shoulder of the road to consider this more deeply. He processes the idea with the same focus he uses to study the Owls' offensive playbook the night before a game. Forever wanting to be the hero, he imagines one of the plays breaking down in real time, and he improvises. In his imagination, he is scrambling, but he also knows that the opponent's inside linebacker is terrible in coverage and the Owls' running back is about to break free for a wide-open reception because of it. The inside linebacker is the opponent's weakness, and Chet is trained to ruthlessly exploit weakness. With a cocky smirk, Chet hits the running back on a slant route for a big first down. The crowd goes wild.

No, Chet decides, *I'm innocent.* Barry and Lich are weak, and it's his job to exploit them. That's just the way things work. It's not his fault if they snap and start killing people. Just like it's not his fault if the inside linebacker who sucks in coverage gets demoted to second string following Chet's masterful dismantling of that team's secondary. It's survival of the fittest.

With that settled, he continues his trek into town.

As he walks past Pistol River Pizza, he glances at the front window to see a missing-persons poster with Patrick's face on it. Must've forgotten to take it down after they discovered his body in the woods. Another poster in the window is a photo collage of the many lives lost during the Grafting quake. A duplicate of the poster hangs in the windows of Movie Knight and Buck's Five & Dime and a whole bunch of other places around town. Streetlamps are stapled with pleas for donations and information about upcoming fundraisers for the victims' families. The fundraisers are to be held at the Methodist church on Surline Road and at Saint Joseph's Cathedral on Higgins. All are urged to attend.

Chet's jaw clenches as he concludes in this moment that he *must* be the one to save Grafting, just like he does every autumn Friday night. He's the only one that can do it. But for this play to work, he'll need someone to catch his pass, so he takes a right on Creek Road and heads in the direction of George's house. He soon finds himself waiting on the front porch until he sees his star tight end approaching from the closest bus stop.

AT SOME POINT in the conversation, George has to lie down on his couch so that he can better listen to Chet's semi-coherent ramblings about the Grafting quake, the murders, the knocking on his window, and everything the quarterback intends to do about it. The sky outside has started to darken, and George is beginning to feel the pressure of five o'clock chiming from the grandfather clock alongside the stairs behind the couch. His dad will be clocking out from the mill soon, and if he comes home to see George and Chet loitering around the living room where the television is, he's gonna be pissed. The man likes his solitude.

"Well?" Chet asks.

George scratches his nose. "You honestly think those two nerds killed Patrick and Corbin? Is that even possible? I mean, Lich weighs like ninety pounds soaking wet."

Chet doesn't hesitate. "I know it's true. And I know I'm next. Why else would they be knocking on my window every night? It's a fucking omen, man."

George sits up. "I hate to say it, dude, but I think you're overreacting. I mean, I get that things around town have been weird lately, but—"

"Then why were the cops trying to arrest them, huh? Don't you think they know something?"

"Maybe. Or maybe they're still trying to figure stuff out. I mean, they could have been questioning Barry and Lich about the fight at the Sandpit. Would make sense, ya know. Patrick did give Barry a wicked black eye."

Chet nods condescendingly. He was expecting George to say this, and he's already prepared his reply. "Innocent people don't run from the cops," he says coldly. *Try and make sense of that one, George!*

George tries but can't. He looks weary, like all he wants to do is fall asleep.

"I know it sounds crazy. *Trust me,* I do. But the facts are the facts, George. Patrick is dead, Corbin is dead, Corbin's *parents* are dead, and we're probably gonna be dead next if we don't do something about it first."

George looks up. "Okay. How?"

"Remember that game against Sterling?"

A reluctant half-smile creeps at George's mouth. "They thought they had us dead to rights."

"And what happened?"

"You put that ball right in my chest."

"And then what? Three broken tackles?"

"Four."

"And nothing but green grass for forty yards."

George nods. His face is devoid of expression, but his eyes smile at the memory.

"Remember what I told you in the huddle?"

"Fuck Coach. George, get open. It's coming to you."

"Damn right. And that's what I'm telling you now. Fuck Coach. Fuck Comely. Fuck the sheriff's department. And especially fuck Barry and Lich. You and I got the ball, and it's time for a game-winning drive."

THE TWO HIGH school football stars slip out the back of George's house right as George's dad gets home, and they head over to Chet's.

It's barely six o'clock in the evening when they arrive, which means they still have another nine hours until the 3:00 a.m. knocking, so they microwave some pizza rolls and marathon *Madden '94* on the Super Nintendo in Chet's bedroom while formulating some semblance of a plan.

What they come up with is not complicated.

See that baseball bat leaning against the wall beside the TV? When 2:59 a.m. hits, George will ready it over his shoulder and wait for Chet to rip on the window-blinds pullcord precisely at 3:00 a.m. When he does, George is gonna swing that sweet, machined aluminum as hard as he can into the window's double-paned glass and, with any luck, send some really nasty shards straight into Barry's fat fucking face. Then, Chet will grab his State Championship MVP trophy, a heavy chunk of painted stone shaped like a football, and chuck that thing right into

Lich's long ugly nose. Blood will go everywhere. From then on, it will be a scramble drill.

Five minutes before 3:00 a.m., Chet shuts off the video game and turns out all the lights. He places the MVP trophy next to him on the bed and wraps the window-blinds pullcord around his non-throwing hand twice. George, meanwhile, paces the room and twists the bat's worn grip in his hands. It's a long five minutes. An eternity to stoke the fires burning inside them both. Thoughts of Patrick and Corbin flash through Chet's mind.

The clock changes to 2:59 a.m.

"Ready?" Chet whispers.

"Ready," George grunts.

Knock. Knock. Knock.

And there's the snap.

Chet rips that window-blinds pullcord with all the force bottled up in his non-throwing arm, and before those blinds have accordioned their way out of sight, George is swinging. The window shatters into a million pieces, and a wet thud fills Chet's ears as George's bat connects with something fleshy on the other side. Chet grabs the MVP trophy, wraps his fingers around its golden laces, and quickly assesses the remaining defense.

Even in the moonlight, he knows their silhouettes. Knows that the short, fat little dork writhing on the ground from George's blow is Barry. Knows that the tall, skinny freak with the long hair is Lich, and he's about twenty yards deep and running a fly route to get away. But he won't make it far. This is Chet we're talking about, the star quarterback of the Ottawa Heights Owls. They call him Grafting's Savior. Of course he nails his target with the painted stone football, hits him right where the pads would be. And that skinny geek goes sprawling to the ground.

But the play isn't over.

"Man coverage, George!"

Chet shoves the shattered window open and vaults through it with abandon, lands on the broken grass twenty feet below. George immediately lands beside him, baseball bat still firmly in his grip.

And that's when Chet realizes: he's just the quarterback. He distributes the ball to his receivers, then watches from behind the line of scrimmage while *they* fight through the defenders, break the tackles, gain the tough yards after the catch. Chet doesn't make plays down field. He stays in the damn pocket.

He freezes, watches George charge into the fray and take that baseball bat to Barry, swinging it hard against the pudgy dork's ribs. But the tall one, Lich, is already recovering from the MVP trophy's collision with the C7 vertebrae in his spine. He's also carrying something. Something heavy. But it's hard to see in the dark. Chet doesn't know what it is until Lich stumbles another ten yards ahead and inadvertently triggers the motion-sensing floodlights atop the roof of the backyard shed. Now able to see things clearly, Chet understands immediately that he has misread his opponent. Misread him terribly.

Lich doesn't look like Lich anymore, not when you look at his face. He has one glowing yellow eye and a serpentine tongue that flits back and forth atop a row of serrated teeth. His spindly fingers drag a gas-powered chainsaw along the ground.

The monster locks its one eye onto Chet.

"W-what the fuck?" is all that Chet can manage to say.

In response, the chainsaw roars to life, and with a blood-soaked smile, the lanky aberration hoists the hungry machine high above its head and just lets the monster rip. A plume of black exhaust consumes the nightmare face as it laughs. Without waiting for the smoke to dissipate, the skinny demon charges.

If this was a game under the Friday night lights, and the pass rusher was baring down on him like this monster was now, Chet would just take a knee. It wasn't his job to get pummeled. He had a Division-III scholarship to protect. The refs would blow their whistles and wave the play dead. Better luck next down.

So, that's what Chet does now. He takes a stupid fucking knee. And to the shock of no one, except for maybe Chet, not a single whistle blows, and the chainsaw-wielding maniac doesn't stop. But lucky for the star QB, George is fired up and still making highlight-reel plays. The tight end comes out of nowhere and swings his baseball bat right into the churning blade of the chainsaw. Sparks fly as both weapons reject one another and pinwheel off into the night.

Chet watches the battle. It's just like that game against Sterling. His tight end is breaking tackles beneath the brightest lights in Grafting. There's still hope. They can still win this game. Chet stands tall. He's the savior of Grafting, isn't he? He'll fight alongside George until the game clock hits triple zeros.

But that's when the blow comes from behind.

As Chet lays on the grass outside his bedroom window, he can't help but shake his head at the irony. He was too focused on the play down field, he forgot to watch his blindside. He always forgets to watch his blindside. He looks up to see that George is running away. His number one offensive weapon is abandoning the play. And worse, that chainsaw motherfucker is heading back for Chet.

Chet closes his eyes and stifles a pathetic whimper. He can feel it now, the toothy, lanky fuck standing over him. Demon-Barry stands beside Demon-Lich now, a toxic vapor emanating from his eyes. His smushed warthog snout leaks slimy purple snot over a grin that glows like hot ember, two large tusks protruding from the mouth's corners. Fur-tufted ears twitch atop a mop of curly hair. When Demon-Lich huddles with Barry to hear the play, Chet can see the C7 vertebrae protruding from the skin in a bloody, purple mess. Dead spider legs hang limp from the open wound.

The demons break their huddle and turn their attention back to Chet. Wasting no time, Demon-Barry raises a bludgeon above its head and strikes.

Chet knows the weapon well. Even as it splatters his memories across the lawn, he can still vividly recall standing tall atop that stage after the State Championship game and holding that MVP trophy high in the air, triumphant. It was the best night of his life.

INCIDENT
REPORT

Apex Door Field Assessment Unit 3
Incident/Assessment Report

Today's Date: Tuesday, November 7, 1995

Time: 4:38 AM

Assessor Number: 7

Assessor's Handler: Orson Caster

Location of incident: Grafting, Michigan

Person(s) affected: Chet Springs

Reason(s) for field assessment dispatch:

7 and I were in the vicinity, at a local 24-hour diner, eating pie. We sat at a bar against the front-facing window so that we our view of downtown Grafting was directly ahead of us. As we were eating, a young male adolescent sprinted by. Given the time we've spent in Grafting, we've been able to assess the typical cadence of the town. What we witnessed fell outside of that cadence. 7 merely stood without alert, exited the building, and swiftly chased down the boy. In a frantic state, he claimed two individuals had just murdered his friend. The description recounted matched roughly the profile of

the anomalies currently targeted by the
local Apex Door Field Lab.

**Key Indicators mentioned (please refer to
the latest edition of the APEX DOOR FIELD
ASSESSMENT MANUAL for updated glossary
of Key Indicators to choose from):**

* NA

**Please describe the incident(s), including
any anomalous phenomena:**

7 was able to guide me on foot to the
scene. He described a sort of aroma
that trailed from a fresh Bleed. I could
smell sulfur, but only as we were within
close proximity. The murder was quite
fresh, just outside a two-story residential home. The body of a young man
lay in the back lawn. The victim appeared bludgeoned by an object, his face
unrecognizable as a face. The apparent weapon, a football trophy, had been
discarded close by. Footprints had been
tramped into the grass, many of them
emitting a violet glow. Seven observed
these tracks closely, appearing grim as
he did so.

Our joint investigation was disrupted
when 7 raised his head suddenly, audi-
bly sniffing at the air. At that time,
I could hear an odd sound coming from
around the corner of the house. The

sound would best be described as a combination of two things: a chewing sort of slurp, and a skittering. As I headed toward the sound, 7 stopped me. He communicated fear to me. That was the word he used: fear.

Upon appeal, 7 allowed me to investigate the sound alone. I was too late to witness the cause of the sound, but I did discover two puddles of a viscous material, thick like molasses and glowing with the same hue as the footprints seen in the yard, but with a more intense luminosity

Assessor Response:

7 offered no more than a glance at the scene I described, then walked back toward the diner without reply. His behavior was unlike anything I've witnessed from him before. Our pies were still where we left them, and 7 sat down to eat. After finishing his slice of pie, he informed me that a coming Bleed event would be from an origin unlike most Bleeds. That this would be an incident comparable to One Horse, if not worse. Without any clear evidence, he indicated to me that the fleeing boy who'd prompted this investigation should be surveilled. 7's overall demeanor made it difficult for me to enjoy the remainder of my own slice of pie, which I felt was unfair given that he'd finished his.

Conclusion & Recommended Next Steps:

As I type this, 7 remains close to the police scanner in our hotel room. He's instructed that I prepare to leave at a moment's notice. It's my recommendation that the local field lab identify the boy we witnessed sprinting from the scene. I will fax 7's sketch along with this report. If the local field lab is able to spare personnel from the extraction team, they should keep this individual's residence under close surveillance. 7 has informed me that this fax is unlikely to be processed and delivered to the field lab in time, but in time for what, he did not say. I'm tired and will attempt sleep now.

GRAFTING, MICHIGAN

Tuesday, November 7, 1995

COURAGE UNDER FIRE

SHERIFF KELLER'S FATHER wakes up multiple times throughout the night, ready to fight the Imperial Japanese Army each and every time. The first time, Keller is startled awake when his father starts barking orders to an imaginary platoon under heavy fire on the beaches of Okinawa. Luckily, Keller is able to calmly talk his father down and put him back to bed without incident. But before Keller can get back to sleep himself, it happens again…and again…and again.

In the morning, Keller drinks black coffee from a mug shaped like the head of Yoda. "Tired, I fucking am," he mumbles to the face on the cup.

The phone rings, and he rips it from the cradle. "Fuck off," he says into the receiver.

"…Sheriff?"

It's Art.

Keller pinches the bridge of his nose to help alleviate the pounding headache behind his eyes. "Oh. Hey, Art."

A pause. "Everything okay?"

"Yeah. Just had a long night. What's up?"

"There's been another one, sheriff."

"Another what?"

"Murder. Last night. Victim is Chet Springs."

A long pause.

"Sheriff? You there?"

Keller hangs up the phone without responding. He thinks for a moment, then grabs his Yoda mug, clenches his teeth, and hurls the ceramic novelty across the kitchen. It crashes into the toaster on the countertop and splatters hot coffee all over the counters and appliances. Keller watches the contents drip around the jagged remains of the mug, over the edges of the countertop. It's a mess he doubts he could clean up even if he tried. A lot of those kinds of messes lately.

SIX-LETTER WORDS

WHEN DAWN'S EARLY light peeks through the trees and strikes the Wolfmobile's bubble-window, it refracts just enough to smack a slumbering Randall directly in the eyes, which causes the boy to wake. Blinking away the sleep, he props himself up on one elbow and looks to his friends for any signs of life.

Lich is curled into a lanky version of the fetal position, shivering, his arms wrapped tightly around his legs for warmth. Sammy lays on her side in the reclined passenger seat and whimpers in her sleep. And Barry is splayed out on his back, arms and legs akimbo, looking like he just fell from a tree and stayed there, snoring away, unconscious. A river of drool flows from the corner of his mouth to the dirty shag carpeting beneath him.

Randall is deciding whether or not to wake his friends when his stomach grumbles, which reminds him that he hasn't eaten since yesterday morning—none of them have—and he soon gets an idea.

Quiet as he can, he exits the van through the back and carefully shuts the rear doors behind him. A light snowfall now dusts the ground, but not so much that it stops him from grabbing his silver Magna mountain bike from its resting spot beside the van, taking a firm seat on the saddle, and pedaling like the wind. The Magna is made for this. Two wheels, all-terrain. Mother Nature is gonna have to do better than a little frost if she wants to stop him from riding roughshod across her face.

He takes the two-track that connects the Sandpit to Grey Road, and from there, heads south back into town. Lucky for him, the Sandpit is at the top of the highest hill to Grafting's north, so it's mostly just coasting for the remainder of the way. The ride back to the Sandpit is gonna be hell, but Randall tells himself it'll be worth it when he finally gets to see the looks on his friends' faces after he returns to the van with four Donner Cherry Pies and a sweaty jug of Sunny D.

After soaring down Grey Road, Randall hooks a left along a side road that will lead him north to Fairview, and from Fairview to Rotten Roscoe's little gas station at the corner of Fairview and Higgins. The forest gives way to stretches of farmland, and Randall moos to the cows as he pedals by.

Rotten Roscoe's pumps are empty when Randall rides his bike up to the building and props it against the white-painted brick. He thinks about chaining the Magna to the payphone out front, but decides not to bother since he'll only be gone a minute. He heads inside and makes his way to the refrigerated drinks in back.

He's crouched down next to the glass-door refrigerators, still searching for that elusive Sunny D when he hears a woman's voice address him from behind.

"Getting some refreshments before school?"

Randall turns slightly on his heels and looks up to see a stern-looking sheriff's deputy perusing the refrigerated inventory from a stance most closely resembling parade rest. Randall immediately snaps his attention back to the glass-door refrigerators so as to hide his shocked expression from the officer's gaze. "Uh, yeah," is all he manages to say.

"What are you looking for?" the deputy asks.

The way she's acting... It freaks Randall out. She's obviously trying to make polite conversation, but she's doing so in the most off-putting way possible. There's almost no intonation in her voice. No inflection. Just words.

"Sunny D."

"Come again?"

"Sunny Delight."

The deputy steps to the refrigerator on Randall's right and opens the glass door. She retrieves a ten-ounce bottle of Sunny D and offers it to him. "You know this isn't real juice, right?"

"I, uh, need the big one," he says, pointing to the jug of Sunny D on the shelf below the individual serving sizes… Please." His knees start to tremble.

The deputy exchanges the ten-ounce bottle for the sixty-four-ounce jug and hands it to Randall. "You havin' a class party or something?"

"Um, no. Just thirsty, I guess." His knees are quaking now.

The deputy cocks a suspicious eyebrow, then points to the fridge in front of Randall. "You mind?"

"Oh, sorry." Randall mumbles. He stands on wobbly legs, hugging the jug of Sunny D to his chest and backs away from the fridge door to allow the deputy access. The deputy opens the vacated door and grabs a twelve-ounce bottle of Pepsi for herself. She turns and nods at the giant orange jug in Randall's arms. "I hope you're allowed lots of bathroom breaks."

Randall forces a polite chuckle, but it comes out sounding more like a nervous squeak.

The deputy ignores the awkwardness and takes her drink to the register up front, where Roscoe works on one of his crossword books while he waits.

Randall cautiously follows.

As he approaches the register, he hears Roscoe say, "Pie? For breakfast?" He can tell by the man's smirk that the question is meant to be in jest, but something about the way he says it feels sad, like he's just going through the motions. There's a lot of that in Grafting these days.

The deputy sets her bottle of Pepsi down upon the checkout counter beside a delicious Donner Cherry Pie snatched from the carousel next to the register. "I need all the sugar I can get this morning," she says.

At the sound of the deputy's voice, Suzanna steps out from her office and waves to the officer. "Good morning, Tam," she says flatly.

"Morning," Tam says back.

Suzanna frowns. "I heard about the Springs boy on the radio just now."

Springs boy? Randall thinks. *Chet Springs?*

Tam's back stiffens. She peers slowly back at Randall. Her gaze falls heavy.

Randall is certain she sees panic in his eyes.

Tam returns her attention to Suzanna. "I'm not really at liberty to talk about that right now," she states. "But I should warn you that the victim's name has not yet been made public. It would be wise to keep quiet about whatever you've heard."

Victim?

"Oh, come on, Tam," Roscoe interjects. "This is Grafting. Everyone who's up and moving has already heard the news. Hell, I heard it twice before sun-up and you're my third customer."

"The devil is in Grafting, Tam," Suzanna says. "This ain't no time to be politically correct."

Roscoe rings up the two items on the register and accepts a five-dollar bill from Tam as payment. He returns the proper change to her hand. Tam takes the Pepsi and cherry pie. "I'm not at liberty to talk about an ongoing investigation," she says again. She nods a silent thank-you to Roscoe and exits the store. Suzanna retreats back into her office.

"Can I help you," Roscoe says to Randall.

Randall places the jug of Sunny D on the counter. "This and four Donner Cherry Pies, please," he says.

Roscoe points to the carousel of Donner Cherry Pies beside the register. "Help yourself," he says, already ringing up the items.

Randall grabs four cherry pies from the carousel and puts them on the counter so that Roscoe can bag them when ready. On the rack below the counter, he sees this morning's edition of the *Ottawa Herald*. The headline reads: "PINE MOUNTAIN MASSACRE." The lead story is accompanied by a photograph of the smiling Reese family at some ski resort in Colorado. He takes a paper from the rack and puts it on the counter with the pies and orange drink. "I'll take one of these, too."

Roscoe keys the cost of the paper into the register. "Just tragic," he says, his eyes pointing to the front-page story.

"Totally," says Randall. "But what's this news about Chet Springs?" He's trying his best to sound casual. He checks the register's display to see the amount owed and hands Roscoe a small wad of cash.

Roscoe uncrumples the ball of dollar bills, counts them, places them one at a time in the register's cash tray. While counting out Randall's change, Roscoe watches Tam through the store's front window. Once Tam's police cruiser has exited the gas station to head south on Fairview, he drops a handful of coins into Randall's open palm and says, "Chet Springs is dead. Murdered last night in his own backyard. Probably by the same sickos that slaughtered Patrick Smith and the Reese family." He again points with his eyes to the newspaper. He bags up the Donner Cherry Pies and the newspaper in one bag and the jug of Sunny D in another, pushes the two plastic bundles across the counter to Randall. "But if Tam asks, you didn't hear it from me." Transaction complete, he returns his attention to his crosswords.

Randall goes to take the bags but stops when he sees the lower headline on the bottom half of the folded newspaper's front page: "POLICE ASK FOR HELP IDENTIFYING SUSPECTS." Below the headline is a child's illustration in crayon of two monsters, both with sharp teeth and claws and glowing purple eyes. One of the monsters is short and squat and has the face of a pig…er, wolf…er, *wolf-pig*? And the other one is tall and lanky, with crazy hair and a serpentine tongue. The caption below the picture reads: "Illustration of the suspected killers by six-year-old survivor, Kelly Reese." *And is that…?* Yep, both monsters have purple scribbled on the bottoms of their feet.

Fuck.

Randall grabs his bags and is about to leave when Roscoe stops him. "Hey, before you go, can you help an old man out?" He taps the point of his pen against an empty square in his crossword. "What's a six-letter word for 'hopeless?' Starts with an 'F.'"

Randall takes a second to think. "Fucked," he says.

Roscoe erupts so hard with laughter that he accidentally spits a bit into Randall's face. "'Fucked!' That's a good one, kid." Then as if struck by epiphany—or maybe he knew the answer all along—he writes the correct word on the paper instead: *futile*. "I needed that laugh. Thanks."

Randall fakes a knowing smile. Smiles like he had been kidding, like he *didn't* think "fucked" was the perfect word. He quickly exits the store.

Back outside, he switches from a stroll to a speed-walk and motors over to the payphone. He drops his bags to the ground, grabs the newspaper, and opens it to page three, where the story about identifying the suspects continues. Placed amid the text there is another picture, smaller than the illustration, but of even more importance. It's a close-up photograph of the *Hurtz Donut?!* patch from Barry's black denim vest. The caption for this one reads: "Evidence found at the scene of the crime." Randall folds the newspaper back up and shoves it into his waistline. He then grabs the phone book that hangs from the payphone by a chain.

What's George's last name again? Jankowski?

Figuring that time is precious, Randall opens the phone book to the "J"s and… *Aha!* There it is, halfway down the page. He looks over both shoulders to check if the coast is clear, then tears that page from the book. He folds the paper into quarters and stuffs it in his pocket. Sighs. *Desperate times*, he thinks.

Time to tell his new friends everything.

REVELATIONS

THE BIKE RIDE back to the Sandpit is a pain, but despite having to pedal uphill while a heavy bag of fake orange juice hangs tenuously from the Magna's handlebars, Randall makes it back to the Wolfmobile in seemingly record time. Once there, he throws the rear doors open with abandon to let as much sunlight in as possible.

"Wake up!" he shouts.

Lich and Sammy spasm out of their sleep, but Barry barely moves—just wipes away some drool with a fist.

"Randall…?" Sammy says groggily, "What the hell is going on? What time is it?"

"I'll tell you, but first I need you all to get up. Now! Oh, and I brought pies!"

Upon hearing the magic words, Barry shoots up groggily to a sitting position. "Donner Cherry?"

"Yes, dude, come on!" Randall grabs the bag of pies from his bike's handlebars and tosses it at Barry. He then unhooks the bag of Sunny D and rolls the jug across the van's carpeted floor to Lich.

"Holy shit, you're serious!" Barry exclaims. "Where did you get these?" He looks up from the bag of pies to see Lich holding sixty-four ounces of chilled Sunny D, the lanky drummer ready to crack the seal and chug—just give him the word. "Am I still dreaming?" Barry wonders aloud.

By the time Randall climbs into the van, Barry has already torn open the waxy paper on a pie and taken several ferocious chomps of the flaky perfection inside. Lich, however, is still holding the jug of Sunny D expectantly. He looks to Randall, who nods in the affirmative. "Drink up, buddy," Randall says. Lich beams and happily does as instructed. Randall grabs a pie from the bag and tosses it up to Sammy in the passenger seat.

"Seriously, though, where did you get these?" she asks.

Randall hands a pie to Lich and takes the last one for himself. "Rotten Roscoe's. Now eat."

Barry nearly coughs a mouthful of cherry filling across the van. "That's like a hundred miles away. How'd you get there? Call a taxi?" But before Randall can respond, another possibility occurs to Barry, and his brow furrows in response. "Wait a sec… We're still parked at the Sandpit, right?" He leaps up to look out the bubble-window and confirm their location.

Randall chews through his first bite of delicious cherry goodness before responding. "I took my bike."

All eyes turn to Randall.

"Whoa," Lich says. The awe in his voice is hard to miss. He passes the jug of Sunny D to Randall, who takes a long, gulping swig, pulls it from his lips, panting, to hurriedly say, "Chet Springs is dead."

"That's not funny, Randall," Sammy says.

"Yeah, dude," Lich says. "Not cool."

"I'm serious. I heard a cop talking about it with Roscoe and his wife while I was waiting in line. Supposedly, the news is all over town already."

"You're really not joking?" Sammy asks. She looks like she's gonna be sick.

"When did it happen?" Lich asks.

"Last night. But that's all I know."

"Barry," Sammy says, "I'm using your radio." She turns the ignition key enough to start the battery, then turns on the radio. She switches from FM to AM bandwidth—a first for the Wolfmobile—and twists the frequency knob until she finds the local news station for Grafting and the neighboring counties. Chet's murder is the top story. After listening silently for a few gut-churning minutes, Sammy turns the radio off.

"They're totally gonna think we did it," Randall says.

"And why wouldn't they?" Sammy says, her voice breaking on the word *wouldn't*. Her eyes are welling with tears. "The same day we flee from the cops, another jock gets killed." She throws her hands in the air and pretends to be a stumped police officer, says, "Whomever could it be?!"

"I think I know the answer to that," Randall says. He pulls *The Ottawa Herald* newspaper from his waistband and flattens it out on the van's carpeting so that everyone can see the full front page, top to bottom.

"Sick illustration," Barry says, pointing to Kelly Reese's drawing.

"Oh, yeah?" says Randall. "You know what's *not* sick?" He turns to page three and presses a finger to the photograph of the *Hurtz Donut?!* patch, allows Barry time to read the caption.

"Holy shit," Barry mumbles. "I'm being framed."

"What does it say?" Sammy asks. She snatches the paper from the floor so that she can read it for herself. Her mouth falls open when she does.

Barry turns to Lich and makes eye contact, holds it so he can speak to his best friend, man-to-man. "Dude, they *really* think I killed people."

"No," Randall interjects. "They think you *both* killed people. You, too, Lich." He points to the open newspaper in Sammy's hands, to Kelly Reese's illustration of Lanky.

"He's right," Sammy says from behind the paper. "According to this, they're looking for two suspects, and the descriptions match the two of you to a tee."

"Wait!" Lich blurts. "Are our names in there?"

"No. Lucky for you guys, you're minors."

Lich breathes a heavy sigh of relief. He's not sure what the twins would do if he had to flee to Mexico without them.

"But there *is* a description of the Wolfmobile," Sammy adds.

"Fuck," Barry says.

"They're baiting you," Randall says. "They want you to see this and turn yourself in. Probably gonna increase the pressure now that Chet's been killed."

Sammy looks up from the paper again, having finally finished the article. "Are we sure Barry and Lich are innocent?" she asks. The look in her eyes says she's only half joking.

"I'm sure," says Randall. He leans over to grab Barry's black denim vest from off the floor next to the Gibson Explorer. It's a wrinkled mess after Randall had bunched it up and used it as a pillow to sleep on.

Barry's eyes grow wide with horror at the sight of the wrinkles. "Dude! Did you use my battle vest as a pillow last night?"

Randall grimaces. "Sorry, dude. But you should be happy I did, because it was last night that I noticed this…" He turns the vest from back to front and points to where the *Hurtz Donut?!* patch is stitched securely to the black denim. "The patch they found at the Reese home isn't yours."

Barry snatches his vest from Randall and puts it on, lovingly pats the *Hurtz Donut?!* patch on his chest. "Case closed then. Let's go over to the sheriff's station right now, show 'em my alibi."

"I don't think it's gonna be that easy," Sammy says.

"Yeah," says Lich. "You could have just bought a new one."

"Thanks for the vote of confidence, buddy," Barry says flatly. Lich just shrugs.

"They're right," says Randall. "Good news is I have a plan to fix all this. But in order for the plan to make sense, I need to confess something first."

The van falls silent. Randall can feel the anticipation in the air. "My dad isn't my real dad," he says. "And he's not here to scout a new Walmart location."

Sammy and Lich look at each other, confused. Barry wonders if all that biking caused Randall to lose too much oxygen to his brain. Just more proof it was unsafe to exercise.

"So, like, you're adopted?" Sammy says. She's trying to understand.

Randall shrugs. "Eh, more like in foster care."

"Okay," says Barry. "So you're a foster kid. Big whoop. What does that have to do with your plan?"

"I'm getting there," Randall says. "See, my foster dad doesn't work for Walmart. He's a leading scientist for a secret organization called Apex Door."

Sammy scoffs. "We don't have time for this?"

Lich perks up. "What's Apex Door?"

Randall takes some time to explain everything he knows about Apex Door and the strange work they do: multiverse theory, Bleeds, extractions, assessors, doppelgangers. He does his best to deflect the many questions along the way.

"This is ridiculous," Sammy says. She looks annoyed by the way Barry and Lich are lapping up Randall's claims without question. "Even if any of this were true, what makes either of you believe that Randall would be in the know? He's just a kid. I doubt his dad comes home every night and just spills all the beans about his top-secret work over dinner. Think about it!"

"Maybe he and his dad are actually cool with each other," Lich says.

"He's lying!" Sammy blurts. She turns to Randall, her face humorless. "Are you done playing for attention yet? Because I think it's time we get serious again."

"I can prove it," Randall says. He reaches into his back pocket and retrieves a tri-fold Velcro wallet with the Nirvana logo stitched into the nylon exterior. There's no money inside, no ID. Just a wallet-sized photograph and a folded newspaper clipping from eighteen months ago. He removes the photograph from its window in the wallet and hands it to Barry. "That's me with my real parents and my two sisters, just outside our home in West Virginia."

Barry studies the photo. "What happened to them? I mean, if you're in foster care, something must have happened. Right?" He hands the photo to Lich, who studies it and hands it over to Sammy.

"*This* happened." Randall retrieves the folded newspaper clipping and hands it to Barry.

"You have a weird love of newspapers, dude," Barry says, accepting the folded square with trepidation. "How many more periodicals you got stashed in there?" He points with his eyes to Randall's many pockets.

"Just read it," says Randall.

Barry unfolds the clipping and starts to read. His eyes grow wide within seconds. He looks up at Randall. "What the hell is this, dude?"

Randall sighs. "My obituary."

"Let me see that!" Sammy says and snatches the paper from Barry. Her eyes well with tears as she reads. It's been an emotional twenty-four hours. "This says you were killed in a car accident on March 3, 1994."

"No way," says Lich. He crawls over to Sammy and looks over her shoulder at the clipping in her hand. "It's the same picture," he says.

"What do you mean?" Sammy says.

Lich points at the wallet-sized photo of Randall's family in Sammy's other hand and then back to the same photo printed in the newspaper as part of the obituary.

"You'll see that my entire family died that day," Randall says. "Earthquake. Biggest in West Virginia history. Split the road in front of my family's car. Nothing my dad could do. He tried to swerve, but that stretch of mountainous road is narrow and the drop-off alongside it is…steep."

"What are you saying, dude?" Barry asks. "That you're a ghost?"

Randall shrugs. "In a way, yes."

"Multiverse theory," Lich says. "You're not a ghost. You're a— What did you call them? A doppelganger." Lich always knew his conspiracy knowledge would come in handy one day.

"Not a doppelganger. That's something else. I'm just a Randall from another dimension, another reality, similar enough to this one, but different. In my world, I was riding my bike down that stretch of West Virginia road when the quake hit. I had just gotten the Magna for my birthday and wanted to take it for a ride. I don't know why things were different here, why I was with my family in our car instead of on my bike, but for whatever reason, this world's version of me died when my family's car went off that cliff. In my world, though, I didn't swerve, wasn't quick enough, so I lived. Just crashed my bike into the crater that had opened up in front of me. Hurt like hell. Broke my wrist pretty bad in three places. But I didn't die, not for-real die anyway. I can still remember the smell of sulfur steaming inside that pit, the glowing purple core at its center. But that's all I remember before blacking out. The next thing I knew, I was somewhere else, locked up in an Apex Door holding cell, awaiting what the white coats there like to call 'extraction.'"

"What does 'extraction' mean?" Sammy asks.

Randall pretends to slit his throat with his thumb.

"Gnarly," Barry says.

"I get it, though. Can't have people roaming realities that aren't their own," says Randall.

"Why not?" says Lich.

"Don't know. They never told me. Something to do with the space-time continuum, I bet."

"Like *Back to the Future*," says Barry.

"That was time travel," says Lich.

"How did you escape?" Sammy asks. She's still not entirely convinced, but her skepticism is quickly waning.

"I didn't. My foster dad saved me. He convinced the Apex Board of Directors that I had value as a case study. Said he would do all the work himself, if need be. The rest is history."

"So, what? Do they, like, run tests on you and stuff?" Barry asks. A dark thought occurs to him, and his eyes narrow. "Do they probe you? Like, in the butt?"

"No probing. They do run tests on me, though. About once a week. Simple stuff like MRIs, EKGs, blood draws. Nothing you wouldn't see at a hospital. Really, they're just trying to make sure I'm still human."

"Come again," Sammy says, aghast.

"Well, see, that's the other reason for extraction. When people fall through the Bleeds, the interdimensional…

whatever...tends to—I don't know—scramble their DNA or something. And that's assuming they survive the trip. According to my foster dad, those that do survive tend to mutate over time, sometimes within days. But I've been lucky so far. Almost two years in a strange dimension and I'm still one-hundred-percent human. One time, I thought I was starting to grow a horn, but turned out it was just a bad pimple."

Sammy holds up the wallet-sized photo of Randall and his family. "I'm confused. Is this picture from your dimension?"

"Yeah."

"Then how is it in this dimension's newspaper?"

"Our dimensions must be really similar. When they are, stuff like that happens—the same picture being taken, the same families being formed, the same people becoming friends." He glances at Barry, then Lich. "But some dimensions are nothing like this one. Places where the world is so different, it would melt your brain."

"So, like, there could be a real-life Dungeons & Dragons plane like The Underdark?" Barry says. "With real highland warriors?"

"Anything's possible, man. But that's really not the point I'm trying to—"

"Dude!" Barry says to Lich. The two halves of Wolf Harp share an excited smile.

"Guys! My point is that there are real life monsters out there, and sometimes they Bleed into other worlds—into *this* world. Like they did in West Virginia. Like they did in One Horse, Kentucky." Randall points to Kelly Reese's drawing in the newspaper. "Like they're doing right now in Grafting."

Barry raises an eyebrow. "The pig-thing and the one-eyed freak? They're real? Like, real monsters? Not just the kid's imagination?"

"I think so. This purple on the feet. It's Bleed membrane. The goop that exists between worlds. These guys, the ones killing all the jocks, they're from another dimension, I just know it. A violent one, if I had to guess."

"The Grafting quake," Sammy says. "That was the Bleed, wasn't it?"

"One of them," Randall says.

"So, where the hell is your fake dad's company in all this?" Barry says. "I thought it was their job to take care of stuff like this. You know—" He drags his thumb across his neck to mimic Randall's earlier explanation.

"That's what I don't get," says Randall. "Most Bleed events are over by now. Don't last more than a few days, max. Apex Door goes in, takes care of business, gets out. It's when they last longer than normal that…" He falls silent.

"What?" Sammy demands. "If they last longer than normal, what?"

Randall shakes his head. "The last time a Bleed got out of control, it took an entire town with it."

"Sinkhole," Barry says. "One Horse, Kentucky. It's the town that got swallowed up, isn't it? The one that Suzanna was going on about with Roscoe. Holy shit."

"Sinkholed," Lich whispers.

Randall nods. "And that's what will happen to Grafting if something isn't done to stop it."

"But how do they stop it?" Sammy asks.

"I don't know, but I think it has something to do with these two maniacs going crazy all over town. And I think I know where they're headed next." Randall retrieves the torn page from the Ottawa County phone book and lays it down on the van's carpeting.

"More newspaper?!" Barry blurts.

"Phone book," says Lich.

Barry snorts. "Oh, way more interesting."

Randall points to a listing on the page. "They're headed to 114 Northeast Branch Drive. I'd bet my life on it."

"Which is?" Barry and Sammy say simultaneously.

"George Jankowski's house."

"What the fuck, Randall?" Barry says.

"Think about it. These killers are following a pattern. First Patrick, then Corbin, now Chet—"

"They're hunting goons," Barry says. "I get it. But what do you want us to do about it?" Barry says. "I mean, me and Bludzorg can definitely throw down, but I'm not so sure about the rest of you."

"We're not gonna fight them. We wouldn't win. We just have to get George and his family to safety."

"What? Why?" Barry says.

"Because they're human beings," Sammy scolds.

"George? Barely. Guy's a trog. If this is the plan, I'm out," Barry states firmly. "I'm not risking my neck for George fucking Jankowski."

"Me neither," says Lich. Nods at Barry in solidarity.

"Fine," says Randall. "Sammy and I will go."

To which Sammy replies, "Hold on a second…"

To which Randall adds, "Or maybe I'll just do it myself." He turns to appeal to Sammy. "But I'm gonna need your camcorder."

"No way," Sammy says. She grabs her camcorder from its resting spot on the driver's seat and clutches it to her chest. "There's only one tape in here and it's full. I'm not letting you tape over it."

"What's on it?" Lich asks.

"Oh, I don't know, Lich. Only the best movie since *Jason Goes to Hell*," says Sammy. "It's all my footage for *Creeps*. Duh."

"What do you need her camera for anyway?" Barry says, his tone dripping with suspicion. He's not keen on *Creeps* being erased from existence either. Some of his best acting is on that tape. And besides, it means a lot to Sammy, so it means a lot to him, too.

"After I get George to safety, I'm going to hide outside his house and film the killers as they try and break in. I'm gonna get the cold hard evidence needed to exonerate you and Lich for good."

Barry scratches his chin while processing this new information. "Okay, I'm starting to like this plan again."

"This might be our last chance to prove your innocence," Randall continues. "Once Apex Door catches these guys, and they will, the only people left to blame in Grafting will be you two." He points at Barry and Lich. "Even with this new evidence, you guys will probably still be forced into witness protection or something, maybe even have your memories wiped, but that's better than spending the rest of your lives in prison."

Barry looks at Lich, then Sammy. "Our memories would be wiped? We'll still remember each other, though, right?" He looks at Sammy again.

"Don't know. It's never been done to me." Randall pauses, scrunches up his face. "At least, I don't think it has."

Sammy looks down at her camcorder. All the shots captured within, those perfect angles, those exceptional scenes executed just as she'd directed. She glances up at Barry and Lich, weighs all that against the plight of her two friends.

"Okay, fine," she says. "We can use my camcorder, but only if I'm the one behind the camera."

"Sammy…" Barry says, trailing off.

She shoots him a wounded look. "What? I've always wanted to try my hand at cinéma vérité, and I don't trust that Randall won't break my camera. He's kind of klutz."

Randall shrugs and nods, like, *Guilty.*

"Besides, a good director never falls in love with her first cut. It'll probably be good for me to start over."

"You sure?" says Barry.

"I'm sure."

Barry sighs. "Well, fuck. I guess I'm coming too, then."

"Me too," says Lich.

"When do we leave?" Sammy says. "I just need some time to make room on the tape."

"You can do it on the way," says Randall. "We have to go now."

BEST LAID PLANS

ON THE DRIVE to George Jankowski's, Barry and the others opt for silence. Each of them has fixed a gaze on whatever might help anchor their thoughts, help them process everything that Randall has told them and prepare them for whatever might come next. Sammy stares into the view screen on her camcorder while Lich stares into space, and Barry glances back and forth between the two of them, Lich to his right and Sammy in the rearview mirror.

When Barry looks at Sammy, he feels like shit. He knows that she's saying goodbye to whatever footage she's captured of her fading magnum opus as she rewinds her grand vision one final time. Shit like this just reminds him how so much of life is unfair, and how much he especially hates when life's unfair to her.

When he looks at Lich, though, he feels his angry grip on the steering wheel soften a bit. His lanky counterpart is lost somewhere in the middle distance, a dopey half-smile hanging off his face, and Barry can't help but smirk. He likes to think that Lich is zen, like a legendary samurai at peace with whatever fate awaits him, but in reality, he knows that Lich is probably just running through Neil Peart's Birmingham '88 "XYZ" drum solo again. They way he paradiddles his drumsticks against his knee.

Barry doesn't bother looking back at Randall, because that kid's on his shit list right now. None of this is really his fault, but also, it kind of is.

Driving into downtown Grafting has Barry feeling like he just plunged into an arctic lake in nothing but his boxers and came out wearing less than that. He feels exposed, watched, observed. Every passing car contains at least one pair of eyes that may have read this morning's edition of *The Ottawa Herald*, and they all seem to be glassing his van as it drives by. He watches every car as they pass, certain that at any moment, the brake lights will light up and the car will swerve into the nearest parking lot with a payphone to make a quick call to 9-1-1.

So, Barry, he's driving like he's never driven before: five miles under the speed limit, blinkers thrown when merging, initiating a slow stop ahead of the next sign at least one hundred feet in advance. All the while, excruciatingly aware that not only were he and Lich named as the primary suspects in the serial killings that have all of Grafting locked in a state of fear, but also that the Wolfmobile has been identified and described with an accuracy that makes it hard to miss. Barry trying to drive his van through town incognito right now is like Batman trying to drive the Batmobile through Gotham in hopes that no one notices.

"You said Branch Drive?" Barry asks as he scans the crisscross of street signs.

"Yeah," Randall says. "One-fourteen."

Barry hangs a quick left, watching for the house numbers as he slows the van. "Guys, watch for the house."

Everyone snaps out of their own thought-porridge at once. Lich aims a finger at every house they pass, mouthing wordlessly the number nailed beside a garage door or a porch beam, or whatever still-legible numbers are spray-painted on the curb.

"There!" Sammy shouts. "One-fourteen. There it is."

Barry pulls the van to a stop in front of the house. "Okay," he says, "Now what?"

"We explain the situation to George and wait until he leaves," Sammy says. "Just like we discussed."

Staring now at George Jankowski's house a mere fifty feet away, actually being in its physical presence, has Barry feeling once more like this entire plan is ridiculous. "Oh, hey, George," he says in a mocking, dopey voice. "Remember me? The guy who you and your buddies are always shitting on, beating up, and otherwise tormenting? And who, as far as you know, just got done killing all your friends? Boy, do we have a wild story to tell you. Can we please come in?"

Lich snickers despite the seriousness of the situation.

"Oh, is this funny to you guys?" Sammy says. "Ha-fucking-ha. How about this? Your stupid ass can stay in the van, Barry. You, too, Lich." She hangs the camera around her neck.

"Yeah," says Randall. "Come on, Sammy. Let's go." He starts to get up off the carpeted floor of the van, but Sammy stops him.

"As if, new kid," she says coldly. "I'm not going within a mile of that house with any of you three dorks. If this is gonna work, I'm gonna need to go alone."

As she slides open the side door, Barry says, "What is that supposed to mean?"

"You know what it means," she says, as seductively as a girl like Sammy can. She hops out, winks at Barry and blows him a fake kiss, then slams the door shut between them.

Barry is stunned. He looks over at Lich, desperate for some sort of explanation that doesn't involve Sammy flirting with George. "Dude?"

Lich just shrugs.

The three boys watch Sammy saunter up to George's front porch, then slow to a cautious stop after climbing the three short stairs to the front door.

"Something's wrong," Randall says.

Suddenly, Sammy turns and frantically starts waving her fiends over. After a quick glance between them, the three boys erupt from the van and sprint across the lawn to join her.

"What is it?" Barry is panting.

Sammy just points at the front door.

"Oh, cool, a front door. Never seen one of those before."

"Barry, look," says Randall.

"It's been broken in," Lich says.

The door frame is splintered, as if the door had been kicked in, and the door is still ajar, resting ominously now against the deadbolt. The handle is covered in purple goop.

"Shit. They're already here," says Randall.

"Welp, we tried," says Barry, turning on his heels and ready to run.

Sammy grabs his arm to stop him. "What if George and his family are still alive? We have to help them." She pushes the door the rest of the way open and steps inside. The others follow behind her.

For daytime, the house is incredibly dark.

"What the hell?" Barry whispers. "Why's it so fucking dark in here? Are the Jankowskis secretly vampires or something?"

"We need to find a light," Sammy says. "My camera can't pick up anything right now."

At the end of the hall they turn into a room as black as a crypt. Sammy feels along for entryway for a light switch and finds one, presses it.

Click.

The four teens can't help but wince at the sudden brightness, eyes having just finished adjusting to the transition from daylight to dark. One by one, each of them sees they are in the Jankowski living room, where the horrid angle of light from the fallen lamp the light switch was connected to casts terrible shadows on the walls. But most horrifying of all, is what stands in the center of the room.

No one makes a sound. No one except for the figure before them, who is breathing with a slow, wet wheeze. Steam curls from the almond nostrils of a pig-like snout that drips with a mixture of pale mucus and purple residue. An arrowhead-shaped ear flicks at the top of its mangy scalp, a very human gaze regarding them from beneath a moist brow, where fur extends into greasy bangs. Its shoulders rise and fall with each ragged breath. It wears what looks like Barry's vest, all crusted and stained, denim threads hanging from the empty spot on the vest where the *Hurtz Donut?!* patch used to be.

The monster looks down, and with a gruesome *slurch*, pulls a sword from the corpse of George Jankowski, the star tight end eviscerated at the creature's feet.

Sammy gasps at the horrific sight. Has to cover her mouth in case she vomits.

Barry recognizes the sword immediately. *Bludzorg*. But not his Bludzorg, a duplicate. The hilt is slightly different.

The grotesque version of Barry raises the sword slowly and steps toward the intruders. The teens turn to run, but behind them, in the hallway, the light that'd been coming through the open front door is suddenly obscured. Another impossibility. A silhouette of Lich so familiar that Barry must glance over his shoulder to make sure his *real* friend is still behind him. The real Lich's eyes are wide, tearing up, and his skin is drained of blood, staring like a ghost at the impostor looming before them. Whatever affliction has morphed Barry's own doppelganger into a demonic parody of himself has also affected this evil version of Lich. It's much taller than real-Lich, more exaggerated. Lankier. Its face is like a banshee in perpetual shriek, the mouth split wide, constantly agape and bearing a haphazard cluster of sharp, pointed teeth. A serpentine tongue dangles over the bottom row of jagged enamel and drips a viscous mix of blood and purple saliva onto a gore-stained XXXL Misfits T-shirt. A lone yellow eye peers out from a black eyehole in the face. The other eyehole is empty. The grotesque parody of Barry's best friend holds the chainsaw that Lich normally uses for his lawn maintenance gig at the courthouse, the one Barry is always pining after, but this one is more rusted, the teeth more serrated, and the blade is stained with human blood.

Barry feels a small hand grip his upper arm. It's Sammy, pulling herself close. She's raised her camcorder and has started recording, is doing her best to courageously wield the camera like a needed weapon of truth. This tape will set them free. Her tear-stricken eyes watch the viewfinder as her trembling hand does its best to keep the monstrosity in frame. She pans quickly back to the monster version of Barry, holds it in frame for a second, and then returns the camera's eye to monster-Lich.

She shrieks as the Lich monster rips the pull-cord on the chainsaw, filling the room with a terrifying roar that promises no way out alive. But just as monster-Lich raises the chainsaw high enough for the whirring blade to shred the plaster ceiling above, a new sound, louder than the chainsaw, punches through the air.

It's the sound of gunfire.

The Lich monster stumbles forward as if hit, then straightens to reveal a smoking golf-ball-sized bullet hole in its chest. A shout comes from outside, then another gunshot booms and the monster stumbles again. Then four more booms punch four more golf-ball-sized holes in the monster's stomach, shoulder, and neck. With blood now spurting from its carotid, the monster drops the chainsaw and collapses to the floor, uses both hands to clutch the wound in its neck. The chainsaw's safety throttle must be engaged, because the machine's roar dies upon impact with the floor. Monster-Lich grabs the chainsaw and crawls as fast as its wounded body will allow, to take cover behind some furniture.

A new silhouette then steps into the bright doorframe, the sunlight like a halo behind them. It's Sheriff Keller. He levels the barrel of his gun at Barry—the human Barry—and starts firing.

ART HAD BEEN quick to reply when Keller radioed him to say he was finally on his way to the Chet Springs crime scene, but Art didn't have much to offer other than anxious gratitude.

Hooking a left on Branch Drive, Keller studies the homes there. Everything looks normal, save for the one house that still needs to take its Halloween decorations down. A twelve-foot inflatable skeleton doesn't age well after October 31st, especially when the real specter of death is already so omnipresent in Grafting.

And then he sees the van parked outside house number 114. THE VAN. The one that looks like it's been to hell and back. The van with the airbrushed graphic on its side of three wolves howling at a bubble-window that's been painted to look like the moon.

"No fucking way," Keller mumbles to himself. He radios his deputies: "Art, Tam, I've got our fugitives. The four kids from Ottawa Heights. One-Fourteen Branch Drive. I need everyone here now. Over."

Keller slams his patrol car to a stop behind the van.

"Sending out the APB now," Art radios back.

Keller reaches for his firearm, checks the cylinder of his magnum. He remembers his dad's words the day John-David was elected sheriff: "*It's not the size of your gun, it's how you use it.*" He'd said it with a wink after handing his son the largest hand-cannon that Keller had ever seen. He then drunkenly joked that the magnum had always been the only backup he ever trusted.

Keller checks the van. The barrel of his magnum is like the snout of a bird dog, searching for the scent of Keller's suspects. He pounds his fist against the graphic of three wolves and shouts for anyone in there to come out. When no one does, Keller throws the rear doors open, his scanning gaze affixed with the aim of the gun's barrel.

There's no one inside.

On approach to the house, Keller can see the back of a lanky individual standing outside the front door, shoulders as high as the top of the doorframe. As the sheriff levels the barrel of his magnum, ready to order the individual to the ground, he is reminded of Kelly Reese's picture. One of the perps was tall and lanky. And then he sees the weapon the lanky figure wields: a rusty fucking chainsaw. *It's him. One of the killers.* But before Keller can stop him, the lanky giant ducks beneath the doorframe and steps into the darkness of the home.

That's when Keller hears the roar of the chainsaw and a young woman's shriek from inside the home. He has to act quick, and he has to act decisively. Would the maniac even hear Keller's order to step out with his hands up? Almost certainly not. Probably wouldn't comply even if he did. That settles it then.

Keller rushes to up to the front porch, aims his magnum at the figure in the doorway and fires.

The first pull of the magnum's trigger is followed quickly by Keller's adrenaline-riddled order, "Drop your weapon!" But the command is only symbolic. Before the lanky thing can respond in any meaningful way, Keller fires again. When it still doesn't drop, he empties the rest of the gun's chamber. After the thing falls forward into the home, wounded, Keller pops the cylinder on the magnum and reloads six bullets as he approaches the front door. Standing upon the threshold now, he sees something so far beyond the pale, it makes him question reality.

A stout, hairy creature with a drooling maw, wet snout, and spade ears like a pig's, is charging down the hallway at him, giant sword in hands, raised as if ready to strike. The creature is dressed like Barry—Scorpions T-shirt, Converse sneakers, black denim vest with patches—but it's not Barry. It's the wolf-pig from Kelly Reese's drawing. *Killer number two.*

Barry and his friends are huddled in the hallway, in the space between Keller and the creature that charges. The girl is filming everything she can with a camcorder. She's sobbing.

Keller aims at the creature, waits for the four kids to drop to the floor in frightful shouts, and fires until the chamber is empty once more and smoking.

The wolf-pig version of Barry recoils and stumbles backwards at the heavy caliber that just punched it six times in the shoulder and chest. It clutches the wound nearest its heart, purple ooze spewing out between its fingers, and with a dry hiss, darts with inhuman speed towards the lanky chainsaw wielder that has collapsed behind the nearest couch.

Keller reloads his magnum.

Lanky throws a too-long, too-skinny arm over Wolf-Pig's shoulders, and Wolf-Pig helps him to his feet. Lanky leans on his monstrous counterpart and allows Wolf-Pig to do the walking for the both of them. They leave slimy purple foot-prints in their wake.

"It's feeding time, Lich," Wolf-Pig says to Lanky.

Lanky nods.

Keller aims his reloaded magnum at Wolf-Pig but stops when he sees something strange on the creature's back.

"The fuck…?" he murmurs.

A spider-like creature with too many legs and needle-teeth is crawling up Wolf-Pig's spine. It's somehow the size of a small mouse. The sight of the ten-legged freak makes Keller suddenly double over, nauseous and dizzy. That spider… He's seen it before. Hasn't he? And why does he suddenly feel the urge to vomit? He paws at the back of his neck, but he doesn't know what's compelling him to do so. Is there something in there, at the base of his skull? Or is it a memory of someone else?

More spiders appear, start crawling out of the many gunshot wounds that smoke in Wolf-Pig's black denim vest. They are covered in purple goop. Some start bursting from tumors along the creature's collarbone. Spiders are appearing on the Lanky one now, too, crawling from the gunshot wounds and out the neck of its oversized Misfits T-shirt. Tumors on its spine burst open in sprays of purple goo and even more spiders join the growing horde.

Keller watches in horror as the spiders cover the two monsters from head to toe and start biting them with their needle-teeth, the sound like wet squelches. They rip, tear, and chomp their way through clothing, flesh, hair, and bone. They work fast, like a swirling tornado of gore, and within seconds, Wolf-Pig and Lanky are no more—eaten alive. Not a single thread of fabric, skin cell, or strand of hair remains. The dozens of remaining spiders collapse to the floor in a heap and melt away into nothing amid a hiss of steaming purple vapor.

The sheriff looks to the four teens huddled on the floor. "Did anyone else see that?"

None of them answer except for the girl. "This did," she says quietly, offering up her camcorder like it was the Holy fucking Grail.

The sound of sirens and police cruisers screeching to a stop outside is followed by a chorus of voices closing in on the house. Keller turns to see Art leading the way. He's the first one in, Tam close behind. With them are two squad cars of state police, most likely from the Chet Springs crime scene.

"Sheriff!" Art shouts as he approaches Keller. "You okay? What happened?"

Keller doesn't know what to say. Has trouble even attempting an answer. Instead, he points weakly to Barry, Lich, Sammy, and Randall, the four friends still huddled in the hallway, their eyes wide with fright. "Arrest them", Keller says flatly. "Bring them to the station for questioning."

It's the only command that makes sense.

INCIDENT REPORT

Apex Door Field Assessment Unit 3

Incident/Assessment Report

Today's Date: Tuesday, November 7, 1995

Time: 11:11 AM

Assessor Number: 7

Assessor's Handler: Orson Caster

Location of incident: Grafting, Michigan

Person(s) affected: George Jankowski

Reason(s) for field assessment dispatch:

Local P.D. dispatch intercepted, describing recent murder following the patterns of the prior homicides. Strong indication of the two anomalies.

Key Indicators mentioned (please refer to the latest edition of the APEX DOOR FIELD ASSESSMENT MANUAL for updated glossary of Key Indicators to choose from):

- N/A

Please describe the incident(s), including any anomalous phenomena:

Unfortunately, local P.D. was already on
site at the time of our arrival. We witnessed the arrest of several adolescents.
We waited until the scene was mostly clear
before investigating. I chatted briefly
with a deputy who stayed behind to wait
for a forensics unit. She was taping off
the scene.

The deputy identified herself as Tam. She
was unpleasant and not forthcoming about
what had happened despite myself showing
federal clearance. She told me only that
this was the scene of an active homicide
investigation, and that the killers had
been apprehended and she was about to take
them to the sheriff's station. Her recommendation was that myself and 7 proceed
there to discuss with Sheriff Keller if I
had more questions.

Her overall hostility and generally dis-
agreeable nature, along with the late
arrival of the murder victim's parents,
compelled me to evacuate the immediate
area. However, with Deputy Tam's attention
focused on the parents and their high
emotional state, 7 had the opportunity to
briefly search the location.

Assessor response:

7 was able to glean critical information
while eavesdropping on conversations
between law enforcement and the four
murder suspects. The suspects claimed
to be innocent, and the county sheriff

seemed willing to listen. 7 believes that the four suspects and the sheriff witnessed a horde of Bleed spiders devour what they could only describe as two monsters. 7 believes the monsters they described and the Bleed anomalies are one and the same. Furthermore, 7 has strong reason to believe that the anomalies are using the Bleed spiders to create Bleeds and travel across dimensions. 7 theorizes that the key to this interdimensional travel lies within the mouths and digestive systems of the spiders. The anomalies allow themselves to be eaten and digested by the spiders, because the spider's digestive system acts as a portal to alternate planes.

Conclusion & Recommended Next Steps:

Myself and 7 will be making an appearance at the Apex Door field laboratory in the vacant factory building in Grafting. It is critical that this issue is dealt with swiftly now that local law enforcement is involved. The risk of national attention is currently high. I'll impress upon Director Cleeve the need for decisive action, as I believe it to be paramount. While at the lab, we will present 7's theory and discuss next steps.

ANIMUS OR ANIMOSITY?

EN ROUTE TO the station, the morning passing by in a kaleidoscope of muted oranges and grays, Barry looks to Lich to check on his buddy, but the guy isn't looking too good—looks kind of like he's gonna hurl. Barry glances up at the cage separating him and Lich from the female deputy in the driver's seat—Keller called her "Tam"—makes sure she's busy, then looks back to Lich and whispers, "You saw what I did, right? Back at George's house. I wasn't imagining those things."

Lich, more pale-faced than usual, only looks back at Barry in reply. Nothing to say.

"Who were those guys?" Barry asks.

Lich looks down at his own shoes on the cruiser's floor.

"Talk to me, Lich. Did you get the same feeling I got?"

Lich looks up. He nods.

"They were *us*," says Barry.

"I know."

"So, like, demon versions of ourselves murdered Chet and his goons? Do I have that right? Maybe there's, like, a hell world or something. Like from *DOOM*."

Lich looks up at Barry. "But what if they're not from a hell world? What if they're from a dimension just like ours? Like Randall. What if…we're not so different from them?"

"What are you talking about, bud? Those things weren't us. They just looked like us…in monster form."

"Yeah, but Randall said that jumping dimensions scrambles human DNA. What if they weren't always monsters? They just became that way. What if they started out just like us?"

"That's crazy talk," Barry says.

"Is it. We've talked about it before, ya know, about killing Chet and those guys. I know it was always just a joke, but sometimes, late at night, when I couldn't sleep after a shitty day, I did more than just joke about it, ya know? I imagined it, even planned how I would do it." Lich has tears in his eyes. "I've never told anyone that before, but if I can't tell you, who can I tell? It's just… It's eating me up inside, dude. Been eating me up inside ever since Patrick's murder. And after what we just saw, I don't know. I'm starting to wonder if I imagined whatever those things are into existence. Anything seems possible at this point."

Barry hears that. *Really* hears that. And he finds himself unable to respond immediately. A rarity for him, one that almost disturbs him more than how much he can relate with Lich's account of those late nights..

"Be honest with me, dude," Lich says. "Have you ever imagined it? Imagined how you'd do it? Like…in detail."

Barry levels his gaze at Lich, but he doesn't see his friend. He sees all the years of bullying at the hands of Patrick, Corbin, Chet, and George. Even now, he can remember every insult hurled, every fist connecting with his body. He can even remember everything he didn't say back, all those smart-ass replies that died inside his hunching submission. All those fantasies of catching the fists before they connected. Of raising *Bludzorg*, of bringing it down upon George and pulling it from his lifeless corpse just like the wolf-pig version of Barry had done. Fantasies conjured from his sweat-stained mattress on the floor of his mom's trailer; conjured while his mom's latest boyfriend calls Barry a dipshit loser loud enough for Barry to hear through the paper-thin wall; conjured while Barry bleeds from his latest beating.

"Yeah," Barry says. "But I don't regret it. I'm allowed to think what I want." Suddenly feeling the weight of someone else's gaze, he glances up at the car's rearview mirror to see Deputy Tam's inquiring eyes staring back at him with intensity.

BACK AT THE station, Keller is seated at his desk and rewinding his memory all the way back to his years as a deputy under his father. Rewinds it just like he did with the VHS tape on his desk after watching it for the umpteenth time this morning—the tape from inside the camcorder he confiscated from Sammy Walters. Keller is starting and stopping the videotape in his brain until a voice drifts into his mind—his father's voice. Like tetrominos, stage props fall out of the void and fill in around the image of his old man until the mental scene is set. Billowing drapes reach across vinyl flooring, striped wallpaper on the walls, dead monstera adansonii wilting in its pot. His dad, he's drunk, hunched over the kitchen table like he's one missing puzzle piece away from some great mystery being solved. Police work.

"A good cop assesses the situation before acting," Keller's dad says from inside the memory. "He makes sure he *knows*. If he doesn't, he's bound to make bad decisions. Hurt himself. Hurt someone else. Shoot a man in the back over twenty bucks and change. So tell me, son. What do you know?"

Keller's twenty-three-year-old self steps into the frame and says, "I feel like I don't know anything anymore."

"That's a start, at least. Do you remember the Aguilar kid, yet? Barry? Remember who his dad was?"

"I don't see how that's relevant."

"If that's the truth, you're gonna be mighty surprised when they come for you next."

"'They'? I don't understand."

But before Keller's father can answer, the vision of him shatters. Back in reality, a knock raps against Keller's office door. Art enters, and he has that odor of stale ashtray about him that makes Keller want to light up for the first time in years, start smoking two packs a day again. Instead, the sheriff just breathes deep.

"What are you thinkin' about, sheriff?" Art asks.

"Just trying to figure out what we know," says Keller. "It's a lot to process. Hey, do you happen to know who the Aguilar kid's dad is?"

"No. But I can find out. Is that what you called me in for?"

"Oh, no. Just thinking out loud. I called you in because I have something I want you to see." Keller grabs the videotape from his desk, holds it up. "I want you to—"

Tam joins Art at the doorway, interrupts Keller immediately. "Hey, sheriff. Just put Aguilar and Adams in with Walters and Foster. Cell's gettin' a bit crowded, but it's the only one we got, so…"

Keller sets the VHS tape back down upon his desk. "That tank once held two drunk Zimmer boys and a junkie on heroin withdrawal in the same night. It can handle four sober high-schoolers."

"That's one hell of a way to say 'four murder suspects,'" Tam says.

"They're not suspects anymore," Keller says. "At least, I don't think they are."

"What the hell are you talking about, sheriff?" Art says. "We caught 'em at the scene of the crime. Plus we've got the patch connecting the Reese case, and motive. They're guilty as sin."

"I know what it looks like, but this tape, there's something on it I need you to—"

Keller is unable to finish before Debs shoves her way through the two deputies and into the office. "Sheriff, you have calls from the mayor, the district attorney, the state PD, a reporter from *The Ottawa Herald*, and someone named Daniel Cleeve—says he's important, but sounds to me like your run-of-the-mill government type. I told them all you'd call them back as soon as you can." She holds up a bright pink sticky note. "Where do you want me to put these numbers?"

"Hand 'em here," Keller says. He reaches out his hand and receives the note from Debs, sticks it to the phone on his desk.

"Don't wait too long," Debs says as she squeezes past the deputies again. "I don't want them calling me back. I'm busy enough as it is."

Once Debs is down the hallway, Art steps inside Keller's office. "I don't get it, sheriff. Why do you think those kids are innocent?"

Keller holds up the videotape once more. "Do me a favor, Art. Just take this videotape to the VCR in the conference room and watch it. You too, Tam. After you've both watched it in full, we can talk. There's not much else to discuss until you've seen what was recorded at the Jankowski place."

"I don't understand," says Art. "What about the kids?"

"Can't interrogate them until their lawyer shows up."

"Those kids have a lawyer?" Tam says.

"A good one," Keller says. "Called the station within thirty minutes of their arrest. Represents the Foster kid's dad. Or his company. Something like that. Either way, we're handcuffed until he gets here. Now go. And don't come back until you've watched that tape."

After Art and Tam leave with the videotape, Keller looks to the bright pink sticky note on his phone. *Who the hell is Daniel Cleeve?* he wonders. He then spends the remainder of the morning and some of the afternoon on the phone with everyone on the list besides Daniel Cleeve, this guy who has nothing other than his own assurance that he's important. Probably some low-level aide for Grafting's state rep. No one he expects to hear from or see anytime soon.

"HOW LONG HAVE we been in here?" Randall says. He's seated in the corner of the jail cell and tracing cracks in the cement floor with a finger.

"Five hours, at least," Barry says. He's laying on his back on one of the benches, practicing guitar licks in his mind.

"More than five," Sammy murmurs. Her eyes are red from crying off and on throughout the afternoon. "It's almost six o'clock at night."

"How do you know that?" says Barry.

Sammy points to the small reinforced window in the drunk tank's door. "I can see the wall clock in the other room."

Barry sighs. "Hey, Randall," he says.

"Yeah?"

"Why did your dad's company make demon versions of me and Lich?"

Lich looks up from his knees, intrigued to hear the answer.

"Apex Door doesn't create the monsters that come through the Bleeds, they just kill them," Randall says flatly. "We've been over this already."

"Where did they come from then?" Lich asks. "Some kind of hell world? Like in *DOOM*? An entire dimension of demon versions?"

"I don't think so. Not in this case. My guess is they come from a dimension pretty similar to this one. That's why they look so much like you guys, and why the Barry and Lich from their dimension are friends. They also seem pretty familiar with Grafting. The odds of that being the case for a dimension super different than this one—"

"The odds can kiss my butt," says Barry.

Lich offers a guess: "So, they're just similar versions of us, but with scrambled DNA or whatever? That's why they look the way they do."

"Yeah. Probably. I don't know for sure. All I know is what I've overheard and read from papers my foster dad left around."

"Oh," says Lich. He slumps toward the concrete. Not the answer he was looking for, apparently.

Barry doesn't like seeing his best buddy looking so defeated. "But these other dimensions, they don't have anything to do with us, right? Even the ones that are similar. They're not, like, our dark sides or anything. It's more like when Luke went into that cave and saw himself in Vader's suit. It didn't mean nothing as long as Luke chose the right path for himself."

"You and Lich aren't killers," Sammy says.

"Yeah," says Barry, "I know. But I want to hear it from Bill Nye the Science Guy over here."

"I'm not the science guy," says Randall. "That would be my dad. You'll have to ask him."

"Oh, I can't wait to meet that dude," says Barry, his brow suddenly furrowed. "Him and the rest of his stupid Apex

Door flunkies. Definitely gonna be hearing from my lawyer, if you catch my drift."

"You have a lawyer?" Sammy says.

Barry snorts. "No, but I'll get one. Jeez, Sammy. You're supposed to be the smart one."

"Oh, God!" Sammy huffs. "You come up with one lousy *Star Wars* analogy and suddenly you think you're Mark fucking Twain. Free wit and wisdom for everyone!"

Barry guffaws. "Jokes on you, Sammy. I don't even know who Mark Twain is. I bet George does, though." He bats his eyelashes in mock flirtation. "Why don't you go ask him? Oh, wait..."

Sammy jumps to her feet, furious and ready to unleash a verbal assault on Barry. But before she can serve up a biting response, the power goes out in the station.

"ANY WORD FROM the kids' lawyer?" Art asks after stopping for a moment in Keller's office. It's almost six o'clock, and he's ready to go home.

Keller shakes his head no.

"And what about the videotape? Have you decided what to do with that?"

"I don't know, Art. What do you think? Should we send it to the FBI, the CIA, or Area 51?"

"Sorry, sheriff. It's just, we're not equipped for this kind of stuff here."

"I know," says Keller.

"Sorry I didn't believe you."

"I know," says Keller again. "But if it's any consolation, I'm still not sure I believe myself."

That's when Debs's voice comes through the speakerphone on Keller's desk. "Sheriff?"

"I'm here, Debs. Go ahead."

"There's an urgent call for you on line one. It's from the FBI."

"Speak of the devil," says Art.

"Thanks, Debs," Keller says. "I'm taking it now."

"Should I go?" Art asks.

"No, you can stay. This won't take long."

Keller picks up the phone and puts it to his ear, then hits the button for line one. The voice on the other end speaks first.

"Sheriff Keller. My name is Daniel Cleeve. And I'm calling to tell you that your life and the lives of everyone else in your station are in immediate danger."

"Cleeve? Hey, didn't you call—"

"No time for chit chat, sheriff. Just listen. An Apex Door extraction team is on its way to your location now. I will need you and the four teenagers you currently have detained to go with the team them when they arrive, no questions asked. If you try and stop them, you will be taken by force. ETA is in ten minutes."

"What the hell is an apex door?" he asks, but he finds himself speaking into a dial tone following the sharp click of a phone line disconnecting.

"The FBI doesn't mince words, do they?" Art says after Keller hangs up.

"I don't think that was the FBI."

And that's when the power goes out in the station.

Keller and Art blink at each other in the sudden dark and then head out into the hallway to investigate. The emergency lights above the exit signs have already kicked on and are projecting their eerie spotlights onto the floor in front of the doors. Everything else is dim or dark.

From somewhere else in the station they hear screaming, followed by the sound of gunshots.

Moments later, one of the doors down the hall flies open, the aggressive sound of which causes Keller and Art to spin on their heels, hands on holsters, jumpy and on high alert. But when Tam comes through the door alone, they relax.

"Oh, thank God," she says after seeing them. She's breathing heavy, muscles tense, face fraught, like she's been hauling ass to get here and the last thing she expected to see after coming through that door were the good guys. "Sheriff, we have a problem. It's one of those…things, monsters, whatever you wanna call them—from the tape. It's inside the station. It killed Sandra, sheriff. Cut half her head off with that goddamn chainsaw, horizontally through the nose." Tam cups her hand over her mouth to stop from retching. "I unloaded a full clip into it, but it didn't do shit. We're outmatched, sheriff."

"Where is it now, Tam?" Keller says.

"Lobby."

"Where's Debs?"

Tam winces at the thought. "Shit. I don't know."

"What about the wolf-pig? The one with the sword? Did you see him anywhere?"

"No, sheriff. Just the tall one."

"Okay, you and Art go check on the kids. I'm gonna go try and stop this psycho. Radio me if you need help."

"You got it, sheriff." Art draws his pistol and jogs down the hall to the drunk tank.

"Are you sure you're gonna be okay, J. D.?" Tam asks. She has never once called Keller by anything other than "sheriff" until now. Always thought it was too informal.

"I'll be fine, Tam," Keller says. "You just watch Art's back, okay? He needs a good officer like you at his side."

Tam cracks a half smile, the most she'll allow herself, and jogs after Art.

DEATH OF A DEPUTY, PART TWO

WHEN ART OPENS the door to the drunk tank, all four teenagers jump to their feet.

"What the hell is going on out there," Barry says. "We heard gunshots."

"We've got a bit of situation on our hands," Art says, "But Deputy Tam and myself are here to keep you safe."

"What kind of situation?" Sammy asks.

"A serious one," says Art. He turns to Tam. "Now what? Should we stay here or move?"

"I vote we fucking move," Barry interjects.

"Cool it, Ace of Spades," Tam says. "No one asked you."

Barry tries to grumble, but secretly he's digging the nickname. Senior would be proud.

"Quickest way out is through the exit in back," Art says.

"Shit," Tam says. "Are we *sure* they're innocent? They could be accessories to the crime."

"Oh, come on!" Sammy blurts.

"Tam, there's a monster on the loose," Art says calmly, trying his best to reason with his unflinching colleague. "And these four kids in danger. Serve and protect, remember?"

Tam glares at Barry for longer than is probably necessary. "Okay," she says. "Let's get the hell out of here. But we should probably cuff that one just in case." She points to Barry.

"Get bent," says Barry. He shoves his way past Art into the dim hallway that hums with emergency light and power. "Where to?"

"We're going this way," Art says, pointing down the hallway toward the only exit in back, the one that opens to the impound lot full of abandoned vehicles.

As the group makes their way to the exit, Barry glances at an open door and stops. "Hey! That's my guitar!" he shouts. He points to the black Gibson Explorer that is leaning haphazardly against rusty storage shelving inside a room the size of a utility closet, locked behind a flimsy metal cage no thicker or more secure than your standard chain link fence.

"That's the evidence locker," Tam says, urging him forward.

Barry plants his shoes. "But what's it doing in there?"

"Being evidence. We confiscated it from your van before it was impounded."

"You took the Wolfmobile?!"

"Barry," Sammy says gently, "we can figure this out later. C'mon."

"Not without my guitar," Barry insists. He shakes himself free of Tam's grip on his arm and darts for the steel cage.

"Good luck getting in there without the key," Tam chides.

But when Barry grabs the door handle and twists, the latch releases without a fight. He swings the cage door open.

"Dammit, Art," Tam groans.

Art winces. "Must have forgotten to lock it. Sorry."

"Well would you look at that," Barry says with a grin. "I spy with my little eye a pair of stainless steel drumsticks. I think I know someone who can hang on to these." He grabs the stainless steel drumsticks from one of the storage shelves, then retrieves his guitar from the floor and slings the leather strap around his neck. He returns to the group a conquering hero and hands Lich his sticks.

"*Danke*," Lich says. He twirls one of the sticks in his fingers, then shoves both into his back pocket. But when he looks down the hall, his smile disappears. "Oh, fuck," he says. "It's me."

The group turns to see Lanky looming in the hallway beneath a flickering emergency light. The emaciated giant seems to have grown even taller since the morning, having to duck it's head now just to keep it from touching the tubes of fluorescent light flickering inside the eight-foot ceiling. Its arms hang so freakishly long that despite its towering height, the chainsaw drags along the concrete floor behind it.

Art and Tam draw their guns and train them on the killer.

"Drop your weapon!" Tam shouts.

"Put your hands on your head!" Art shouts at the same time.

To both of their surprise, the monster stops.

Tam takes a step forward, gun still held out in front of her, trained on the monster's center mass. She shouts again, "Drop your weapon!" Another step. And then another.

"Tam!" Art snaps. "What are you doing? Get the fuck back here."

"Get the kids to the exit," Tam says flatly. "I'll be right behind you."

"You're gonna get yourself killed!"

Lanky tilts its grinning head to the side and watches with one curious yellow eye as Deputy Tam refuses to cede any ground.

"Get out of here!" she shouts over her shoulder, refusing to take her eyes off Lanky. "Get the kids to safety, Art."

"Go!" Art says to the teens, pointing them down the hallway toward the single exit in back and their only means of escape. The teens do quickly as they're told and rush down the hall. Sammy is the fastest. "Tam, let's go," Art says to her. He's on the verge of pleading.

Finally, Tam complies, thank God, but that's also when the attack occurs. Not from in front of her, but from the side.

She barely glimpses the flash of steel to her left before the blood-soaked blade comes down heavily on her elbow, severing her arm clean off at the joint. She immediately crumples to the floor in shock, can't soften the scream that bursts out of her. Blood pools on the floor at her knees.

"TAM!" Art shouts.

From the shadowy alcove beside her, Wolf-Pig emerges. It has also grown larger since the morning. Stockier, but also stronger, more sturdy. Smellier, too. "Hurts, don't it?" it snarls. He and Lanky share a soulless snicker.

Art is trembling, but he doesn't hesitate, just unloads a full clip into the beast. The muzzle flashes are nearly blinding in the dark, but his aim stays true. When the smoke clears, he drops his aim in defeat. Even at close range, the bullets have done nothing. The wolf-pig just laughs.

"Go," says Tam. "Make sure the kids are safe." She lifts her gun with her one remaining arm and fires three steady shots at Lanky, then three more at Wolf-Pig. The wolf-pig responds by chopping off her other arm, then plunging its sword straight through Tam's heart. She exhales a dying gasp.

Art pulls the trigger on his gun a half-dozen more times before remembering the clip is empty.

Tam falls backward, tries to catch herself with an arm that's not there, but just flings blood from the stump at her shoulder. She falls onto her back and rolls onto her belly. She attempts to crawl pitifully towards Art, and when she calls out to him, she only coughs blood.

But Art knows exactly what she's trying to say. He can see it in her eyes. *"Please, Art,"* they say. *"Go."* Art just nods a silent thank-you through wet eyes and turns to chase after the teens.

Behind him, he hears the roar of the chainsaw, but he refuses to turn, to watch, as the whirring blade digs into Tam's spine between the shoulder blades, then tears upward through her brainstem and out the top of her skull.

SINS OF THE FATHER

KELLER KNOWS HE should stand on one side of the closed door to dispatch, then kick the door open and clear the room as quickly as he can, but he doesn't do that. Something tells him there's no point. And when he opens the door casually to reveal the horror that's inside, he's proven right.

What he sees inside the dispatch office is an old switchboard against the back wall, with its quarter-inch jacks gleaming through years of dust beneath the single emergency light bolted to the wall. He sees blood. A lot of blood. He sees the mangled remains of Sandra splattered across the switches. He takes a deep breath to snuff the urge to upchuck.

"Debs?" he shouts. But the only response is his own echo as he looks from dispatch to the front of the station down the hall.

The lobby and the admin desk appear empty. No lanky serial killer or Debs in sight.

That's when Debs hears screaming, followed by another volley of gunshots. Lots of them.

Art!

Tam!

Keller sprints through the maze-like halls of the sheriff's station, back toward the drunk tank, hears six more gunshots and the roar of a chainsaw along the way. When he arrives, he sees Tam's ravaged corpse. Her final expression calcified over her face. Fear. Pain. Confusion. Art and the teens are nowhere in sight.

Standing over Tam's body, shoulder to shoulder, watching with yellow eyes through the eyelets of cheap rubber Halloween masks now become animated flesh, fused to their skulls as if by some demonic spell, are the grotesque parodies of Grafting's two most infamous outcasts: Barry and Lich. Their wounds from the Jankowski house have appeared already to heal. And they look bigger, stronger, more invincible than before. New tumors the size of softballs pulse along their shoulders and necks.

Keller raises his magnum. The muscles in his arms have tightened to concrete, his stance gone statuesque. He doesn't pull the trigger. Not yet, at least. Just stares.

The wolf-pig's hideous voice speaks, the words distorted by a mouthful of spurting tusks. "What are you waiting for?"

"Don't test me," Keller warns. "I *will* shoot you."

"Oh, no," says the voice. It's all soot and ember. "He's gonna shoot us, Lich."

Lanky's shoulders hitch with a single-syllable laugh coughed from a throat full of sludge.

Crack!

The hallway erupts with Keller's magnum firing off its first round. A twist of smoke burns off an acrid sulfuric smell. He hears the wet punch of bullet into flesh. He knows he's hit his target.

"Damn," says the wolf-pig. "You got me."

Crack! Another round.

The wolf-pig brushes away the slug in his chest, amused. "That's not gonna work on us this time, sheriff."

Crack!

"Keep trying, Sheriff Killer," says the wolf-pig. "I want this moment to last."

Sheriff Killer? That's what Barry called Keller during his questioning at Ottawa Heights.

"Why did you call me that?" Keller shouts. "'Killer.' What's that supposed to mean?"

The voice of Keller's father echoes in his brain. *"Remember the Aguilar kid, yet? Remember who his dad was?"*

"It took us a long time to find this place," the wolf-pig says, "this near-identical dimension to our own. But on the way, me and Lich, we went somewhere that changed us. Now we can go anywhere and everywhere, and never get hurt. Pretty rad, huh?"

"What do you want?"

"Back where we come from, you're just a happy-go-lucky sheriff with a wife and two kids, walking around town without a care in the fucking world. But that version of you will never know justice. It took a long time for me to accept that, but eventually I did. I must admit, though, my acceptance was made easier after learning that a near-identical version of you exists here in this world, along with a few more of Barry and Lich's most wanted."

"You mean Chet and his friends."

Lanky gazes with a singular yellow eye, nods *yes*, grins a mouthful of dagger teeth.

"You know it," says the wolf-pig. "Funny thing, though: we killed those guys once already back home. Just couldn't take any more of their shit, ya know? Killed them so brutal it made a quake that shook us straight to Hell. But for as much as I hate Chet and his goons, getting to kill them a second time here was really just gravy. But you, sheriff... We didn't get to kill you back home. So this time will be special."

"I don't understand. What did I do that makes you hate me so much?" Keller asks.

The wolf-pig tilts its head as if surprised the answer isn't obvious. "You exist."

Do you remember who his dad was.

"Shit," Keller says. "Your dad was Barry Aguilar Senior. The guy my dad shot dead."

The wolf-pig takes a step towards the sheriff. A spider crawls out from its vest and up the back of its neck. "Your pops killed Senior in this dimension, too?"

He's asking. He doesn't know.

"Lich," the wolf-pig snarls, "it's time. Let's butcher this little piggy."

And that's when the entire wall beside them explodes in a cloud of blasted cinder block and dust.

FOSTER DAD

WHAT A BEAUTIFUL morning. Yeah, it's cold as the other side of Hell outside, but in here? In Dale Foster's kitchen? Toasty and cozy and *mmm*. The coffee maker sputters and spits fresh arabica coffee into a carafe. It will go great with the eggs and sausage frying in the pan. Over on the kitchen island, two slices of homemade sourdough have been buttered and placed upon two waiting plates—one for him and one for Randall.

Foster searches for his pager but can't find it. *Fuck it.* If it ain't in the bowl by the door, in the dish on the dresser, or clipped to yesterday's khakis, it ain't nowhere. Must've left it at the office. *Whoops.* Foster retrieves the pan of eggs and sausage and puts two of each on both plates.

"Rand!" he calls up the stairs. "Got breakfast ready down here!"

He takes a few bites of his eggs, mops at his mouth with a paper towel. Still no sign of Randall. "Rand?" Foster makes his way upstairs and knocks on his son's door. "Rand, you up?"

Nothing.

"I'm coming in." He opens the door slowly and peaks inside. The bed is empty, his son is nowhere. Foster sighs. "Must have gone off to school without saying goodbye."

This kind of thing was beginning to happen more frequently now that Randall was a teenager. The One Horse Bleed was the worst. Somehow, Randall had a way of getting mixed up with the wrong kind of kids at school, and before Foster knew it, the kid was AWOL for days at a time. No hellos, no good-byes, no "How was your day, Dad?" Foster should have seen this coming after Randall showed up so late on the night of Halloween and refused to tell his dad where'd he been. He's been trying to give the boy more space, allow him to grow as he must, but maybe Grafting wasn't the right place for him to stop pushing back. Maybe he shouldn't have allowed him use of that damn bike again. Probably just gave him an easier way to run off.

Glancing around the walls of his son's room, Dr. Foster sees posters for bands he's never heard of and movies he never knew existed. If only he had more time to spend with the boy, maybe this wouldn't happen. He could learn about his interests, maybe get into some of the music. Maybe after the Grafting Bleed is contained, the two of them can go out for ice cream or something and catch up. Does Rand even like ice cream anymore? As he closes the door to Randall's room, he understands why almost no one else at Apex Door has a family. He wonders if his own desire to start one was selfish.

Back in the kitchen, he puts the breakfast he made for his son in a Tupperware container and sticks it in the fridge for later. *Is that the coffee sputtering its final drip?* He snags a carton of half-and-half while the fridge door is still open, pours a splash into his *Star Trek: Deep Space Nine* coffee mug. Then comes the squirt of honey from the bear-shaped bottle that always makes him smile. And then, finally, the coffee. He plunges the smallest silver spoon in there. Stirs, sniffs, sips.

He walks his coffee over to the master bathroom, looks at himself in the mirror while he sips. "You're Dr. Dale Foster," he says to himself. "You've got what it takes to be a great father. You're among the top scientific minds in the world, gosh darn-it. It's just going to take hard work and effort. No different than when you earned your third PhD." He sheds his terry cloth robe and showers, then gets dressed and ready for the day. He doesn't have to be into work until noon, so he spends the next few hours reading quietly on the sofa.

Thirty minutes before noon, he snatches his keys from the hook beside the door, pushes his feet into a pair of slippers, and scuttles out to the driveway to start his Ford Taurus, let it warm up and defrost. Hurries back inside.

While the car idles, he packs a quick lunch, throws a pre-tied necktie around his neck and tightens it, puts on a pair of white cotton athletic socks, followed by a pair of plain white sneakers with added arch support, bundles himself in his heaviest winter coat and hat, and slips his hands into a pair of high-performance ski gloves that he bought for comfort and insulation, not skiing. He's never skied a day in his life. Wouldn't know how.

The drive to Apex Door's field ops lab isn't far. Just enough to catch the morning DJ on Z93.4 get goofy about the weather with his cohort, a woman's voice identified as one Highway Helen.

"Hey, Helen, looks like Jack Frost is about to dump one on you over there in Grafting," the DJ says.

"Not until he buys me dinner first!" Helen replies, laughing a fake laugh.

"Hey, now! How about Bobby Dylan's 'Winterlude' to keep us warm this chilly afternoon?"

Foster chuckles as he pulls into the gravel lot outside the old Grafting door factory. He hurries into the cold warehouse and finds the hidden door beneath a collapsing staircase. Enters the thirteen-digit alphanumeric code and retinal scan. Heads ten floors down.

When the door opens, he's back in the lab, and oh, if there's one thing that could make this day better, it's the bustling lab before him, full of personnel he'd personally interviewed, selected, vetted, recruited, all busy at work. God bless them. Some gems in there, to be sure. He'd know, anyway. A gem himself, back in the day. Maybe the next Head of the Science Division is among those white lab coats, just like he was. He smiles, then saunters on.

But before he can make it past the first ring of consoles, his heart plummets. Cleeve is striding toward him, looking royally pissed off, but not pissed-off enough to break his perpetual cool. *Never* pissed-off enough to break his cool. And shit, Logan Rhett is on his heels. Cleeve is clutching a cigarette in one hand and a sheet of paper in the other.

Foster quickly yanks the ski gloves from each hand with his teeth and puts them in his coat pocket. Grabs the winter hat from his head and does the same. Cleeve demands decorum.

"Why weren't you responding to your pager alerts?" Cleeve says, now a foot from Foster's face. He smells like a chain restaurant smoking section.

"I—I didn't have my pager with me. I must have forgotten to take it home last night. I—"

Cleeve shoves the paper he's holding into Foster's chest, takes a hard drag from his cigarette. "Read it!" he orders. Foster waves away the cloud of smoke and coughs, then takes the paper and starts reading. He stops after the first few lines.

"This is an incident report."

"I know. Read it."

"But I thought Apex Door stopped using assessors for prediction. Isn't the purpose of my machine"—he motions around at the many consoles and computer screens—"to replace the work of assessors so we don't have to rely on them anymore? What have I been doing these last ten years of my life if that's no longer the case?"

"Don't worry, doctor, your life's work is still very much a part of Apex Door's future. But your machine is not perfected yet, not ready for global implementation."

"But I thought every assessor was terminated months ago."

"You thought wrong. While it's true that there aren't many active assessors left, a small number do still remain. The Board uses them sparingly, assigns them only to the highest profile cases, like this one. They spared Number Seven for this. Show's you how important the Grafting—"

"*Assessor 7?*" Foster blurts. He checks the incident report to confirm, sees Seven's identification on the document. His blood runs cold, and not just because of the weather. If you're an Apex Door employee, you've heard all about Assessor 7, the Apex Door bogeyman. No one knows if the stories about Seven are true, but they can tell them to you if you ask.

"Seven was assigned to Grafting following the disaster at One Horse."

"This report is from today," Foster says. "It's my understanding that assessors were—*are*—re-assigned after a field-ops lab like this one is established. Their investigation is only supposed to be preliminary."

"The Board decided to extend their stay after learning of our two anomalies. You see, doctor, your machine can spit out impressive graphs, but it can't think like an assessor can. Can't *feel* like an assessor can. Besides, assessors used to do a lot more than just preliminary investigations. Let's not forget their origin."

Instead of answering the question, Foster just grumbles as he holds up the sheet of paper like he's never seen one before, adjusts his glasses, pinches his face at the text. When he gets to the "Conclusion and Recommended Next Steps" section of the document, his eyes grow wide. He finishes reading and looks to Cleeve. "You don't actually believe this, do you? The spiders? There's obviously another explanation—"

"Don't waste you breath debating their findings with me, doctor. Tell them yourself."

Foster falls silent. Tries to speak, stops, tries again: "They're here? In the lab?"

Cleeve flicks his cigarette butt into a metal trash can. "Five minutes out. Now follow me. I have a lot to catch you up on, starting with the murders of Chet Springs and George Jankowski."

SEVEN

CLEEVE, FOSTER, AND Logan wait in the lab's glass-walled conference room for Seven and its handler to arrive. One of Logan's armed men guards the only door.

"I confess," Cleeve says to Foster and Logan from his seat across the glass conference table, "I'm not entirely sure what's about to unfold here. When I was regional manager, I saw my own director enter a room with an assessor for questioning, and after the assessor and its handler left, my director was… no longer fit to direct. Less than forty-eight hours later, I was tapped to fill the vacancy."

The conversation is interrupted when the elevator door across the lab opens and two figures step out. Foster watches as his dozens of loyal lab techs quickly part like the Red Sea so as to allow their visitors a wide berth. The armed guard at the conference room door shifts uneasily from foot to foot until the two visitors arrive and the one hands the guard his credentials. The guard barely glances at the identification before handing it back and allowing both guests inside. It's clear he's avoiding eye contact with them.

The first visitor to enter is a squat man in a charcoal tweed suit. His nose is a beak plucked from the face of a crow, and his small gray eyes rest inside deep, shadowy sockets. He has a sickly pallor, his mouth is turned down into a perpetual frown, and he has a prominent hump on his back from decades of hunching over a desk or hunching over his notepad out in the field. The hump is so severe, in fact, that he looks more like a turtle struggling to walk on its two hind legs than an adult human male. He carries a large, reinforced briefcase with a carbon fiber shell.

"The handler," Cleeve whispers. "Orson Caster."

The second visitor to enter is tall, *long*. Gangly limbs stuffed into a narrow black suit. It's hairless, and its jaundiced skin glistens with beads of stale sweat. Its eyes are hidden behind a pair of Roy-Orbison-style sunglasses, and a coiling wire leads from the earpiece in its…*ear?*…to something hidden beneath its white shirt. Assessor 7.

"And you probably know who that is," Cleeve whispers.

The air in the conference room suddenly reeks of sulfur. Orson Caster sits at the head of the table while Seven stands behind him.

Seven looks in Foster's direction, tilts its head as if curious. It rests a bony hand with long, gangly fingers on Caster's shoulder. It doesn't stop looking at Foster.

Caster looks up at Seven. "What's that? You don't say…" It appears as though he's talking to Seven, despite his partner's silence. Its thin, nearly lipless mouth remains sealed shut. Caster turns to look with Seven at Foster. "You're Dr. Dale Foster, the one who discovered the reverse bleed."

Foster's throat feels coated in sawdust. He clears it with a loud *"Ahem!"* and then simply says, "I am."

Caster listens to the silence for a moment, then says, "Seven would like to congratulate you on your groundbreaking discovery."

"Oh," squeaks Foster, choking on his own surprise. "Well, please tell Seven thank—"

"It makes him hate you slightly less for trying to replace him with a computer," Caster adds.

Foster's face drops.

Logan chuckles.

"And you must be Logan Rhett, Head of Security and Field Extraction," Caster says.

Logan nods.

"And Director Cleeve," Caster says. He and Cleeve share a nod of mutual respect. "I trust you all have read our latest incident report."

"About that," Cleeve says, "Dr. Foster here would like to dispute your conclusion. Says the findings don't warrant—"

Cleeve is silenced when Seven pounds an angry fist on the table, its face void of expression. Caster turns to his partner, listens, then turns to Foster. "Seven says there is nothing to discuss. He knows what he saw. But more importantly, he knows what he sensed."

"In fairness—"

"The anomalies are influencing the spiders to intentionally open up Bleeds, Mr. Cleeve. That is our conclusion, and our conclusions are final."

Foster shivers beneath the cold gaze of Seven's Roy Orbison glasses. He gathers the courage to speak. "We've known about the spiders for decades—killed them, captured them, studied them, even…*nurtured* them." He points through the glass wall of the conference room to Baby's tank at the center of the lab, to the giant monster inside. "I just find it hard to believe that no one—no scientist *or* assessor—has, until now, made the discovery you have claimed to make. That the spiders are the means to interdimensional travel."

Caster puts his left hand on the table. It looks plastic and rigid, as if stricken by rigor mortis. "You know what's interesting about this hand?" With his right hand, he plucks the left hand from its socket and holds it aloft, independent of his left arm. "It's fake. You know why? Because I lost that hand nearly a decade ago when one of those spiders bit it off."

Cleeve retrieves a Lucky Strike from his pocket and goes to light it.

"DO NOT SMOKE IN THE PRESENCE OF SEVEN!" Caster booms. He's pointing at Cleeve with his left hand, which is still being held by his right hand.

Cleeve holds up his hands like a bank teller in a stick-up, then quickly returns the cigarette and lighter to his pockets. Neither

Foster nor Logan have ever seen Cleeve cave so quickly to a demand, especially without rebuttal.

Caster returns to his story: "I never thought much of it—losing the hand—until I started getting these phantom feelings whenever Seven and I were assessing a new Bleed. Felt like the hand was still alive somewhere, just not here. But wherever it was, I had this feeling that it wasn't in the belly of the spider that took it."

Seven puts a hand on Caster's shoulder, and Caster pauses, listening to nothing. He returns his prosthetic hand to its socket. "I'm getting to that," he says. He then proceeds to describe the events from the latest incident report: how Seven overheard talk of the spiders and decided to use his "sight" to look back in time at the event; how in the vision, Seven witnessed the spiders eating the two anomalies inside the Jankowski house; how witnessing this event caused something inside Seven to click; and how according to Seven, the spiders weren't digesting what they ate, they were ingesting it into another dimension.

"But we know why the Bleeds occur," Cleeve says. "And it has nothing to do with the spiders. The spiders are simply a byproduct, something that leaks into our dimension during Bleed events."

Caster listens to Seven, then relays the message to Cleeve and company: "Seven believes the spiders come from a source dimension of all Bleeds, a sort of limbo that is the membrane separating realities—what many of you colloquially refer to as The Wound. Just like our own bodies are governed by gravity, theirs is governed by the dominant force of the world they come from. A force that opens doors to other realities."

"Is that where these anomalies come from?" Logan asks.

"We don't believe so. Judging by their apparent familiarity with Grafting, we think they come from a dimension strikingly similar to ours."

Foster pipes up: "So, what? The first two people to discover a way to open controlled Bleeds and use them to jump realities aren't physicists, they're serial killers?" He can't hide the dejection in his voice.

Caster shrugs. "We don't know for sure they're the first, but yes."

Foster sighs. "Wonderful."

"So, what now?" Logan asks. "My men are ready for orders."

"Extraction," says Caster.

Logan grins. "Extract the anomalies. Now you're speaking my language."

"Not the anomalies," says Caster. "You'll be extracting their next targets: Sheriff John-David Keller and two adolescent males—go by the names Barry and Lich. Luckily for you, all three targets are currently in the same location: the Ottawa County sheriff's station."

"We'll need surveillance on the sheriff's station while I put together a briefing for my men. I don't want them leaving the premises," says Logan.

"They won't," says Caster. "Our attorneys have already made sure of that."

"How do we know the anomalies will be targeting them?" Cleeve asks.

Seven puts a hand on Caster's shoulder, and Caster pauses to hear his silent partner out.

"Seven says the pattern is obvious, but he understands why you would be confused, since confusion is part of human nature."

Foster rolls his eyes and snorts. "The four victims are friends. You don't have to be a genius at pattern recognition to—"

"That's not the pattern Seven is referring to," Caster snaps. "He's referring to the Bleed pattern. The Bleeds the anomalies create are intentional, premeditated, which makes their Bleed signatures stronger, easier for Seven to sense. Seven describes each reality as having its own aroma. With the evidence we've gathered, Seven is certain that these two have been to many realities." He pauses to reflect on the gravity of what he's about to say next, then continues: "Including the Bleed source dimension."

Seven shifts his weight from one foot to the other, wrings his hands, then wipes them on his pants. It's the most he's moved all meeting.

"Impossible," says Cleeve. "They wouldn't survive two seconds in The Wound. No human would. Apex Door assessors have long assured us that—"

"You have the most acclaimed assessor in all of Apex Door history sitting right in front of you and telling you different," Caster says. "Are you saying you don't trust Seven's judgment?"

Cleeve immediately clams up, reaches for his bolo tie to mindlessly adjust its ornamental clip. "Uh, no, not at all. My apologies, Seven. It wasn't my intention to imply—"

"Our anomalies have been to the source dimension many times and for extended durations. It appears they're using it as a base of operations of sorts. A place where they can rest and get stronger—"

"Mutate," says Logan.

Caster nods. "And a place where they have seemingly tamed the spiders. Travel with them. Call on them to do their bidding."

"What will we do with the extracted targets?" Foster asks.

Seven puts a hand on Caster's shoulder, and Caster nods his agreement.

"All you need to know is that you are to extract the three targets from the Ottawa County sheriff's station so that the anomalies can be properly dealt with."

"Dealt with how?" says Logan.

"Thermonuclear annihilation," Caster says flatly.

Cleeve and Foster remain stoic, look to each other for a reaction. Logan, meanwhile, chuckles, but his smile quickly fades when Caster gives him a hard stare.

Caster hoists the large, reinforced briefcase from the floor besides his seat and drops it onto the glass conference table with a loud clunk. "The payload is en route via airlift from HQ. Specially designed by R&D," he states. He opens his briefcase, and from inside it retrieves various diagrams and photographs of a large warhead, places them on the table. "Detailed instructions for the handling and arming of the device are in this packet of materials. Please utilize discretion when briefing your staff."

Logan reacts first: "You gotta be fucking kidding—"

"Logan!" Cleeve barks. "Decorum! Please."

"The Board has voted unanimously to terminate our two anomalies with prejudice," Caster explains. "In their eyes, the risk of trying to capture them alive now greatly outweighs the reward. They know this will be worse than One Horse. A Bleed from the source dimension may never be contained. Time is running out."

"Orders, please," Cleeve says.

"The anomalies will Bleed into this world at"—Caster looks at Seven's hand on his shoulder, nods—"1800 hours, two hundred yards south of the Ottawa County sheriff's station. It is Seven's and my belief that the anomalies will then storm the station by force. Your first job is to let them."

Cleeve and Logan share an uneasy look.

"If the sheriff and two teenagers are eliminated before you can extract them, fine. But The Board strongly urges that you extract as many of them alive as you can. If you have to choose, the two adolescents take precedence."

"If you want them alive, then why use them as bait?" Logan asks.

"A necessary evil, Mr. Rhett. I know you of all people can understand."

"And what about the anomalies? We strap the nuke to their back and hope for the best?"

Caster chuckles. "No, no. Dr. Foster will be overseeing the nuclear device. It will be your job to tag the anomalies with this…" Caster reaches into the briefcase and removes a small tracking beacon. The beacon is roughly the same size and shape as a high-school kid's graphing calculator.

"Goodness," says Foster.

"Once the tracking device has been placed, you will severely injure the anomalies to the point that they are forced to jump back to the source dimension to recover. Once they do, this little beacon will signal from across the interdimensional web. When it does, Dr. Foster will drop the payload."

"Drop the payload?" Foster says. "Goodness. Drop it where?"

"Into the source dimension, doctor. Into The Wound."

"And how am I supposed to do that?"

Caster turns to look at Baby's tank through the glass conference room walls. "Babylon is always hungry, doctor. And according to your test logs, it appears the subject is indiscriminate about what you feed it."

Foster's eyes widen as he looks at Baby's tank through the office window, then back to Caster. "You want me to—"

"Feed her the payload."

Logan whistles. "Christ almighty, you fellas have lost your goddamn minds."

"Logan!" Cleeve scolds.

Seven places a hand on Caster's shoulder. Caster relays the message: "Seven would like to inform you that he doesn't have a mind to lose. Not in the way you're thinking, at least."

"Will you and Seven be assisting with the mission?" Cleeve asks.

"We will assist with the staging. Seven will provide Mr. Rhett with a blueprint for when, where, and how to best strike to the sheriff's station so as to achieve optimal results. And I will assist your scientists with prepping and arming the payload. Once staging is complete, Seven and I will be on our way. We will not stick around for mission execution. We have other more important matters to attend."

Logan grunts. "What's more important than this?"

Caster grins in a way that makes everyone in the room feel uncomfortable. "You'd be surprised, Mr. Rhett. Now, no more wasting time. We have a mission to prepare."

ARACHNOIDPHOBIA

AFTER EXITING THROUGH the back door of the sheriff's station, Art, Barry, Lich, Sammy, and Randall slow to a halt outside and double over. With hands on knees, they gasp at the cold air and fight back the emotions threatening to overwhelm them. The makings of a heavy snowstorm has begun, the snowflakes of which fall gently atop their slumped shoulders and heads.

"Dammit, Tam," Art laments. He rubs his arms to warm himself up, breathes a cloud of warm air into his hands.

"I don't get it," Barry says. "If those guys are me and Lich from another dimension, why do they want to kill us?"

"Ow!" Sammy blurts. She winces, then reaches back to rub the nape of her neck. "This headache… It keeps getting worse."

Randall eyes Sammy with concern. "When did you start getting a headache?"

"Sometime after we were arrested. It started hurting while I was in the back of the police car. Probably from stress or shock or something. I've never had a headache like this before."

"Where does it hurt the most?"

"Right here, actually. On the back of my neck."

Randall frowns. "Mind if I take a look?"

Randall approaches Sammy with caution. When he's close, she turns and removes her hand from her neck to show him.

"What the fuck is that?!" Barry blurts. He's pointing to the pulsing purple tumor on Sammy's brainstem.

"She's been infected," Randall says matter-of-factly. "Quick, I need something sharp."

"Wait, what?" Sammy stammers. "Why do you need something sharp? What is it?" She reaches for the back of her neck, but Randall swats her hand away.

"Don't," he says. "You'll make it worse."

"Make *what* worse?"

Art retrieves a Swiss Army knife from his pocket and hands it to Randall. "Here, but be careful with that. It was a gift."

Randall rolls his eyes and takes the knife, places the tip gently upon the tumor, tracks the agitated creature inside with his eyes. "Hey, Sammy," he says.

"Yeah?" she says, her voice trembling.

"Name three Nirvana songs."

"Are you fucking seri—"

"Good enough," he says and thrusts the knife into her neck. With a nasty squelch, it pops the tumor, spilling blood and purple goo down her neck.

"Shit! I missed," Randall says.

"Missed *what*?!" Sammy shouts.

"I don't think you wanna know," Barry says. He grimaces while watching a spider-like leg curl out from the wound.

At the sight of the spider-thing, Lich goes from pale to paler.

Randall pulls back the blade and readies it to stab again at the spider, but before he can make another attempt, the spider leaps from the wound in Sammy's neck and erratically toward Lich. At the sight of what just exited her neck, Sammy faints into Randall, who catches her beneath the arms and lays her gently down upon the snowy ground.

Lich, meanwhile, yelps and sprints gingerly toward a pair of rusty metal dumpsters.

"Run, Lich!" Barry shouts.

Right before the spider can pounce, Lich vaults himself into the safety of the smelly container, which causes the pursuing spider to slam full-speed into the heavy metal exterior. A loud *BONG!* rings out in the night.

The spider wobbles a bit on its ten legs, then quickly rights itself and skitters full-speed at Sammy, who is still laying unconscious on the ground. Randall turns and brandishes the Swiss Army knife in quivering hand. Art draws his pistol and pops off a few shots at the spider, but the thing is moving too fast for him and every bullet ends in a spray of snow around it. Closing in on Sammy, it leaps for her face and soars through the air, its needle-mouth open wide, teeth dripping with some kind of purple venom, hungry.

Sammy awakens just in time to see the angry mouth descending, but before its needle-teeth can inject themselves into her eyeballs, the creature is swatted away in an explosion of purple goop by the battleaxe body of a black Gibson Explorer.

Sammy looks up to see Barry standing over her, his head haloed by a nearby streetlight, purple goop all over his neck and face, holding his guitar by the neck and watching the spider soar across the heavens as if he were Babe Ruth watching his called-shot clear the center field bleachers.

The spider flies damn near a country mile through the air and tumbles a half-dozen times across the accumulating snow upon the pavement before falling dead, where it vanishes into a purple vapor.

When Sammy looks back at Barry, she feels like she's seeing him for the first time. She gently brushes a strand of hair behind her ear.

"Touchdown!" Barry shouts.

For a brief moment, he and Sammy lock eyes, and a warmth floods his chest. When she doesn't immediately break eye contact like she usually does, his cheeks flush.

Blind to the tender moment, Lich pops his head out of the dumpster like some strung-out Whac-A-Mole that's just hit rock bottom and blurts: "Is it safe to come out now?"

Barry shakes the rose-colored tint from his eyes. "Yeah, dude. It's safe."

But as Lich climbs awkwardly out of the dumpster, a loud bang comes from metal door to the sheriff's station behind them.

"What was that?" Barry asks, turning to see.

"I don't know," says Art, "but I think it's past time we get out of here."

Another bang.

Then another.

More bangs in quick succession, each one now leaving a hefty dent in the heavy metal door where the mass behind the noise had struck. The last bang, the loudest of them all, hits with such force that it buckles the door at its hinges.

"Run!" says Randall.

But it's too late for that. The door to the sheriff's station has already been breached by the weight and determination from a massive cluster of ten-legged, needle-teethed, bloodthirsty spidery creatures, some as big as watermelons, all charging at the five hapless humans with deadly intent.

Art immediately starts firing on the biggest of the bunch, causing it to explode like a rotten fruit and dissolve into purple vapor. The smell that wafts from the kill is rancid.

Barry is able to swat a few of the smaller ones away with his guitar, but he's soon overwhelmed. So is Lich.

The spiders take no interest in Randall, Sammy, or Art, the three of whom watch in horror as Barry and Lich are quickly engulfed by the horde of arachnid nightmares and consumed in a cloud of dark purple vapor. The sounds of clattering spider legs and wet mastication are nearly deafening. Neither boy cries out for help because they can't. The spiders are in their throats.

Soon, nothing remains of the two best friends or the spiders that devoured them, save for two steaming puddles of glowing purple goo, bubbling on the pockmarked pavement like boiling Jell-O. Even Barry's black Gibson Explorer is no more.

Sammy wants to scream, wants to fall to her knees and weep, but before she can, the sheriff's station is rocked by an explosion so heavy, it sends her stumbling backward in surprise. Somewhere else a car alarm goes off as a plume of fiery debris shoots skyward into the night.

EXTRACTION

THE APEX DOOR armored transport rumbles down the neglected back roads of Grafting with the power of an Abrams tank and the fury of a charging bison. Its windowless, bullet-proof body shrugs of the falling snow, while its large, heavy tires make mincemeat of every empty, snow-dusted can of Molson, an iced-over Happy Meal box, every inconvenient piece of trash that locals discarded from a car window on a random Tuesday night, thinking no one would notice or care.

Inside the reinforced vehicle, Logan's eight-man unit sits stone-faced across from one another on two benches that run lengthwise down the narrow bay. They dip tobacco, check weapons, tighten straps. You know, soldier things. The space is cramped and their knees are constantly touching, neither of which is a suitable environment for these kind of men, but soon they will be loosed upon the world, no holds barred, and all will be right with them again. The things they've seen, man. The lives they've taken. Would make your head spin. They haven't seen action since taking Babylon in One Horse, and they crave more. Can't wait for it. Right now, in the small, sweaty space of this transport, their chests heave for more oxygen like caged dogs ready for a fight.

Up front in the transport's cab, Cleeve is seated in the passenger seat, a cigarette wilting to ash between a lopsided grin. Logan's ears prick as the director raises an AN/PRC-6 walkie-talkie and presses it against his lips. "All set, doctor?" he asks.

After a silence, Foster's voice crackles in the speaker. "The payload is being processed. Will be standing by for the order. Over."

Cleeve notices Logan watching him, so he turns to stare back at the man, force him to confront his own reflection in Cleeve's aviators. "Understood. Over."

"Night vision," Logan says to his men, and every mercenary under his command flips a pair of night-vision goggles down over their eyes.

Suddenly, a sharp turn slams half the occupants against one side of the cabin, leans the other half forward against their straps. A chorus of groans from the soldiers is followed by another sharp turn, the opposite direction this time, and everyone rocks toward the front when the vehicle screeches to a halt. Straps unlatch as the two men closest to the rear fling the double doors open, and four members of the eight-member crew exit the vehicle faster than Cleeve can put out his cigarette. Cleeve zips up a tactical jacket for warmth and exits the vehicle out the passenger-side door to join the four soldiers waiting in the gusting snowstorm.

Cleeve bites a fresh Lucky Strike. "Godspeed you bloodthirsty little bastards," he says, and reaches for his gold Zippo.

The vehicle's rear doors are then slammed shut and the remaining three extraction team members along with Logan are whisked around to the front of the sheriff's station. Logan's team—team Alpha—is going in through the front. The team that already exited—team Bravo, led by ex-IRA soldier O'Connor—will breach using explosives on the exterior wall closer to where the anomalies were detected, once Logan gives them the word.

"Those little shits better be in there," Logan says under his breath, consulting the blueprint laid out for them by Seven.

The transport vehicle screeches to another halt and team Alpha jumps out. Some Desert Storm vet named Kimball hurries through the biting winds, across snow-covered cement to the front door of the sheriff's station and kneels down to check a handheld motion-sensing device that had been clipped to his gear. "Lobby is clear," he says.

Logan raises his CAR-15 assault rifle and stares down the sights at whatever monsters might be waiting beyond that tempered glass door and the two "Vote for Keller" signs plastered on it. He smiles at the thought.

"Let's eat," he says.

He leads his men into the station and across a dimly lit lobby that smells like a slaughterhouse. Veins of glowing purple goo cover the walls, pulsing neon-green in Logan's night-vision. According to Kimball, the goo's heat signature is off the charts.

"Fresh out of the fryer," Logan says. He spies a trail of blood coming from the room labeled *Dispatch* and orders one of his men to check it out. While he waits, he speaks to the radio in his helmet: "Bravo, this is Alpha. What's your status? Over."

A crackle of static, then the brogue-heavy voice of O'Connor: "Charges are almost set. Will let you know when we're ready to breach. Over."

The soldier tasked with checking Dispatch returns and delivers grave news to Logan. The dispatcher is dead. Logan feels for the victim, but it's not his job to save lives. He's here to hunt. It's what Apex Door hired him to do when they first approached him on that last flight out of Saigon.

Kimball approaches next with the handheld motion-sensing device. "I've got two heat signatures coming from the opposite end of the station. Body temps of 120 degrees Fahrenheit."

"Sounds like our anomalies," says Logan.

"Ah, fuck. I've got a third signature now. It's human. And it's heading in the direction of the anomalies."

"Better get a move on then. Let's go."

As Logan and his men move stealthily through the halls like SEAL Team Six on steroids, another burst of static crackles in Logan's helmet radio, then: "Alpha, this is Bravo. Charges are set. Ready on your mark. Over."

"We're on our way now," Logan replies as he continues to proceed with careful haste through the bloody, pulsating halls. "You have a read on the two hostiles?"

"Affirmative."

"Good. Keep an eye on that readout. There's a civilian non-combatant heading your way, and it might be one of our extraction targets. Try not to kill them, okay?"

"We'll do our best," O'Connor says mock-cheerfully.

A few more hurried paces forward and Logan hears the crack of a large-caliber gunshot from the direction Alpha team is headed.

A crackle of static. "Alpha, this is Bravo. We've got shots fired. Was that you?"

Another gunshot cracks through the dark hallways. And then another. Logan breaks into a jog.

O'Connor's voice crackles in Logan's helmet: "Alpha team, we need orders. Should we breach?"

"The anomalies are just around this corner," Kimball says, looking down at the motion-sensing device as he runs.

"Bravo team, this is Alpha," Logan says. "You're clear to breach. Over."

"Alpha, this is Bravo. Breaching now. Sláinte."

WHEN O'CONNOR SQUEEZES the trigger on the detonator and ignites the C-4 explosives glued to the exterior cinder block wall of the sheriff's station, a deafening boom rocks the building to its foundation and sends a dense cloud of super-heated dust and debris mushrooming into the hallway where the two anomalies are located. Keller's motion signal goes dead after his unconscious body is thrown by the blast and quickly buried beneath a small pile of rubble.

"Alrighty, boys! Switch yer night vision to thermal and light the fuckers up!" O'Connor shouts to his team. His brogue is thicker than a brick.

Before the smoke can clear, rifle fire erupts from Bravo team's CAR-15 assault rifles, muzzle flashes lighting up the night like the Fourth of July as they push forward into the building. The soldiers unload 30-round box magazines at 810 meters-per-second into the red-hot, glowing masses that are the heat signatures for Wolf-Pig and Lanky. They can't see it yet, but they're painting the opposite wall with purple guts and viscera.

After Bravo team pauses their fire to reload, a chainsaw roars to life, and a wild boar squeals its fury.

Then suddenly from out of the darkness, a ten-legged spider leaps at the face of a former Russian Spetsnaz officer. The man-of-war easily pries the spider away with the butt of his rifle, but when he turns to fire his reloaded weapon at the sounds of chaos, the last thing he sees is the revving blade of a chainsaw slam into his forehead to split his face in half. Quickly following the Russian's death, an AWOL member of the French GIGN is beheaded with one swing of a sword, and a dishonorably discharged Delta Force officer with time in Grenada, Panama, and Kuwait, is thrown to the ground by Lanky. From a supine position, the downed mercenary fires a dozen bullets into Wolf-Pig's center mass, but to no effect. He cries out to his maker as Wolf-Pig stomps a Converse-size-30 hole in his chest, grinds the heart and aorta to a sticky paste.

Lanky raises its roaring chainsaw over O'Connor, ready to bring it down on the man's skull. But before it can, it's struck down by the relentless spitfire from an M134 minigun, every round punching haymakers into the hell spawn. The tumors on Lanky's neck and back explode in majestic sprays of purple goop and amputated spider limbs. The parasitic arachnoids spared the spray of bullets burst from their lee-side tumors and scatter into the shadows.

O'Connor glances down the hall to see Logan wielding the bulky weapon like the goddamn Terminator. Logan shifts his aim to mow down the now-charging wolf-pig with prejudice. More spiders explode from their fleshy fluid sacs, some alive, some dead. The surviving creatures flee in their repulsive twitching skitter.

With Lanky and Wolf-Pig now laying in steaming piles of their own disemboweled organs, Logan releases the M134's trigger so that the whirring rotor stops feeding the belt of 7.62

mm bullets into the six rotating barrels. He mumbles one word into his helmet radio: "Clear."

Waiting patiently in the falling snow, Cleeve sticks out a pink tongue, catches a snowflake, smiles.

"Reckon ya've killed the bastards," O'Connor says.

"They're not dead," says Cleeve. "Stick to the plan." He nudges his aviators up the bridge of his nose and steps through the demolished cinder block wall and into the station, where the cold of the winter storm gives way to the stifling heat of battle.

Cleeve unzips his jacket pocket and from it retrieves the handheld homing beacon that Caster and Seven provided—the one that looks like a school supply but somehow syncs across dimensions with a portable nuclear weapon that fits neatly inside a briefcase. He kneels down besides the snoring body of the wolf-pig and stuffs the beacon into one of the foul-smelling wounds as quickly as he can without gagging. Once he's done so, he stands to his feet and wipes his hand off on his pants.

"Back up," Cleeve tells his men. "They're gonna need a little room." The men do as he says, and Cleeve steps back a number of paces to match them. Calmly, he draws a nickel plated Colt government model, with wooden handle and "M1911A1 US Army" engraved on the stock. He aims the handgun's polished barrel at the wolf-pig's head and fires a single round directly into one of the smelly beast's closed eyelids, popping the squishy yellow eyeball beneath.

The wolf-pig squeals awake. Enraged, it struggles hastily to its feet, where it has trouble standing. It squeals again, louder this time, as if calling to something far away. Blood and spit spray from its maw. Vitreous jelly leaks from its blinded eye. It points to Cleeve. "Congratulations, asshole. You just made the shit list." It levels its gore-slicked broadsword at Logan down the hall. "You, too, dickwad! We'll be seeing you again real soon."

O'Connor raises his rifle to fire on the wolf-pig, but Cleeve puts a hand on the barrel and pushes the gun back down.

"Easy now, soldier," Cleeve says.

That's when Alpha and Bravo teams notice the horde of surviving spiders emerge from the shadows. The creatures crawl from every hidden crevice, out from beneath ruined desks, swarming around the soldiers' ankles. No part of the floor is visible beneath their millions of clattering, talon-tipped legs. In layers, the myriad organisms cover the wolf-pig and lanky anomalies like sickly black waves, piling thicker and thicker over themselves.

"Sweet Jesus, Mary, and Joseph." O'Connor draws the sign of the cross over his chest.

And it's here, when Daniel Cleeve knows what he must do. What Caster has told him that The Board requires he do. They want an eyewitness account of the process taking place beneath that blanket of spiders. From the one pair of eyes unlike any other in all of Apex Door: Cleeve's.

When Logan glances at the director and sees Cleeve removing his sunglasses for the first time in ages, he goes rigid. He wants to stop Cleeve, urge him to think hard about this, remind him of all the risks involved.

Cleeve is now staring down at the two spider-infested anomalies with his naked violet eyes. The cloudy irises glow from within their foggy sclera like poorly rendered simu-lacra, double-exposed and motion-blurred. He suddenly appears weak, starts showing signs of seizure. He tries to raise his aviator sunglasses back to his face, but is failing.

Logan rushes over, snatches the sunglasses from Cleeve's feeble grasp, and gently places them over Cleeve's eyes once more.

Cleeve's knees give out, and he falls against Logan, who catches and steadies the man. "Mission objective complete," Cleeve says with a frail smile. "I don't know if The Board will believe what I've just seen, though." He gestures with his chin back to the anomalies, but nothing remains of them or the spiders other than a dissipating purple gas over two bubbling puddles of ooze. "Hand me my walkie," Cleeve says. Logan holds the receiver against Cleeve's mouth and presses the talk button. "Ball's in your court now, Foster. Stand by for orders."

Foster's voice crackles in the walkie: "What about the kids? Randall? Have they been located?"

Logan allows Cleeve to stand on his own weight, hands him the walkie. Reaching for another cigarette, Cleeve says into the walkie, "I told you not to get too attached, doctor." He walks to the pile of rubble where Keller is buried and motions for O'Connor to help with removing the debris from the sheriff's body.

"Wait a second," the voice of Foster says. It sounds urgent. "Something's happening. Every indicator is spiking."

The earth starts to rumble beneath Cleeve's feet. He looks to Logan and down the hall to the rest of Alpha team. "Head back!" he shouts to them. "To the front entrance. I'll meet you at the rendezvous point."

Logan and his team hesitate, eyes darting in confusion from behind their night vision goggles.

But when a steaming fissure splits the ground between them and Cleeve, widens to the size of small chasm, they understand. The smell of sulfur is so overpowering, it causes Kimball to gag. The walls of the sheriff's station start to buckle, and sections of the roof begin to cave in. The pit of the jagged fissure glows ultraviolet.

"You heard the director," Logan says. "Back to the front exit." He drops the dead weight of the M134 and retrieves the CAR-15 from his shoulder.

"Oh, no," crackles the voice of Foster. "This is the big one."

THE GROUND CONTINUES to quake as Bravo team jogs with purpose back through the station toward the front exit. More fissures crack open at their feet, plaster and insulation rains down upon them and water bursts from damaged pipes. The building will not survive, and Logan figures he's survived too much shit in his life to end up buried beneath the collapse.

His team turns the corner near dispatch and heads toward the lobby, sees open air on the other side of the front doors, some thirty yards away.

But before they make it halfway there, the glowing veins on the wall crack open, and a fissure splits the floor like lightning.

From out of the walls and floor, ghoulish arms reach. They look like the flayed arms of a corpse, bloody flesh hanging ragged from the bones. They claw wildly at the air.

Logan and his men immediately open fire, light the arms up in sprays of purple mist. But whenever one arm goes down, another reaches through the cracks. And then another. And another. Soon there are more limbs than Bravo team can train their rifles at, and they watch in horror as the dozens of skeletal hands push against the walls and floor for leverage and extract themselves from their hellish prisons as if hoisting themselves from a pit. Once free, their flayed bodies flop wet and bloody onto the ground like beached seals borne from a sea of purple ooze. And when they finally stand like shaky newborn foals, all limbs and joints, the goop drips from them in long, viscous tendrils like some kind of cursed embryonic fluid. Their faces are featureless, like bloody, unmolded clay.

No one on Bravo team has seen this kind of thing before. Not even Logan. And suddenly, decades of cumulative experience and training are lost in the presence of whatever these abominations are standing before them.

"Hold your fire," Logan says. He needs to reassess. Improvise. This was not in the debriefing. He watches as one of the creatures slowly approaches him. With each practiced step, the unmolded clay on the thing's face forms itself into recognizable features. Sickly gray skin wraps in tendrils around swelling flesh, and the pigmentation darkens as those reaching tendrils knit themselves into a face. Logan stares, dumbfounded, at a naked replication himself. "What are you?" he whispers.

The doppelganger's voice is a harsh wind over gravel. "You," it says, then opens its mouth, baring teeth as it lunges toward Logan's throat.

But before the teeth reach their target, Logan watches the copy of his head explode in a spray of brain matter and skull fragments, coating his night vision and spraying into his mouth. He spits and turns to see that the bullet had been fired by Kimball—against a direct order. But when Logan nods his gratitude, thankful for the soldier's flagrant disobedience in the moment, the rest of Bravo team takes the gesture as the green light to engage. The four soldiers open fire, and the fight descends into chaos.

THE WOUND

AFTER TUMBLING FOREVER through an endless black abyss, a glowing point of light suddenly appears in the ill-defined distance, glorious and…*irradiated?*

As it gets closer, things get hot. Really hot. *Too fucking hot.*

And is Barry…*falling?*

Suddenly, the doughy body of Barry Aguilar Junior pierces a giant cloud of scalding-hot steam and slams into an unforgiving planetary surface with the force of a two-hundred-pound meteor strike, and the impact sends a mushroom cloud of ash and dust billowing into the air like some demented Wile E. Coyote cartoon. Once the dust settles, a small crater remains, and at the epicenter of the crater is Barry, completely unharmed, his skin, hair, and clothing dripping with a smelly purple goop. Before Barry can get his bearings, Lich hops into Barry's crater and helps his friend to his feet. Once the world stops spinning, Barry looks around to see a plane of craggy, igneous rock cut through by rivers of flowing magma. Surface cracks vent plumes of sulfurous gas into an atmosphere already thick with it, while bright flashes of lightning illuminate a blanket of black clouds that move slowly across a crimson sky the consistency of coagulated blood.

"Where are we?" Barry asks, but he's afraid he already knows the answer.

"I think we're in Hell, dude," Lich says. He wrinkles his nose to fight back the scent of rotten eggs.

"No way," Barry says, wiping the purple goop from his arms and chest. "Me going to Hell, I can understand. But you? You're destined for Valhalla, dude. This can't be Hell. Not as long as you're here."

"I don't know. I ran from that spider pretty quick," Lich says. He also wipes the goop from his arms and chest.

Barry shrugs. "Eh. I'm sure even the bravest Viking warriors have moments of weakness now and then." He feels his guitar at his back, slings it around for a quick inspection. The axe is unscathed.

"You were pretty awesome, though," Lich says.

The two fist bump.

"Did we just get eaten by a fuckload of spider-things?" Barry says, looking out over the scorched landscape. "Because it sure doesn't feel like it. Some stings here and there, but honestly, I thought something like that would hurt way more."

"I thought it hurt a lot," says Lich.

Barry scans the flaming horizon. "So, what do we do now?"

"Don't know, dude. Your guess is as good as mine."

"Well, what about all those bootlegged UFO documentaries you have on VHS? What do they say about traversing other dimensions? Any tips?"

"Man, I wish. But aliens are extraterrestrial, not extradimensional. So unless this is, like, Mars or something, I got nothing"

"Don't think this is Mars, dude."

"Know what I really wish?"

"What."

"That we had Sammy's camcorder. Think about the footage we could bring back, dude. We'd be celebrities in the paranormal scene."

"Not interested, compadre. I don't want the CIA watching me every time I leave the house. How will I ever take a morning shit at Roscoe's again? I won't be able to focus knowing some pervy government dude might be listening through the walls. You know how I am. I already get stage fright whenever

I hear Suzanna messing around outside the bathroom door. That's not the life for me, partner. Not for me."

"True. I hadn't thought of that."

Barry spits at the ground and watches it steam. "Well, might as well see what in the fuck we're dealing with. No better place to walk than somewhere else, right?" he says. "There's gotta be some way back."

Lich isn't sure he believes that, but he shrugs an agreeable shrug anyway. Beats just standing around.

"If you see those ten-legged little shits, go easy on them, okay?" Barry says. "We might need them."

A light bulb goes on in Lich's mind. The same one that must have lit up Barry's. "The spiders. Yeah. Maybe we can use them to get home. Einstein-level thinking, dude."

"Elementary, my dude Watson. Now we just gotta find out where they're hiding."

They walk for what feels like hours. Time moves differently here. They can sense as much. For all they know, only a couple minutes have passed where they come from. What they *do* know is that they're hot as fuck, tired as hell, and thirsty as shit. More thirsty than they've ever been before. But an ice-cold Sunny D right now, all fresh and sweaty from the freezers at Rotten Roscoe's. Can you imagine?

After summiting a particularly treacherous ridge, they pause to gape at what lies before them on the other side.

"Is that…a battleship?" Barry asks.

"Looks like one," says Lich.

"What's it doing here?"

"Don't know."

"What's that building in front of it?"

"Don't know."

"Think the spiders live there?"

"Maybe."

"Only one way to find out."

Barry leads the way as the two friends descend the other side of the ridge and trudge across a barren valley of brimstone until they reach the edge of a deep canyon that circles the building and battleship like a moat. A rickety old rope bridge is all that connects one side of the canyon to the other. A number of wooden planks are damaged or missing.

"Just like *Temple of Doom*," Barry says. He can't help but smile. "Rad."

Lich looks like he's gonna be sick.

Barry crosses first, with Lich hesitantly following. What might as well be a mile below them, a river of molten lava flows, burping giant clouds of sulfur gas that look so tiny from way up here. But even from this distance, they can see them, know they're big. Barry's eyes bulge when he catches sight of some slithering leviathan down there in the lava, its serpentine back breaching the flowing fire lazily.

Once across the bridge, they are faced with a tall, chain link fence topped with coils of rusted razor wire that also runs the perimeter of the building and ship. An empty guard booth sits outside the fence, next to a sliding metal gate and a sign that warns against trespassing. Barry shoves open the guard booth door and searches an old control panel for a button that opens the gate. Instead of trying to deduce anything, he quickly tries all the buttons until he's successful. The gate lurches unlocked with a clank and squeals slowly open with the grinding clatter of gears in need of lubrication. When it rattles fully open in a cloud of ash and dust, the boys cough and wave away the foul air. Beyond the gate is an abandoned courtyard.

With a somber look between them, they navigate the perilous terrain until they come to the building's crumbling facade, the entrance reduced to a dilapidated wall of crumbling brickwork and torched lumber. They step over the wall onto a floor of cracked stone tile. The remaining walls of what appears to have once been a lobby reach up to open sky where clearly there was once a ceiling. The hull of the battleship can be seen clearly from this distance, rising up from beyond the open-air structure.

Lich looks up at the vessel with reverence. "That's a United States Navy Cannon-class destroyer escort from the 1940s. Dude, I know this ship. It's the *USS Eldridge*."

"Wrong, dude," Barry says. He points to the name emblazoned on the hull. "Says *USS Eldritch*; -itch not -ridge."

"But I could swear…" Lich looks away, but his eyes stop on something as they go: the edges of a symbol in the floor, peeking out from beneath a pile of collapsed ceiling. He pushes enough of the debris away to uncover the rest of the image: an upside-down pyramid held aloft by a spread of eagle's wings. Circling the image are the words: *Wall Abyss.*

"What the hell is an 'abyss wall?'" Barry asks, reading the words in the wrong order.

Lich shrugs. "Looks like some CIA shit to me."

The two make their way toward what was clearly once a reception desk now covered in papers aged and brittle papyrus. They look ready to crumble at first touch, and they do. Buried beneath them, however, are a few papers that have been protected to some degree but are still mostly scraps. Only one page contains legible type: the closing lines of what was once a full-page letter. The type reads:

```
Find solace in your fight knowing
that Stargaze has not failed. It's
simply re-affixed. You're good men.
There can be no apex as long as
there is abyss. I'll see you on the
other side.

                          —D. Hatchet
```

Barry finds the metal knob of a drawer beneath the desktop and throws it open in a cloud of dust. As he reaches in, several ten-legged spiders skitter out. He jumps back in fright.

"Oh fuck!" he shouts. "We need those!"

Lich is in a panic. He wants to make up for running from the spider outside the sheriff's station, but before he can gather any kind of useful courage, the spiders have fled the scene.

Barry starts to sprint after them, but an awfully familiar sound arrests him entirely. It's the sound of a van engine trying its best to turn over.

Before Barry can turn around to face what he already knows is there, a pair of square headlights pierce the smoke and ash, blinding him and Lich. The struggling engine roars to life and revs, tires peel out. Then from the courtyard, a copper, rust-bitten van blasts through the crumbling half-wall and accelerates across the bizarre lobby in the direction of Barry and Lich.

The boys jump aside as the van crashes through the reception desk in a spray of splinters and paper, and screeches to a smoking halt before slamming into the far wall. A scorched graphic is painted on the van's broadside: three wolves, howling at a bubble-window moon. The vehicle rumbles with a downshift and idles in park as two creatures emerge from the cab. It's them. And they have been renewed by the dark power of this world. Healed. More powerful. And more monstrous, further possessed by their animal moiety.

Wolf-Pig gazes with glowing eyes beneath the unmoving folds of a deep brow covered in synthetic fur singed by Hell's flame. Spearhead ears aim right at Barry. White tusks curl up around a glistening pig's snout that sniffs wetly for its prey. It wields Bludzorg with hairy werewolf hands.

Lanky unfolds from the passenger side, stretching immediately to a height twice the size of the van. A single yellow eye blinks as a wide grin cuts across its face, and a slimy tongue uncoils, hangs from a mouthful of needle teeth that drip with blood and saliva. It rips the starter cord on a bloodstained chainsaw and raises the roaring machine above its head.

Lich's voice is a quivering whisper. "What did we do to ourselves," he says of their monstrous counterparts.

Barry stares at Wolf-Pig. He thinks of Chet's fist striking his eye. Of his stolen backpack. He thinks of being shoved to the ground, straddled by Chet while Patrick and Corbin pin his wrists to the grass. He thinks of the snide remarks, the comments, the shouldered shoves in passing that sent him smashing into lockers. The humiliation. And how this wolf-pig version of himself put an end to all that, finally got revenge for the both of them, and what the act clearly required. To embrace the dark side so completely that the first victims were not Barry's bullies, but Barry and his best friend. Barry feels utter repulsion as he watches this cursed reflection of his worst self closing in slowly.

Barry looks to Lich as he unshoulders his Gibson Explorer. He remembers the things Chet and Patrick and Corbin and George would do to Lich in the locker room, in the showers. What they would make him do. What they would make him see. Barry remembers all the times he found his best friend beat up, but how in those moments, Lich would never think about himself, just ask in a daze to be taken home since he was late watching the twins, and they couldn't be left alone.

Barry turns the guitar around and grips it with two hands at the first fret, rests the body of the guitar against his shoulder like a battle axe. "Whatever those things are," he says through gritted teeth. "They ain't us. Never will be."

Lich lets out a heavy sigh of relief. "I thought so," he said. He then removes the pair of stainless steel drumsticks from his back pocket and holds them in each hand like daggers—not much for a weapon, but in his hands they feel electric, pulsing with energy that courses through him. "Are we about to do what I think we're about to do?"

"These bitches ain't nothing but a couple of posers. Let's fuck 'em up."

With that, Barry raises his battle axe guitar and shouts a war cry. Lich raises his drumsticks and shrieks a falsetto battle cry of his own. Together, they sprint toward their foes faster than either of them thought the other capable.

Wolf-Pig smiles and raises Bludzorg. Lanky cackles and revs its chainsaw.

LEARNING TO LOVE
THE BOMB, PART ONE

DR. FOSTER STANDS before the main monitor above the master console inside the Apex Door field lab and leans heavily on Meghan's chair, a walkie-talkie in one hand. Meghan sits in the chair and watches the monitor with him.

The monitor is segmented into eight smaller screens arranged to provide a live look-in on the field extraction in progress, with each screen being a separate extraction member's perspective, streamed via the pinhole cameras embedded in each soldier's helmet. Each live feed has a name attached, so Foster knows which screen belongs to which soldier's perspective. Three of the screens are already motionless. Two are on their sides and filming a few inches from the ground, one of which films the headless body to which it was once attached. Another camera films the ceiling. Five screens are still active. O'Connor's screen shows him helping Cleeve attend to the injured town sheriff, while the other four strobe with bursts of rifle fire. One of those flaring screens belongs to Logan.

"Oh my God!" Meghan gasps. "You think he's okay?"

"Who?"

"Screen number two: Kimball." She points to the blood-soaked screen, where only moments ago a clawed hand had pulled away from the screen clutching what looked to be a still-beating heart. Foster watches that same hand smash the heart straight into Kimball's face, causing the feed to go blurry and the camera to fall to the floor.

"No, Meghan, I don't think Kimball is okay."

The lab shutters with the echo of metal clanging against metal, and Foster looks up at the catwalk above Babylon's tank and the two lab techs guiding a wheeled winch. They are looking back at Foster in hopes their boss somehow didn't hear that.

"What's going on up there?" Foster shouts at them. "The payload needs to be in position. Get a move on, for goodness sake! We're running out of time!"

One of the techs regards the winch and the nuke suspended from its chain. The warhead is painted to resemble the head of a cartoon shark showing off a toothy grin. It doesn't appear like it's about to explode, so the two techs continue to guide the winch and bomb toward the feeding tube above Babylon's tank.

"Shit!" Meghan blurts, and Dale glances at the monitor just in time to see another feed go dead, this time ending in static.

"What happened?" he asks.

"We lost another one. Espinoza. Looked painful." She sighs.

Foster shakes his head. He fears the final order is coming soon. He looks back up at the techs who have finally arrived at Babylon's feeding tube without blowing all of Grafting off the map.

One of the three remaining video feeds, a soldier named Ito, turns to see what looks like a copy of Kimball rise from the dead, his arm ending in a fleshy shield that absorbs every bullet fired by Ito in sprays of purple goo.

Foster's eyes flick to Kimball's feed, which continues to be a blood-soaked shot of Logan's boots. The Kimball fighting Ito is another doppelganger, like Logan before.

"Oh, God bless it, they've got doppelgangers at their location now? This is going to be *worse* than One Horse."

Ito's feed pans down toward his rifle to watch as he ejects an empty magazine and quickly reloads, but when it pans back up, the shield has morphed into a spearhead. Ito screams, and

Foster's eyes flick to Logan's feed, where he watches the arm-spear plunge through Ito's mouth and out the other side.

"Get out of there, Logan!" Foster says into his walkie.

To his relief, he watches Logan's feed turn from the fight and move quickly toward the exit. After clearing the doors and stomping through a driving snow, the feed turns to watch a grenade explode and drop two pursuing ghouls in their tracks, before turning and moving onward to the rendezvous point.

"Where the heck did those kids come from?" Meghan says.

"Kids?" Foster looks to O'Connor's feed. "A sheriff's deputy and two teenagers are standing outside the detonated hole in the sheriff's station and slowly approaching. One of the teens is a girl who Foster doesn't recognize. The other is Randall.

DEATH OF A SMALL TOWN SHERIFF*

"SHERIFF!" A VOICE calls. "Sheriff, are you okay?"

Keller, who is being helped to his feet by two men he doesn't recognize—some cowboy and a soldier—looks up to see Art, Sammy, and Randall standing outside the giant hole in the sheriff's station—the same hole detonated by the C-4 that had knocked Keller unconscious. Keller is bleeding from his forehead.

"Art! You're alive!"

"T'aint the time for tearful reunions," the soldier quips. He has a thick Irish accent.

He's right, of course. The entire station is crumbling around them. Little fissures in the earth's crust are opening everywhere and spewing forth that same purple liquid Keller discovered at multiple crime scenes. Outside the station, it appears as though all of Grafting is suffering another massive quake.

"Who are you?" Keller asks.

"Yer knight in shinin' armor," O'Connor says.

"What about you?" Keller asks the cowboy.

"Director Cleeve," Cleeve says. "We spoke on the phone earlier. Pleasure to meet you."

Keller narrows his eyes to better study Cleeve's face: the angular features, the mustache, the aviator sunglasses at night. "Have we met?"

"I guess I just have one of those faces," Cleeve lies. He turns to Art. "Wait right there. We'll bring him to you."

At O'Connor's instruction, Keller wraps his arms around his and Cleeve's shoulders. The two men quickly usher him to the makeshift exit, where Art, Sammy, and Randall wait.

"Where are Barry and Lich?" Keller asks on approach.

Art just shakes his head somberly.

"They're dead?" Cleeve asks. Keller must be kept alive if true. The Board will be furious if all three targets are eliminated.

"Yeah," Art says.

"No," Randall says, "they're not."

Cleeve's eyes narrow in recognition. "Experiment 113. What the hell are you doing here?"

"I told you, Mr. Cleeve, like a million times, my name's Randall. And just like I told Deputy Art already, Barry and Lich aren't dead. They're just gone."

"Gone? Where?"

"Not here, Mr. Cleeve."

"What is that supposed to mean?"

"You of all people should know."

"How?"

"Spiders."

"You saw it happen?"

Randall nods.

"Where?"

"Out back behind the station, by the dumpsters. It's where we just came from."

Cleeve turns to O'Connor. "Change of plan. You go with the sheriff and his friends here, meet up with Logan at the rendezvous point. I have other matters to oversee."

That's when Sammy screams, points.

Cleeve and O'Connor turn to see skinless, faceless ghouls tearing their way through the fissures in the floors and walls. They release Keller and wheel around to start firing on the creatures. Sprays of purple goop explode from every entry wound.

More ghouls pull themselves into this dimension, and some begin twitching, transform into something vaguely more human.

When Cleeve feels a hand on his shoulder, he turns to see Keller raising his magnum to Cleeve's head. But before the sheriff can pull the trigger, his ribs are blown out and he staggers backward. Keller—the real Keller—is kneeling on the floor, a smoking magnum gripped in both hands. The real Keller fires three more times into the gutted body of his doppelganger as it writhes on its back.

"Christ!" O'Connor shouts. His rifle is caught in the clay-like fist of an otherwise perfect copy of himself. The rifle is flung aside, effortlessly torn from the Irishman's grip. That same clayish appendage then forms into a pike and O'Connor's doppelganger lances it straight into the real O'Connor's gut. Art and Keller shoot the O'Connor doppelganger dead before it can move on to Cleeve. The real O'Connor is left to bleed out on the floor.

"Doppelgangers," Randall whispers.

"Get up, sheriff!" Cleeve orders. He grabs Keller by the arm and pulls him to his feet. "We're getting out of here." They step out into the snow to join Art and the kids. "This way," Cleeve says. "Transport will be waiting for us at the rendezvous point."

The group runs through the snowfall, and the ghouls pursue. Ahead, Logan throws open the rear double doors of the transport. Cleeve turns and raises his Colt to the lagging pursuers. One ghoul in particular really stokes his ire, so he fires two heavy shots and drops the naked duplicate of himself in its tracks.

Logan provides covering fire while the group piles into the back of the empty transport. As the last of them pile inside, he stops firing and jumps into the vehicle, slams the doors behind him. The transport lurches forward and roars with acceleration.

Cleeve raises his walkie to his lips. "Foster, you there?"

A crackle of static, then, "I'm here. Randall? Can you hear me? Are you okay?"

"I'm here, dad," Randall says, loud enough for the doctor to hear.

"Foster, listen to me," Cleeve says. "It's time. Nuke the fuckers."

LEARNING TO LOVE
THE BOMB, PART TWO

THE FIRST THING Foster does after receiving Cleeve's command is rush over to Babylon's tank to scold the two lab techs punching in codes on a keypad there. He tells them all the ways they're doing it wrong.

"No, we need that sent with a two-digit trail," Foster says. He references the clipboard he's holding. "Zero, nine. Punch it."

"That's an override code, doctor," the tech says.

"Thank you, yes," Foster says. "Zero, nine. Punch it."

"But we've never opened the tank before—"

"Hence the override!"

"It's just, we've spent a lot of time coding safeguards—"

"Will your safeguards prevent a nuke from detonating if Babylon refuses to eat it?"

"Uh…"

"Precisely. If Baby refuses to eat the nuke, we need to flush that tank as quickly as possible so we can disarm the warhead before it destroys us all. So… Zero, nine. Punch it."

"Yes, sir."

An underground tremor shakes the lab.

Foster turns back to the master console. "Meghan!" he shouts. "Readout!"

"Spikes all over the place" she says. "Multiple Bleeds, all concentrated around the sheriff's station and getting worse. It looks just like One Horse. If we don't act soon, this whole town is going to be history."

Foster looks up at the two techs on the catwalk. The warhead they were moving via winch is now resting safely inside Baby's closed feeding tube, ready to be dropped into the tank

"Are we good to go up there?" Foster shouts.

One of the techs gives a thumbs up.

Foster looks to the two techs beside him. "And how about here?"

"Are you sure this is going to work?" the tech says.

"No," says Foster. "So unless you have a better idea, I'll ask again. Are we good to go?"

"Yes, Dr. Foster."

Foster shouts to Meghan, "Do we still have a lock on the beacon?"

"We do," Meghan shouts back. "Whatever dimension it's in, it's not ours."

Good enough for me, Foster thinks. He's never been much of a religious man, but in this moment, he's praying.

"Okay, Meghan," he shouts. "Drop it."

THE END OF A WORLD

BARRY AND WOLF-PIG rush at each other, the horrid version raising Bludzorg high above his head as they close in on one another. Barry eyes the crusty blade as he runs, anticipating when it will drop.

Lanky, meanwhile, drags his chainsaw in a rooster tail of slag across the hellish earth and waits for Lich to come to it. Lich crosses his drumsticks in an "X" over his head. Metal for metal.

Wolf-pig brings his sword down on Barry, who raises his guitar to catch the blade in the mahogany body. A blue bolt of lightning cracks in the sky above. The notched blade of Bludzorg cleaves into the guitar, stops short of the pickups beneath the strings. Another bolt of lightning cracks, striking the *USS Eldritch.*

Lanky's chainsaw is heavy as it crashes against Lich's crossed drumsticks. A shower of sparks fly from the stainless steel drumsticks and wash over Lich's face. Lanky is screaming as it presses harder against that crux. A spray of syrupy saliva erupts from its lizard mouth, tongue whipping around as micro eruptions of lava burst through the cracks in the linoleum floor around them.

With Bludzorg caught in the Gibson Explorer, Barry yanks on the guitar, ripping the sword's hilt from Wolf-Pig's hands. With the sword lodged in his guitar, Barry swings the instrument, broadside. It's enough to make the monster stumble into a newly formed crick of magma, where its black Converse shoes ignite immediately, and the flames crawl up Wolf-Pig's legs. Stepping back out of the lava, Wolf-Pig's entire body is quickly consumed by fire. It rushes at Barry with werewolf claws bared and pig-like snout agape with its two curling tusks.

Lich, meanwhile, is struggling. He's barely holding back the grinding blade of Lanky's chainsaw. He falls backward onto the ground, where that ragged chainsaw blade roars inches from his face, spits pricks of steel slag that burn into Lich's skin.

Lich feels like he's losing. Again. He's always losing. And this time, losing means death. Where did this shitty copy of himself get its immense strength from anyway? *Do I have that same strength inside me?* Lich wonders.

The burning body of Wolf-Pig lunges at Barry, arms wide, claws sharp, ready to wrap Barry up in its unholy conflagration. And it looks like that's just what it's about to do. But something about this world makes Barry feel strong. Like, physically strong. Stronger than ten men. So instead of turning tail and running, he loads the weight of the sword-stricken guitar on his shoulder, aims where he wants the pointy end of the sword to go, and swings his guitar like it's a bat with nail sticking out the end. The point of Bludzorg glints once with the blazing hot hellscape before punching through the bridge of Wolf-Pig's snout, all the way into its corrupted and rotten brain.

The wolf-pig drops to the earth and is quickly consumed by flames. As the bonfire spreads and grows hotter, spiders emerge from beneath the wolf-pig's clothes and abandon the blazing host-body to its demise.

Barry is too hopped up on adrenaline to care about the flames that have leapt over to his guitar, the heat of which releases the sword from the wood. Barry looks up at the red sky, raises his burning guitar high, and howls. "Awooooo!"

But Lich.

Lich is screaming.

Barry turns to see his friend on his back. Lanky has already chainsawed through Lich's wrists and is now driving the roaring blade slowly into Lich's chest.

Barry is screaming now, too.

He plucks Bludzorg from the molten rock. It's heavier than he remembers. The blade is cherry-red, the hilt hot in his hand. With sword in one hand and flaming guitar in the other, he charges at Lanky with all the rage the two abominations had unleashed upon Grafting.

The blow from the guitar comes first. It's a discordant melody of splitting wood and snapping guitar strings that sends a pyrotechny of sparks flying. Lanky is sent reeling backward against the Wolfmobile. As Barry approaches, the obscene caricature of Lich climbs to its knees. Even kneeling, it's taller than Barry, but that just makes the exposed neck easier to strike.

Seeing his opening, Barry drops the guitar and raises Bludzorg aloft with both hands. Then, with all his might, he brings the sword down upon the nape of Lanky's neck and slices clean through to the ground. The decapitated head rolls into a tributary of molten rock and lights on fire while a horde of ten-legged spiders flee en masse from the severed neck.

Synthetic hair vaporizes, rendering fat bubbles, a single yellow eyeball pops like a pus-filled balloon.

Barry takes no time to gloat. He sprints to Lich and drops to the ground beside him. He doesn't want to cry, tries to hide it, but the tears are impossible to stop.

Lich coughs, and a spray of blood and sputum paints his chest.

Barry wants to say something reassuring. He wants to sound confident that everything will be okay. But all he can manage is a stuttering whimper: "No, no, no…"

Lich tries to look down at his wound, but Barry won't let him. Instead, the two friends lock eyes. Barry tries to smile at Lich, tries to counter the sobs that hitch his pal's shoulders.

"I couldn't do it," says Lich, a wet whisper.

Barry can only shake his head, "Don't say that. You did great. You went to Hell and fought." His words choked within a tightened throat.

"No I didn't. I was pushed to the ground and beaten, just like always. Only this time, I'm gonna die."

Barry simply cannot allow that. "You're not dying."

Lich closes his eyes. "Did we fuck those posers up?"

"Yeah," Barry says. "We did."

Lich's head lolls to the side, eyes shut tight.

"Don't go, Lich. You're our drummer, dude! The foundation of the band. There's no rhythm without you."

"Are the twins okay?" Lich whispers.

That's when the blood from his wound stops pumping and his stuttering breaths cease.

Barry holds his friend. Holds him tight, like if he squeezes hard enough, he can block the life from leaving Lich's body. But it's too late. Barry closes his eyes, weeps for his friend.

"What am I supposed to do without you?"

He looks up to the sky in search of answers but sees only the fiery tail of a falling comet. But that's not a comet, is it? Falling straight toward them? It sure doesn't feel like it.

"Fuck," Barry says out loud.

And that's when the comet that isn't a comet explodes in a blinding flash of light just above the horizon. Barry covers Lich's body with his own to protect them from the sudden rush of superheated blowing everything apart around them. When Barry turns back to the source of the explosion, he sees a billowing mushroom cloud the size of fucking Godzilla. He's seen that glitchy black-and-white footage from World War II, movies about it, learned about the Cold War and the Bay of Pigs, the falling of the Berlin Wall. You don't have to tell him what that cloud means.

"Looks like neither of us is gonna make it," Barry says to Lich. "Guess I'll see you in Valhalla now. I bet Senior is there, too, since technically he died in battle."

That's when Barry feels movement in his arms. He looks down at his friend, sees Lich's lips wordlessly ask, *Barry?*

Suddenly, Barry's vision is filled with a bright purplish light so blinding, it makes the light from the atomic bomb feel like a camera flash.

The spiders. They're back. And apparently, they're fucking famished.

EVERY BITE TAKEN in that hellish dimension is actualized in Grafting, Michigan, circa 1995. But not just anywhere in Grafting. Right...*there.* On the snowy cement out back behind the Ottawa County sheriff's station. Bite by ragged bite, Barry materializes on that spot, coughing and wheezing like a two-pack-a-day smoker.

The stark contrast between where he was and where he is now, and how in the hell he got there, leaves Barry blinking in the snowfall. When he sees the dumpsters behind the Ottawa County sheriff's station, he stands and howls mightily at a moon obscured behind the clouds.

"Lich, we fucking did it, dude!" He turns to wrap an arm around his pal, but sees nobody beside him. "Lich?" He looks around frantically. "Lich, where are you?"

"I had a feeling you'd make it back," a voice says.

From out of the nearby shadows, a man in a tweed suit, bolo tie, and snakeskin boots steps into the light, adjusts a pair of wine-red aviator sunglasses.

"Nice sunglasses. Who are you? Corey Hart?"

"Funny," Cleeve says. He retrieves a pack of Lucky Strikes from his coat pocket and plants one in his mouth. Aiming the open pack at Barry, he asks, "Want one?"

Barry climbs gingerly to his feet. "Where's Lich?" He accepts a cigarette and the two light up with Cleeve's gold Zippo.

"Name is Daniel Cleeve," the man says. "And you must be Barry." He offers up a hand to shake.

Barry takes a drag from the cigarette and tries with everything left in him to hold back the cough tickling his throat. He only looks at the waiting hand.

"You're covered in blood, dude."

"That makes two of us," says Cleeve. "Mind telling me what happened?"

"You wouldn't believe me if I told you."

"Try me."

Barry flicks the still-lit cigarette into the night. "I gotta go. My friend, he's missing, and—"

"Lich has the twins to get home to."

Barry freezes. The cowboy grins.

"Who are you?" Barry says. "CIA? Are you here to kill me? For the stuff I've seen?"

Cleeve laughs. "Not at all. I'm here to offer you some assistance."

"What kind of assistance?"

"I'd like to help you find your friend."

Barry watches Cleeve for a moment. "He's going to die if I don't find him soon."

"You won't." Cleeve takes a thoughtful drag from his cigarette. "Not here, anyway."

Barry suddenly feels the hours of adrenaline-fueled momentum come crashing down on him. He drags a calloused hand over his face.

"If you come with me, I can help you find him."

"And what if I say no?"

Cleeve shrugs. "You go back to your life at Pistol River Sunrise. Navigate high school without your friend. But hey, at least your bullies won't be there." Cleeve twirls his cigarette between his forefinger and thumb, stares at it as if its smoldering cherry is far more interesting than whatever decision this kid is about to make. "Of course, that would come with a cost."

"What kind of cost?"

"Your memories. Specifically, any memory following the night you and your friend drove out to the MOW. Just a blackout that lasts from that point until this one. You'll never know how you ended up here, let alone anything you and your friends did up to this point. It'll be like it never happened. But you won't be alone. Everyone in Grafting will suffer the same amnesia. You'll be fed Apex-Door-written articles about what happened, a name for the collective memory loss, and it'll all be convincing enough that no one will ask questions. Because like you, everyone will be afraid to question it, at least aloud. Always afraid. Always knowing those articles don't really explain anything. Only the conspiracy theorists will speak out, and who listens to them?"

"I'll forget everything?"

"Mostly. You might recall images, feelings. Enough for you to explain it away as a series of bad dreams or an eerie sense of deja vu. But then again, maybe no such explanation will ever really sit right with you. Results vary."

Barry looks up at the snowfall and closes his eyes to feel every snowflake against his skin. Takes a deep breath. "You promise we'll find Lich?"

"No. But you won't find him without me."

Barry opens his eyes and takes a moment to size up this man. "You hungry?"

Cleeve smiles. "I could eat."

Barry grins. "Ever had a Donner Cherry Pie?"

SUMMARY
REPORT

Apex Door Field Assessment Unit 3

Summary Report for Case #1-26-35-1

I. EXECUTIVE SUMMARY

Date of Bleed Event: Wednesday, November 8, 1995

Location of Bleed event: Grafting, Michigan

Date of Board Notification: Sunday, November 12, 1995

II. INVOLVED PARTIES

Assessor Number: 7

Assessor's Handler: Orson Caster

Field Director: Daniel Cleeve

Head of Security and Field Extraction: Logan Rhett

Field Science Officer: Dale Foster, PhD

Other: Sheriff John-David Keller, Deputy Arthur Novak, Barry Aguilar Jr., William Adams, Samantha Walters, Randall Foster

III. SUMMARY OF INVESTIGATION

The scale of the Bleed event occurring on Wednesday, November 8, 1995 within

Grafting, Michigan, exceeds any on record since the incidents occurring in Vietnam, 1970. The origin of this Bleed appears to be The Source, and early signs indicate that the Bleed remains ongoing, spreading. The event remains uncontained.

IV: FINAL NOTES

During the Bleed, 7 evacuated our hotel room without communication and I followed shortly thereafter, finding him seated in our transport, parked outside the hotel. His extreme perspiration was enough to begin dissolving his deeply yellowed skin.

It was in the transport that 7 broke protocol and spoke aloud. He spoke one word: hurry. This was the first time I'd ever heard his voice outside my head.

After blacking out, I awoke two days later to find myself in the Apex Door field lab's medical unit. The field lab was in a hurried state of evacuation when I awoke, having just completed Dream Protocol earlier that day.

It is from my bed inside the field lab infirmary that I inform you of my grave diagnosis: Post-Auditory Sickness. And as a victim of post-voice, the troubled history of 7's previous assessors weighs heavily on me. Since my awakening, 7 has yet to leave my bedside. And even though he has yet to speak aloud or via telepathy, I continue to hear his voice inside my head, his lone audible command to "hurry." I sense he feels guilty, even ashamed, but his feelings are not my concern at the moment.

I am not well, and I'm requesting immediate medical attention from the doctors at HQ. You know my service record, my accolades. I am a valuable asset to Apex Door and will continue to be if given the opportunity. Had it not been for me, 7 would still be without a handler, and should I become incapacitated or perish, he will be without one again. I implore The Board to help me. Take pity on me if you must Please.

GRAFTING, MICHIGAN

Saturday, November 25, 1995

EPILOGUE

DEATH OF A BARRY

SHERIFF JOHN-DAVID KELLER is having one of those early mornings that crawls forth from a relentless night. A night full of problems, like a hydra. Vanquish one, two more appear. That means a Dixie Cup cocktail, and Keller has stoppered the silver flask, tucks it back within his inside breast pocket. He steadies himself against his desk to sip, won't dare sit in that chair on the other side of it. Sleep beckons him there.

It's been, how long since he and his staff had to relocate to this cluster of trailers? Days? No. Weeks? Feels like a hundred fuckton years. The pace of construction for the new station is painstakingly slow this time of year. But hey, new station, that's cool. Silver lining and all that. If he wins that reelection next year, he might even be around to enjoy the new digs.

But let's not get ahead of ourselves. Keller takes a sip of hot coffee mixed with bourbon, recollecting all that's happened even as the temporary station was being constructed in the lot across from the abandoned door factory. The "Big One" had hit Grafting—an earthquake unlike any in Michigan's recorded history. The epicenter of which was right there in Keller's station. How about that? Keller figured he'd never had much luck with women, so why should Mother Earth feel any different about him? Point is, the earthquake was national news, and that meant all kinds of flatlanders from down south crowding him every chance they got with questions about what had happened and what he was doing about it.

There had been Sammy's parents to deal with. Keller hadn't known that Mr. and Mrs. Walters had only ever had one kid, and that meant little Samantha Walters was basically the center of their universe. Everything she did was righteous, her shits gold, and well, let's just say they were less than thrilled with the state that the sheriff had returned her in. With no explanation forthcoming, Keller shouldered all the blame right there outside her hospital room, where she was recovering from lacerations to the base of her neck. And boy did the Walters pile it on, thick enough for just about every staff member in the hospital to hear. Likely a good number of the patients, too, of which there were many.

Then there were the three boys: Barry, Lich, and Randall, each of whom simply vanished from custody when the earth-quake struck. For all the needs of a crippled Grafting, these missing boys had plagued Keller the hardest. Two of them were still key suspects in a series of killings that had led up to the earthquake. The other boy, Randall, was at best an accessory at this point. Records indicated they had been booked, thrown behind bars in anticipation of questioning. Then… Well, it's all sort of a blur. The quake hit, and what staff at the station had survived had all been knocked unconscious. Not a single one of them had any memory whatsoever of the entire day leading up to that. And that amnesia had selectively gone and plucked key moments from throughout the investigation straight from their brains like weeds. Attempting recall of these specifics only dredged up a banger of a headache for Keller, and after chatting with Art about it, same went for the deputy, too.

Keller's decision was to back-burner that shit. Not great—Keller even admitted as much—but there was a hydra at large, and Keller told Art they had to deal with the heads that were snapping at them first: the national media attention, the fam-ilies with missing loved ones, buildings reduced to ruin, a hospital suddenly inundated overnight, and a shoe-string staff here at the station.

United now, the locals are picking up the pieces. Keller, meanwhile, has found the chair on the other side of his desk. But he's only closing his eyes for, like, ten minutes tops.

KELLER IS PULLED straight out of REM, straight out of a dream filled with monsters and demonic spiders and glowing ooze so vivid, he gasps upon reintroduction to the waking world. And it takes him a minute of darting his slowly focusing eyes around the room to realize where he is. And who the man is that's just shaken him awake.

"Sorry, sheriff," says Art. "I got here a little bit ago. Ten a.m., like you said. And, well, it's been a little bit since then, even."

"What time is it?"

"About noon?"

"Christ." Keller stands quickly.

"Sorry, sheriff," Art says again. "It's just, I know sleep doesn't exactly come easy anymore, and when it does, you just have to take it when you can get it. Whenever that is, right?"

Keller shuffles around his desk for the bag of pepperoni sticks he'd been working on throughout the night. "Sounds about right. But I was just going to give myself a few minutes." He finds the bag empty. "Hell."

Art glances at the resealable bag amid the mess of papers on Keller's desk. "Hungry? Cause I could eat a damn hippo."

"Yeah, I am," Keller admits, turning the plastic bag around now in his hand, recalling better times when it was full.

"Rotten Roscoe's?"

"Yeah."

"I'll drive."

"Like hell you are. You'll be too busy telling me all about your surveillance at the Aguilar kid's place."

Art's shoulders drop. "Fine. But you're not gonna like it."

"That's okay, Art," Keller says as he shoulders into his jacket, zips it up. "I don't really like anything much these days."

The two make their way through the claustrophobic hall of the trailer and bust into the wintry day outside. They hurry across the snow-covered dirt lot to Keller's cruiser and throw themselves inside as if it isn't just a dryer cold that awaits them inside. Keller stabs the keys into the ignition and a blast of freezing air hits them both from the dash vents.

As they're waiting for the car to warm up, Keller, hands tucked into his armpits, says, "So? You've been out there, what? A week now?"

"Roughly." Art's holding the same pose as the sheriff. "Still no sign of the suspect, though. Never showed up once."

The defroster slowly opens a single oval of transparent windshield behind the layer of ice coating. Keller leans forward, looking through that defrosted patch, contemplating whether it was good enough to navigate the cruiser. *Better not.* "And nothing out of the ordinary in their little Pistol River Sunrise double-wide paradise?"

"Well, it depends what you mean by 'out of the ordinary.'"

Keller wonders about that. Doesn't really know. What the fuck *isn't* out of the ordinary these days? "Anyone showing up or taking off who isn't Barry or his mother?"

"I mean, yeah." The air is warm enough now that Art places his gloved hands against the vents. "Bunch of guys for the most part. Just Grafting's finest, you know?"

It's time. Keller puts the cruiser in drive and makes his way to Higgins Avenue. Hangs a left.

"Most of them are local to Pistol River Sunrise," Art continues. "Some of them been in and out of custody at the station."

"Uh-huh," Keller says.

Higgins Avenue through downtown Grafting reveals a site that Keller has still not gotten used to seeing. It starts with Scott's hardware. All that remains is the old bank vault in the back of the store. Rob hadn't used that vault to hole himself up against the commies like he always said he might have to, but it ended up being a pretty good place to wait out an earthquake. Pistol River Pies is collapsed into the Cinema 3. Movie Knight stands mostly unscathed, which Keller knows Cal must be quite proud of, given the field of debris that his arch-nemesis Blockbuster has turned into.

"But last night, there were these other guys," Art says, "and they didn't look like they were from around here."

Keller glances at his deputy. "In what way?"

"I don't know. They were both in suits, for starters."

Keller navigates the cruiser around coned-off gaps of asphalt, pits, and riots pockmarking the length of the street. "Suits?"

"Yeah. And sunglasses and fedora hats like a couple of Dick Tracy's all in black."

Keller hangs a left on Plainview and pulls into Rotten Roscoe's lot. *If you need proof of God,* Keller thinks, *it's right here.* Roscoe's remains untouched by the earthquake.

Art continues: "The Chevy they drove up in looked like it came right off the lot. Also black. And shiny. I don't know, sheriff, I got a bad vibe from them."

Keller nods. "Come on," he says. "Let's get something to snack on."

The view from inside Rotten Roscoe's is just like it was a week ago, a month ago, a year ago, a decade ago, complete with Roscoe himself hunched over a crossword puzzle next to the register. The only thing that's changed is the lack of obscene banter he'd normally lob towards Keller or Art. All he does now is nod as they approach the counter. Art snags two Donner Cherry Pies, and Keller reaches to the display stand full of cured meats. He hesitates.

"I'll take a pack of Camel Reds," says Keller.

That's enough for Roscoe to peel his gaze from the cross-word book. "You sure about that, sheriff?"

"Don't hassle me about it, okay? Goes for you, too," he says to Art. "Heartburn and ulcers from the pep sticks or lung cancer from the cigs. Might as well roll the dice when I can. Make it two packs, Roscoe."

Roscoe obliges wordlessly, another divergence for him. He rings them up and they make their way out of the gas station mart while Brick, the old black lab, barks at them from Roscoe and Suzanne's house out back.

Yeah, Keller feels bad about what he's just decided to do. No, it doesn't sit well with him. He knows the first cigarette in two years is on its way, resents how excited he is about that, and delays it all by tearing back the waxy paper of the Donner Cherry Pie and stuffing it into his gullet. Through a mouthful of neon-red cherry filling and a mustache full of flaky crumbs, he beckons Art to continue.

"So? You followed their vehicle, and it led to…?"

"Well, no," Art relents. "I stayed put. You know, just in case."

"In case what?" The two officers plop down into the cruiser, and Keller drives. He's already decided they're headed next.

"In case the suspect showed up. Barry Aguilar."

Keller can't blame the deputy. After all, he was only sticking to orders. They pass by a stretch of golf course alongside Plainview. Slopes of snowdrifts whisk ice from the sand traps. A barbed wire fence stretches off into a distant wood, dividing the golf course from Zimmer Farms.

"Well, I think we both know what's coming next," Keller says.

Art does. As they pull a right into the trailer park, he says sarcastically, "Can't wait to talk to Emily Aguilar."

The drive isn't far. Barry's trailer is just a few down, right where all the snaking lanes of Pistol River Sunrise coalesce into a daily bottleneck at the turnoff to Plainview.

"Look familiar?" Keller asks Art as he stares down the wilting double-wide.

"Yes, sir."

"Miss it?"

"Gotta admit," Art shrugs, "better after a Donner Cherry. And with a friend, too. That also helps." He laughs, then quickly finds a more stoic expression. "Better with backup, I mean."

Keller smiles. "Is that what you think we are? Friends?"

The deputy shakes his head like *Who in the hell could ever think such a thing?* "No, sir, that's not what I—"

Keller stops the deputy with a heavy hand on Art's shoulder. "Times like these, it's good to know who your friends are. Glad I got you on my side, Art. Now let's go see what in the hell is going on with Mrs. Emily Aguilar, shall we?"

Keller throws the car door open and steps once more into the Grafting winter. Slamming the door shut behind him, he doesn't see Art grin the way he does, doesn't hear him whisper to himself "Friends," or glimpse the way he nods in affirmation at that. Keller doesn't see Art take a breath like it's the first breath he's taken in a while. Like the validation of their friendship is the first real foundation Art has been able to stand upon since the Big One hit. Hell, since before that.

They walk up the three steps to the deck in front of the door. Find themselves standing shoulder-to-shoulder on a square stoop of rotting two-by-fours barely large enough to hold both of them. Keller knocks.

They wait.

He knocks again.

Sounds of life inside. A rustling. Then silence.

Keller wraps his knuckles against the door with more force. "Hello?"

Movement again. "Just a goddamn minute," comes the shrill voice of Barry's mother.

When the door opens, it's not her, it's someone else. A man. Shirtless. Rail thin, on that user diet, a thousand ribs rippling over his whiter-than-white torso. A man who the sheriff and his deputy both recognize immediately. This little ray of sunshine is in and out of the drunk tank so often that the three of them basically have a whole routine worked out for those late nights after he's been picked up outside the tavern for... Well, you name it. Fighting? Yeah. Public intoxication? Check. Dude even got himself on the registered sex offender's list for whipping his dick out and pissing in front of a group of school girls on their way to the Cinema 3.

He's now holding the storm door open with a splayed hand, venting from within the trailer a smell of rot and mold to assault the lawmen. "Keller," he says.

"Jesse Lyons," says the sheriff.

"See you brought your bitch," says Jesse Lyons. "See he ain't leashed. That's fine. Girl ain't got no teeth anyhow."

Art takes a swift step forward, and Keller has to catch him by the shoulder. The deputy breathes deeply through flared nostrils, pushes up his glasses.

"I need to speak with Emily please," says Keller. "You should go back inside."

"Em's busy," says Jesse Lyons. "I'm free, however."

"You're not Barry's mother, are you?"

"Who?" Jesse scratches defiantly at his crotch.

Keller's smile is dripping with acid. "Barry's mom. Emily Aguilar. I need to speak with her."

From somewhere in the dark, Emily shouts hoarsely, "Tell 'em to fuck off, Jesse!"

Jesse Lyons grins with a mouthful of rotten corn-on-the-cob for teeth. "You heard the lady."

"Ma'am," Keller shouts over Jesse Lyons's shoulder. "We need to have a few words about your son."

"She gets cranky," Jesse Lyons explains. "Best let her be, sheriff."

"We understand he's been missing for a while now, and we're trying to locate him," Keller continues.

"I said fuck off!" she shouts from somewhere.

Jesse Lyons is lighting a cigarette. "That time of month and all."

"Ma'am, if you'd please come to the door," Art tries.

"Don't make me get a warrant and bring a bunch of armed men here to knock down your door," says Keller. He doesn't know if he can get one. Doesn't know who in the hell these armed men are, or if they exist, but he's leveraging the show *COPS* to his advantage here. "They might just knock the whole trailer down, Emily."

From the putrid dark, Emily emerges just behind Jesse Lyons. "You knock my shit down, and I'll sue your whole department!" she shouts, with a bony finger shifting aim between Sheriff Keller and Deputy Art.

Keller nods with sarcastic stoicism. "That is your right, ma'am. Do you know where your son might be?"

"Read my lips," Emily points at her dry mouth. "Like. I. Give. A. Fuck. That's where."

"When did you last see him?" Keller asks.

Art has his notepad pulled out. Scribbles furiously.

The way Emily says *I don't know* comes like one word. *Ayunno.*

"You heard the woman," says Jessie Lyons. "Guess you got what you need."

And then that hairpin trigger flips in Keller's brain. The kind that makes him do the sort of small-town-cop shit like…

Grab that motherfucker Jesse Lyons by both shoulders, knee him in the balls, and bend him over the flimsy two-by-four railing Emily calls a porch. I'm not saying it's right, but the sheriff draws his firearm and aims it at Jesse Lyons, who squirms and whimpers in the melting snow on the railing.

"How about I shoot your fucking brains out, Jesse?"

Jesse Lyons has his hands up. He's pleading. He's so sorry all of the sudden.

It's Art who has to dampen Keller's fire. "Sheriff," is all he says.

Keller's jaw feels like he's about to bite all the way through his own teeth.

"J. D.," says the deputy softly.

Keller holsters his firearm with shaky hand, aims his gaze hard at Jesse Lyons. Then he aims that same locked-and-loaded look at Emily. He steps inside the trailer, Emily backing up. Fear, that's the look on her face. That's what's melting away her defiance.

"Tell me about the last time you saw your son," Keller says with a mix of kindness and barely contained rage. Like Mister Rogers had one too many.

He's backed her all the way up to a countertop in something meant to be a kitchen. A countertop that's turned into an open-concept trash bin. A deconstructed garbage pail of maggot-sodden dishes, of heaps of fast-food bags crawling with flies.

"I ain't seen him in weeks," says Emily quietly.

Keller turns to check on Art through the opened door. Art looks nervous as shit. Back to Emily.

"How about two men dressed in black suits? That ring a bell? Matching hats?"

Emily, usually flush and pockmarked with a zillion red dots, she goes pale. "I don't know what you mean, sheriff."

"Mrs. Aguilar, we saw them. Let's just get to the part where you tell us what they told you, okay?"

With a quick glance to Jesse Lyons all bent over her front deck rail, she sighs. "I wanted to call you, J.D. Believe it or not."

It's been a long time since this woman has referred to him as J. D., so Keller needs to take a moment. *When was that last? High School?* "Okay, but you didn't. Why?"

"They said."

"Said what?"

"Not to."

"Not to what, Emily?"

"Call you!"

"Why did these two men not want you to call the police?"

"Not just the police, J. D. They said not to call you, specifically." Emily Aguilar brushes a fried tangle of hair away from her brow. "Said don't be calling the police or Sheriff Keller."

"And then?"

"They said…" Emily's eyes begin to well up. "They said my Barry is dead, J. D." She burst into a hitching sob. "Said don't bother." She manages to say between wails, "Don't go lookin'!"

Keller swallows. Calms himself. Pats hesitantly at her back. "Okay, Mrs. Aguilar. Did they say anything else? Anything to indicate where they came from?" But she's gone. Long past consolation. Keller looks hard at the ceiling to try and crack the tension bubbling in his neck. It doesn't work. "Okay," he says.

Keller walks out of the trailer, kicking a couple of Olympia beer cans on the way out. He makes his way down the steps, and without any order to disengage, Art does too. They both climb into the cruiser, shutting their doors, and with that, shutting out the whiny threats of Jesse Lyons's impending lawsuit that will never happen.

The cruiser pulls out of the gravel road from Pistol River Sunrise. Art tries a conversation about what in the hell just happened, but Keller just shakes his head no.

WHEN SAMMY COMES to, it takes her several moments to realize she's lying in a hospital bed. In the corner, next to a machine that beeps in sync with her heart rate, she sees her parents. They've collapsed over each other in sleep. When she looks to her other side, the knot of confusion on her face loosens a bit.

"Randall?"

Randall looks just about as serious as he ever has. "They're not dead, Sammy."

Sammy blinks. Looks around the room. "Who?"

"Barry and Lich. At least," he hesitates, "I don't think so. Barry, at least. I know that much for sure."

Barry? Lich? Sammy can't recall anything. When she tries, it's like a clamp is tightening around her temples.

"Where are they?" she says, eyes shut tight against the headache.

"I don't know," Randall says. He holds up a pair of old keys. "But I know where to start looking."

Sammy recognizes those keys. Clipped to Barry's black jeans every single day for as long as she's known him.

"You want to steal his van?"

Randall leans against her bed. "It's in the impound lot next to the old sheriff's station. No one is there to guard it. Keller has no one left. I'm going to get Barry. Are you coming with me?"

Sammy stares for a moment at the keys dangling from Randall's clutch. She glances over at her parents sleeping on the other side of that beeping machine. They look so tired. Exhausted. Even in sleep, they look concerned.

"Coming with you where?" she says without looking back to Randall.

"HQ," is all he says.

"HQ? What HQ?"

Randall sighs. "I can fill you in on everything that happened on the way."

"You sure Barry will be there?"

"No. But I'm willing to bet money he is."

"What about Lich?"

"Don't know. I just know Barry went with the Apex Door guys, and I know where the Apex Door guys go. Maybe Lich is there, too. Are you coming with me or not?"

WHEN KELLER AND Art arrive back at the temporary sheriff's station, Debs is in the gravel lot outside, waiting for them. She looks worried. When they exit the vehicle, Keller sees her pawing at an envelope in her hand.

"It's for you, J. D."

Keller takes the envelope, sees his name written on it in sloppy handwriting. A small skull and crossbones grins rictus beneath the writing:

SHERIFF JOHN-DAVID KILLER

"Debs?"

She knows what Keller is asking. "No more than an hour ago. That boy was here. It was right after you'd left. Seemed like he was waiting for you to go, like he didn't want you here when he showed up."

Keller regards the envelope. "Thanks." He smiles hollowly.

"That's not all J. D.," Debs says quietly.

"What else?"

"There was a break-in at the impound lot. The one outside the old station."

The old station. Keller thinks about that. "And?" he asks?

"That van, the one from the Jankowski scene? It's gone."

The hydra is dangerously close, Keller thinks. "One thing at a time here, Debs."

"I'm just saying," Debs says, heading toward Keller's trailer.

Keller and Art follow Debs through the narrow door of the temporary sheriff's office. Keller stops there while Debs plops down behind a foldout table and answers a ringing phone. The sheriff rubs his thumb over that Jolly Roger next to his slurred name on the envelope she'd handed him.

Art is holding the door open. "You okay, sheriff?"

Keller looks up at Art and smiles. He places a hand gently on his deputy's shoulder. "You've been at it pretty hard, Art."

Art is too tired to hide just how much he agrees with that.

"A lot of long hours," Keller adds.

"Yeah." Art nods. "Kinda."

"Why don't you go home? Get some rest. Don't come back tomorrow."

Art pushes up his glasses. "You sure?"

Keller nods. "I'm sure. Go fart yourself to sleep." He slaps Art's back.

Art smiles. "Hell," he shrugs, "if you insist." He tips his hat on the way out.

Keller makes his way to Debs and her new desk.

"Temporary," she says as he approaches.

"What is?"

Debs pats the tabletop with two flattened hands. "This."

"What?" says Keller. "You don't like your new office?"

"Excuse me," she says, "this is not an office, this is a trailer. And this is not my new desk. It's temporary. I'm here until you hire someone to handle dispatch."

"Maybe I like you here." Keller folds his arms over his chest, that envelope clutched in one hand. "Maybe I like to start my mornings seeing you right when I walk in the door."

Debs is blushing now. "Oh, please," she says. "You can see me down the hall just like normal if you want."

Keller slaps the table lightly. "Since you said please." He winks and makes his way back to his office.

There, Keller doesn't hesitate to find the well-used chair behind his new desk. Falls right into it like it's a baseball mitt and he's a… Well, you get it.

He's got his Dixie Cup cocktail, drags a red stir-straw through it, takes a sip, goes *Ahh*. Then, after cracking the window behind him, he does something he hasn't done in a hell of a long while. He lights a cigarette, and it burns just right. Sorry.

Keller stares at the envelope for a minute, then tears vertically through one end, slides a tri-folded paper out, opens it up, reads that sloppy chicken scratch scrawled in stark contrast against the clean Apex Door letterhead.

"You bastard," he says to the ceiling after reading the brief note.

He takes a another look, reads it again, and crumples it up. Tosses the letter in the waste basket beside his desk. He smiles, knowing the kid won't get away that easy. Keller will fill out the paperwork later, fudge the truth as needed. He's even more determined to catch this killer now, even if he has to bend a few laws along the way.

But the note, you ask, what does it say?

It says this:

HEY KILLER.

GLAD WE DIDN'T DIE.

FOR WHAT IT'S WORTH, IT WASN'T ME OR LICH WHO COMMITTED THOSE MURDERS, SO DON'T COME LOOKING FOR ME. I'M THE ONE LOOKING NOW.

GRAFTING NEEDS YOU. HOPE I WON'T.

CLEEVE SAYS HI.

I SAY FUCK YOURSELF.

Barry. He's got a way with words, doesn't he?

ACKNOWLEDGMENTS

IT WAS THE winter of 2001 when my family and I packed up the U-Haul and drove up I-75 to a town in Northern Michigan called West Branch. We hadn't made it to the new digs on 8th Street quite yet before a stop at my dad's Free Methodist church. Now, having grown up in the Midwest, I was no stranger to snow. But this? This was the super deluxe version of it. Enough to get the U-Haul stuck in the parking lot. After the drive from Atlanta, this was no fun. But it was the correct introduction, I think. Not an omen, not really, more of a too-firm handshake. A word of advice. *Careful*—that's what Northern Michigan was saying—you just might get stuck here like everyone else.

Anyway, it wasn't the '90s when this happened, as is the setting of this novel, in Grafting, the homage to my little town up there in the Mitten. But wasn't it? See, when you get into a county with a population of three thousand people, where the cattle outnumber the people, you end up in a place that's last in line for the amenities that something like the turn of the century might have to offer. I was only eleven years old in that '01 winter. Not quite a child of the nineties, not like Barry and Lich. But the nineties, it felt, was still in full swing. We were just behind. We were the twentieth century's ellipses.

Just down the street from our new home was a giant empty building that would become a wellspring of inspiration for decades to come. In a town where the only thing to do was sneak the candy you bought from Fox Five & Dime into the Cinema 3 (PG movies only, that's what you get when all of cinema runs through the lens of a Calvinist), something like an abandoned bicycle factory is about as good as it gets. As I entered my teenage years, the conspiracies my pals and I would hatch about the place became increasingly more complex. I've got stories about that place, man. We didn't call the shadow agency we knew must be in the hidden basement "Apex Door," but it was there. We knew that much.

So, yeah. As far as acknowledgments go, I'd like to acknowledge West Branch, Michigan. Grafting is twenty years of dreamlike memories from that place.

Can't get too far without mentioning my family, which is maybe how I should have started this. When I was a kid, there were nights during family prayer when my parents would let me close out the evening of devotion with my latest story, usually something involving dinosaurs, and my sister Andrea has reacted only with pure joy and excitement at every story I've written since. Her enthusiasm has provided a shining light at the end of a tunnel. Thanks, Sis.

My dad, Father Vic. When I was four years old, my dad taught me to spell. If it started anywhere for me, it was there at that kitchen table in Kansas City. As a preacher, he wrote roughly fifteen hundred words per week, and from this experience, he taught me the discipline required to write, and how to write with purpose. Up there in front of a couple hundred hungry souls every week, he also taught me that the words you write don't mean much without a story to tell. Thanks, Pop.

Speaking of family, well, here's more on that. While I was writing this book, I met a woman. She is now my wife. She met the tortured author and decided that was fine by her. She also brought to our relationship two girls, and between them, they taught me just how far a heart can be stretched, how deep the capacity for love. You met them on the dedication page. There was this one day where I had to submit my manuscript. It was a Saturday. Rose guarded my office like a three-headed dog (before it became Delilah's room). She knew from the outset who I was. And since then, she's given me not only the heart of a powerful woman to prop me up, but two girls who I love with every blood cell coursing through my veins. These two girls carry the strength and inclination towards joy that their mother has, and though we met late in life, I couldn't be prouder of my two daughters. Purpose, daily. They've given me that. I wake up each morning with a reason, and that reason is my Rose, my Delilah, and my Bella. Fuck, you have no idea how much I love them.

My friends, always spurring me on. From the outset, inspiring me from everything like what it means to be an artist, to what it means to be a dad. They have found that perfect balance of making me think all the cool shit I do is cool shit, but also, with love and perfect timing, reminding me that I am also full of shit. Jarrod, Jeff, Mark, Steve… Hell, there's too many to name. Love you guys. My brothers.

Can't believe I've gotten this far without mentioning the legendary Sadie Hartman, Mother Horror herself. Sadie and her business partner, Ashley Sawyers, did something really special in 2022 when they co-edited the Bram Stoker Award-nominated *Human Monsters* horror anthology, a lineup of stories without a single dud. I've never read an anthology quite like it. And somehow, my little story "Barry & Lich" was a included in the book. The day I received the anthology acceptance email was the same day that my Grandpa Fox died. I was only hours removed from my last conversation with him, a moment of grace when I was able to tell him that I loved him while he was still able to acknowledge he'd heard me. Red-eyed and feeling the darkness of life's cruel inevitability, I received an email that said my first story ever would be published. What a day.

Man, how about Rob Carroll, Editor-in-Chief and mastermind behind the incomparable *Dark Matter Magazine* and trade imprint Dark Matter Ink? A few months after *Human Monsters* was unleashed, Rob hit me up to ask if I'd ever thought of expanding the Barry and Lich story into a novel. What else could I say? "No," I told him. "I hadn't. But I will."

And I did. If not for his prompt, none of this happens. He recognized something in "Barry & Lich" that turned me into a novelist. This is shortly after Dark Matter Ink's inception, and look what's happened since then. Some fantastic novels now available to anyone who is hungry for them. Without his genuine investment, his humility, and his willingness to fire off every synapse available, entire chapters and subplots in this novel simply would never have seen the light of day. He helped get the manuscript to what it is today. But it doesn't stop with my book. There are so many stories, so many characters and settings, so many words printed to paper that would never have happened without his clear vision and relentless work ethic. I can't express my gratitude to Rob enough, and neither can you.

I also want to thank fellow authors Angela Sylvaine, Steph Nelson, Drew Huff, and R. L. Meza for their generosity in not only reading through an early, unedited copy, but also for their willingness to provide blurbs for the novel. My appreciation cannot be overstated. I understand the effort that takes.

Thank you to artist, Butcher Billy. I'm absolutely thrilled with the cover art he created for this book. The way he was able to capture the chaos of the world and bring to life the characters in this novel is remarkable. To have worked with such an incredibly talented artist will forever be a point of pride.

I'm about to wrap this up, but first, bear with me a moment. I promise I won't go too hard into the paint on this. I never saw it coming, and I won't get into why, but suddenly out of nowhere I found myself entirely alone shortly before I began this novel. And when I say alone, man, I was a ghost haunting my own house. Nights were long, and days piled up on me whether I wanted them or not. Sometimes, there was no point in leaving the house. Hell, why even eat? Well, my boy had to be walked. He had to eat. He didn't ask for crushing solitude, and if you looked at his big brown eyes, you'd see that he didn't even know something like loneliness was a thing. Because he had me. And boy did I have him. My boy is a French bulldog/

Boston terrier mix. There was this stretch where Hux was the reason I left the house, the reason I ate, the reason I slept. Huxley, you abolished the cruel shadow of solitude with the purity of your little heart's flame. You and me buddy. Forever. That's a good boy.

I suppose you've made it this far, so to you, my friend, I offer my final word of gratitude. Thank you for the time you set aside to read my novel. Thank you for sticking with it all the way to this point. These words on these pages don't exist until you read them. And despite all the late nights, the pints, the sweat, the sacrifice, despite all the logistics involved with edits, last-minute oh-nos, industrial printers, this book was never complete until you read it. So, thanks, reader, for getting this novel to its ending. Can't wait to do this again with you.

—Stephen S. Schreffler

ABOUT THE AUTHOR

STEPHEN S. SCHREFFLER is an author of science fiction and horror. His imaginative stories feature unique worlds and complex characters that explore themes of loneliness, loss, identity, and growth. Stephen lives in Bend, Oregon with his wife and two daughters, and their cat and dog. He spends his non-writing time asking his wife what they should make their daughters for dinner, exploring the Pacific Northwest, and playing guitar in various musical projects.

ABOUT THE COVER ARTIST

BUTCHER BILLY is a Brazilian artist and graphic designer known for his art pieces and illustration series based on the contemporary pop art movement. His work has a strong vintage comic book and street art influence while also making use of pop cultural references in music, cinema, art, literature, games, history and politics. His work has appeared as part of promotions and productions for the TV shows *Black Mirror* and *Stranger Things*.

Frost Bite by Angela Sylvaine
ISBN 978-1-958598-03-0

Free Burn by Drew Huff
ISBN 978-1-958598-26-9

The House at the End of Lacelean Street
by Catherine McCarthy
ISBN 978-1-958598-23-8

When the Gods Are Away by Robert E. Harpold
ISBN 978-1-958598-47-4

The Dead Spot: Stories of Lost Girls
by Angela Sylvaine
ISBN 978-1-958598-27-6

Grim Root by Bonnie Jo Stufflebeam
ISBN 978-1-958598-36-8

Voracious by Belicia Rhea
ISBN 978-1-958598-25-2

Chopping Spree by Angela Sylvaine
ISBN 978-1-958598-31-3

The Off-Season: An Anthology of Coastal New Weird
Edited by Marissa van Uden
ISBN 978-1-958598-24-5

Saturday Fright at the Movies
by Amanda Cecelia Lang
ISBN 978-1-958598-75-7

The Threshing Floor by Steph Nelson
ISBN 978-1-958598-49-8

Club Contango by Eliane Boey
ISBN 978-1-958598-57-3

The Divine Flesh by Drew Huff
ISBN 978-1-958598-59-7

Psychopomp by Maria Dong
ISBN 978-1-958598-52-8

Darkly Through the Glass Place by Kirk Bueckert
ISBN 978-1-958598-48-1

Disgraced Return of the Kap's Needle
by Renan Bernardo
ISBN 978-1-958598-74-0

Soul Couriers by Caleb Stephens
ISBN 978-1-958598-76-4

Abducted by Patrick Barb
ISBN 978-1-958598-37-5

Little Red Flags: Stories of Cults, Cons, and Control
Edited by Noelle W. Ihli & Steph Nelson
ISBN 978-1-958598-54-2

Frost Bite 2 by Angela Sylvaine
ISBN 978-1-958598-55-9

Dark Matter Presents: Fear City
ISBN 978-1-958598-90-0

Part of the Dark Hart Collection

Rootwork by Tracy Cross
ISBN 978-1-958598-01-6

Mosaic by Catherine McCarthy
ISBN 978-1-958598-06-1

Apparitions by Adam Pottle
ISBN 978-1-958598-18-4

I Can See Your Lies by Izzy Lee
ISBN 978-1-958598-28-3

A Gathering of Weapons by Tracy Cross
ISBN 978-1-958598-38-2